The Enchanted

Works by
MARTIN FLAVIN

NOVELS
JOURNEY IN THE DARK

CORPORAL CAT

MR. LITTLEJOHN

PLAYS
CHILDREN OF THE MOON

LADY OF THE ROSE

SERVICE FOR TWO

THE CRIMINAL CODE

BROKEN DISHES

CROSS ROADS

SPINDRIFT

DANCING DAYS

AMACO

ACHILLES HAD A HEEL

TAPESTRY IN GRAY

AROUND THE CORNER

BLUE JEANS

SIX ONE ACT PLAYS

THE

By

ENCHANTED
MARTIN FLAVIN

With drawings by
CYRUS LEROY BALDRIDGE

HARPER & BROTHERS PUBLISHERS
NEW YORK *and* LONDON

4-7

THE ENCHANTED

AMERICAN BOOK–STRATFORD PRESS, INC., NEW YORK

To

My Mother

The Enchanted

1

THE DAY WAS BREAKING WHEN THE WOMAN
came out of the house.

The children did not know her name. They called her *she*.
They said, "Look out, she is coming" or "Take care, she is
watching." Among themselves they called her things with humorous
and derisive implications. As for example: the Little One had given
her the name of Pussy Mouth, because the woman's lip had long hairs
growing on it, like the whiskers of a cat. She was not a prepossessing
woman; she had other infirmities which lent themselves to ridicule,
like the way she walked tilted back upon her heels with her belly
sticking out, and her voice which was raucous as a crow's. Sometimes
they said, "Old crow," even in her presence, which would set them all
to giggling. But there was no hazard in the matter because she did not
understand their language.

She had told them her name when they first came, but they had
not paid attention. They did not know any French. Only the older
ones, Gil and Juan and Rosa, had picked up a few words. But mainly
they responded to familiar sounds and gestures which meant do this

or that—the multiple but simple tasks performed about the farm. They had learned by imitation, ignoring the voluble instruction. Perhaps if there had been two or three instead of seven of them, they would have made an effort. But they were a social unit in themselves, a group of *displaced* children—or so, in later times, they would have been described—and they felt no need to make an adaptation. It had been the same in the place where they had come from, where there had been hundreds of them. They had not known each other then, excepting Gil and Juan who had been friends almost as long as either could remember, even before they came to France out of the shadowy chaos which they rarely thought about and which had no remembered continuity. But they had a solidarity: a common language and the heritage of orphans; they knew what hunger was and they knew what war was like—what it was like to children. They were not aliens; the world was alien. They were not foreigners; *she* was a foreigner. The woman felt this—dully, for she was a stupid woman. She did not find it pleasant being with these children; she wished every day she had not taken them.

Her name was Mme. Bigard. Gil saw her leave the house. A while before, when it was still dark, he had been wakened by the barking of the dog and he had not gone to sleep again, lying on the straw tick which he shared with Juan who was curled up close against him with the stump of his arm against his shoulder. Juan had lost an arm, the left one; it had been wounded by a bomb and had gone uncared for until it was too late. It had happened long ago and he did not remember much about it. And he did not seem to miss it; he could do with one arm almost everything that Gil could do with two.

Beyond them in the blackness of the granary were the others: Rosa and Teresa on the straw tick next to theirs, then Pablo and Rafael. Rafael was the crippled one who walked sideways like a crab, but they did not make fun of him. And last of all there was the Little One, who had no other name, to whom everything had happened before she could remember, who had always been *displaced* and was blissfully unaware of any other status. She was so small that she slept in a box which had had apples in it and still smelled strongly of them. The fragrant odor clung to her. Sometimes they said she smelled good enough to eat.

Gil heard the house door close and raising on his elbow, through a narrow window in the stonework of the granary, he could see the farmhouse with its rough slate roof and the green moss growing on it. He saw the woman coming from the house, and he thought she was coming to wake them, as she came every morning. But she did not come across the yard; she turned the other way, toward the road, then toward the village, hurrying on her heels with her belly sticking out. The dog went with her, but no farther than the hedge that lined the road. He was a small black dog; his name was Trictrac—or so it sounded when the woman called him. He was fond of the children and preferred to be with them.

Gil exclaimed beneath his breath. Well, it was strange: where was she going so early in the morning?—and would they have no break-fast?

And then, when she was scarcely out of sight, the door opened again and a man came out, a soldier with a gun and a bayonet on the end of it. He stood in the doorway, leaning on the gun, as though he was un-certain what to do. Gil's breath caught in his throat. He pushed Juan with his foot—

"Look!" Gil whispered, pointing through the window. "There is a man—a soldier."

"A soldier?" Juan crawled to look. "But where is *she*?"

"She went away." Gil nodded toward the road. And suddenly he understood: it was when the dog had barked that the man had come, and then he had driven the woman from the house, or she had run away.

"What does he want?" Juan asked with a tremor in his voice.

Gil shrugged.

"But perhaps he doesn't know that we are here?"

"Perhaps—" Gil thought about it. "Wake them up," he said. "But they mustn't make a noise."

And presently he heard protesting sleepy voices, subsiding into whispers; the rattle of the straw and shuffling feet; but he did not turn his head. He pulled on his ragged shirt and trousers, and he was dressed. He had no shoes or stockings; none of them had. But it didn't matter now; it was springtime, almost summer. He waited by the win-dow, watching with keen brown eyes from beneath a thatch of thick black hair that fell across his forehead. He was not a handsome boy; his features were too sharp, not at all like Juan's, whose sensitive oval face was of a finer molding; nor had he Juan's gracefulness of figure. He was of rougher texture, angular and rugged.

The man had not moved; he stood by the door, leaning on his gun, as if not yet decided what he meant to do. It was lighter now and Gil could see his face, black with stubbly beard; and the uniform he wore was caked with dirt. His aspect was not reassuring. And the situation was not more so; the granary was a long, narrow room built against the stone wall of the barnyard; the windows and the door faced toward the house; in the back wall there were slits which looked into the barnyard, but they were too narrow to crawl through. There was no way of escape.

Rosa came and stood beside him.

"War has come here," he said.

She nodded, peeking through the window. She was a pretty child, with straight dark hair bobbed high upon her neck. She looked like a Madonna with the figure of a child, angular and thin. But they were all thin. Presently the others came. They did not ask any questions and were not much concerned. Only the Little One was complaining plaintively: she could not find her doll in the dimness of the granary; and Pablo had teased her, suggesting that a rat had carried it away. And then she cried a little, whimpering sleepily.

"Be quiet," Gil admonished.

"But I want her," the Little One insisted. The doll was carved out of a piece of wood and was named Juana, because Juan had made it for her. He was clever at such things, though he had only one arm; he would sit on the ground with the work clamped fast between his knees; and he had the patient perseverance of an artist. Teresa had made the costume for the doll out of scraps of rags and ribbons, quite regal in effect, like a sort of gypsy queen. But the face of the doll was not a happy one; it was thin and pinched and wrinkled like a mummy —like the face of an early Christian martyr. Still, the Little One adored the grotesque creature.

Rosa found the doll beneath a grain sack, and then she sat down on the floor to button the child's dress. She was always saying to the Little One, "You are a big girl now; you should button up yourself." But still she did it for her. There was just the dress, and a shirt and panties—not very clean ones, though the panties had real lace. The in her that conveyed a sense of quality—a quietness and poise which Gil completely lacked. In Juan there was a softness that suggested Andalusia—a city like Seville. But he had not any memories behind the slug of steel that had burned into his arm. As for the Little One, there could be no doubt about her, with her sky-blue eyes and golden curls: a Catalan of course, perhaps from Barcelona. She might have been the daughter of a duchess. There was something in the way she held her head—coquettish and imperious, and almost irresistible. But she was a privileged character. And she lived in a world which was her own—a world which could not be understood at all except in terms of Teresa's Fairy stories.

Their pasts were far apart, but they were very close. They quarreled sometimes, imposed on one another; but these were surface matters. Underneath they were united by the strongest of all bonds: defense against a common enemy. And an enemy was standing now outside the farmhouse door—a man with a gun and a bayonet on the end of it.

It was Trictrac who betrayed them, not intentionally of course, for Trictrac was their friend. The dog had loitered by the road when the woman went, but then he came back toward the house, looking doubtfully at the man. And when he came sniffing near, the man spoke to him roughly, motioning him away. He went a little distance with his tail between his legs; then suddenly remembering he had friends near by, he gave utterance to a bark of joyful recollection, and came running toward the granary, straight to the door. And they could hear him jumping up against it, expecting them to open it as they always did. Indeed, from force of habit, Pablo ran to raise the latch.

"No, Pablo, don't," Gil warned. And then his heart stood still.

For now, as if the action of the dog had roused him to decision, the man came striding toward the granary, with his gun beneath his arm, muttering fiercely to himself—a terrifying figure. Spellbound, they watched him come across the littered yard; there was nothing else to do. And then when he was almost there, suddenly it seemed he was not coming to the door, nor conscious of the dog who was still pawing at it. His eyes were somewhere else, and in another moment he passed out of their view, outside the focus of the narrow window in the thick stone wall. They breathed again.

"Where has he gone?" they questioned.

dress, like Rosa's and Teresa's, had long since been discar
fortunate children; they were faded now and worn and ol
and not very clean, though they were sometimes washed. T
wooden tub in the corner of the granary, and occasionally
a day of washing, for their clothing and themselves, with b
hot water carried from the kitchen. And in the suds in wh
scrubbed their garments, they would finally scrub themselves—
and luxurious occasions.

The clothing of the boys was more haphazard: Juan and G
trousers, long ones like men's, but the smaller boys wore shorts
were no protection against the winter wind. But to compensat
this inequity Pablo had a sweater with a turtle neck, and Rafael h
jacket which came almost to his knees; he had to stoop to reach
pockets of it. In this jacket, scuttling sideways like a crab, he presen
a comical appearance.

An odd lot of little scarecrows, of interest to a student of ethnolog
who might study their appearance and the way they spoke and acted
speculating on their racial origins and more recent antecedents, con-
cluding reasonably that Pablo's roots were deep in Africa, that the darkness of his skin came from his Moorish blood, that he was of peasant
stock, from the square flat shape of him and the way he put his feet
down; that Rafael was obviously Semitic, a Spanish Jew in fact, from
his features and quality of voice, and his sensitive eyes and hands;
that Teresa was a gypsy, with her coppery piquant face and graceful
indolence, not much concerned with matters if she could sing and dance
—a ribbon for her hair made all the difference. She was something of an
actress, an intriguing story teller with a gift of mimicry. It was amusing
when she walked tilted backward on her heels, screeching like a crow,
"*Voilà, mes enfants*"—whatever that might mean.

With the others the distinctions would be finer: Gil and Rosa, the
observer might suggest, were probably Castilian, from the tableland
about Madrid, or from Madrid itself. It was the way they spoke, and a
certain independence and dignity of manner. But in Gil there was something of the gamin, an inheritance from gutters; and indeed he had
vague memories of shabby crowded streets and the lurid fronts of
cinemas. Rosa had memories too, of quite a different sort, of a big house
with a garden, of a room that had been hers. And there was something

"Maybe the barn," Gil said.

They scrambled across the floor to look out through the slits into the barnyard—all but the Little One who was not tall enough, and who did not care about it. She was talking to Trictrac through the door. She would have opened it but she could not reach the latch.

Yes, the man had gone into the barn, and through it to the open door which looked into the barnyard—looked down upon it really, for the barnyard was lower than the granary or the barn—a stone-walled square with a great manure pile and some chickens scratching in it. There were two cows in the barnyard, a red one and a white one, which twice a day Gil milked. The white one was docile, but the red one kicked sometimes and had once upset the pail when it was nearly full; and then Gil had been scolded and had gone without his supper. He did not like the red cow.

There was also a big black horse. Pablo cared for him, and could hitch him to the two-wheeled cart which was standing in the yard, when the woman went to market. He was a plow horse too, and together they had plowed the field behind the barnyard—he and Pablo and the horse. The woman had showed them and helped them for a while, but they had managed well enough without her. In a corner of the barnyard was a sow with a litter of young pigs. One of them was spotted and cuter than the others, and the Little One had claimed this one was hers. The mother pig did not seem to mind when the Little One came close and even took the baby in her arms.

The man was standing in the doorway of the barn, looking down into the barnyard, leaning on his gun, as though his decision and his haste had suddenly expired as unaccountably as they began. They could plainly see his face, the expression in his eyes, a distracted angry look; but they were no longer frightened, for he did not even glance in their direction. They watched him through the slits, consumed with curiosity. What would happen now?

"Will he steal the cows?" they whispered.

"Or the horse?" suggested Pablo.

"Or the pigs?" Teresa ventured.

There was a sound of planes flying very high; and the man started quickly and looked up into the sky. And it was as if the sound served to rouse and activate him, to drag decision from him. For suddenly he flung the gun against his shoulder, mumbling to himself, and scarcely taking time to aim, he fired.

Bang! The echoes crashed against the walls. The white cow bellowed once and rolled over on its back with its four feet in the air, and a bright red spot flooding from its neck. The red cow and the pig paid no attention to it; but the horse went galloping around, snorting with terror and pawing at the ground. Even Trictrac howled and ran away to hide. The Little One came running from the door—

"What?" she cried, pulling Teresa's skirt. "Oh, what was that?"

But Teresa was absorbed and would not answer.

"Rosa, lift me up."

"No—" Rosa shook her head.

"I want to see," she wailed. And Pablo lifted her. "What is it? What has happened?"

"The man has killed the cow," Teresa said. "The white one. Look!"

"Why, Teresa? Why did he kill the cow?" But no one answered her. "Why, Rafael? You tell me why." She pulled his hair.

"Perhaps he has gone crazy," Rafael said.

"Oh crazy! Crazy, yes—" She sang the words. "A crazy man, a crazy man. Please hold me higher, Pablo." She stopped and held her ears, for the man had put the gun back to his shoulder and was aiming it again.

"He will kill the red one this time," Gil said cheerfully.

The cow was standing still, a dozen paces from the man, looking at him mournfully, patient and resigned. They waited breathlessly while the moments ticked away, but the gun did not go off; the barrel of it shook and the man was shaking too. And then he made a sound, almost like a sob; and he seized the gun in both his hands, with the bayonet pointed, and ran stumbling down the slope into the barnyard, straight toward the corner where the sow lay with her pigs.

"Oh—" they gasped. "What is he doing now?"

The sow got on her feet out of the ooze of mud, grunting at the man; and he shouted back at her and jabbed her with the bayonet, but not very hard or deep. And then she backed away, still grunting savagely and baring yellow teeth; and the little pigs were scattered, some this way and some that. Perhaps that was his purpose, for he let the mother be and ran after the young ones, jabbing at them with the bayonet, but at first not hitting one, for they dodged and scuttled quickly from the point, squealing with all their might.

"No, no, no," the Little One commanded. "Stop, bad man! Stop!" But then she laughed with glee and clapped her hands, for the man had slipped and fallen in the muck of fresh manure. He scrambled to his feet and went running off again; and this time he got one, speared it like a fish and threw it dead behind him, its little legs still kicking. It was not the spotted one, but the spotted one was next. "Stop, bad man! Stop!" But there was no stopping now. The little pig was trapped in a corner of the yard, and the bayonet pierced its belly and came out the other side. The man stood looking at it, level with his eyes, with the gun butt on the ground. "Put me down, Pablo," she sobbed. "Please put me down." She got her doll out of the apple box and sat on a grain sack on the floor, crying softly to herself.

The sun had risen now. The man wiped his face on his sleeve and brushed the manure from his clothes; and he walked to the white cow and pushed it with his foot, looking at it sadly. He did not seem angry now. But then there was the sound of planes again, and this seemed to rouse him as it had before. He looked about and found the other pig and snagged it on the bayonet with the spotted one, and went hurrying up the slope into the barn, with the gun across his shoulder and the little pigs hung on it. The mother pig was wallowing in the mud again, and the rest of the little ones had found their way back to her. The red cow wasn't doing anything. The horse was as far away as he could get, still snorting and pawing now and then.

The children ran across the granary to the window, chattering with excitement—

"Where is he going now?"

"What will happen to the cow?"

"What will *she* say when she knows?"

"What does crazy mean?" the Little One kept asking. But no one answered her. "What is crazy?" she insisted. Juan came and sat beside her on the floor. "What is crazy, Juan?"

"Crazy?" He thought about it. "Crazy is when you don't know what you're doing."

"Oh, that is crazy." She nodded, smiling through her tears. "Then only men are crazy."

"Yes, only men," Juan said.

2

MME. BIGARD HURRIED TOWARD THE VILLAGE, a kilometer away, walking stiffly on her heels along the narrow tree-lined road which was empty of traffic at this hour. In the fields on either side the grain dipped with the dew and the poppies hung their heads, not yet awakened.

The village street was empty—a narrow street of old stone houses; only in the baker's shop was there a sign of life: the shop door open and a smell of new baked bread. Mme. Bigard hurried on to the end of the street where, next to the church, the curé lived. Père Joseph was his name. She was not acquainted with him. He had not long been resident in the parish, and of late Mme. Bigard had neglected her devotions. She had simply not had time. Knocking on the door now, she was conscious of a mildly guilty feeling.

The priest saw her coming from the window of his bedroom and recognized her from the way she walked. She had been pointed out to him as the wife of a farmer who was serving in the army. He knew no more than that, or no more that he remembered. And he watched her approach with mild annoyance. He could smell his breakfast coffee in

10

the kitchen where the woman who attended on his needs was now preparing it. He assumed that Mme. Bigard was coming in such haste
at this hour of the morning to summon his attendance on a moribund,
and that he would be obliged to go without his breakfast. He was not
a young man; neither was he old; but he was closely wedded to his
habits. And a woman who does not come to Mass, might at least come
after breakfast, if she must come at all. This thought was in his mind
as he buttoned his soutane, hung his crucifix around his neck, and
firmly crossed himself—a gesture designed to relieve his irritation. In
response to the knock upon the door he went himself to open it, and his
apprehensions were immediately confirmed, for his visitor was breathless
and in tears. It could be nothing else but attendance on the dying—

Mme. Bigard introduced herself and mumbled some confused words
of apology, which he gently put aside. "But what is it, Mme. Bigard?"

"The Boche," she gasped.

"Oh, the Germans!" Père Joseph was relieved.

"They are coming, *mon père.*"

"Yes, yes—" He smiled indulgently. He would have his coffee after
all, for this matter was not urgent. "But please come in," he said; and
he placed a chair for her and called to the woman in the kitchen
that she should bring two cups as he would have a guest.

Mme. Bigard was too excited to sit down. She repeated in her hoarse
and raucous voice that the Germans were coming, might arrive at any
moment.

Père Joseph nodded as one nods to a child. "The army of France—"
he began a little vaguely, for in fact he did not know anything about it.

But Mme. Bigard took the words out his mouth. "The army of France
—" She clasped her hands dramatically. "But it exists no more."

"Come, come—" Père Joseph smiled again. For days there had been
wild rumors in the air, but the life of the countryside had not been
interrupted and the Paris radio was reassuring. "Please compose yourself," he said, aware now that the overwrought condition of his guest
had its origin in fright and not in grief. "We may safely leave these
matters to the government. And to God," he added as an afterthought.
He took the breakfast tray which the woman now presented at the door,
and poured two cups of coffee. "A cup of coffee, Mme. Bigard," he suggested.

Mme. Bigard took the cup. She had not stopped talking for a moment, but now he was conscious of something she was saying—

"*Mon père*, please understand: my husband has come home."

"Ah, your husband has come home—" He nodded absently.

"Yes, home, Père Joseph. He arrived an hour ago. In such a state—" She sobbed.

"But I thought—" The priest broke a piece of bread and spread it thick with honey. "That is to say, I understood your husband was a soldier in the army."

"Alas!" Mme. Bigard spread her hands in a gesture of despair. "But it exists no more. The army is in flight, fleeing from the Boche who are close upon its heels."

Père Joseph looked appropriately solemn, but he was not much impressed. He suggested hopefully that there were other armies—

"As to that—" Mme. Bigard shrugged her shoulders. "But my husband has come home and we must leave at once."

"Leave?" The priest looked doubtful.

"Yes, leave our farm. My husband would be killed or made a prisoner if the Boche should find him. We must leave immediately. We will take the horse and cart. We will go to the Midi where his mother lives. And there is no room to carry anyone except ourselves. So you see, it is impossible. Well, definitely impossible."

Père Joseph was confused. "Impossible?" he echoed.

"Yes, impossible, *mon père*, to take the children with us."

"Children?" The priest put down his cup. "Surely you do not mean you would go without your children?"

"But no, I have no children—" Mme. Bigard choked.

"Then what children would you leave?"

"*Mon père*, the Spanish children—"

"Spanish children, do you say?" He began to remember something he had heard.

"Of a certainty, *mon père*." Mme. Bigard clasped her hands. "The little bolsheviks."

"Bolsheviks?" Père Joseph frowned.

"Well, perhaps they are not that," Mme. Bigard added hastily, "since they are only children. But one of them is Jewish, to judge by his appearance; and another one is black, like an African in fact; and there is one without an arm and the Jewish one is sickly; and there is the smallest one who is really just a baby. Oh, I was deceived about them. I was deceived, *mon père*." She paused to catch her breath. "I said I would take four and they sent me seven. Only think of that! They came on a bus two months ago, with tags pinned on their clothes, addressed to me, here to the village. And what was I to do? I couldn't send them back, for there was no place to send them."

"Yes, yes—" Père Joseph nodded, remembering some scraps of village gossip to which he had not paid much attention at the time: Mme. Bigard had responded to a notice in the paper and had written for some children to be sent to her from a refugee camp close by the Spanish border—one of those social undertakings sponsored by the communists, that Popular Front which was no longer popular. In fact, the advertisement no doubt signified liquidation of the project, for the communists had now other things to think about, and neither time nor money to devote to Spanish orphans. It was said that Mme. Bigard had not been activated by purely philanthropic motives, but had seized an opportunity to get the farm work done, in the absence of her husband, with no expense beyond a minimium of food.—Yes, that much he remembered.

Mme. Bigard was still talking, in a kind of plaintive screech. "And they did not tell the truth about their ages," she complained. "They pretended not to know how old they were, but assured me they were old enough to do a good day's work. And they are only children. I have been imposed upon, really cheated is the word. Imagine, seven of them when I only asked for four. And they did not tell me they could not speak French, and so it is impossible to make them understand. And they are not friendly children, not pleasant in the least."

"Not pleasant?" Père Joseph echoed vaguely.

"No." Mme. Bigard shook her head. "I would not like to know what they say among themselves. But of course they do not come from decent homes—picked up in the gutters or sleeping in the fields, and with bolsheviks for fathers."

"Little children strayed from God," Père Joseph murmured sadly.

"Very true, *mon père*—" Mme. Bigard sighed and altered her lament to a more charitable note. "I have done my best," she said. "I have turned the other cheek, have repaid these swindling communists with kindness. I have cared for these children as if they were my own. But unfortunately I can do no more. We are leaving at once, my husband and myself, and we cannot take the children. Well, please figure to yourself: a small cart and a horse, and there are seven of them. No, no, it is impossible." She stopped for lack of breath.

Père Joseph wiped his face which had begun to sweat from the coffee or confusion. "I am afraid," he said, "that I have not understood the purpose of your visit."

Mme. Bigard begged a thousand pardons. She had come, she explained, at her husband's command; and, indeed, there had been no alternative. The children must be left—well, that was obvious—and where could they be left save under the protection of the Church?

"Of the Church?" Père Joseph had a sinking feeling.

"Of the Church." Mme. Bigard nodded blandly. Nowhere else would they be safe, in the actual care of God who would overlook the fact of their dubious origins—

Père Joseph interrupted this pious declaration, clutching at a straw. He admitted the soundness of the argument. "But," he protested, "the solution you suggest is unfortunately not practical. My house is very small; there is certainly not room for seven children. If the question involved only one or two—" He smiled and shrugged, suggesting the frustration of benevolence.

"But no, *mon père*—" Mme. Bigard laughed, sounding strangely like a crow, "—you have not understood me. Of a certainty I would not dream of imposing these children on your household. That is not what I have in mind at all. The orphanage of Sainte-Cécile—"

"Ah, the orphanage of Sainte-Cécile!" Père Joseph breathed again. "Yes, yes, I see, of course. Excellent, Mme. Bigard, an excellent idea! And you wish me to write a letter to the convent?"

"A letter, *mon père?*" Mme. Bigard shrugged her shoulders. "Well, a letter if you like. But no doubt it would be better if you took the children there."

"If *I* took them, Mme. Bigard?" Père Joseph felt a chill of apprehension. The orphanage of Sainte Cécile was in a suburb of Le Havre, some thirty kilometers away. "Really, Mme. Bigard—" He frowned reproachfully. "—I could scarcely leave the parish for so long a time. Well, it would take all day on the bus to go and come. And let me see—"

He affected to remember. "—I believe there is a christening to solem-
nize at noon." The christening was tomorrow, but he might be excused
for confusion of the date. "No, I am afraid it is not possible." He sighed.
"But I will write a letter—" He moved as if to do so. "And you can
take the children on the bus or in your cart. Yes, that will work out
nicely."

"But no, *mon père.*" Mme. Bigard shook her head, sadly but firmly.
"Unfortunately we go in the opposite direction. So it would not be
possible."

"But only a few hours, surely that would make no difference in
your plans—"

Mme. Bigard grimly reverted to her thesis: the Germans were coming,
might arrive at any moment, and her husband's urgency would admit
of no delay. She put down her empty cup with a gesture of finality.

"But, Mme. Bigard—" Père Joseph was suddenly inspired, "—if as
you say, the Germans are at hand, how can I leave this village which
is my post of duty, and where I may be needed to attend upon the
wounded or administer the sacrament?" This argument was in the
realm of the rhetorical, for he did not expect any such development.
But Mme. Bigard was apparently impressed.

"Yes, that is true," she sighed. "Well then, I do not know. I have
done all that I could, and there is nothing else but to pray God's
mercy for them."

"You mean that you will take them?"

"On the contrary, *mon père.*"

"But then what will you do?"

"I will leave them where they are."

"Alone there on the farm?"

"Alas, I have no choice."

"Ah, ah—" Père Joseph paced the floor.

Mme. Bigard was aware that she had won, but she added for good
measure, "Perhaps the Germans will not harm them, though one of
them is Jewish and another one is black. Still, even so—"

Père Joseph muttered something and hastily crossed himself. He
detested Mme. Bigard at this moment. "Let us go then," he said calmly,
and he got his wide black hat from a hook upon the wall. "The bus for
Le Havre will pass by at eight o'clock." He was calculating briskly in

his mind: an hour and an hour, and an hour to come back; by noon it might be finished if there was no delay.

"The bus fare—" Mme. Bigard began, and stopped abruptly, thriftily regretting she had spoken.

"Yes?—the bus fare?" Père Joseph waited with his hand upon the latch. He was not disposed to let this matter drop.

"Well, I will pay the bus fare," Mme. Bigard sighed, "though really the communists should do so."

"You are generous, Mme. Bigard," Père Joseph murmured dryly. "The fare? Now let me see: one franc fifty for each child, and to go and come would be six francs for myself—sixteen fifty, I believe."

"I did not bring my purse." Mme. Bigard in her victory felt the sharp tooth of defeat.

"It will be soon enough—" Père Joseph smiled, "—when the children are delivered to my care."

As they came into the street there was a rumbling sound like distant thunder, and the earth seemed to tremble for a moment. But the day was fine; there were no clouds in the sky and the sun was shining brightly. The village was awake; shops were being opened and farm carts passing by. Père Joseph dismissed the matter from his mind: the big guns at Le Havre were practicing perhaps, as they sometimes did. He absently returned the greetings of the villagers, for he was preoccupied. And presently he said, from a context in his thought:

"Not pleasant, Mme. Bigard, I believe you mentioned?"

"Not pleasant, *mon père?*"

"These Spanish children."

"Oh! Oh yes!" But she did not go on.

"In what way are they unpleasant?"

"But, *mon père*, it is difficult to say—" And it was difficult because she didn't know; she had asked herself the question many times but had never pursued it to an answer.

"Are they disobedient?" Père Joseph suggested.

"Well no, not disobedient, when they understand."

"Are they quarrelsome or destructive?"

"No, *mon père*—"

"Lazy and provoking?"

"No, I would not say that—"

"Do they pilfer things?"

"Oh no—"

"Are they perhaps unclean about their habits?"

"Well, no—"

"Would you say that they were stupid?"

"On the contrary, *mon père.*"

"But they have not gone to school?"

"That is true, no doubt."

"They cannot read or write?"

Mme. Bigard shrugged. She had not explored the matter.

"And they have not had instruction in religion?"

"As to that—" Mme. Bigard sighed. "But what would one expect from little bolsheviks?"

"Hum—" Père Joseph nodded and came back to the question in his mind. "In what way are they unpleasant?"

"In what way?" Mme. Bigard struggled with the problem, hurrying on her heels with her belly sticking out. They had passed through the village into the narrow lane with the trees on either side in their vivid new spring dresses. The grain in the fields was holding up its heads, and the poppies were opening, like slowly spreading bloodstains. "In what way?" she repeated. "Well, they are not very friendly."

"Friendly?" Père Joseph was persistent. He must give some account to the nuns at Sainte-Cécile. "How not friendly, Mme. Bigard?"

"How?" Mme. Bigard reflected in silence for some moments. "It is as if—as if—"

"As if?" Père Joseph prompted.

"As if they were not children, like children that one knows. They are foreigners of course, but that is not what I mean."

"Do they romp and play like children?"

"Oh yes, they romp and play."

"Then in what way are they different?"

"I do not know, *mon père.*" Mme. Bigard shook her head. "But they are not like children, and they are not like adults."

"Perhaps they are afraid?"

"No, they are not afraid." Mme. Bigard answered with conviction. "It is something else entirely. I do not know how to say it, but as though you were shut out, regarded with suspicion, as an enemy in fact. Yes, that is it exactly: an enemy, *mon père*. And so it is not pleasant being with these children, not pleasant in the least."

"Humph!" Père Joseph shrugged. He thought that Mme. Bigard was a very stupid woman; and so, indeed, she was. But she had expressed herself with a flash of rare intelligence.

3

THE CHILDREN SAW THEM COMING—GIL AND
Juan and Rosa who were watching through the window. The
others had lost interest in the matter. Pablo and Teresa were
playing a game, hopping on one foot through a pattern of
squares chalked on the floor, and the Little One was acting as an
umpire, deciding points against them when they cheated. Rafael
was lying on his bed because his back was hurting. He had a wooden
whistle with three squeaky, plaintive notes, and he was blowing on it,
softly to himself.

They had not forgotten to wash their hands and faces in the metal
basin underneath the tap, and had given attention to other morning
matters, in a noisome cubby at the far end of the granary, roughly
improvised with a hole cut in the floor. They had combed or brushed
their hair—such is the force of habit. Rosa had helped the Little One,
brushing the long blond curls around her finger, saying as she always
said, "You are a big girl now, you should do this for yourself." And
the Little One had laughed and changed the subject.

They were hungry and bored, no longer intrigued by the crazy
man's behavior.

After he had killed the cow and little pigs, he had done other things equally absurd. He had rushed from the barn across the yard into the house, leaving his gun outside with the pigs stuck on the bayonet. And he had carried out a quantity of things: clothing and utensils, mattresses and quilts, even chairs and tables and pictures from the walls—until there was a pile that reached above his head. And then he had gone to the rooms above and thrown more things from the windows. All kinds of things came crashing down, and some of them were broken. It had been exciting for a while.

"He is stealing all her things," they said.

"What will she say when she comes back?"

"Maybe he will stick her on the bayonet with the pigs."

The idea was amusing. But as the pile grew bigger there was doubt of his intention.

"How can he carry all the things away?"

"Perhaps he'll burn them up," suggested Gil.

"And the house too," Pablo said.

"And the granary and the barn," Teresa added hopefully. But then she and Pablo had gone away to play.

But the man had not set fire to the things. Instead, he had gone back to the barnyard and driven the horse into the barn, and then had led him out with the harness hung upon him, and had hitched him to the cart. He had had some trouble doing it because the horse was frightened and would not stand still or do as it was told. His purpose was now plain: he would steal the horse and cart to take the things away.

"And the cow, too?" Rosa asked.

"Yes, the cow," Gil said, "if he has room for it."

But, as it turned out, there was no room for the cow, nor for half the stuff he had carried from the house. He filled the cart and still there was a great pile on the ground. And then he took things out and put others in their place, tugging and lifting till the sweat ran down his face, and shouting when something would not go in where he wanted it; and once he hit the horse in the belly with his fist because it pawed the ground, but it could not get away because he had it tied to a stout post by the door. And it was sweating, too, and its legs were trembling, and it kept looking back with frightened eyes to see what the crazy man was doing.

Finally no more things would go into the cart, and it was no use to try. And the man stuck his gun in at the back, with the two pigs hanging from it, and kicked some scattered things back into the pile. And then he stood there waiting, leaning with his back against the stone wall of the house, looking all around—at the barn and the granary and the orchard, at some blossoms that were growing on a vine beside the door. And he plucked one from the stem and held it in his hand. And then he rubbed his sleeve across his eyes.

"He is crying," Rosa said.

"No," Gil shook his head. "Why should he be crying?"

The others came to look.

"Maybe," ventured Pablo, "because all the things won't go in the cart."

"Anyway, he's crying," they agreed. And so in fact he was.

It was then they saw them—the woman and Père Joseph, approaching on the path.

"Look! *She* is coming back."

"There is someone with her."

"A woman."

"No, a man."

"But see the long black dress."

"Look at his hat—a man."

"A woman, I tell you."

"No," Gil said, "it is not a woman and it is not a man. It is a priest."

"Oh yes, a priest," they chorused.

"What is a priest?" the Little One demanded. But no one answered her, for the moment was exciting.

"What will she do?"

"She has brought the priest to help her."

"The priest will make him give back everything he's stolen."

"No, he won't," Gil said. "Men are not afraid of priests."

"Maybe," suggested Pablo, "the man will kill them both."

"Oh no," cried Rosa. "No." And Juan went away and would not look.

But the man did not do what anyone expected. He untied the horse and climbed into the cart.

"He will run away," they said, relieved and disappointed.

But he did not run away, though the horse was pulling at the reins, impatient to be off. Instead, he waited, holding back the horse, and shouting a word with which they were familiar—a word which meant to hurry. The woman came running toward him and he motioned to her to get into the cart. He did not speak to the priest or take any notice of him. The woman hurried on, looking back over her shoulder, screeching to Père Joseph, pointing at the granary—

"The children are there, in the granary, *mon père*. I regret I—"

"Come now," her husband shouted. "Enough of this. Get in." The horse was snorting and pushing back the cart. "Get in, I say. Get in."

"In the granary, *mon père*." She climbed into the cart beside the man. "You will find them in the granary."

Père Joseph gently took the bridle of the horse and put his other hand upon its neck. "I understand," he said. "But there is a final matter which has been overlooked."

"A final matter? What?" M. Bigard raised his whip, as if to strike the priest—or so it seemed to the children who were watching.

"The bus fare, Mme. Bigard."

"Ah yes, *mon père*," she groaned. "It had escaped my mind."

"Bus fare?" M. Bigard fumbled in his pocket, cursing bolsheviks and brats.

"Sixteen francs fifty." Père Joseph waited calmly with his hand upon the bridle.

"Ah bah!" And grumbling furiously, M. Bigard took the money from his pocket and counted it out into Père Joseph's hand.

Mme. Bigard had remembered something else and was screeching again. "Trictrac! Trictrac!" she called, looking everywhere about the yard. "Come here, Trictrac! Come here!"

The children wriggled with delight. They knew where Trictrac was —close by the kitchen door, under the currant bushes, in a hole he had dug for occasions of this kind. And he would not come out.

"Trictrac!" she shrieked. "Trictrac!"

The man brought his whip down on the horse which bolted with a jerk that nearly overturned Mme. Bigard on her back. The cart went rattling off and some things fell out of it, but the gun stayed in its place, the little dead pigs bouncing playfully up and down.

Père Joseph stood for some moments without moving, looking at the money in his hand. And then he crossed himself, and crossed himself again, atoning in good measure for something he was thinking.

The children were bewildered. They had followed the affair with comment and discussion deriving from a drama without words: the man had tried to run away but the priest had stopped him; yet in the end he went and took the woman with him, not unwillingly it seemed. It was completely crazy, as were most adult matters.

"She is stealing her own things," Teresa giggled.

"The priest has told the man," suggested Pablo, "that if he steals the things, he must take the woman too."

"But she wants to go with him."

"No, she wants her things."

Then the priest held the horse so the man could not drive off; and the man raised his whip as if to hit the priest; but instead of that—

"Oh look!" they cried. "He is giving money to him."

"Certainly." Gil nodded. "That is what they do: when they have sinned they give money to the priest."

"Of course," said Teresa, "and then God will forgive them."

"Does God want money?" Rafael asked.

But no one answered him because at this moment the cart went rattling off, with things falling out of it and banging on the ground. And when the noise had died away, there was another sound—like distant thunder, and the granary seemed to tremble. Père Joseph turned his head and looked back at the sky: on the far-off horizon there was a great white cloud swelling like a mushroom. The attention of the children was diverted—

"There will be a storm," they said. "Listen to the thunder."

Juan listened critically. "It sounds like war," he muttered.

"War? What is war?" the Little One demanded. But her question went unanswered because Père Joseph had moved from where he stood and was walking toward the door.

"He is coming here," they whispered, looking at each other with anxious inquiry.

"What does he want of us?"

"What will he do?"

"Nothing," Gil said scornfully, with a confidence he did not altogether feel. "He will not do anything, because he is a priest."

They waited in a group close by the window. Père Joseph could not see them very well at first: it was dim in the granary and the light from the window was directly in his eyes. He spoke with gentle amiability—

"Good day, my children."

They were familiar with these words, and they answered him in Spanish. "Good day," they said.

Père Joseph knew no Spanish but he was aware they had returned his greeting. He began to see more clearly, picking out the black one first—not really black, he thought, but with a swarthy skin; and then the Jewish boy who looked very frail indeed, and pathetic in a jacket which came almost to his knees. And there was a girl with the face of a Madonna; and another, rather pert, with a ribbon in her hair; and a sensitive-looking boy with one arm missing; and another of like age, or perhaps a little older. This one stood apart, feet spread and firmly planted, arms folded on his breast—not defiant exactly, but certainly not friendly. None of them was smiling, nor had smiled when they spoke.

Still, they did not look like communists—as Père Joseph imagined communists would look. He had never, to his knowledge, seen a communist, but he had a vague idea that the mark of Cain would be apparent somewhere, or at least a suggestion of rudimentary horns. These children looked like any other children, and perhaps they were not communists. The orphans of a civil war were not easily classified. He felt relieved. Mme. Bigard was a fool. If it should turn out that there was among them a subversive element, the nuns at Sainte-Cécile would know what to do about it.

Three boys and three girls, six of them in all. But then he remembered: Mme. Bigard had said seven. At this moment the Little One stepped out into his view from where she had been screened behind the others.—Ah yes, of course, the smallest one—a merry little face in a halo of blond curls; and she was really smiling. It would be well, he thought, to start with her. So he came closer, squatting on the floor with his soutane spread around him, smiling back at her, actually grimacing, as unenlightened adults do with children, and making chirping sounds—

"Well, well—" he said. "We shall be friends, shall we not, my pretty one?"

And the Little One replied, with smiling eyes, in her most coquettish voice, "The priest looks like a frog."

The children could not keep their faces straight, and then a giggle overwhelmed them. He did look like a frog, squatting on his haunches in his long black dress, with his wide flat hat and big pop eyes, and his funny croaking voice.

"Humph!" Père Joseph rose and shook the dust from his soutane. He was embarrassed and annoyed; he knew that he was being laughed at but he did not know why, and this, for priest or layman, is a trying situation. He did not feel so sure of his first impression. There *was* something unpleasant in their attitude, quite aside from the laughter they were trying to control.—What had that small one said to set them all to giggling? Well, no matter—

He went on talking in his thin, high, nasal voice, to cover his confusion. "You are to go with me, my children, on a motorbus, through the pretty country—and that will be amusing, will it not? You are going to a lovely home where they will be kind to you, where you will hear many stories—about the infant Jesus and his Mother. And we must hurry, for the bus will soon be leaving.—Well now, where are your things?—some articles of clothing, I suppose?" But there was no sign of understanding in their faces.

"What does he want?" they whispered.

"When shall we have our breakfast?"

"Perhaps he will stay here and tell us what to do."

"What is he doing now?"

Père Joseph had discovered two ragged canvas rucksacks hanging on the wall, and went to take them down. "Ah yes, these will serve nicely in place of a valise." He undid the straps and opened them. "Now children, bring your things." He made signs of putting things into the rucksacks.

They understood the pantomime: they were to put their things into those bags—as they had done when they came; they were to go away—

from the farm, the dismal granary. They rushed to gather their possessions, chattering with excitement—

"Oh good!" they said.

"We are going away."

"On a motorbus perhaps?"

"Like the one we came on."

"We are going. We are going."

Only Gil said nothing and moved deliberately. He was excited, too, but he did not mean to let the priest know that.

They brought their things and crammed them in the rucksacks; there was not much to bring and the sacks were not half full. Gil took one upon his back and Juan the other—as they had done when they came.

"Good!" Père Joseph said. "Very good indeed, my children. But have we forgotten anything?—no shoes or stockings?—no hats of course?—nothing left that we should take?" He looked about, but the granary was bare. "Yes, well—" He opened the door and the children ran out into the sunshine.

They were terribly excited. They had even forgotten they were hungry. Trictrac came bounding out from beneath the currant bushes, wagging his tail and barking joyously.

"There is Trictrac," they exclaimed.

"He has been waiting for us."

"We will take him on the motorbus."

"But will the priest allow it?"

"Then he can run behind."

"Oh no, it goes too fast."

Trictrac was ecstatic; he jumped on the Little One and licked her hands and face.

Père Joseph arranged them in a kind of procession. His forebodings were allayed: they seemed like normal children, like children anywhere. Introducing them at Sainte-Cécile would not be hazardous; they would soon resemble all the other orphans. "Now let me see," he said, "in what order we must go.—Come now, you two!" He motioned Pablo and Rafael that they should walk with him—the black boy and the Jew at the near hand of God's vicar. But that was not in his mind. "Now the three girls behind us, with the small one in the middle. Yes, that's the way, my children." The one with the Madonna

face had an air of refinement, of gentility in fact. It seemed unlikely
she could derive from communists. The other, with the ribbon in her
hair, looked like a gypsy—not quite dependable. There might be
some question about her. "And last, you two big boys with the knap-
sacks on your shoulders—like a rear guard, so to speak." The one who
lacked an arm seemed a gentle, thoughtful boy. The other was much
rougher and rather sullen looking, and perhaps he would bear watching. "Now, off we go!" And away they went across the yard.

Trictrac came along beside the column, his high spirits undiminished.
Père Joseph paused at the edge of the road and admonished him
severely. "Go home," he said and pointed, and even stamped his foot.
"Go home," I say. Trictrac stopped doubtfully with his tail between
his legs. The children were depressed—

"He is sending Trictrac back."

"The mean old priest!"

"Who will take care of Trictrac?"

"Who will feed him?"

They went on a little way, till Père Joseph, looking back, found
that Trictrac was still following. "Go home," he shouted sternly, and
he picked up a pebble and threw it toward the dog, but not far enough
to hit him. "Go home, I say. Go home!" Trictrac stopped and sat down
in the road.

"The priest is bad," they said.

"The priest is like a man."

"Gil said he was a priest."

"Yes, I said he was a priest," Gil answered from the back, "but I
didn't say that he was not a man."

Père Joseph walked along. He was conscious of a change, of something hostile in the atmosphere, but he was unable to define it. It
occurred to him that song was a leveler of barriers, and might be helpful
in the present situation. So he began to sing, in his high thin voice,
an old folk song of Normandy, with words which were easy to repeat.
And he urged the children to join in. "Come now, my children, let us
all sing together. I will begin again." And he did so, looking back over
his shoulder and urging with his arms.

It was quite plain what he meant and they understood him perfectly.
But they did not feel like singing: they were hungry, and both grieved

and angry about Trictrac, though the dog was still following at a distance. Whenever he stopped, Gil would look back with an inviting gesture, even whistling to him softly, so it sounded like a bird. No, they did not like the priest and they did not feel like singing, and so they did not sing.

Only the Little One made response to the appeal, with words which she fitted to the simple melody: "The priest is bad—the priest looks like a frog—"

Père Joseph gave it up after a decent effort.—They were not like other children, he decided. It was difficult to say, but the feeling they inspired was not pleasant.

4

THEY WAITED FOR THE BUS ON THE VILLAGE
street outside the baker's shop. The tantalizing smell was
almost insupportable and they could not keep their eyes from
straying to the window where the long brown loaves were
piled. And Trictrac waited, too, sprawled on the sidewalk at a
respectful distance. Père Joseph knew that he was there, but pretended
not to notice. It did not occur to him that the children might be hungry,
that they had had no breakfast. He was preoccupied: people were
passing by, exchanging greetings with him and pausing to ask questions.

The baker came into the door, a big man with bare arms. "Good
day," he said, and nodding toward the children with humorous
curiosity, "I see you have a handful. Do they by any chance belong to
you?"

"From the Bigard place," Père Joseph explained, smiling faint ap-
preciation of the jest. "Spanish orphans, I believe."

"Oh, the little bolsheviks!"

"Well, possibly—" Père Joseph changed the subject. He remarked that Mme. Bigard had been called away. He did not say more than that. He suspected that Bigard had deserted from the army, but he did not wish to indulge in any gossip. "I am taking them to Sainte-Cécile," he said.

"Ah, to Sainte-Cécile." The baker wagged his head. "They will not be bolsheviks when they get through with that."

There was laughter among others who had stopped to listen. Père Joseph wished the bus would come, already it was late.

A man said, pointing at the western sky, "It would seem there might be fire over there." The white cloud had diffused, no longer like a mushroom. "And there was a sound like guns," another added.

"Bah!" The baker shrugged. "They are always shooting guns there at Le Havre, burning up their powder. That's where the money goes. Politics!" He spat.

"But it could be the Germans," someone ventured.

"It could be your sister's cat," the baker said. There was more laughter.

Two women, market baskets on their arms, exchanged remarks with frank provincial rudeness:

"What little scarecrows!"

"Well, they are foreigners."

"And bolsheviks, I hear."

"No doubt."

"How thin they are!"

"But one would not get fat at Mme. Bigard's." They laughed maliciously.

"See, there is the black one."

"Like a little savage."

"And there, the Jewish one." She pointed at Rafael who was sitting on the sidewalk with his feet in the gutter. He had sat down because his back was hurting.

"Ah, but he is pale and sickly."

"Look! The one without an arm."

"Yes, you are right. Not much use around a farm."

"Mme. Bigard did not know it till they came."

"It served her right. Something for nothing was what she was after."
They laughed again.

The children had experienced this sort of thing before, being stared at and discussed. They drew closer to each other, looking straight before them, silent and impassive.

The bus came rattling down the cobbled street and stopped before the door. It was an old, ramshackle bus, open at the sides, with seats that ran across it. There was no one in it but a surly-looking driver who got down from his seat to issue tickets. Père Joseph paid the fares and then arranged the children in the bus, in the order of their walk: Pablo and Rafael in the seat behind the driver, then Rosa and Teresa with the Little One between them. But the Little One protested and her blue eyes filled with tears. She wanted to sit on the edge where she could see, and she had her way about it. Then Gil and Juan. Trictrac got in, too. He had been sneaking closer a little at a time, and at the end he wriggled in and crawled under the seat. Père Joseph saw this from the corner of his eye but did not think it wise to offer an objection. The driver, who was busy with the tickets, did not notice.

"Trictrac is in the bus," they whispered.

"No. Where?"

"Under the seat with Gil and Juan."

"What will the priest say?"

"He doesn't know."

"But if Trictrac barks?"

"Gil will keep him quiet."

The driver got in and the bus began to move. The baker waved his hand. "A pleasant trip," he called. The children were ecstatic—

"See! We are not going back the way we came."

"We are going to a new place."

"A nicer one perhaps."

"A new one anyway."

"We are going to a new place," the Little One sang blithely, holding Juana up to see. "To a new place—to a new place—"

Père Joseph drew a deep breath of relief. When they were no longer rattling over cobblestones, he spoke to the driver, pointing through the windshield, for he was not entirely reassured about the smoke. "It would seem," he suggested, "that there might be a fire near Le Havre?"

"A fire?" The driver looked and shrugged. "It is always smoky there," he said ungraciously.

After some moments Père Joseph spoke again. "Is there any news," he asked, "about the Germans?"

"The Germans?" The driver looked around. He had no news, he said, nor time to listen to it. Anyway, the news was all a pack of lies invented by the thieving politicians. "As for me," he added viciously, "between Blum and Hitler there is very little choice."

Père Joseph acknowledged this treasonable statement with a noncommittal smile, and refrained from further questions.

The children had again forgotten they were hungry. The day was fine; the sun was shining brightly from a deep blue sky. The narrow, tree-lined road slid away beneath the wheels, crisscrossed with light and shadow. Birds sang in the hedges, beyond which were green fields of grain, thick sprinkled with red poppies; or meadows smooth as velvet, with herds of grazing cattle and cows with little calves. And there were farmhouses, like the one that they had left—low, flat houses built of stone, roofed with rough-cut slate on which the moss was growing; stone barns and granaries, too. Dogs rushed out and barked and were quickly left behind. Occasionally a farm cart was passed or overtaken, but there was little traffic on the road. Now and then they came into a village—sleepy little places, even smaller than the one that they had left. But no passengers embarked, and in a moment they would be off again.

After one such unprofitable pause Père Joseph ventured to remark that people did not seem to be traveling very much.

"Good thing," the driver grunted. "They are better off at home."

Père Joseph gave it up. He was really enjoying this unexpected holiday; that's why he wished to talk, to share his warmth of feeling with his fellow man. He looked back at the children, unable to resist his opulence of mood. "It is lovely," he smiled, "is it not, my children? —the sunshine and the birds, this pretty land of France."

They stared at him suspiciously, their happy chatter silenced. Trictrac was breathing hard, and Gil shoved him with his foot. Père Joseph sighed and said no more, reflecting that the absence of a common language was a stubborn barrier to understanding. Still, the barrier existed among very many people who spoke a common tongue, whose thoughts and feelings were so far apart that communication could not make them clear to one another.

And this was true of children on the whole. They inhabited another world in which the adult symbols had no meaning. For example, neither time nor space represented to children what they did to adults. Men lived by clocks which were ignored by children. And kilometers meant nothing to a child. If a thing was out of sight, it was gone, it was away. Its spatial location had no bearing on the matter: out of sight was gone completely, as far off as Arabia, as far away as death—as far off and as near. It was here or it was not here, that was all there was about it.

There was little common ground on which children and adults could intelligently meet. And though they might converse with some apparent freedom, this freedom was deceptive, lip service in fact—breeding and training on the part of children, and patience and forbearance on the part of adults. To spend one's life with children would be a lonely business. For some hours in the day such a life might be intriguing. There were women and teachers who insisted this was true, but they had other lives to which they had free access and could return again. But suppose—he allowed imagination to run loose—suppose one were alone in a world of children, the only adult in it! He could not repress a shudder at the thought. And then he remembered, with a slight sense of discomfort, something Christ had said, according to St. Mark: "Suffer the little children to come unto me, and forbid them not; for of such is the kingdom of heaven."

"Yes, well—" Père Joseph murmured, fingering his crucifix. But then, he reflected, it was scarcely likely Our Lord had had in mind the progeny of bolsheviks.

His meditation was abruptly interrupted as a motorcar went by, going very fast, the back piled high with luggage and things tied on the sides; and then there was another and another, flashing by like streaks. The children were excited, looking forward, looking back—

"It is a race," they cried.

The driver was beside himself with fury. He had never, he affirmed, seen such driving on this road. He would take the numbers of these motorcars and report them to the *préfecture* when he reached Le Havre.

But the cars went by so quickly and the dust was so thick that he could not see the numbers.

"They are crazy," he said, "or the devil is behind them."

Père Joseph said nothing, partly because he did not wish to divert the driver's attention from the road. But he was aware of a sense of vague discomfort; the warmth of his feeling had gone cold. And the aspect of the day itself had changed: the sun no longer shone but appeared, through a screen of yellow haze, like a plate of burnished gold. And there was the smell of smoke, but not ordinary smoke, for it had an acrid taste and was burning in the nostrils. Trictrac was panting underneath the seat, and the children coughed and rubbed their eyes—

"It is the dust," they said.

"No, it is smoke."

"It has a funny smell."

"It tickles in my throat."

"It smells—" Juan sniffed suspiciously, "—it smells like war."

They were near their destination. The orphanage of Sainte-Cécile stood in a park with a stone wall around it, in a suburb of the city. But first they would come into the highway—the *grande route nationale*. Père Joseph was certain it could not be much farther. He had visited the convent and remembered certain landmarks. They would soon be there, he thought. Above the chugging of the engine and the rattling of the bus he was conscious of a sound which he could not classify: a rumbling as of traffic but with other sounds mixed in—the noise a crowd might make, a crowd that was in motion.

And then around a curve, debouching on the highway, they came suddenly upon it—a tangled stream of traffic: motorcars and carts, bicycles and wagons, and vehicles men pushed or dragged behind them—wheelbarrows, perambulators with little children in them or piled with household goods. And there were many walking, with packs upon their backs or babies in their arms—men and women, young and old, even cripples on their crutches; and so the whole procession, blocked and snarled, was moving at a snail's pace. The drivers blew their horns and shouted angrily and the walkers shouted back. But even when they crowded to the roadside to make way, it was all to do again a moment later, for the traffic flowed like a stream of muddy water, filling the road from side to side and trickling in the ditches and in the fields beyond. The clamor of the horns and shouting voices had a shrill and ugly sound. Now and then a car would diverge onto the road where the bus had stopped, perhaps in desperation, for this was not the direction of their choice.

"But what—" the driver gasped, and said no more; his tongue was paralyzed. Père Joseph was shocked but not very much surprised; he had been expecting something of this sort. The children stood up, staring—

"They are running away."

"Away from what?"

"They are angry."

"No, afraid."

"Afraid of what?"

"Of war," Juan said. His face was pale and he was trembling.

"Maybe they are crazy," the Little One suggested.

The driver found his voice, shouting at a passing car, "Say now, what is all this?" And a man shouted back so that part of it was heard—

"The Germans. They are bombing—"

"Ha!" The driver shook his head as if to shake his wits together. "In that case we go no farther." A gratuitous remark since the bus could in no way have gone on against the traffic. He began to turn the clumsy thing around.

"But wait," Père Joseph said. "We are not going back."

"Then get out," the driver snapped.

"Thank you," Père Joseph said. And he got out of the bus, motioning to the children. He had made his decision without any hesitation: there was nothing else to do, no other place to take them. The orphanage was almost within sight, ten minutes walk away; and there they would be safe. He did not think about himself or how he would return. He spoke with cheerful, reassuring words, forgetting that they could not understand. "Come now, my children, there is no cause for alarm. The bus is going back—" It had already started and was almost out of sight. "We must walk a little distance and keep very close together so we are not separated. Now then—" He arranged the procession in somewhat different order, with Gil and Juan in front, then the younger boys, and then the girls with the Little One between, while he himself walked at the side where he could keep them all under his eye. He no

longer pretended to be unaware of Trictrac, acknowledging his presence
and assigning him to walk with Gil and Juan. "Let us be off," he said.
And in a moment they had threaded through the traffic into the ditch
upon the other side where they could make their way against the
stream.

It was exciting for a while: the honking horns, and funny-looking
people crowding and pushing and getting in the way. There were old
ones leaning on the arms of sons and daughters, and some who had
been hurt were being helped along; and there were many children, and
some of them were tired and frightened and were crying.

Père Joseph made inquiry of the passers-by and received fragmentary
answers: the German planes had bombed Le Havre that morning—
the city was in flames and many people had been killed and injured—
the ships in the harbor had been sunk, but a few had got away—the
Germans themselves might arrive at any minute—no one knew where
they were.—Père Joseph walked on with his crucifix held tightly in
his hand.

The children were not happy; they were hungry and they did not
feel like walking. The excitement of the road soon wore away, and
they began to grumble—

"Where is he taking us?"

"Why don't we run away like everybody else?"

"Are we going to the war?"

Juan walked reluctantly, with his eyes upon the ground. He said to
Gil, "It was like this before, when my arm got hurt."

"No matter," Gil replied, "there are no soldiers here." But Juan
was not encouraged.

"I am hungry," the Little One protested, hanging back upon the
hands of her companions. "And I am tired of walking."

"Please—" chided Rosa. "You are not a baby."

"But I am hungry, hungry—"

"We are all hungry."

"But where are we going, Rosa?"

"See! There is Trictrac. He is not complaining."

"I don't care. I am hungry, and I am tired too."

"If you are good," Teresa said, "I will tell a story."

"Well—" The Little One smiled through her tears. "Well, tell it
then, Teresa."

And Teresa began, "Once upon a time—"

Rafael was limping painfully. It was difficult for him, walking in the ditch where the ground was rough and lumpy; once he almost fell and grabbed at Pablo's arm.

"Hi!" shouted Pablo. "What's the matter with you now?"

"My back is hurting."

"Humph!" The black boy hesitated. "Well, you can have my cane." And he gave Rafael a stick which he had picked up.

Père Joseph was peering through the pall of yellow smoke for the tower which would mark the site of Sainte-Cécile—a sixteenth century tower, so the nuns had told him. And the convent itself was very old— a rugged Norman building with thick stone walls and roof of ancient slate which time and the elements had mellowed.—Yes, there was the tower, rising high above the trees of the park in which it stood. He saw it with a deep sense of relief; he had known it would be there, and yet, in such a world, who could be sure?

"Come now, my children," he cried cheerfully. "We are at our journey's end, and soon you will be safe, out of turmoil and confusion—in the house of God, my children—in that lovely park of trees you can see behind the wall. And there are gardens, too, with pretty flowers. Come now, let us hurry—" And he mended his pace, thinking for a moment of himself, that perhaps he could remain at Sainte-Cécile until the bedlam of the road had passed—possibly until tomorrow, for the convent had a hospice where he could be housed. But still, he thought, perhaps he should return, even though he had to walk, for it might be they would need him in the village. Well, he would see—

They went on beside the wall and came to iron gates—great ornamental ones which had stood open when he came before. But they were closed. Père Joseph looked around for a bell to ring, for he knew there was a gatehouse where the gardener lived. And he saw the cord and pulled it, and heard the mellow chime inside the gate. And then he saw a man sitting on the footstone of a buttress—an old man with white hair, in a gardener's smock. The man was looking at him—

"What do you want?" he said.

"I—" Père Joseph approached. "Well, I have brought some children."

"Heh?" The old man cupped his ear.

Père Joseph raised his voice. "I have brought these orphaned children to remain at Sainte-Cécile."

"At Sainte-Cécile?" The old man laughed—a thin, dry cackling sound. "But it exists no more."

"What?" Père Joseph stared.

"The Germans came this morning from the sky."

"But—"

"Look!" He pointed to the gate. "Look for yourself."

Père Joseph went and looked between the iron bars, up the avenue of trees; and now he saw through the murk of yellow smoke which hung among the trees like a ragged dirty blanket—saw what at first he had not noticed, for at a casual glance everything appeared unchanged. The massive building stood, its walls unharmed, but the thick slate roof had vanished, the chimneys gone; it looked like a tin whose lid has been ripped off; and through the empty windows, as blank as sightless eyes, he could see the waving foliage of the trees. The building had been gutted, was empty as a drum. "Ah, ah—" he groaned, and crossed himself, and crossed himself again. And then he turned away and went back to the man—

"But the orphans?—and the nuns?"

"Some are dead, the others gone."

"Gone? But where?"

The old man shrugged and looked away, as if there was nothing further to be said.

"Yes, I see—" Père Joseph murmured, and remembered suddenly why he had come.

The children had not noticed anything. They were sitting on a patch of smooth clipped lawn close by the gate, listening to Teresa, to the story she was telling, sitting close together so as not to miss a word. The story was about a Witch, a good Witch actually, who turned herself into a goose to carry a small boy to liberate a Princess whom some wicked Moors had captured and imprisoned in Granada. It was very much involved, but in the end they had all been saved from death by a bag of clover seeds—four-leafed ones of course. And then in thankfulness they flew around the world, scattering four-leafed clover seeds everywhere they went, so that all the people of the earth would always have good luck.

The children had heard this story many times—a rather childish story for the older ones, but still they always listened because Teresa had a way of telling stories that made them both amusing and exciting.

She was crouching in the center of the group, sitting on her heels, pretending at the moment that she was a Witch, and they were leaning closer, watching every move she made and the changing expressions on her face, oblivious to the bedlam of the road a few short steps away, to the honking horns and angry, frightened voices, forgetful of the priest, not remembering they were hungry, not anything in fact. Even Trictrac was attentive, listening with his ears cocked.

"And so," Teresa concluded with a flourish, "they all lived happily ever after."

"I have found one," cried the Little One.

"Found one? Found what?"

"A four-leaf clover." She held up her hand with fingers closed.

"You haven't?"

"Yes, I have."

"Then show it."

"That will spoil it."

"You are fooling."

"No, I'm not."

"Then show us," they insisted.

"I will show it to Juan, but no one else."

"All right, show it to Juan."

"Juan—" She snuggled close to him, their heads together. "Look quickly. I will only show you once." She opened her fingers and snapped them shut again. There was nothing in her hand except a blade of grass. And then she laughed and laughed; she had played this trick before.

"Come now, my children," Père Joseph interrupted with a hint of sharpness in his voice. It was strange that they could laugh, it did not seem quite human. "You see, my children, there has been a great disaster—a dreadful thing has happened. So we must change our plans. Yes, we must rearrange—"

They waited on the grass, watching him with eyes in which there was no laughter, silent and impassive. Suspiciously, he thought—or callously perhaps—yes, that might be the word. But certainly not friendly.

"Well, well now, let me see—" Père Joseph felt very helpless and alone.

5

PERE JOSEPH LEFT THE CHILDREN ON THE
sidewalk while he went into the *préfecture* to appeal to the
police for assistance in solution of his problem. He expected
that his errand would be brief.

He had continued on into the city because he could think of nothing
else to do. He could not retrace his steps; neither he nor the children
were equal to the trip of twenty odd kilometers on foot. And if the
journey should be undertaken and completed, there was no solution
waiting at the end of it. Finally, the road that they had come was one
on which the Germans would be likely to advance, and so they might
be met with on the way. Père Joseph did not fear the Germans, nor
anticipate mistreatment at their hands, but still—it was difficult to say
what their temper really was, or that they would respect a Catholic
priest if they should come upon him on the road. And there was the
Jewish child and the other black one! He did not feel certain how

the Germans would react if they came upon these two, nor assured that his cloth would be effective to protect them.

It would be better, he reflected, to go on into the city where municipal authority was functioning. It was possible indeed that the nuns from Sainte-Cécile had taken refuge there in temporary quarters with the orphans who survived. The police would know about this and be able to direct him; and if it should turn out not to be the case, and no other institution was suited to receive them, then no doubt the police would undertake their care and provide for their removal to a place of safety.

All this he had debated and had come to a decision, standing with his back to the lofty iron gates, looking at the children sitting close together on the grass, with their eyes upon his face—

"We must go on, my children." He motioned them to rise and form the same procession, with the big boys at the head. "We will go into the city. It is not far to walk. If it were not so smoky we could see the city now. And beyond it is the sea, which perhaps you've never seen, with big stone docks and ships. Come now, let us be off!"

The children trudged in silence. The air was hot and heavy, and the thickening yellow smoke made them cough and burned their eyes. Even Trictrac was depressed, slouching at the rear with his tail between his legs.

They came into the city on the Rue de Normandie, a long and ugly thoroughfare in which the stream of traffic still persisted, but diminishing in volume toward its source. Père Joseph was relieved to find that the city still existed. Indeed, in this section no great damage was apparent: here and there a house was missing, like a tooth out of a jaw, and some were still on fire; from others the residents were removing their possessions which were piled upon the sidewalk. The children were aroused to fleeting interest—

"Look! A house has fallen down."

"It didn't fall."

"What then?"

"They knock them down with bombs."

"Why do they do that?"

"That is war," Gil said.

"Look! One is burning up."

"They are putting water on it."

"How did it catch fire?"

"They drop the fire down from airplanes in the sky."

"Why do they do that?" the Little One inquired.

"Oh, that is war," they said impatiently.

Only Juan did not ask or answer questions, walking with his eyes upon the pavement, looking neither to the right nor left. Père Joseph remarked the pallor of his face and feared the boy was ill. They came into a square in which there was a fountain, and ran toward it eagerly. They were perishing of thirst, so thirsty that their hunger had long since been forgotten. There were other people drinking, or waiting for their turn, but the children did not wait to reach the bubbling cups; they drank like Trictrac, from the basin of the fountain.

Père Joseph while he waited, asked some questions. They told him that the damage had been greater in the center of the city near the docks. The planes might come again—no one could say. The Germans? Who could tell? They had not seen any yet. The people who had fled would no doubt run into them. It was stupid, they agreed, to run away. The nuns of Sainte-Cécile? No, they had not heard of them. Perhaps at the *préfecture* information could be had. They directed Père Joseph how to find it.

They went on into the city.

"This is a big village," Pablo said.

"Ho!" Gil laughed. "It is not a village but a city—like Madrid."

"Madrid? How do you know?"

"Because I used to live there." He liked to believe that this was true, but he wasn't sure of it.

"Yes, a city," Rosa said, "like one where I lived, too."

"When, Rosa?"

"Oh, long ago. I can only remember a little bit about it."

"Look!" Gil pointed. "There is a cinema."

"A cinema? Oh, where?"

"There! Across the street." But the walls had fallen in and there was nothing left except the colored posters, cowboys on prancing horses.

"Oh—" They stared in disappointment. "Is that a cinema?"

"Wait, Rosa, wait!" The Little One pulled back. She had caught a glimpse of something in a window—an enormous cake, it seemed, tier on tier of snow-white frosting, a cake as tall as she was. "Rosa, please, I want to see."

Just then Père Joseph stopped. The *préfecture* was in a narrow street and had escaped destruction by a hair, for the cinema across the way had been utterly demolished; and the building at the side, which had housed a pastry shop, had nothing left of it except the front, in which remained the window with the decorated cake. Behind the window men were working in the wreckage, going in and out through the narrow doorway.

There was scarcely any traffic; the shops were closed, most of them tightly shuttered; but people were going and coming from the *préfecture*, quite a number of them, hurrying up and down the steps between the iron lanterns.

It was here that Père Joseph left the children on the sidewalk, expecting that his absence would be brief. He motioned them to wait, explaining volubly—

"I must attend to matters here, my children—matters in your interest. And you must wait for me till I return. You may sit here on the steps." He nodded approval of Rafael and Juan who had anticipated the suggestion. "Yes, that is it exactly—sit down and wait for me. I shall only be a minute." And he disappeared into the *préfecture.*

The children understood. They sat on the steps, staring at the posters of the vanished cinema. Only Juan did not look up, sitting by himself with his chin sunk on his breast, and Trictrac sprawling limply at his feet.

"What are they doing, Gil?—the men on horses."

"They are hunting," Gil replied. He had never been inside a cinema, or one that he remembered, but he seemed to know about them.

"Hunting what?"

"Wild beasts or Indians."

"But where?"

"In America of course."

"Oh, America." They nodded.

"Where is that?" said Pablo.

"Across the sea," they told him.

"But where is the sea?"

They couldn't answer that. Gil was painfully spelling out some words upon the poster.

"What does it say?" they urged.

"They are foreign words," he said and shrugged contemptuously.

Rafael asked a question: "Do they have war in America?"

But no one knew the answer.

The Little One was not attending. She was pulling Rosa's sleeve, pleading in an undertone: she wanted to go back to the window of the shop where she had caught a glimpse of something wonderful. "Rosa, please! Teresa!" She found their hands and tugged.

And at last they went with her and stood before the window, with breathless gasps of startled admiration, speechless and enthralled. It was wonderful and beautiful, an incredible confection towering high above their heads, with snowy terraces adorned with golden ornaments and multi-colored flowers; and at the very top were two tiny life-like figures, a girl in a white dress and a boy in a black suit, standing with clasped hands. The window glass was broken; they could almost reach to touch the tempting object—almost but not quite, for there were jagged edges of the glass.

"But, Rosa, is it real?—a cake to eat?"

She nodded.

"Oh, Juana, look!" The Little One held up the monstrous doll.

"It is a wedding cake."

"How can you tell?"

"See!" Teresa pointed. "The bride and groom are standing on the top."

"Yes, I see." The Little One leaned closer. "I would like a piece to eat."

"Would you?" Rosa smiled. "When you are married you can have a cake like that."

"But I am hungry now."

"Well, you will have to wait till you are grown up."

"And married," said Teresa, "like a Princess in a story."

"But perhaps I will not be hungry then—" The Little One considered: not being hungry was not easy to imagine. "Anyway," she said, "if I were grown up I would not need to ask. I would take the cake and eat it."

"Then God would punish you."

"But he couldn't punish me until I ate the cake."

"That is wicked," Rosa said and took her hand. It was too tantalizing, looking at the cake; it was putting evil thoughts into her head. "Come, we must go back."

"Please, Rosa, let me stay." The Little One was tearful.

"Well—" Rosa hesitated. "But you must not touch the cake."

"No, I will only look."

So they went back to the steps and left her staring through the broken glass.

In a dingy, musty hallway of the *préfecture* Père Joseph was waiting in a long queue of people. The line moved very slowly and presently he realized that his errand must occupy some time. He thought perhaps he should go back and see about the children, but to do so he would sacrifice his place and multiply delay. So he waited with what patience he could muster. It was now midafternoon, and he was reminded by a gnawing in his stomach that he had had no food since early morning. And it occurred to him that the children must be hungry, though he had not thought of this before. But he consoled himself with the reflection that the end was now in sight, and their mutual needs would soon be satisfied.

He counted the people who were still ahead of him: there were twenty, men and women, some of them in distress, weeping or with dazed expressions on their faces. For the most part they were silent. An *agent* at the door let them in one at a time when it opened to let somebody out. Yes, he was making progress, though it seemed interminable. Now there were a dozen in advance of him, now eight, now five. He closed his eyes, aware of his fatigue, continuing to move forward in little shuffling steps, pushed on by the person at his back. Now there was one; he would be next. He closed his eyes again, not to open them until—

The chief of the police was sitting at a desk in the center of the room, a pudgy little man with bristling hair, in policeman's uniform and with medals on his breast. He did not look up from a paper he was scanning—

"You wish?" he queried curtly. And then glancing up, he observed that his visitor was a priest, and he nodded toward a chair, but not graciously at all. He was harried and frightened and buried in the debris of a task which no one could fulfill. Père Joseph did not sit down but drew nearer to the desk—

"*Monsieur le préfet?*" he inquired.

But the chief of the police had no time for the amenities. "You wish?" he repeated with an accent of impatience.

Père Joseph answered briefly: he was seeking the nuns of Sainte-Cécile—where, or if, they could be found.

"Nuns of Sainte-Cécile?" The *préfet* shrugged. "I have no knowledge of them."

"But the orphanage has been destroyed—"

The *préfet* shrugged again. "You wish?" he insisted, as if up to this moment nothing had been said.

"I have brought some children—"

"Children?"

"Orphans, *monsieur le préfet*. There are seven of them."

"Orphans? Where?" The *préfet* stared, as if he half expected seven orphans to emerge out of Père Joseph's pocket.

"They are waiting in the street."

"Are they residents of Le Havre?"

"No, *monsieur le préfet*." Père Joseph made an effort to explain.

"But why do you bring them here?"

"I have not known what to do—"

"Bringing orphans to Le Havre—" the *préfet* fumed, "—with the city burning up and the Germans at our gates. We have orphans of our own."

"Yes, I know," Père Joseph said, "but I have had no choice."

"No choice? No choice?" The *préfet* bounced up and down upon his chair. "I do not understand you, but no matter. There is more important business with claim to my attention."

"Yes, no doubt, *monsieur le préfet*. But these children are homeless and hungry and in need, and so I am appealing to municipal authority to provide for them, or arrange for their removal to a place of safety."

"Provide for them? And how?" the *préfet* shouted.

Père Joseph did not answer. He was suddenly so weary that he could hardly stand.

"Remove them to a place of safety?" The *préfet* thumped his desk. "Really, *monsieur le curé*, your demands are very modest. And where is a place of safety? Would you kindly tell me that?"

"Then what would you suggest?" Père Joseph asked.

"Suggest? Suggest? I have nothing to suggest." And he at once suggested: "Take them back to the place from which they came."

"But that is hardly possible—"

"Why not?"

"They came from Spain," Père Joseph said.

"From Spain?" the *préfet* scowled.

"They are Spanish children—refugees, *monsieur le préfet*, from the civil war in Spain."

"Spanish children!" the *préfet* fairly screamed. "And you occupy my time on behalf of Spanish children?"

"They are children, little children—"

"Then send them back to Spain, *monsieur le curé*. Yes, embark them on a ship and send them home."

"A ship?" Père Joseph started, clutching at a straw.

"But certainly. Why not?" The *préfet* was sardonic, but Père Joseph was too weary and too wretched to remark it.

"And where would I find a ship?"

"In the harbor, naturally." He pointed through the wall. He was strongly anticlerical and thoroughly enjoying his performance. "At the docks beside the *quai*."

"The docks, beside the *quai*—" Père Joseph nodded. "There are ships there now?"

"There *were* ships yesterday."

"And a ship would take the children to a place of safety?"

"Yes, certainly." The *préfet* waved his arms. "To Spain or to England—to America perhaps where they have room to spare for refugees."

"Yes, America perhaps—" Père Joseph murmured gratefully, moving toward the door. "Thank you, *monsieur le préfet*. Thank you very much."

"Pray do not mention it, *monsieur le curé*." The *préfet's* tongue was sweet with malice. "I rejoice that I have been of service in this matter."

The children waited on the steps. Pablo had a piece of chalk with which he drew some squares upon the pavement, resuming with Teresa the game they had been playing in the granary, hopping from square to square, but the idle foot was not to touch the ground—

"No," objected Pablo, "you are cheating."

"I didn't."

"Yes, you did."

"I never touched. I didn't."

They appealed to Rafael for decision in the matter, but Rafael was not looking; he was blowing his whistle, three melancholy notes. Then to Gil and Rosa, but they were not looking either; and Juan did not answer when they appealed to him. He was still sitting by himself with his chin sunk on his breast. Trictrac was asleep. He opened one eye as the argument progressed, but quickly closed it.

"Very well," Teresa said, "then I will start again."

"No." Pablo shook his head. "That's what you always say. You cheat and then you want to start again. I won't play any more."

But they went on with the game.

"When I was little," Rosa said, half to herself, "every night I had a cup of chocolate. It was very sweet and creamy. A woman brought it to me—not my mother; she wore a big white cap. I had it in my bed before I said my prayers."

"Ho!" Gil shrugged. "I never said my prayers."

"And nobody brought you chocolate."

"I don't like chocolate," he asserted glumly. But that wasn't true. There was something about the luxury of the idea—the chocolate and the woman with the cap, that nettled him a little. It seemed to make a gulf between himself and Rosa, though he had no notion why. He didn't like to hear about the things that she remembered.

"Anyway," sighed Rosa, "I wish I had some chocolate now." Her eyes strayed to the window of the pastry shop where the Little One was standing, staring through the broken glass. "I am so hungry."

"It is better to be hungry than thirsty," Gil said cheerfully. "One time when Juan and I were with the soldiers we did not have any water."

"What did you do?" she asked. But then abruptly something happened—

Some men came from the pastry shop, carrying a litter. It was wider than the narrow doorway, and so they had a time to get it through. And this attracted the attention of the children—

"What's that?" they said. "What are they doing?"

"Kicking down the door."

"Carrying something out."

"A dead one," Gil suggested.

"Maybe the house fell on him?"

"And they have dug him out?"

The litter bearers cleared the door and came along the sidewalk, directly past the steps.

"It's not a man," said Pablo. "It's a woman."

Rosa only glanced and quickly looked away. The face was black, resembling nothing human, but it was a woman because it wore a dress.

"The one that made the cake," Teresa ventured.

"Hi, Juan!" Pablo nudged him with his foot. "Look! Here is a dead one."

Juan stood up quickly, shrinking from the litter which was almost at his feet, stumbling backwards with his heels against the steps—

"No, no, no!" he cried in a high-pitched faltering voice. "I don't want to see it. Please—" And suddenly he tottered and fell down on the steps, rolling limply to the bottom like a sack of grain, till he lay on his back upon the sidewalk, with his eyes half open and his face as white as the chalk marks on the pavement.

The children stared in horrified amazement. The litter bearers had passed by, but other people stopped, coming from the *préfecture*.

"Juan! Oh, Juan—" Rosa knelt beside him and tried to lift his head.

"He is sick," Gil said. "He doesn't like the dead ones. It happened once before, when we were with the soldiers."

But now the people who had stopped were closing in upon them, commenting to each other: "The boy is sick."—"He's had a fit."— "But see, he has one arm."—"He has been hurt."—"Why don't they pick him up?"—"Take him in the *préfecture*." But instead of doing so, they now addressed the children: "What is the matter with him?"— "Is he sick?"—"Say now, why don't you answer?"—One took Gil by the arm: "Have you lost your tongue, young fellow?"

Gil jerked out of his grasp but stood his ground. "Good day," he mumbled sullenly in Spanish.

"But they are foreigners!"

"Germans," one suggested.

"No, the boy spoke Spanish."

"Well, take the sick one in to the police."

"Be quick and pick him up."

And two men moved to do so, but Gil thrust himself between, crouching on the sidewalk facing them, with his back against Juan's body.

"No!" he shouted, sobbing. "Help me, Pablo! Quick!" And Pablo came crawling on his knees. "Don't let them take him, Pablo. Hold on tightly, Rosa."

"Yes, Gil, I will." She nodded, sitting on the sidewalk with Juan's head upon her lap, and her arms wrapped tight around it.—No, they would not take Juan away.

"Trictrac!" cried Teresa. "Don't let them take him, Trictrac!"

Trictrac was wide awake; he growled and showed his teeth. And Rafael gripped his stick, as if planning to attack.

The men were hesitant: there was the dog which might be dangerous; and there was something in the faces of the children—They laughed uncomfortably, embarrassed and uncertain.

"They resemble little savages," an onlooker remarked.

"Little wolves," another said. "As if they might snarl and snap."

"Well, they are foreigners."

"Yes, foreigners of course." There was murmur of assent.

At this moment Père Joseph came from the *préfecture*, intent upon the matter in his mind, repeating to himself: "The docks beside the *quai*—" trying to remember in what precise direction the *préfet* had pointed through the wall. And then he saw the group upon the sidewalk. "Ah, ah! What now?" he groaned, and came hurrying down the steps.

Juan was waking up, and the color coming back into his face.

"Look, Gil!" Rosa cried. "He is all right again." She raised his head, and he sat up limply, leaning back against the step.

And now Père Joseph was among them, addressing them and everybody else. The child had fainted, from fatigue no doubt; they had had a trying day. "Are you all right now, my child? Are you quite all right again?" He continued in a flutter of excitement, "They are orphans, Spanish orphans—refugees in fact. Thank you very much for your assistance, but the child is quite restored. I was taking them to Sainte-Cécile, but it exists no more. So now they are to go upon a ship, as the *préfet* has suggested—to America perhaps. We are going at this moment to the docks. But we must find the *quai*—"

They called directions to him: directly down this street, if it were not so smoky he would see the harbor, it was only a few steps; and dispersed about their business, grumbling to each other: "America! Now think of that!"—"Lucky little brats!"—"Refugees have the best of everything."—"The Church looks after them."—"And the politicians, too."—"Yes, politics of course!"

"Come now, my children—" Père Joseph was once more arranging the procession, but in somewhat different order: Pablo would walk with Gil, with the knapsack Juan had carried; and then the girls—But stop, something was wrong: one of them was missing. He looked anxiously about, but the child was not in sight.

"What is the matter now?" the children grumbled.

"He is looking for something—something he has lost."

"But what?"

It was Rosa who remembered. "The Little One," she stammered. "Where is the Little One?"

"Yes, the Little One," they chorused.

"She was standing by that shop, looking in the window."

"She's not there now."

"Perhaps she has been stolen," Teresa volunteered.

"Or she's lost," suggested Rafael.

"Or hiding," added Pablo.

"She has not gone far," Gil said. He ran across the street to look behind the posters of the cinema. And they all began to look, running here and there, and calling her to come. "Come quickly or you will be left behind."

Père Joseph was accosting passers-by: "Pardon, monsieur, have you seen a child of five?—a little girl with long blond curls?—No?—Thank you very much." And he would stop another.

It was Trictrac who found her, where no one had thought to look. He had gone charging after them, infected with excitement; but then suddenly he stopped at the doorway of the shop, with his four paws firmly planted and his tail straight out behind him, barking furiously.

"Yes, she is here," Gil shouted. And they all came running to the door, with Père Joseph at their heels, holding up his skirt.

The Little One was sitting on the floor behind the window, munching an enormous piece of cake which had been torn out of the heart of the confection, leaving a gaping hole. Indeed, the monument had sagged in her direction, and the tiny figures on the top were leaning dangerously. Her hands and face were encrusted in white frosting.

"Oh, how could you?" Rosa groaned.

"Didn't you hear us calling?" Teresa questioned sternly.

"Yes, I heard you—" The Little One swallowed with an effort. "But I couldn't answer because my mouth was full."

Père Joseph wiped his dripping face. "Come now, my child—" he said. And then he hesitated, calling to a man who was digging with a pickax in the wreckage at the back—

"Monsieur—"

The man came out into the light, leaning on his pickax. "*Mon père?*" he said respectfully.

"This cake, monsieur, I regret it has been damaged. One of the children—"

The man looked at the cake and nodded dully.

"They are orphan children and they are very hungry—" Père Joseph wet his lips. "It has occurred to me, since the cake is badly damaged, perhaps the owner would not mind if now—" He paused expectantly.

"No, *mon père.*" The man shook his head. "The owner will not mind, for she is dead."

"Oh, dead—" Père Joseph crossed himself.

"Yes, dead, *mon père.* A little while ago we found her body." He turned and went back into the shadows.

"Yes, I see," Père Joseph murmured. "Thank you very much." And he broke a piece out of the cake, broke it with his hands—a big piece thick with frosting. "Come now, my children, let us eat," he said.

6

CAPTAIN ARISTIDE WAS STANDING ON THE bridge of the vessel he commanded—a ship with an historic name, *Le Bellérophon*. But there distinction ended, for the ship of Captain Aristide was a wretched little freighter, untidy and decrepit, caked with rust, alive with rats and roaches, and stinking horribly of the cargoes which it brought at uncertain intervals from far-off Martinique: sugar and rum, than which, when thick and stale with age, there is no more repulsive and nauseating odor. The engine of the ship was no better than the hulk. The engineer, a silent, gloomy man whose name was Samson, kept it running somehow; but each voyage that he made he swore would be the last.

The engineer was on the bridge with Captain Aristide who was also very gloomy. He was tall and emaciated-looking, resembling Don

53

Quixote in the angles of his figure and his melancholy visage which was creased and long and narrow. He had been standing there most of the day, on the navigating bridge outside the superstructure, in which he and Samson had their cabins, which was directly forward of the vessel's single funnel. Samson, who was short and fat, was sitting on a stool, puffing at a pipe in the English fashion; he was in his shirt and dungarees which were black with grime and oil. Captain Aristide stood at the rail, also in his shirt but with his captain's cap which had gold braid on it. He was looking down the dock which was deserted, and had been deserted all day long.

He did not know what to do. Half his cargo was on board and half was on the dock: a general cargo, but much of it was wine—great piles of clean new cases waiting to be loaded. The loading of the vessel had not been completed on the night before, and with the dawn the planes had come.

There had been other ships tied up at neighboring docks, loading or unloading. Some of them had fled, and some remained, resting on the bottom with their funnels sticking up out of the greasy water. The *Bellérophon* had been unprepared for flight, its fires banked, and the stokers—blacks from Martinique—sleeping in their hammocks. The ship had escaped destruction by a miracle: bombs had fallen all around it, flinging geysers of water high into the air and carving ragged craters in the granite dock. And when the bombs were finished they had come back with machine guns, raking everything in sight, so that sections of the deck were like a sieve, and nearly all the windows of the deckhouse had been shattered. There were holes in the funnel, in the cabins, everywhere. And the cases on the dock had been riddled through and through, so that wine was leaking out and the smell of it was mixed with the smell of oil and smoke.

Captain Aristide had not known what to do, and knew no better now. Half his crew had gone ashore the night before, and not one had yet returned. Among the missing members was the cook, whom, because of his dyspepsia, the captain greatly cherished. The ship at sea would be dangerously short handed. But on the other hand the Germans might come back, might return at any moment to finish the affair. It was a real dilemma. All day long Captain Aristide had struggled with the problem, standing on the bridge, not knowing what to do. He had had no nourishment except a cup of coffee which had not been fit to drink and had caused him indigestion. He had thought of many things: as for example to hoist a neutral flag; but he had no neutral flag nor any flag at all except the flag of France which hung limply at the stern. And there were holes in it where bullets had gone through.

He had not been idle; he had performed his duty. When the planes had departed he had vigorously directed the extinction of some fires which incendiary bullets had kindled here and there. Luckily enough there had been no casualties, for the crew had taken refuge at the bottom of the ship and had not emerged until the planes were gone. Captain Aristide himself had remained upon the bridge; several bullets had come close but he had not been hit. Some goats in a crate, left standing on the deck, had not been so fortunate. Captain Aristide had them thrown overboard. He did not regret their loss, though indeed the smell of goats could contribute very little to the smell in which he lived, but to that he was accustomed. He gave orders to the engineer to get up steam at once; and the stokers, who were eager to get back to Martinique, set to work with right good will. And then when a semblance of order was restored and he had caught his breath, he summoned the mate and sent him off to call on the agent in Le Havre for instructions what to do—whether to remain and await the loading of the balance of the cargo, or to sail without it, shorthanded though he was. But the mate did not return. The man was badly frightened and no doubt had run away.

In the early afternoon Captain Aristide dispatched a second messenger, a common sailor this time, but one on whom he thought he could rely, giving him a letter for the agent, which had taken an hour to compose, and minute instructions how to find the office. It was, he explained, opposite the *préfecture*, up a flight of stairs above a cinema. But the hours dragged away and the man did not come back.

Captain Aristide did not know what to do. Steam was up and had been up since noon. Smoke rose from the funnel and trickled through the holes which had perforated it. The hatches had been closed and the hoisting tackle stowed. There was nothing left except the gangplank which was level with the dock, out of view behind the deckhouse, and the creaking hawsers at the bow and stern. The remnant of the crew was lounging on the hatches.

threading through the debris, skirting craters in the granite, urging them with cheerful words: "We are coming to our journey's end my children, and soon you will be safe on board that pretty ship, in the care of honest sailors who will take good care of you. All will be well, my children—" They were drawing near the ship, and he could see a man standing on the bridge—a man in a cap with gold braid on it. The children saw him, too—

"Look, there is a man!"

"Where?"

"Up there by the chimney."

"Perhaps the ship belongs to him."

"Can we go on it?"

"Will the priest allow it?"

"Then why did he bring us here?"

"Perhaps," suggested Rafael, "we are going to America."

"To America?" They caught their breath again. "Yes, going on the ship. Going to America."

"And Trictrac, too," the Little One insisted.

"Maybe the man won't take him?"

"Then I won't go."

"Hush!" Rosa took her hand. The priest was talking to the man.

"Good day," Père Joseph said politely, gazing upward at the bridge.

"Good day," Captain Aristide replied ungraciously, leaning on the rail, staring glumly at his visitors.

"You are," Père Joseph ventured, "the captain of the ship?"

The captain nodded brusquely, admitting this was true.

"You are sailing to America?"

"To Martinique."

"Oh, Martinique—" Père Joseph nodded vaguely. "But that is near America?"

"It is near enough," the captain said. "Near enough for me."

"And you are sailing soon?"

But Captain Aristide would not commit himself.

"Well, at least—" Père Joseph wiped the perspiration from his face. "At least I am in time."

"In time?" the captain said suspiciously. "In time for what?"

"Oh yes! Forgive me, please—" Père Joseph felt confused; his reception had not been what he'd hoped. "I have not explained my errand—"

"Errand?" the captain interrupted, hope springing in his heart. "A message from the agent?"

"Agent?" Père Joseph shook his head. "I have come from the *préfecture*—from the *préfet de police*."

"The *préfet de police*?" echoed Captain Aristide. "What have I to do with the *préfet de police*?" But then he thought of something and abruptly changed his tone. "With reference, you mean, to some members of my crew?"

"Your crew? Oh no!"

"Then what?"

"With reference to these children—"

"Children?" Captain Aristide repeated, as if the word did not make sense.

"I have brought the children here at suggestion of the *préfet*—"

Captain Aristide was speechless with confusion.

"Orphan children," Père Joseph hurried on. "And we wish to have them taken to a place of safety."

"Will you kindly have the goodness to tell me what you mean?"

"But yes—well, I am trying—" Père Joseph raised his voice to a note of desperation. "I have brought these orphan children to place them in your care and embark them on your ship; and though there is no money with which to pay their fares—yet in such a time as this, God will certainly reward you."

"What?" the captain bellowed. He had missed the final words, for the air was filled with sound to which his attention did not at once respond: the sirens in the city shrieking out a warning. "What's that? What did you say?"

"I said—" Père Joseph cupped his hands and shouted. "I said that God would certainly reward you."

"You are crazy," Captain Aristide roared back, or meant to roar. But at this moment the sirens caught his ear and drove every other thought out of his head: the planes were coming back. Long-delayed decision was determined in a moment. He rushed across the bridge and jerked the indicator signal to "Standby," shouting for the wheelsman and the crew—"Get the gangplank in! Cast off the lines!" running back and forth from side to side, looking for someone to obey his orders. But the crew had vanished. There was not a soul in sight but the priest and the children standing on the dock. He dashed into the wheelhouse and seized the whistle cord and blew it savagely, and then dashed back again. He did not know what to do—

And now the planes were on him, diving with vicious screams.— Whiz—crash!—Fragments of wood and bottles went sailing through the air from the boxes on the dock.—Whiz—crash!—A geyser of water sprang up at the bow and drenched the bridge with spray. Captain Aristide ran back and forth like a chicken with its head off, pulling the whistle cord and shouting for the crew, but he might have saved the steam and saved his breath.

Samson was at his post in the engine room, with his hand on the throttle and his eyes fixed on the dial which recorded the orders from the bridge. The bell had tinkled sharply and the signal hand had swung, pointing to "Standby."—"What now?" he muttered. "Is the old fool getting started?" Then he heard the whistle which seemed to have no purpose. He cursed beneath his breath, trembling with impatience.

"Standby" the signal said, and said no more. "Well, I am standing by," the engineer repeated through his teeth from which the pipe had fallen. "But standing by for what?" And then the screaming bedlam was upon them. The concussions were so violent that the ship shook and quivered like a sick man with a chill, and it seemed her rusty plates must fall apart.

The moments ticked away. From the corner of his eye he could see the frightened faces of the blacks, huddled in the opening of the bulkhead. He heard the whistle blow again—short, frantic blasts; and it passed through his mind that the captain had gone crazy, succumbed to indecision. "The fool, the fool!" he groaned. "He can't make up his mind. He sits here like a goose—an ugly, stupid goose, sitting on a duckpond, waiting for a hunter. He has all day to get away and he sits here like a goose, while the rest of us are murdered."

The whistle had stopped blowing and Samson decided Captain Aristide was dead—dead on the bridge where a captain should remain in time of peril. "And serve him right," he said. He was tempted to go up and gaze upon the captain weltering in his blood, but he dared not leave his post—and, in simple truth, he felt safer where he was. He continued to wait, with his eyes fixed on the dial, while the sweat rolled down his face and dripped onto the floor.

Père Joseph had no warning. He did not hear the sirens, or, if he did, was unconscious of their meaning. The captain had concluded by shouting something at him, which he did not understand, and then had disappeared. He was afraid he had not made things clear; it was difficult to talk at such a distance. Then he heard the whistle which alarmed him: possibly the ship was preparing to depart. It crossed his mind to go on board and take the children with him, relying on more intimate appeal. The gangplank to the deck was close at hand. But still he hesitated, not knowing what rules such an action might infringe, or the etiquette which governed ships and captains.

The children were gathered close behind him in the shadow of a pile of wooden boxes. There were other boxes scattered at the bottom, and Rafael, Juan, and Rosa were sitting on them. They were all engrossed, fascinated by the ship, but still they heard the sirens, heard them at the start—

"What is that noise?" they asked uncomfortably.

"Maybe motorcars?"

"No, not motorcars."

"Then what?"

Juan had begun to tremble and was growing pale again, and Rosa was afraid he might be sick. The Little One had gone to comfort Trictrac who was whining, cowering back against a box. Gil stepped out to look, staring at the sky. But there was nothing to be seen through the greasy, yellow smoke.

And then it happened. And no one could describe it or say exactly what—not Captain Aristide, nor Père Joseph, nor the children: a screaming roar of sound, and the air was full of things, flashes of flame and whistling, crashing objects, fragments of wood and glass, water spouting from the sea and falling in a shower on the dock. And everything was shaking—the granite blocks, the ship which quivered like soft jelly; and you could hardly see, or breathe the poisonous fumes.

Trictrac howled with terror and suddenly ran out from the shelter of the boxes.

"Trictrac!" screamed the Little One. "Trictrac, come back!" And she ran after him.

Père Joseph raised his head—he had been thrown down by the concussion—and saw the Little One running out onto the dock—

"Come back!" he cried. "Come back!" And he scrambled to his feet, dizzy and confused, and ran stumbling in pursuit, heedless of a plane which came sweeping down the dock scarcely higher than his head, spraying streaks of flame from tracer bullets which spattered on the stone in puffs of granite dust. He overtook the child and threw her down, falling across her on his hands and knees, arching his body over her, hardly conscious of a blow upon his shoulder but finding that he could not lean upon that arm, seeing, half a dozen paces in advance, the dog stretched on its side, its legs still twitching.

The plane had vanished. He scrambled to his feet, dragging the child away.

"Trictrac," she wailed. "Trictrac—"

He held her hand, calling to the others, "Are any of you injured?" He saw that they were not—there were six of them huddled in the shelter of the boxes which miraculously had not collapsed upon them. "Come now, my children, quickly!" But he could not raise his arm to motion them; and he saw now that his hand was dripping blood—blood running down his arm, soaking through his sleeve, dripping from his fingers. "We must go upon the ship, for there we will be safe." He herded them along in frantic haste. The Little One was crying, wailing for the dog—

"Trictrac," she sobbed. "Trictrac—"

"Trictrac is dead," they told her. Teresa held her hand.

"No, he isn't dead. Anyway, I want him."

"But we're going on the ship."

"I won't go without him."

"Going to America."

"No, no, no!" But Teresa dragged her and Pablo pushed behind.

"Go on!" Père Joseph pointed. They were at the gangplank now. "Go on, my children, quickly!" He pushed them on ahead, thinking he would follow once they were safe on board, for he felt near to exhaustion and his wound must have attention—but waiting to look back, to make sure all had gone. And then he heard a shout, and there was the captain looking down at him from the very place where he had been before—in a time as remote as something in a dream, though not more than a minute had elapsed. The captain looking down and saying something—

"Would you have the kindness—" But the end of it was lost.

"What do you say?" Père Joseph shouted back.

"Cast off my lines." He was pointing to a heavy rope looped on an iron stanchion on the dock.

"Ah, the rope!" Père Joseph nodded. "How can I be of service?"

"Cast it off," the captain bellowed.

"You mean—untie the ship?"

"Yes, yes, yes," Captain Aristide replied, on fire with impatience, expecting every moment the resumption of attack, for the air still echoed with the crash of detonations, though nothing could be seen now through the smoke. The boxes on the dock were burning briskly, adding to the smoke from the straw that wrapped the bottles.

"I will try," Père Joseph said and hurried toward the stanchion, reflecting that the captain, behind his gruff exterior, was a kind and generous man: he had waited for the children until they were safe on board. But he was wrong in this assumption. Captain Aristide had not perceived the children, and could not from the bridge since the deckhouse was between them. Indeed he had forgotten them completely. In frantic desperation he had looked over the rail and seen the priest, standing quite alone beside the gangplank.

Père Joseph hurried, stumbling, for he was weak and faint from loss of blood; his gown was soaked with it and it was dripping faster from his hand. But Captain Aristide could not see this from the bridge. He watched the priest fumbling with the rope—fumbling with one hand and tripping on his skirt. "These priests!" he groaned. "What a good-for-nothing lot!" And aloud he shouted—

"When the tide lifts toward the dock the line will slack."

"I see," Père Joseph answered. He waited till the rope seemed somewhat looser, and then it slipped off easily and dropped into the water.

"Good!" the captain shouted. "Now the other at the bow."

"Oh yes, the other—" Père Joseph staggered toward it, weaving like a drunk man. When he finally reached it he could no longer stand and sat beside the stanchion, tugging at the rope.

"Now!" the captain ordered, and the rope came off at last. "Thank you very much."

"Not at all," Père Joseph answered, sitting on the dock leaning back against the stanchion, not seeing very clearly, for things were getting blurred. He felt for his crucifix and held it in his hand, and added in a whisper, though he thought that he was shouting, "You have been very kind. God will certainly reward you—" But Captain Aristide had disappeared from view.

The gangplank tore away with a sound of splintering wood and fell into the sea. The ship came toward Père Joseph, edging slowly from the dock. There was the captain, in a little house, pulling and pushing on the spokes of a big wheel. And now the children came—clustered close together, just their heads above the railing. He thought they were looking, but he could not see their faces. He smiled and waved his hand and called to them, or thought he called, "Good-by. Good-by, my children."

But they did not answer or wave back. They were not looking at him, did not even see him. They were looking at the dog—

"Poor Trictrac," they said.

The Little One was crying. "Hold me up," she begged. "Please hold me up." Rosa lifted her. "Good-by, Trictrac," she sobbed.

It was an hour later when the engineer climbed the ladder to the bridge. In the pilothouse a sailor had the wheel. Captain Aristide was standing at the rail, feeling rather proud of his behavior. He saw his engineer rising from the hatch and could not repress a note of exultation—

"Well, you were wrong," he said.

"Wrong?" Samson stood beside him with his pipe between his teeth, clinging to the railing, for the open sea was rough and the ship, with half a cargo, rolled and pitched. "About what was I wrong?"

"You said that God would not smile on us again."

"Oh that!" The engineer considered and spat over the side. "It is still a long way to Martinique."

"But at least," the captain chuckled, "we have made a start."

"Humph!" grunted Samson and was silent for a while. And then he remarked with studied casualness, "I see we have some passengers."

"What?" Captain Aristide thought he had not heard correctly.

"Some children—" Samson jerked his thumb over his shoulder. "Back there behind the deckhouse."

"Children?" Captain Aristide stared blankly. "But you are jesting."

"Well, see for yourself," the engineer replied. "Children, I repeat, and there are seven of them."

"Seven?" gasped the captain. And then suddenly he saw; he remembered everything. "That priest! That priest!" he groaned. "And he was laughing at me. I think he had been drinking. I am sure he was drunk."

"As to that—" The engineer could not conceal his satisfaction. "But what will you do with seven children?"

Captain Aristide was silent, staring gloomily at the sky.

"You cannot throw them overboard."

"They are stowaways," the captain growled. "And they must work their passage."

"But they are children."

"No matter." And then Captain Aristide had an inspiration. "They are old enough to cook. I will have a talk with them."

"Ah that—" said Samson dryly. "Well, it may be difficult."

"Difficult? But why?"

"They do not speak French."

"What?"

"They are foreign children—Spanish, I believe."

Captain Aristide could not find anything to say.

"And anyway—" The engineer puffed his pipe indifferently. "I think they are beginning to be seasick."

"Hah!" said Captain Aristide and paced across the bridge, muttering to himself, "That priest! That priest!"

7

KAPITÄN-LEUTNANT WOLF VON BLOTTNITZ revolved his periscope, searching a narrow field of vision.

The sun was setting, sliding behind a bank of fog which rimmed the sky, and which was closing in upon the ship. The sea was like a mirror made of amethyst, cupped in a platinum setting; there was not a ripple on it.

The U-boat had been lying idly on the surface, but sounds had been detected and it had submerged till their source could be determined. Kapitän von Blottnitz had a rendezvous to keep, an appointment with a mother ship whose visit he was anxiously expecting. He had been long at sea and had sunk several ships. He had one torpedo left, scarcely any ammunition for his deck guns, and he was short of fuel. The mother ship was already three days late, and so he had reason for anxiety.

He was a youthful, dapper fellow, with close-cropped reddish hair and cold blue eyes and the vestige of a mustache with the ends clipped like the Führer's, and he wore a monocle. He did not wear much else: shorts and knitted shirt and canvas sandals, for it was hot beneath the sea—hot on top of it, indeed, where the U-boat had been waiting.

Oberleutnant Gottfried Träger stood at his commander's side, in his hand a scrap of paper on which were penciled figures. He resembled the captain in appearance and in fact—same close-cropped head and keen, cold eyes, though he did not wear shorts because he was bow-legged. They looked like polo players, and in a way they were. War was a game to them, and the sinking of a ship was the making of a goal, an addition to the score. They did not look any further; they had no social or political ideas; they were out to win a game. If you made the goal, all right; but if your opponent made it, then that one was the last—a very thrilling game, make no mistake about it.

At a respectful distance stood Leutnant Otto Dreyer, the junior of the three, a chubby youth with glasses, not looking like a polo player, no matter how he tried. He had planned to devote his life to archae-ology, and even now sometimes he thought about it. This rendered him indifferent as a polo player, and socially suspect, too; his seniors were contemptuous of him and he stood in awe of them. He wanted to be like them but it seemed to be impossible. Still, he was useful in an academic way: the figures on the paper which Träger was consulting, were of his computation.

"Nothing," Blottnitz said, turning his head from the eyepiece of the periscope.

"There," suggested Träger, indicating with his pencil a point upon the azimuth.

"It is getting dark." The captain shrugged. "And the fog is closing in."

"All the same that's where it is, and coming toward us."

"Then it is the mother ship," said Blottnitz confidently.

Träger shook his head.

"I will bet you on it, Gottfried."

"How much?"

"A case of wine."

"Champagne?"

"Champagne."

"Done," said Träger.

"You will lose." The captain laughed. "It is certainly the mother ship. What else would it be?"

"Hum—" Träger grinned, glancing at the paper in his hand. "A single screw," he read aloud. "Probably a freighter and a small one. And there is a rumble like loose bearings on the shaft."

"Nonsense!" Blottnitz snapped, scowling at Otto Dreyer. He looked again, nudging the periscope to point upon the bearing. "Nothing," he grumbled. But suddenly he stiffened. "Yes, now there is something, but I cannot make it out. Wait a bit," he said. "It is clearing for a moment." There was a pause, and then he added glumly, "A single funnel."

"Ha!" crowed Träger. "Now do you say it is the mother ship?"

But the captain ignored this pleasantry. "Riding high," he said, "as if in ballast."

"You have lost a case of wine."

Blottnitz made no answer. He was no longer in a jesting mood; the game was on again, another chukker, and there was no time to lose. He must come closer to the ship and determine its identity, whether enemy or neutral, before the fog and darkness intervened. He raised his head and barked his orders, and his officers and crew sprang to their posts. The engines hummed, and the sea was lightly furrowed by the white wake of the periscope—like a faint flaw in a jewel.

In a matter of minutes the ship was close at hand—a wretched little freighter, wallowing top-heavily as if it had no cargo, chugging and rattling like a concrete mixer, limping so slowly it could not raise a breeze to spread its flag which hung limp and undecipherable. Blottnitz maneuvered closer, circling round the stern to read the vessel's name—

"Le Bell—" he said. "Bell—something." But he could not read the rest of it. Träger was already thumbing through the register. "Bell—er—it looks like, and then there is an o—anyway, it must be French."

"Bellero," mumbled Träger, sliding his pencil down the page. But he could not find a vessel of that name.

"*Le Bellérophon* perhaps?" suggested Otto Dreyer.

"Yes, that's it," cried Blottnitz, as if he had thought of it himself.

"Come, be quick," he added, for it was nearly dark and the fog was thickening. A few seconds later he could not have confirmed it.

"Here it is," said Träger who had found it on the page. "*Bellérophon —Le Havre.*" He began to read a description of the vessel.

"No matter about that," interrupted Blottnitz. "It's French, and that's enough." With his eye upon the ship he gave his orders. And then—"Ah God," he groaned, "now I have lost him!"

"Lost him?" echoed Träger. His hand was raised to signal the discharge of the torpedo.

But the captain did not answer, intent upon the murky blur of night. The ship was there beside him, a cable's length away; he could hear, or feel, the vibration of its screw. But it was out of sight.

"Anyway," said Träger, "we have only to follow him until the fog clears up, or till daylight if we must."

"Humph!" grunted Blottnitz. "You forget we're short of fuel, and we have a date to keep." He was thinking while he spoke: perhaps it was as well if the vessel got away. It seemed a shame to spend his last torpedo on the rusty little tub—a torpedo he might need to save his life.

"Then what?" inquired Träger.

"Nothing," Blottnitz said. "I'll let him go, that's all." But he did not take his eye from the eyepiece of the periscope.

"Oh—" Träger sighed. "Well, good-by, *Bellérophon.*" He mispronounced the name. "A ship with an historic name, if my memory serves me."

Blottnitz mumbled something.

"On a ship of that name," continued Träger brightly, "Napoleon went to Elba."

"You mean, to St. Helena," said the captain.

"No, to Elba."

"You are wrong, to St. Helena."

"Would you care to bet on that?"

"Yes, another case of wine."

"Done," said Träger.

Otto Dreyer held his tongue, though he had an urge to speak. Both of them were wrong; they were nearly always wrong about everything except this stupid game of sinking ships. But all the same he wished he were more like them. It would be easier—

"Wait now!" Blottnitz suddenly exclaimed.

"Is it lifting?"

"No, but—"

"But what?"

"I thought I saw a light."

"A light?" Träger laughed. "He would not be such a fool."

"Yes, by God, a light!" the captain muttered. There was no mistake about it: a tiny yellow blur not far above the water—probably a porthole in the hull, a vagrant light someone had overlooked. Those things did happen, fortunate things for polo players. He gave his orders sharply, and a moment later the torpedo sped away with a hissing sound like air escaping from a tire—like a polo ball aimed neatly at the goal posts. "Now then—" Blottnitz waited with his eye upon the light.

Captain Aristide was on the bridge. He had hardly left it for ten days. The weather had been bad nearly all the way, with winds approaching the velocity of gales; and the ship, with half a cargo, had rolled and pitched like a shaving in a millrace. The cargo had not been carefully stowed, and some of it had suffered damage, for cases had been broken and wine had spilled around over other things; and it had shifted in the holds until the vessel had a dangerous list. Nothing could be done to help the situation until there was a lull, and this had not occurred until the day before. Then the hatches had been opened and the crew, what there was of it, had descended to the holds and done what could be done, so that the vessel rode on a fairly even keel. Several of them had been drunk when they emerged.

Captain Aristide had had his hands full. He would go into his cabin to snatch a wink of sleep and then come back to the bridge. His meals, if meals they could be called, were brought to him on a tray. He had not had a mouthful that was fit to eat, and had been greatly troubled by severe pains in his stomach. The cooking had been done by a common sailor who knew nothing about cooking; and, as it turned out, there had not been much to cook, since most of the stores had been left upon the dock. The captain had not known this at the time, or perhaps he would not have sailed at all. Between being bombed or poisoned there was very little choice—

He was thinking of this now, standing on the bridge, staring gloom-ily into the murky darkness, groaning with distress from the supper he had eaten: onions and potatoes, with some fragments of salt fish which perhaps was slightly spoiled, and coffee that tasted like scrapings from the hull. He had never in his life had a more unpleasant trip, and there still remained some days to Martinique.

It had been uncomfortable in every way, not the least of which was a quarrel he'd had with Samson, arising from the children, those mis-creant young vagrants foisted on him by the priest—a clerical con-spiracy of which he was the victim. And when they came to Martinique, what then? It was likely enough the port authorities would not let the children land, without passports or any kind of papers; and he might be compelled to take them back to France. A dreadful thought assailed him: suppose they would not take them there, since they were Spanish children. He groaned aloud, seeing himself plodding back and forth across the broad Atlantic for the balance of his life, with seven Spanish orphans hung across his shoulders like the fabled albatross.

He had seen the children only once, and that was on the night of their departure. He had gone with Samson down the ladder to the deck, and had found them huddled in a group behind the deckhouse. It had been dark by then, but he had a pocket flash. He had thought that Samson might be exaggerating: no doubt the little rascals were malin-gerers, quite old enough to work, and able to speak French when it served their purpose. The matter called for firmness.

The children were sitting in the shelter of the hatch. Their elation had resolved to apathy. It had been fun at first when the ship began to roll and the floor slid up and down like a teeter-totter. They had made a game of it, excepting Juan and Rafael who preferred to sit and watch, seeing who could stand the longest without holding on or stepping. Gil and Pablo had been best. The trick was to spread your legs and lean the other way, but not too far of course or you would lose your balance. The Little One had been ecstatic, sliding back and forth across the deck, screaming to Rosa or Teresa to catch her, making everybody laugh. "I love the ship," she cried. "I love the sea."

But then they tired of it. It was growing dark and cold, and they began to feel a little dizzy. One by one they lost interest in the game and came to sit with the others on the deck—

"Are we nearly there?" asked Pablo.

"Nearly where?"

"America."

"But we have only started."

"How much longer will it take?"

But no one knew the answer.

"Is it always tippy—like this?"

"This is nothing yet," said Gil. But he hoped that he was wrong.

A man came by and spoke to them. They did not know what he said, but they answered him, "Good day." He was smoking a pipe and the smoke blew in their faces. They turned their heads away.

Suddenly the Little One came and sat by Rosa. "I don't feel good," she said. "I feel bad in my stomach." She cuddled with her head in Rosa's lap, twisting and turning, but still she was uncomfortable. "I don't like the ship," she whimpered. "I would like to go home now." They told her to be quiet, thinking with longing of the cheerless, dismal granary which did not slide up and down. After a while she said, half to herself, "I'm glad I ate the cake."

"Why?" they asked indifferently.

"Because now I wouldn't want it."

"Ugh—" Pablo groaned and leaned back against the hatch.

It was then that Captain Aristide came tramping down the deck with Samson at his heels. They looked smaller than he'd hoped—small and thin and white, huddled like little calves, blinking at the light. But there was one who sat apart, arms folded on his breast, not belligerent in his attitude, but not conciliatory. Of the others he did not take much note—

"You," he said, pointing with his flash and speaking gruffly. "What have you to say?"

But Gil said nothing, pressing with his arms against his stomach which had begun to wriggle in a disturbing way.

"Humph!" Captain Aristide could hear Samson snickering in the dark. "No nonsense now," he threatened. "I know you can speak French, so answer me directly."

The boy stared straight into the light—not defiantly perhaps, but certainly not pleasantly.

Captain Aristide attacked the problem boldly. "Listen now," he said.

"Pay close attention to me. You are guilty of a crime, for you are stow-aways. When we arrive in port you can be sent to jail. Yes, to jail, that is a fact. Do you understand me?"

No answer. The childish eyes were unwavering and expressionless. But they were not childish eyes; they were and they were not.

The captain continued with a shade less confidence, "Very good. If you persist it will be the worse for you. Come now, speak up, what have you to say?"

The children were whispering to each other—

"Who is that man?"

"The one who was standing by the chimney."

"Does the ship belong to him?"

"What does he want?"

"Why is he angry?" But they were too wretched to care about the answers.

Captain Aristide did not know what to do, and so he turned to Samson who he knew was grinning, though he could not see his face and was careful not to turn the light upon it. "They are lying," he affirmed, which was a gross misstatement since they had not said a word. "Put them to work," he stormed, "at least the bigger ones—that boy there, for example."

"To work?" retorted Samson. "Work at what?"

"Anything you like," the captain mumbled vaguely.

"There is nothing they could do in my engine room."

"I did not say the engine room," Captain Aristide corrected irritably. "Let them help in the galley—help someone to cook. They can peel potatoes certainly."

"No doubt," said Samson dryly, "but I am an engineer and not a cook."

"I ask you—" said the captain with a note of desperation, aware that he had gone too far now to draw back, "I ask you to relieve me of this matter."

"But no," protested Samson, "it is no affair of mine."

"I order you in fact," Captain Aristide said sternly.

"Bah!" said the engineer.

Captain Aristide ignored the exclamation. "As you know," he said, "we are shorthanded. And—and—" he stammered, "the country is at war. I am appealing to you as a patriotic Frenchman."

"I am an engineer," insisted Samson stubbornly, "and you have no right to treat me like a purser."

Captain Aristide completely lost his temper. "This is mutiny," he shouted.

"Mutiny?" sneered Samson, and added a word which is unfit to print —the same with which, according to the legend, Cambronne replied at Waterloo when called on by the British to surrender.

"I could have you put in irons," growled Captain Aristide, albeit rather lamely, for the ship was not equipped with any kind of manacles.

"Do so by all means." The engineer laughed scornfully. "Arrest me if you please, and row your filthy tub to Martinique." And he turned on his heel and strode off into the darkness.

Captain Aristide did not know what to do. And then—

"Oh, oh, oh—" cried the Little One with a dreadful gagging sound, and then there was a "Whush—"

With a start of apprehension the captain flashed his light in her direction; his fears were realized: the child had thrown up, all over everything; and others of them sat with their heads cupped in their hands, making most unpleasant sounds—

"Ah bah!" Captain Aristide exclaimed, with hot saliva gathering in his mouth, for sailors can be seasick and the master of the ship had a very sensitive stomach. "It is really too disgusting," he protested. "Here, take this!" He held out his handkerchief to the bigger of the girls. But a handkerchief was nothing; it should have been a mop.

"Oh, oh, oh—" It was Pablo this time; and there was another "whush" which engulfed the captain's shoes.

"Ugh—" he grunted and hastily withdrew, stamping his feet and slipping on the deck. And then he turned and ran and leaned over the rail. "Oh, oh—" he groaned; then "whush—"

He was thinking of it now, brooding gloomily on the painful recollection, standing on the bridge, blissfully unaware of a ripple in the sea—the ripple of a periscope which sped circling round the stern, like a knife blade in the water, with a crest of foam behind it. He was thinking: It was good the engineer had not been there to witness his humiliation. They had not spoken since. If they met in the companionway on which their cabins opened, they merely nodded brusquely and passed by. The engineer had not been near the bridge, and he himself had seldom left it. In time of peril the captain of a ship should remain upon the bridge, remote from the embarrassment of sulky engineers and seasick children.

He had not seen the children since that night. When his *indisposition*, as he called it in his thought, had sufficiently abated, he had turned the matter over to a sailor, ordering him to put them in a kind of lazaret located near the stern, beneath the deck—a broad but low ceiled den, the full beam of the ship, which the carpenter had used for a storeroom and a workship, which contained his bench and tools, but the carpenter was missing. The lazaret was equipped with several pipe bunks which were not in use. It was a dismal place, dimly lighted by a solitary bulb—not unlike the granary, except for the way it kept jouncing up and down. It was, in fact, the roughest section of the ship, for in a heavy sea the stern would lift, the clattering screw would spin and then come slamming down. At night the rats ran through it, and swarms of flying roaches came out of hidden cracks and filled the stagnant air with the rustling of their wings.

He gave careful instruction to the sailor: to keep the portholes closed when the sea was rough, as it had been all the time till yesterday; and to make certain they were tightly shut at night—they were covered with black paper to render them opaque—so that no ray of light could escape out of the ship. He directed that the children be regularly fed— but they had not wanted feeding for some time.

The sailor made report of the matter every day. He had not liked the job but he had done it, in consideration of some extra compensation which Captain Aristide was providing from his pocket. The smell of the place was terrible, he said, and though he hosed it out and sprayed with disinfectant, it had been almost more than he could bear. But it was much better now, for they had all recovered—all except the crippled one who still lay in his bunk—not seasick any more, the sailor thought, but sick, he suspected, in some other way. He had come with his report a little while ago: they had eaten everything that he had brought for supper—

"Humph!" said Captain Aristide with a reminiscent shudder. "If they have eaten *that*, then they are well indeed."

And he was right, but they had been very ill. Under other circumstances perhaps not all of them would have succumbed. But seasickness
is a persuasive malady, potent in suggestion; the smell and sound of it
invite participation—and there was the wedding cake with which they
had crammed their empty stomachs.

Yes, they were very sick, but not as adults are. They were scarcely
aware of the passage of the days—not saying to themselves: It has been
(so many) now—how many more? Their distress was non-dimensional
—in time, and space as well; they did not say or think: If only I could
get a breath of air!—if I could go outdoors! They did not imagine
things: that they would be worse or better in the morning, that they
might die, though one of them was coming close to death. But neither
he nor they ever thought of such a thing.

They did not waste emotion in self-pity; nor did they chafe and rage
—at the moaning and retching of the others, at sound and smell, at
the pitching of the ship which rolled them back and forth till they
ached in every bone, at the steeply slanting deck on which they had
to crawl on hands and knees, at the dislocating jerks when the hull
came banging down, at the shuddering vibration of the screw which
set their teeth to chattering, at the stagnant fetid air and suffocating
heat, at physical discomfort of torturing quality. They did not think
about it. They were sick but not *afraid*; at no moment, at the worst,
did any one of them feel the finger tip of panic or despair.

And when they were well they forgot the whole affair—forgot it
right away, not saying to each other: Remember when—how terrible
it was—the endless days and nights—and how we suffered! No, they
never mentioned it, could not indeed recall it, except as a vague and
shadowy time when they had been sick.

Now they were well again, all of them but Rafael—thinner and
whiter than they had been, which was thin and white enough, and very
weak. When the man came in the morning he had opened the
windows—one on each side. They had not known those two round
things were windows until he opened them. It had been exciting to
see the light and smell fresh air again. One at a time they had climbed
on a box to look out at the sea—only Rafael had not cared to make the
effort. He could walk if someone helped him but his back was so
painful he preferred to rest in bed. None of them had stayed up very

long. Juan had discovered the workbench and the tools, and had gone
back to his bunk with some chisels and a hammer. All day he had been
busy, making a cane for Rafael, carving something on the handle. Now
and then he held it up for their inspection.

"What is it anyway?"

"A fish."

"A bird."

"A horse."

"It's Trictrac," he explained.

"Oh—" They were polite, but it did not look like Trictrac.

They dozed and waked, and dozed and waked. When the man came
to get their empty supper bowls—only Rafael's was untouched—he
closed the windows. They heard the key turn in the lock when he went
out, and knew he would not come back till morning. It was hot again
and smelly.

The Little One had climbed into Rosa's bunk, asking to have her
hair brushed. Her curls were full of snarls, and they pulled and itched,
she said. Teresa was telling them a story—really telling it to Rafael
who had asked to hear it, but all of them were listening, although it
was a story they had often heard before—

It was about a Prince, a most unpleasant one. He was so conceited
about his face and voice that everyone disliked him. All day he would
sit with a mirror in his hand, singing to himself. His unhappy parents
wanted him to have a bride, and they sent for the loveliest Princesses
in the world to come to their Court so their son could take his choice.
But the disagreeable Prince sent them all away. The King and Queen
were in despair. But then at last there came a Princess whom no one
had ever heard of, and when the Prince saw her face he lost his heart
completely and said that he would marry her at once. But suddenly
the Princess turned into a Witch who had come to punish him for
being so unpleasant—

But there was an interruption to the story, in the most exciting part:
Rafael coughed and choked, gasping for breath. He said, when he
could speak, it was hard for him to breathe with the windows shut.

"Go on, Teresa," urged the Little One.

"Wait!" Gil said. "Maybe I can open it." And he got out of his bunk.

"But the man will be angry," they objected.

"I don't care." Gil shrugged. And he climbed on the box, but the screw was turned so tight he could not budge it.

"You see—" they laughed. "You can't."

Then Juan put down his work and came to help.

"Juan will open it," they said. They thought: If Juan will do it, it must be all right.

"I don't care about the window," the Little One complained.

"Be still!" They silenced her, for Juan had climbed upon the box and Gil was holding him. He slipped a chisel through an eyelet in the screw and turned it open easily, and he pulled the window wide and a breath of air came in.

"Oh, that feels good," sighed Rafael.

"Go on, Teresa, please," the Little One demanded.

"And so—" Teresa continued with the story: the Witch had turned the Prince into a swan, and now he would have nothing else to do but to look at his face reflected in the water; and he was not to sing again, not ever in his life. If he raised his voice in song, then he would die.

So they put him in a pond in the garden of the Palace, and there he lived in misery, getting very tired of looking at his face and afraid to sing a song—still conceited and unpleasant. But one day a little girl who was very poor and crippled, came into the garden and stood looking at the swan. A Fairy had told her that if the swan would sing to her she would be well again and could play and run about like other children. She was talking with her mother and the swan heard what she said. His stony heart was touched, for at last he understood that there were other people unhappier than he. And so, not caring what became of him, he raised his voice and filled the air with music. The little girl cried out and clapped her hands with joy, for she could walk again—

The last words of it were: "She ran to the edge of the pond and as the last notes died away she stood there, her arms stretched toward the water where the swan lay dead."

It was at this moment that Blottnitz muttered tensely, "Yes, by God, a light!"

The children were silent. It was very sad the way Teresa told it.

"What is *dead*?" asked the Little One at last.

"Dead is dead," they said.

"But what is that?"

"Well, Trictrac is dead."

"Yes, I know. But *where* is Trictrac?"

"Trictrac is in heaven."

"Where is heaven?"

"In the sky," they told her.

"No." She shook her head. "There is nothing in the sky."

"The sun and moon and stars."

"But where is heaven?"

"It's too far away to see."

"Then how do you know it's there?"

"Because—" They hesitated.

"Because God lives in heaven," Rosa said.

"And who is God?"

They laughed. "Why God is God," they said.

"Is God a man?"

"Oh no!" They shook their heads. "No, not a man."

"Then what?"

Juan had been listening, although he had not spoken; but now suddenly he did, almost as if he were talking to himself. "God is a child," he said.

"A child!" they exclaimed incredulously. They would have laughed if Gil had said it, for Gil was careless of his words—or if Pablo had, for Pablo liked to tease. But Juan was not careless nor given much to joking, and he was not joking now. "A child?—you mean like us?"

"Yes, like us, but smaller."

"Smaller than me?" the Little One inquired.

"Smaller than you," Juan nodded.

"But—" they objected doubtfully, "—how do you know?"

"Because I have seen God," the boy replied.

"You have seen God?" they cried. "When? Where?"

"Good!" crowed the Little One. "Oh, tell it, Juan."

"Yes, tell it," they urged. And Rafael raised his head, leaning on his elbow, listening eagerly. His face was flushed and his eyes were bright with fever. "Yes, tell it, please," he whispered.

"It was long ago," Juan said. "I had forgotten it, but I remember now. It was in a city—in a street—but I don't know where. There was

a great procession and the people came to watch it, dressed in their
Sunday clothes, for God was there—"

"God was there?" They stared. "But where and how?—Go on."

"He was in a golden cart, drawn by white oxen—"

"White oxen—" they repeated. "Think of that."

"And there were wreaths of flowers on the oxen and the cart. There
were so many flowers that the air was sweet with them. And all the
people kneeled when God went by."

"What was he doing, Juan?"

"He wasn't doing anything—just sitting in his mother's lap."

"In his mother's lap?" they echoed.

"Yes, it was his mother. She was dressed like a Princess, and she had
a crown with jewels—colored jewels that sparkled."

"Ah—" They sighed with bated breath. "But how do you know the
little child was God?"

"Because my father told me," Juan replied. "I asked him who it was,
and he said that it was God."

"Oh—" They nodded slowly. If Juan's father had told him, then it
must be true.

"I am glad—" Rafael sank back with a contented sigh. "I am glad
God is a child—a child like us."

At this moment the torpedo struck the ship.

Samson was in the engine room, dozing in a chair, with his pipe
between his teeth. He saw, half thinking he was dreaming, the skin of
the ship come blistering toward him, caving in upon him—and in this
life saw nothing else.

Captain Aristide saw nothing. The funnel of the ship folded down
as if on hinges, crushing the wheelhouse to splinters on the bridge.

8

VON BLOTTNITZ BROUGHT THE U-BOAT TO THE
surface and directed a powerful searchlight on the scene.

"Ah!" said Träger. "Very pretty."

Otto Dreyer, a respectful pace behind them, wished he had
thought of saying it, and that he could have said it in the way that
Träger did—a careless tribute to the captain of his team who had
neatly scored a goal. But he had not thought of saying it, and if he
had, could not say it in that way, for it was not *pretty*—not to him.

The torpedo had struck near the center of the ship, aft of the
superstructure which was burning briskly, and the vessel was sinking
by the bow; already the stern had lifted so that the screw was visible.
The crew, such of them as survived, were shouting and rushing
frantically about—you could see the sparks of lanterns, like winging

fireflies. They were launching the boats in panic and confusion, as was commonly the case. Halfway to the water the tackle slipped on one, and it hung nose down, spilling the struggling men into the sea. They tried to climb into another boat which had safely reached the surface, but the occupants of that one shouted to them to stay clear and beat them off with oars. That was reasonable enough, for they would have swamped it and gained nothing for themselves. But it was not *pretty*.

Some of them managed to crawl onto a raft which floated near, and the raft and the boat drifted off into the fog. In a matter of minutes the boats had cleared away and disappeared from sight. But for quite a while after they had vanished the creaking oars and frightened voices continued to be audible. And then there was silence—silence so intense that you could plainly hear the crackling of the flames which began to light the scene and project a crimson glow against the fog.

"I do not like that," Blottnitz said uncomfortably.

"What?" asked Träger.

"The fire." He glanced at the sky. "It is possible it might attract attention."

"Oh well—" Träger shrugged. "In ten minutes she will sink."

Otto Dreyer would have liked to challenge that, to say expansively, "Come now, Gottfried, I will make a bet with you: a case of wine she isn't under water in ten minutes, and another case that backs her to float at least an hour." He had been calculating in his academic way: the ship had sunk so far and then had stopped. And there was a reason for this: the ship was light of cargo, with holds perhaps half empty, and air was trapped in them beneath the hatches; and this might keep her floating for many hours yet. As for the fire in the super-structure, when she sank a little deeper by the bow the sea would put it out. These things passed through his mind, but he said nothing.

"All the same I do not like it," Blottnitz said. The fog seemed to be lifting and he thought he saw a star.

"Well," considered Träger, "let us pump some shells into her."

"No." Blottnitz shook his head. "I have no shells to waste." He was silent for a moment and then he gave his orders. And presently the U-boat slunk away, like a predatory beast which has dispatched its prey and lacks appetite to eat it, like an escaping thug when a crime has been committed and policemen are expected—slinking crookedly away upon the surface.

Otto Dreyer stood alone on the conning tower deck, watching the flames grow dim. He felt a wave of sickness, actual nausea. He was sick in every fiber of his being, sick at heart, wanting only to be through with it forever—with Blottnitz and the U-boat, with his life, with everything—with this stupid game in which he was a player, though not a very good one, but a player none the less. And it didn't matter much if you were good or bad, or which side you were on, or if you won or lost; in the end it was the same, devoid of human dignity. He felt he was alone, suspended in a void whence there was no escape. Nostalgia overwhelmed him. He wished with all his heart he were a child again—or that he could have died before his childhood ended.

The flickering light was gone. He paced the narrow deck, keeping lookout for the mother ship, as he had been ordered: that rendezvous which Blottnitz was so anxiously awaiting. And the mother ship, indeed, was not far off, resting peacefully at the bottom of the ocean, where, to anticipate events which will have no further mention in this narrative, the U-boat and its crew of polo players were destined soon to join it, a fate from which—it is possible at least—they might have been preserved by one well-aimed torpedo.

The children were thrown from their bunks when the torpedo hit. But they were not injured, and they were not frightened because they had no idea what had happened. There was a grinding crash and the light went out, and that was the end of it. The Little One had bumped her head and whimpered that it hurt, but Rosa found her in the dark and kissed the place and rubbed it, and then it was all right. They crept close together on the floor which had begun to slant and rapidly grew steeper. They heard shouts on the deck and footsteps running and splashes in the sea, but these things seemed no stranger than everything had seemed. They were not much concerned—

"The ship has stopped," they said, for the churning screw was stilled, and things were not rattling and jiggling as they had been.

"Perhaps it has bumped into a rock?"

"Maybe," Pablo joked, "it has bumped into America."

They laughed at that. But Juan sniffed at the air—

"It is war again," he said.

"War? How can you tell?"

"Because I smell it."

They sniffed—that biting smell that burned your throat and eyes. "Yes, war again—" they sighed resignedly.

The searchlight swept the porthole and was gone, but lingered not far off so that it was less dark.

"It is morning," they exclaimed.

"No, it is the moon."

"No, more like lightning."

"But lightning does not stay."

Gil went to look, but the box was broken and he could not reach the window. The noises on the deck had died away and there was a strange and soothing silence. They had not missed Rafael until now—

"Rafael!" they called. "Where are you?"

There was no answer. But the light swept by again and they saw him for an instant, lying in his bed as they had seen him last. The bed seemed to be broken, twisted out of shape. Still, they did not think of that as meaning anything: Rafael was safe in bed, no doubt asleep.

"Hush!" they said. "Don't wake him."

They were tired, too, and getting sleepy. They thought to climb back into their bunks, but the mattresses and blankets were scattered on the floor and they were too weary to find them and replace them; and anyway, the bunks were so steeply tilted now that they would be hard to lie in. So they lay down where they were, pulling mattresses together so they would be near each other; even then they slipped and slid if they made a sudden movement—

"If it tips any more," commented Pablo, "the ship will soon be standing on its head."

"What will you do," they said, "when it is upside down?"

"I will walk on the ceiling like a fly."

The Little One was intrigued with this idea: a topsy-turvy world. "If everything was upside down," she said delightedly, "then heaven would be here and Trictrac would be back and we would be with God and I could play with him."

"Oh no," chided Rosa, a little shocked and startled. "That is wrong to say."

"Wrong? Why is it wrong?"

"Because God wouldn't like it."

"I don't see why," the Little One complained. "If God is a child he would like to play with me."

No one seemed disposed to answer that. She was silent for a while, turning something in her mind, and then she asked—

"Can God do anything a Fairy can't?"

"Of course," they said.

"Well, what?"

"Oh, lots of things." But the truth is they didn't know just what.

"Ho!" laughed Gil. "There are no such things as Fairies." But he spoke without conviction.

"Oh yes, there are," the Little One said stanchly. "In Teresa's stories."

"Those are only stories."

"Anyway, they're true."

"I don't believe them."

The Little One appealed for confirmation, but Juan was asleep and Rosa wouldn't answer. Rosa didn't know about the Fairies, whether they were or weren't; sometimes she thought one way and sometimes the other. But she *hoped* there were—not like some of those in Teresa's stories who did such silly things, but beautiful and good ones who could help and guide you. But she had never seen one—

"Maybe—" Pablo said in a noncommittal tone. He was certain there were Fairies, and Witches too, and Sorcerers. But he didn't want Gil to laugh at him.

"Aren't they true, Teresa?" the Little One insisted.

"My mother told them to me." Teresa dodged the question, for she was not quite sure.

"You see?" crowed the Little One. "If there were no Fairies how could they get in stories?" And she added a profound philosophical remark, "You can't think about a thing unless it is."

Gil was secretly impressed. "Maybe," he admitted, "there were Fairies long ago, but not any more—not now."

"What happened to them then?" the Little One demanded.

He was discreetly silent.

When they wakened it was morning and sunlight streaming in the open window. The floor still tilted steeply, even steeper than it had, and their mattresses had slid down by the door. And the door itself—

"Oh look!" they cried. "It's open." And so indeed it was, swung open on its hinges, the wooden bulkhead sprung to free the lock. "Let's go and see what's happened."

"Maybe we've come to land?"

"To America at last."

"Then wait, let's take our things."

"Put them in the bags."

"Hurry! Hurry quick!" They were chattering with excitement.

But the Little One, unnoticed, went scurrying through the door, up the ladder to the deck.

They got the rucksacks down from the hooks where they were hanging, and crammed their things into them, in a fever of impatience.

"Here's Rafael's coat," said Pablo.

"Rafael!" they called. "Wake up!" But he did not answer them. They called, and called again. "What's wrong with him?" they grumbled. "Why doesn't he get up?"

"Maybe he's sick," said Rosa.

"Maybe his back is hurting."

"Maybe he's dead," said Gil. But he was only joking.

"Dead?" They laughed uncomfortably. But then they went to look —only Juan did not go with them, climbing the slippery floor, crowding round the bunk. It was dark in the corner and they couldn't see his face. The bunk was twisted out of shape and a piece of iron pipe had fallen down across it. Perhaps it held him fast so he could not get up. Still, he could answer them and tell them what was wrong. "Rafael! Wake up!" They pulled his sleeve and shook him. His arm was strangely limp—the way that it fell back when you let loose of it; and his hand was dry and cold—like something that you didn't want to touch.

"See, there is his whistle," Pablo said, as if it were evidence that nothing could be wrong. He picked it up and put it in his pocket.

"Rafael, we are going."

"What is the matter with you?"

"Why don't you wake up?"

And then suddenly they knew. And they drew back from the bunk, keeping close together, not wanting to come near it. Rosa began to cry, softly to herself—

The Little One climbed the ladder to the deck, quite an undertaking, for the rungs were far apart, but to compensate for this the ladder was no longer up and down but almost horizontal, like a bridge. Anyway, she managed it and emerged upon the deck to confront a scene of appalling devastation. But lacking adult concepts to appraise the situation she was not depressed or frightened. Quite the contrary in fact. The sun was warm, the sky was blue, the sea was like a mirror; everything was beautiful—beautiful and good. But still she did not say this, nor reflect it to herself, as an adult would have done, distinguishing between the observer and observed. She just felt beautiful—beautiful and good, a part of what she saw, of the world in which she lived. For the cankering crust which experience grows around the human soul to cut it off from Life, was still in her case very soft and thin. However that may be, the adult facts were these—

The ship, a littered wreck, was almost standing on its head. The bow had sunk, as Otto Dreyer had foreseen it would, till the hull was half submerged; and the superstructure which had been on fire, was now beneath the sea, though some smoking remnants of it still remained above the water. The stern of the ship reared high in the air, like the tail of a whale about to dive. And indeed the *Bellérophon* might dive at any moment, might have dived at any moment of the night. But the Little One was blissfully unaware of any danger.

She wanted to be first to see America; and she scrambled across the deck and climbed up on the rail, until she could see over. "Oh—" she gasped, for the sight that met her eyes quite took her breath away. Something was coming toward her, from the sky or from the sea. At first she thought it was a bird—a huge and wondrous bird, with a Fairy in its claws. But then she saw it was a ship, and the wings were really sails, and the Fairy was not clutched in claws but standing at the very front, almost in the water. "Oh, oh, oh—" She had never been so thrilled; and she jumped down from the rail, slid back across the deck and squealed into the hatchway—

"Oh! Come quick!"

"What is it?"

"Come and look!"

"Is it America?"

"No, better."

"Well, what?"

"A Fairy ship." She heard them coming now, scrambling up the ladder; and she scuttled back to look, not to lose a precious moment.

It was not a Fairy ship, but a ship out of a dream, out of a comic opera—out of a nightmare really. It came without a sound—a schooner with three masts; but it was not a schooner, nor bark or brig, nor anything that could be named.

It came out of the sun with all its canvas spread, a crazy quilt of patches, like a coat of many colors—four bellying jibs, and then a lateen sail, rust colored like burnt-orange, set from a yard obliquely to the foremast; but the mainmast was square rigged, and, to complete confusion, on the mizzen was a spanker, a small and stubby sail whose boom must scarcely clear the skylight of a cabin in the elevated poop, behind which, in the shelter of the coaming, was the wheel. The forecastle was high to match the poop, and beneath the bowsprit was a gilded figurehead with a trident in its hand—a female figure, possibly a mermaid, but time and the elements had made the question doubtful. On either side of it were vestiges of eyes, carved and painted in the graceful clipper bow, suggesting that the ship had its origin in China, where reasonably enough eyes are given to a ship. "No got eyes, then no can see," the Chinese say, or did say yesterday.

Midship of the waist, with its back against the mainmast, was a shanty with a stovepipe in its roof—a floating shanty, it appeared, for the vessel had scarcely any freeboard, so that at a little distance the masts appeared to be standing in the water. The name of this nautical anachronism was lettered on the bow above the eyes; it was in Arabic, and, in free translation, might be rendered *Flying Virgin*—as misleading as a name could be, for despite its graceful lines it was slow and cranky—ninety days from Istanbul; and as for its virginity—

It had been built in China sixty years ago, for the opium trade; and when that played out it had served its time as a Red Sea slaver, ferrying blacks from Ethiopia, children for the most part, to Jidda in Arabia where there was good market for them, and remains one to this day. Some reminders of this business still persisted: stringers in the hold which had been bored for fetters, worn smooth by chains tethering

leg irons together—irons that cut the flesh, and there would be festering sores, and perhaps the child would die or the leg would be cut off.

But steam had proved more profitable, and better to elude British
men-of-war cruising out of Aden, alert for evildoers when they had no
share in it. And so the *Flying Virgin* had been sold to a rich American
who had used it as a yacht in the Aegean Sea, fitting up the cabin at
the stern with American magnificence. But he had tired of it, and then
it had been wrecked, and plundered too.

Not long ago it had been sold again, by a Jew in Istanbul who had
got it on a debt from some shady undertaking—*chartered* was the word,
but the charter price was twice what it was worth—to an international
scoundrel who had immediate need to evacuate himself and his ill-
gotten wealth from a quarter of the world which threatened to be
hotter than he cared to contemplate. For the Third Reich had a price
set on his head, a price which might be tempting in the Balkans—the
product of an overt act of treachery in connection with the famous
Russian Purge in which he had escaped liquidation by a hair, and by
ruthlessly betraying his employers.

It had been a problem where to go, for there were not many places
where he would be welcome, and where he might with safety disembark
his fortune—English and Turkish gold and a pint of unset jewels,
concealed beneath false bottoms in a dozen earthen jars of olive oil,
of which there were four thousand in the *Flying Virgin's* hold. After
careful preparation he had settled on a small and inconspicuous port
in South America, whence by hook or crook he hoped to reach New
York where an international scoundrel might feel reasonably secure.
And so three months ago he had sailed from Istanbul, under protection
of the neutral Turkish flag, with a crew of thieving rascals, and a
drunken Greek for captain.

His name was Kerch, but this scarcely matters since he frequently
used others; his origin was undetermined, nor was his speech a clue,
for he could speak many languages. His age was doubtful too, but somewhere in the sixties. He was small and slight, with a dark-skinned wizened face, and a thatch of thin gray hair combed down across his
forehead. His manner was mild, and on occasion polished. Like many
dangerous people he did not look alarming, and this had more than
once served to his advantage. He did not smoke or drink or play at

games of chance. But by way of compensation he had a secret vice—
and not so very secret, for several times it had got him into trouble,
even in the Balkans where so many human frailties are indulgently
regarded. Still, one time in Bucharest he had nearly lost his life. In
short he had a weakness: a taste for little girls—to feast his aging
eyes upon their naked bodies, to fondle and caress them—

He was asleep in the spacious cabin underneath the poop, among
the faded souvenirs of American magnificence—the paneled walls and
remnants of brocade which canopied the bed, odds and ends of shabby
elegance. He turned and tossed in the light and troubled sleep of international scoundrels.

On the deck, directly aft of the cabin's open skylight, the captain
steered the ship, lying on his back, his eyes half closed, steering with
the toes of his bare feet, clinging to the spokes from long practice like
an ape, and looking not unlike one in his swarthy, hairy nakedness,
with his ugly bearded face and the brass rings in his ears.

The *Flying Virgin* kept no watch. There was no one else in sight
except the cook, a negro with a wooden leg strapped to the stump
above his knee—an Abyssinian black, deep-chested, tall and lithe,
powerful and beautiful, with a skin like satin bronze and rippling
muscles under it, though he was no longer young, for his hair and
close-trimmed beard were streaked with gray. He wore a single garment, a pair of cotton drawers; and hanging from a cord about his waist
was a gleaming butcher knife whose edge was razor sharp. His name
was Mohammed and he was a Moslem. He was a freeman now, but
for more than half his life he had been a slave in the Hejaz of
Arabia.

He stood before the galley, that crazy wooden shanty in the center
of the ship—stood beside a meat block which was anchored to the
deck, with a cleaver in his hand, cutting up the carcass of a sheep—
one of several living creatures they had loaded when, a month ago, they
had put in at Madeira for supplies, and which dwelt beneath the
galley in a dark and noisome stable: chickens in a crate for the Effendi,
who dined in his cabin in solitary grandeur, and a she-goat with her kids
which would soon be fit for roasting. That night a ewe had lambed, and
there were more creatures now. He had heard her plaintive bleating
and had climbed down the ladder with a lantern in his hand, to help

her with her labor as he knew how to do, speaking to her softly in the Galla tongue, the language of his childhood, feeling in her body with gentle, skillful hands, watching her distress with compassionate, sorrowing eyes.

Yes, there were more creatures now: when one went another came. It was the will of Allah. He was thinking this, cutting up the sheep whose carcass was still warm, when, glancing forward at the sea, he saw upon the *Flying Virgin's* beam and close at hand, the hulk of the derelict rearing high above the water. He gazed a moment at it, not knowing what he saw. But then it seemed to him that something moved upon the wreck—a head above the railing, of a woman or a child. And now he dropped the cleaver and ran back along the deck, up the ladder at the poop till his head would show above it—

"Look!" he shouted, pointing at the sea.

The Greek sat up and looked, heavy with sleep and drink, and then his dull eyes widened and he hammered with his heel upon the deck, calling as he did so—

"Effendi! Effendi!"

Kerch wakened with a start and sat up in his bed. Through the open skylight he could see the captain's legs. "What now?" he questioned anxiously.

"The Germans have been here."

"What?" He caught his breath, scrambling from his bed. "Germans do you say?" He was in such a tremble he could hardly speak, thinking in sweating terror they had found him after all, followed him implacably, thirsting for their vengeance—to rob him of the gold in the jars of olive oil, which no doubt they knew about, for they knew everything —to take him back and torture him. His eyes strayed to a gun case in the paneled wall, in which there was a military rifle—thinking to himself he would sell his life as dearly as he could; they would not take him alive. "How do you know?" he stammered.

"There is a sinking ship."

"A sinking ship—" He climbed on a transom whence he could look out beneath the skylight, and saw the smoking hulk standing on its head a thousand meters off the starboard bow. Yes, the Germans had been there, for the flag of France still flew. And they might not be far off, watching at this moment through a hidden periscope. "Sheer off," he ordered sharply. He wanted only to be gone and out of sight of it, afar from any contact with a German U-boat. And yet, if he had known what was to be, he might have welcomed the hand of the Gestapo, reaching from the sea to strike him down. "Stay clear of it," he warned.

"Yes, Effendi." The Greek obeyed, not unwillingly at all, standing to spin the wheel, edging the *Flying Virgin's* bow to port.

The crew were tumbling up out of the forecastle, gathering at the rail, staring at the wreck—Albanians, Greeks, and Turks, shouting to each other in a polyglot of tongues, in terror of the Germans despite their Turkish flag. Mohammed was still standing on the ladder, shading his eyes to look. He was certain he had seen a head above the rail, of a woman or a child, but he could not see it now, not anything that moved. The *Flying Virgin* began to edge away. He turned with a start, staring at the Greek—

"What now?" he muttered, and ran across the deck, his wooden leg thumping hollowly upon it. "Why do you turn away?"

"The Effendi—" shrugged the Greek, nodding toward the skylight.

"But there is someone there upon that ship."

"There is no one," said the Greek, sullen and indifferent.

"But I tell you that I saw one."

"What is this talk?" cried Kerch, catching phrases in the cabin.

"There is someone on the ship," the black explained respectfully.

"No matter," Kerch retorted, speaking Arabic. "It is no affair of ours."

"But Effendi, there is someone—a woman or a child."

"A child?" repeated Kerch and climbed back upon the transom, staring at the wreck. But he saw no sign of life. "No, you are mistaken."

"Effendi, but I saw."

"No matter. I have spoken."

"No—" The black's face darkened, and he reached his hand as if to take the wheel. But now suddenly he saw them—not one but several of them, their heads above the railing, and they were the heads of children. "Look!" he shouted. "There!"

The Greek stood staring, with his jaw dropped open.

"Go thou and launch the longboat," Mohammed said to him. "And I will take the helm." And he took it from his hands, nursing the ship about into the wind, watching aloft until the canvas slacked and the boom of the spanker swung idly overhead. "Children—little children," he kept saying to himself.

"Children—" mumbled Kerch. He jumped down from the transom and climbed upon another where he could see them better.—Yes, children—little children, and there were six of them. Children abandoned on a sinking ship. *Abandoned* was the word, he told himself, for it did not stand to reason they could have been forgotten—not all six of them. But he was wrong. They had not been abandoned, nor had they been forgotten, for there was not anyone to remember them. They had been *overlooked* which is a different thing, of quite another quality.

"Children—" Kerch repeated.—Boys and—yes, he saw the flutter of a dress. His heart beat faster and there was a tightening in his throat. He stood there watching, clinging with his fingers to the coaming of the skylight—clinging so tightly that his fingernails were white.

"Oh—" the children gasped in amazement and delight, as one by one they emerged out of the hatch—like prisoners who forget the beauty of the world and see it all afresh as something new and wonderful. But they had never really seen the sea till now, the endless circle of it spreading all around them, blue as blue could be, sparkling in the sun as if jewels were strewn on it. And in the sky, where it came down to the sea like an inverted bowl, were fleecy drifting clouds, which while you looked at them, became all sorts of things: elephants and dragons, palaces and castles, Witches on trailing broomsticks—

But these were not the things they saw at first, blinking their eyes against the unaccustomed light, scrambling across the deck to reach the railing—

"Look! Oh look!" they cried, and gazed in silent rapture: the great sails, patched and stained, flapping idly in the breeze; the tall masts swaying gently to the motion of the sea; the figure at the prow with the trident in its hand—a mermaid certainly. Yes, here was a ship as ships should be, as one had pictured them and dreamed about them. They spoke in breathless whispers—

"See the little boat they are putting in the water—"

"Will it come and get us?"

"Are we going on that ship?"

"Of course!" exclaimed the Little One, her hands clasped at her breast and her eyes as bright as stars. "And it *is* a Fairy ship."

They looked at her and smiled, half tempted to believe it.

"And a Fairy Prince will come—"

"Ho!" Gil grinned. "He is coming now, in the little boat—a big black Fairy with a wooden leg."

They laughed and laughed. It was really very funny.

9

MOHAMMED WENT ALONE TO BRING THE children, for there was none who sought to keep him company, who wanted to come closer to the wreck. Once the boat was launched they quickly edged away. He understood and smiled contemptuously but he did not ask for help, though the longboat was heavy for a single pair of oars.

And then he could not take his eyes from them, bending to the oars, with crimson stains upon his arms and hands from the interrupted butchering of the sheep, with the long shiny knife which hung between his knees—not a reassuring figure. But the children scarcely noticed him, their whole attention centered on the ship.

"Little children—" he kept saying in the Galla tongue, nodding to himself, wondering and delighted. And once he stayed the oars to strike his fist against his breast. "Mohammed," he explained. "Mohammed me."—Mamud it sounded like, and Mamud it became.—"And thou?" he questioned one and then another.

They understood and answered him their names. And he repeated each, struggling manfully with the unfamiliar sounds until he had them right, or nearly so. Little One was hardest and they told him several times before he mastered it, amused by his mistakes, for to them it was a name like any other.

They had forgotten Rafael, forgotten him completely. It was the Little One who missed him and reminded them—

"Where is Rafael?" she demanded.

"Rafael—" They remembered with an ache but without a sense of guilt. "Rafael is dead," they told her.

"Oh dead—" She thought about it. "Why are you crying, Rosa?" For tears had welled again in Rosa's eyes, thinking of the patient little boy whom they had left behind and would never never see again.

"Because I am so sorry," Rosa said.

"Sorry?" The Little One shook her golden curls. "But why should you be sorry that Rafael is in heaven with Trictrac and with God?"

"Don't talk so much," they said. But in simple truth they were not *very* sorry. The world was too exciting, and they did not need Rafael, were not emotionally dependent on him. And in point of fact it is not for the dead that people grieve, but for themselves, for something they have lost, for interrupted habit, for the end of a dependence, for an emptiness within them. The little cloud passed quickly and the sun was bright again—

The ship was close at hand—and, yes, it *was* a mermaid, with scales of glittering gold where the fish part of her started. Juan was staring at her. He thought she looked like someone—no, it wasn't Rosa; but someone he had known or seen somewhere.

"Oh look! The ship has eyes."

"Eyes? Where?"

"There, beside the mermaid."

Mohammed laughed aloud, studying their faces, first one and then another. But perhaps it was at Pablo he looked longest, seeing in the dark-skinned little boy a picture of the child that he had been—

He had been about that age when he had been stolen, tending his father's cattle, kidnaped by Arab traders, and in a long procession of boys and girls, and maidens and young men, tethered leg to leg, had made the endless journey from his homeland in farthest Abyssinia—a pleasant temperate country of grazing land and mountains, of green and fertile valleys where even coffee trees grew tall as oaks—through all of Ethiopia, over torrid, barren deserts to the shore of the Red Sea—twelve hundred English miles.

Many children died of exhaustion and disease and were left beside the way for the vultures who were hovering in the sky. But he was a sturdy lad and he survived. Only his leg, wounded by the fetters, as were so many others, had become a festering sore which grew worse upon the slave ship, in the darkness and confinement of the hold, without any care for it—

"Akhs—" he muttered and with tightened lips bent stoutly to his oars. For even now, after fifty years, his heart flamed with resentment at the memory of it.

In Jidda, in a slave pen, the leg had been cut off, hacked off at the knee, and the ragged stump of it plunged in boiling fat to cauterize the wound. But of this he had been mercifully unconscious, for he had long since fainted from the pain. He had waked to find it gone, and childhood vanished with it—

The longboat gently nosed against the schooner's side. Mohammed shipped the oars; and one by one he picked up the children and set them on the deck, as if they had been feathers, and threw the rucksacks after them, and clambered up behind with the painter in his hand. It was not much to climb for the top of the bulwark was no more than shoulder high above the sea.

The ship was still hove to, teetering gently up and down, swinging to and fro, as if not quite decided what to do, its great square sails crackling idly in the breeze, catching a puff of it and then snapping slack again, while playful little waves lap-lapped against her side. And there were all the pleasant smells of the ships of yesterday—of sunburned canvas, hempen ropes, tarred ratlines, seasoned wood—her deck was teak, though you could not have told it for the crust that lay upon it. And there were not any irritating sounds of winches, screws, and engines, nor the trembling that they made—only the crackling sails, and creaking stays and braces, and lapping of the waves.

Yes, this was a ship—a really truly one. The children looked about with fascinated eyes, breathing deep the clean fresh air which did not smell of oil. But then—

"What is that?" gasped Juan, shrinking back among them.

"What? Where?"

"There—" He pointed. "By the little house, on that block of wood."

"Oh there—" They looked with horror, not knowing what they saw.

"Is it—" He had turned his face away and would not look again. "Is it a child?" he stammered.

"A child—" Their hearts stood still. It did not look unlike a child, the carcass of the sheep, its head hung down and blood still dripping from it; and the cleaver, like an ax, stuck in the wood beside it. And the black man with the knife and the red stains on his arms!—They turned their heads to look. He was tying a rope to the railing of the ship, making fast the little boat. But then Gil laughed—

"It is not a child," he said. "It is a sheep."

"A sheep—" They breathed again.

"See! There is the skin, on the floor beside it."

"Oh yes—" They saw it now—gray and woolly, not in the least like theirs. But they quickly looked away at something else—at some men who had come near to stare at them, strange-looking men, ragged and half clothed, with beards and hairy chests and ugly grinning faces—jabbering to each other, staring, pointing. And one came pushing through them, one with brass rings in his ears, saying something in a rough and angry voice. They huddled close together, startled and confused; and then suddenly the black man stood between them and the others.

"I—" Mohammed said, speaking to the Greek, but to be overheard, "I will care for them," not offering to, or asking, but saying what would be, and in a manner not to be denied. But there was none among them to gainsay him, nor, had they been tempted, to make an issue with him. He was apart from them—*dock-scum*, as he named them in his thought. He slept in the galley among his pots and pans, or on the deck outside it; he cooked their food—big iron kettles which they came to fetch. But he held no traffic with them, and they were careful not to tread upon his toes, for his prowess was a legend. It was well known to them that he could hurl a knife with deadly aim—that he had and might again. The Greek knew as much and was no bolder than the rest—

"As you will," he mumbled with a shrug, but then he added something, grinning through his yellow teeth, pointing his finger at Rosa and Teresa. "But for those," he said, and winked and jerked his thumb toward the cabin in the poop, "it may be the Effendi—" He left the rest unsaid. The men around him laughed, which no doubt was what he sought, to recover face with them; for it is unlikely that he, or any of them, knew anything of Kerch—of that unhappy weakness of which he was a victim. It was an ugly jest, no more than that.

And not waiting for an answer, he ordered the men to go about their business, shouting to one to make the longboat fast astern, for there was no tackle rigged to hoist it in; and himself turned away and went aft to take the helm, to bring the ship again upon her course.

Kerch saw him coming and spoke to him through the skylight—

"Are they aboard?" he asked.

"Yes, six of them, Effendi. Three boys and three girls."

"Three girls, you say?"

"Yes, three, Effendi. But one is very small."

"Ah so—" A pause. "What—will you do with them?"

"Nothing, Effendi. The black will care for them."

"The black—" He nodded, frowning. He went to the door and opened it a little, until he could see forward to the deck. But then he thought of something and went feverishly to seek it in his luggage, muttering to himself and throwing things about until his hand closed on it—an opera glass, a woman's, inlaid with mother-of-pearl. He went back to the door, adjusting the focus with a trembling finger. Now he could see them plainly, as if he were beside them—a child with a face like a Madonna—another with a ribbon in her hair—

The *Flying Virgin* came about into the wind, mincing gracefully like a dancer, coquetting with the sea. The yards swung to the breeze; the spanker boom swept through, snapping like a whip; the great sails cracked and filled; the bow dipped low and a pinch of spray sprang high into the air, pattering down like raindrops; the deck tipped sharply, steeply, blue water reaching for it, foaming white against the bulwark; the masts leaned to the sea. The children were dismayed—

"Oh, oh—" they cried. "The ship is tipping over." And they crowded back against the little house as a curl of water washed around their feet. But it quickly ran away, gurgling in the scuppers; the deck tipped back again; the masts stood straight. The *Flying Virgin* steadied on an even keel, settling to her stride with a fair breeze at her heels, riding jauntily on the sea, the mermaid at her prow whisking gaily through the spray.

"No—" they murmured, breathing deeply with relief. "No, it will not tip over."

"Because it is a Fairy ship," the Little One said firmly. "And it could not tip over."

They laughed indulgently. "It's going fast," they said. "Flying like a bird."

Mohammed stood behind them in the doorway of the galley, smiling to himself. At last he spoke to them. "Mohammed me—" he said.

They turned their heads with apprehensive starts—the red stains and the knife, the wooden block with the heap of bleeding flesh, which did look like a child, though of course it was a sheep, and the ax stuck in beside it.

"Mohammed me—" he said again, reassuring and explaining, spreading wide his arms in welcoming gesture, which said as plain as words what was written in his eyes: "Mohammed is your friend, your father and your mother. Be not afraid of anything, neither elements nor men, for Mohammed will protect you."

But they did not understand, or at least were unconvinced; and indeed there was behind them no remembered relationship to serve them as a guide.

"What does he want?" they whispered, cautious and on guard, not to be taken in by nodding smiles and gestures, by words which had no meaning, nor by other words which had.

The negro sighed and shook his head, sensing the probation which their friendship would demand. They had suffered, that was why. He, too, had been like that when he was a child, after he was stolen, expecting only evil at the hands of men. By and by, he thought, by and by—

And perhaps he would have won them if—if—

It was Kerch's custom to walk upon the deck in the afternoon, the weather being suitable—from the door of his cabin to the break of the forecastle, forty level paces from the mizzen to the foremast—back and forth for an hour or until he had his fill, walking slowly and carefully with a slightly mincing step.

He wore on these occasions, and all others, a dark gray suit devoid of character, fitting loosely to his slight, ill-shapen figure, and a collar and a tie—the whole effect completely nondescript—and a flat tweed cap, like a trans-Atlantic tourist, a final incongruous and unbecoming touch. His shoes were soft black leather, soled with rubber.

Sometimes as he strolled he would pause beside the galley to exchange with the negro a word or two in Arabic, to pass the time of day or make some request about his food, which Mohammed carried to him on a tray. But on the whole he was silent and reserved, giving out no information and not asking any questions. Not many of the crew had heard his voice. He would nod as he passed by and that was all.

He strolled today—

The children had been fed. Mohammed had cooked rice and brought it in a kettle with chunks of mutton in it, tender and delicious. He had filled their bowls brimful, and filled them up again, till they could eat no more.

They were sitting on the deck outside the galley door, too stuffed with food to play, or even talk, content to watch the sea sliding smoothly up and down, and the faraway white clouds making pictures in the sky. They did not see the man until he spoke—speaking to Mohammed in the galley door. And then they looked and saw a small mouse-colored man with a narrow mouselike face—not a prepossessing figure and not alarming either, inconspicuous, unimportant. And now he spoke to them, in a voice that matched his looks, tentative and colorless. But they did not understand.

"Good day," they said indifferently.

"I see—" He spoke in Spanish. "You are Spanish children."

"Yes, Spanish," they replied, amazed and pleased. They could scarce believe their ears: a man who spoke their tongue. It had been long since such a thing had happened. "Are you Spanish, too?" they asked.

"No, I am not Spanish." He seemed to speak to Rosa and Teresa, to one and then the other, not noticing the rest except with special effort. "But I have been in Spain. I know your country well."

"I—" Gil interrupted, "I am of Madrid."

"Indeed?" Kerch glanced at him and glanced away speaking again to Rosa. "Whence have you come?" he said.

She shook her head. His eyes made her uncomfortable—staring, mouselike eyes. The others answered for her—

"From France," they said.

"From France?" He nodded, looking at Teresa. "But why and how?"

They told him, haltingly at first but eagerly enough once they were fairly started, what they knew and could remember, not the nebulous dim past but beginning with the farm, strange jumble of realities and interpretation of them: the slaughtered cow and pigs, the priest and motorbus, the cinema, the cake, the ship—of Trictrac and of Rafael.

Kerch listened absently, toying with his watch chain, twisting it in and out around his fingers, shifting his eyes from Rosa to Teresa, seeing through their ragged garments the naked little bodies, angular and thin, of children who are coming to be women—buds still tightly folded but soon to be in blossom—appraising and debating: which was the purest symbol of innocence, of virtue? He thought that Rosa was —the oval face and straight dark hair, smooth and fine as silk—the eyes like a Madonna's. But they would not look at his. Yet that was as it should be; that was what he sought: recognition and denial of himself, of the evil he personified.

He groped deeper in the blackness of his life, as he had groped so many times before. He knew himself to be a scoundrel—an international one, a liar and a cheat, a traitor who would sell for the best price he could get a country or a cause, a mistress or a friend, though it was long since he had had a friend. Yes, he was a scoundrel; there was no doubt of that. But the passion that he felt for little girls—to strip their clothing off and gaze upon their bodies, to kiss and fondle them and strain them to his breast—for which society would show no mercy; *that* was not the scoundrel in himself, but only his poor effort to escape it, to recover what was lost, the soul which he had bartered. And it was only then, in fulfillment of perversion—a loathsome, hideous one, as well he knew, and dangerous too; that time in Bucharest it had nearly cost his life—only then he could find peace, could touch the hand of God, for this dreadful malady was his one remaining avenue of prayer. Ironic blasphemy, but it was true.

A physician in Vienna had explained it to him—a psychiatrist of note, whom he had consulted in the early period of the disease, nearly twenty years ago—not so much explaining as confirming his own half-formulated diagnosis. The doctor had been curious, asking many questions that he dared not answer, for already he was well embarked on his career, and not even to a doctor or a priest may such things be safely mentioned. He had said, "I am a scoundrel. We must let it go at that. I cannot enlarge upon it."—"Very well," the doctor said, "but tell me why—why are you a scoundrel?"—"I have always been a scoundrel," he replied.—"No," the doctor said, "you deceive yourself, my friend, for once you were a child."

Yes, he had been a child, that was quite true, and not a scoundrel then—like these children who were chattering at him now, like children everywhere, in process of corruption from the day that they are born, but not yet corrupted—clinging tightly to their souls, struggling vainly to resist a man-made world, being squeezed and trimmed and nailed into its pattern against their futile efforts to prevent it—the helpless victims of an adult Party Line. Yes, he had been a child. He had not much memory of it, save of bitter and degrading poverty, of hunger and ignorance, of a way of life a dog would have rejected.

And he had been a youth, not yet a scoundrel. He saw himself again, sitting with a candle through long winter nights, shivering with the cold, poring over books—seeking from them some method of escape out of the squalid misery with which he was surrounded, an egress from the trap which the world of men had built for themselves and for their children. And he had found the answer, or believed he had: he had become a revolutionist—had thrown himself, with all his heart and soul, into the Cause which promised everything to the wretched of the earth. And he had served it faithfully, ruthlessly and long. He had been persecuted, exiled and imprisoned—fifteen of his first forty years he had spent in prison cells. But the fine flame in his heart had not gone out. Tomorrow, yes tomorrow, he had thought—

But when that morrow came it brought no surcease to him, for a triumphant Cause is a Cause no longer, but a hydra-headed monster. It is bad perhaps to lose, but it is not good to win. Victory gives out a hollow sound; in a parade of conquerors the victors and the vanquished march together. But one only learns these things when it is much too late.—He had not conformed exactly to the pattern of the moment, and he had been denounced, arrested and convicted by his friends of yesterday, by that very Cause he had spent his life defending.

It was then, disillusioned, brokenhearted, that he became a scoundrel, deliberately and coolly, finding little difference in himself when it was done—being a scoundrel for a Cause or for oneself, *agent provocateur* in the interest of the Party or to feather one's own nest, sending comrades to be shot for some minor deviation in dialectic or for an honest dollar in one's pocket. He had not so much become a scoundrel as discovered that he was one—that in pursuit of God he had renounced Him. For he had long since parted with compassion; and he who parts with that, no matter toward what end, is lost beyond redemption.

It was not long after this that the disease came on him—

"Why are you a scoundrel?"—He had answered with a shrug, tempted to say, "Because I am a man," but he had restrained the impulse. They had talked for quite a while. "But how," he questioned at the end, "how may I be cured?"—The doctor smiled. "To begin with," he said, "you should cease to be a scoundrel."—Very simple—yes, no doubt, "And how," he had asked, "may I do that?"

"How?" The doctor drummed with his fingers on the desk—a handsome, healthy, smugly virtuous man. "It might be well to start with an honest occupation."—"What?" he insisted. "What would you suggest?" —"Ah that!" The doctor laughed and spread his soft white hands, ignoring the question as a jest. But it was not a jest.

An honest occupation.—Yes, but what?—What occupation would one choose to escape the company and practices of scoundrels?—One must return to childhood to find the occupations of a child; and there was no road back.—Children had no Causes; they did not subscribe to Principles; they were not intrigued by lofty words and nebulous ideas. They were essentially practical—as practical as Nature, healthy in mind and body, intent upon exploring the mysteries of Life and enjoying the adventure.—They could forget an injury—a scratch, a bump, a fall, a broken heart. That was their great advantage, to forget.

He was looking at Teresa with riveted attention—pert and piquant little gypsy, with the scrap of faded ribbon in her hair, indolent of body, gay of eye—thinking something else in another pocket of his mind, appraising and debating. But then he was aware they were no

longer chattering; they were asking him a question, had already asked
it twice—

"Does the ship belong to you?" That's what they were saying.

"To me?" He bent his thought upon it with an effort, noticing that
sweat was trickling on his face, taking out his handkerchief to wipe it,
seeing that the watch chain had left a livid streak where he had tightly
wound it on his fingers. "No, not to me," he said. "I am, like you, a
passenger."

"Oh—" they nodded. "But where does it go, this ship?"

"To America," he said.

"America!" they cried, and clapped their hands with joy. "And will
it be like home?"

"Like Spain?" He shrugged. "America is like—like everything." And
he added, stammering slightly, looking now at Rosa, "I—I have some
pictures of it in my cabin—" thinking with a shudder of revulsion as
he spoke the words, which he had not willed to say: the classical
technique of seduction—pictures of America, a necklace of matched
pearls, a sweet, a sable coat, a doll that speaks—francs, dollars, pounds—

He tore his gaze from her, looked up and looked around—as a guilty
man would look, to determine if he had been overheard, furtively and
quickly. The black was standing in the doorway of the galley with his
eyes fixed on him—eyes which seemed dark and threatening. But the
man could not have understood his words; and the words themselves
were innocent enough. It was absurd; his sense of guilt was prompting
him. He drew composure tight, like a garment that he buttoned, but
it did not shut the chill out of his heart. When he spoke there was
nothing in his voice—

"They are Spanish children—orphaned refugees," he said.

"Yes, Effendi." The negro nodded slowly, but there was not any
change in the expression of his eyes.

"They have been telling me—" He rubbed his hands, rubbing out the
livid streaks. "They have been telling me of their adventures."

"Yes, Effendi."

The children were afraid he would forget. They asked with eager
voices, "When will you show us the pictures of America?"

"When?" He glanced at them. And suddenly he turned and walked
away, back along the deck whence he had come.—These Abyssinians!

One could not tell about them. And himself and all the fruits of his career at the hazard of this voyage.—It was madness, utter madness to think of such a thing. But he was mad in fact, diseased with madness.—No, no, it would not do—not this time, no. He must not think of it, must think of something else—

He dragged his thought back, groping for the point of interruption: Children could forget. Yes, that was it. That was their strength—a coat of mail which shed or blunted the arrows of experience. They could forget—forget. And if one could forget all one had ever learned—had ever learned from men—one would be a child again. But men could not forget; and there was no road back.

He came to the door and went into the cabin. The opera glass was lying on the bed where he had dropped it. He picked it up and turned it in his hands, debating, hesitating—

The children saw him go into the cabin, and saw him reappear with something in his hand—

"He is coming back," they said, "with the pictures of America."

But he did not come back nor glance in their direction. He went to the rail, not hurrying his step, and stood there for a moment; and it seemed that he dropped what he held into the sea. And then, empty-handed, he went back into the cabin and closed the door behind him.

"No," they sighed. "No, he isn't coming back."

The black man had not moved, still standing in the doorway of the galley. And now he spoke, not smiling, almost sternly, touching his finger to his breast, "Mohammed me—" He took a step and turned his head, looking toward the door where the man had disappeared, then back at them; and he frowned and shook his head.

Their faces fell; they said resentfully—

"He means we are not to see the pictures."

"Yes, but why?"

"Maybe he is angry?"

"Angry about what?"

"Angry with the man."

"Perhaps he doesn't like him."

"I don't like him either," the Little One announced. "He didn't notice me."

"Because you are too small," suggested Pablo.

"I don't like him anyway," the Little One insisted. "He looks like a mouse, an ugly little mouse."

"Like a spider," said Teresa.

"Yes, a spider." Rosa shivered.

"All the same," said Gil, "I would like to see the pictures."

"Yes, the pictures," they agreed.

Mohammed had vanished down a narrow hatchway whose scuttle top was close beside the galley. They had not noticed where he went, but now he reappeared with something in his arms—

"Look!" they cried. "What is it?"

"A dog. A cat."

"No. A baby lamb."

He put it down among them on the deck—a soft, white little thing, hardly able yet to stand upon its legs. They were speechless with delight; in a twinkling they forgot the pictures of America.

Yes, perhaps he would have won them, for he left no stone unturned. He emptied out the rucksacks and scrubbed their wretched garments, and hung them to dry on a line stretched to the mast. He took them to the bow and let them lean far over, one by one, till they could see the mermaid riding through the spray. He fed them till their bodies seemed visibly to swell and color came again into their cheeks.

One day he took them with him down the hatchway, through the storeroom which was underneath the galley, to the halfdeck forward of it where the animals were kept—a dismal, smelly stable where there was not any light save the lantern that he carried, which projected monstrous shadows on the walls. They had stayed close together, feeling very sorry for the creatures: the goats, the ewe and lambs, and some melancholy chickens clucking mournfully in a narrow, slatted prison. They were glad to go back to the deck, to see the sky again.

He taught them Galla words for things about the ship. At night he slept beside them on the deck. They had no relationship with anybody else. Occasionally they glimpsed the mouseman, walking back and forth on the high part at the back where Mamud never took them, but he did not come again to speak with them. The hairy man with the brass rings in his ears would pass by now and then. The sailors came to fetch and bring their kettles, and they would stare and grin; but

Mamud would be there, watchful and alert, and, beneath his gaze, they did not linger.

When he went below to the storeroom or the stable, he would give them warning of it, instructing them with gestures: they were not to wander off, not to leave the narrow space before the galley, whose boundary he had marked with Pablo's chalk.

They understood and they obeyed. They had not been tempted to disregard the order.

Yes, perhaps he would have won them; he was coming close to it. They had almost forgotten the carcass of the sheep and there had not been another to remind them. The headsman's block remained, and the headsman's ax stuck in it, and the long shiny knife ever dangling at his waist; but their shocking implications had drifted far away. Mamud was their friend, not a man like other men. They were on the edge of beginning to believe it, of giving him their confidence without any reservation, of accepting him as one of them. And then—

It was in the afternoon of a hot and sultry day. The gentle following breeze had died out to a calm, and the sky was overcast with a dirty scum of clouds. The sun shone through it like a copper stain in a leaden-colored bowl. And the sea was leaden-colored, with a lazy, greasy swell that rolled the *Flying Virgin* till her stays and braces groaned—a heavy, sickening motion. And though there was no wind, not the barest breath of one, yet there was a sound like wind—a moaning in the sky. The air was thick with portent. The Greek had roused himself, cross-legged at the wheel, eying the darkening sky and sagging canvas. The lateen sail was furled, for it was unwieldy, hard to handle in a squall; but the mainmast carried everything she had: skysail, royal, topsails. It was at these he looked, debating whether he should shorten sail, scanning the sea for the riffle of a squall, waiting undecided.

Mohammed had gone below, disappearing down the hatchway with his lantern, pausing to remind them as he always did: they were not to go away from the space before the galley. He had left them sitting in a circle on the deck. It was too hot to play.

The Little One was to blame for what occurred, though she was only joking at the start. She was bored and irritable. There was nothing to do: Teresa had refused to tell a story; Pablo would not play any

game that she suggested; Juan was busy carving that old head of
Trictrac, which looked more like a sheep; Gil was half asleep and was
angry when she tickled him; even Rosa acted crossly and spoke sharply
when she teased. And it was so hot and sticky; her hair was in a tangle,
and it itched uncomfortably—

"I wish—" she lamented, "I wish I had no hair. I wish my hair was
made of wood like Juana's. I wish—I wish—" She did not know what
she wished; and then suddenly she said, "I know what I wish: I would
like to see the pictures of America."

"The pictures of America." They stirred with languid interest.

"I wish the man would come and show them to us."

"He won't," they said and laughed.

"But if we went and asked him?"

The idea was so absurd they didn't even answer.

"We could go," she insisted.

"No, we couldn't." They dismissed it.

"But why not?"

"Mamud wouldn't like it."

"Mamud needn't know." She wasn't really serious.

"Of course he'd know," they jeered, "when he came and found us
gone."

"Well—" The Little One's invention was unflagging, "—one of us
could go."

"What good would that do?"

"The one that went could ask the man to bring the pictures
here."

"Oh—" They were impressed but unconvinced. "He wouldn't," they
objected.

"He might," the Little One persisted.

"And who would go and ask him?"

"Who?" She considered and decided. "Maybe Gil would go?"

"No," Gil answered shortly. "I don't care about the pictures."

"Then Pablo—"

"I don't care about them either," Pablo lied.

"Then Teresa—"

"Not me." Teresa shivered.

"Well, if you're all afraid," the Little One said boldly, "I will go and ask him." But she had no such intention, and she knew they wouldn't let her.

"Oh you!" They laughed derisively.

"Well—" She was silent for a moment, thinking hard. "I know," she cried triumphantly, "we could draw straws to see."

"Straws?" Gil sat up, for the matter began to be intriguing.

"Yes, broom straws," she explained in high elation. "The way we always do, and whoever gets the shortest must go and ask the man." And she ran into the galley for some straws out of the broom.

That was how it happened. When it became a game no one could refuse—not even Juan and Rosa, despite their disapproval. And it would be fun to see the pictures, and no one expected to draw the shortest straw. The Little One was barred from competition; she was too small to go, they were all agreed on that, but for compensation was allowed to hold the straws, pressed between her palms with just the ends in sight and nothing to suggest their hidden lengths.

"Draw, Gil!" She held her hands out. "Now Pablo—now Teresa—Rosa—Juan." They drew the straws—quickly, hardly looking; or slowly and debating, studying her eyes which were dancing with excitement.

"Rosa!" they cried. "No, Gil's is shorter." But when the straws were measured side by side, it was Rosa who had lost.

She did not want to go. She was not afraid exactly, but she wished with all her heart that Mamud would return, would suddenly appear out of the hatch.

"Go on," they urged.

"But what am I to say?"

"You must ask the man to bring the pictures of America."

"All right—" She took a step.

"Wait." Juan put down his stick. "I'll go with you, Rosa—if you want me."

"No, I lost—" she said.

But Gil went Juan one better, as he was like to do. "If she's afraid," he grumbled, "she can stay and I will go."

"No." She shook her head, as bravely as she could. "I'm not afraid." And she turned and walked away, past the galley and the hatchway, along the rolling deck, with her eyes upon the door—like any other door. But she did not want to touch it, nor to pass beyond it—

They were calling to her: "Hurry, Rosa, hurry!—Mamud may come back.—Hurry quickly, Rosa!"

But she did not answer them or turn her head. She stood before the door, her heart like lead.—If only Mamud would come!—And she raised her hand and knocked—

10

CATASTROPHE PREPARES ITSELF WITH scrupulous attention to detail, developing a rhythm in the timing of events, which, though unnoted by the actors, may be seen in retrospect to have a flawless pattern. The hidden forces move harmoniously together toward the appointed end, converging at the moment in inexorable fatality, which could not have come to pass if this—if that—

If the Greek had not delayed decision, or had promptly converted decision into action, for he knew what he must do. There was no doubt in his mind that he must shorten sail. Yet he waited, as an actor waits a cue, till the movement of the drama calls his entrance on the scene. He had but to blow his whistle seconds sooner than he did to upset the total scheme—

If Mohammed had returned in accordance with his custom. He had gone to feed the beasts as he regularly did at that hour of the day, and had quickly finished with it, noting that the fodder which remained would last but little longer, reflecting sorrowfully that when it was exhausted the beasts must all be slaughtered, which he knew would grieve the children. His foot was on the ladder to ascend when he suddenly remembered that in the hold beneath him were jars of olive oil, which might be packed with something the animals would eat. It would do no harm to look—

He found the hatch and freed the cover of it, prying off the cleats which wedged the battens, and leaned to swing his lantern in the shallow blackness of the hold, seeing with satisfaction a floor of tight-packed straw, which the goats would eat with relish and the sheep would nibble at. Though it had not much sustenance, still it might preserve their lives.

He found a sack to fill and swung down into the hold, hanging the lantern from a stringer at the side, stooping as he moved, for there was barely head room, kneeling to pluck the straw which was packed between the jars. He had filled the sack and was on the point of lifting the lantern from the nail when he noticed in the heavy wooden stringer a hole bored through the timber—a hole which had no purpose. He explored it with his finger: the edges worn smooth, grooved deeply at the bottom, as if something had slid back and forth along it. He held the lantern closer: the groove was shiny black, as wood grows black from metal. He was certain he could see the scars of iron chain—

His heart beat fast and the blood surged to his head—symptoms of resentment he was never to forget, flaming like a torch when memory stirred. He felt along the timber which ran lengthwise of the ship, bolted to its ribs: there were other holes bored in it, spaced evenly apart—all worn deep with grooves and shiny black. And suddenly he knew: this ship or one like it, and this one like enough. The picture spread itself before his eyes, as he had seen it fifty years ago—

There had been another deck which spanned the hold, like the half-deck overhead where the animals were kept—a deck with less than head room, so the Arabs had to stoop going back and forth between the rows of slaves—maidens and young men and little children, squatting on the deck with wooden shackles fastened to their ankles, bound together with a chain whose slack looped through the holes bored in the timber, rattling, clanking, sliding to and fro, wearing those shiny grooves in the oaken beam. And there had been another and another —four rows of them across the belly of the ship, and two more on another deck beneath where the bottom narrowed to the keel—three hundred boys and girls chained in fetid darkness, in suffocating heat. But some of them had died and been cast into the sea. In the morning they would come and drag them out—

The Arab traders had not been unkind—not more unkind than men who drive cattle to the market, not killing them by choice. The slaves had not been whipped or starved, not deliberately abused. They had been fed and watered, from filthy buckets passed along the rows; their shackles had been loosed to provide for their necessities, but not always soon enough—The stench rose to his nostrils with the memory.—He himself had not been fastened to the chain, for his leg had swollen now out of confine of the shackle. And he had been left free—free to turn and toss on the bare planks through endless days and nights of torturing pain and grief, dreaming in the hours when his fever mounted of his pleasant homeland, the trees and grazing herds, of his father and his mother—waking with the tears streaming down his cheeks, with wrenching childish sobs, to new agonies of body and of soul—

"Akhs!" He sat flatly in the straw, feeling the pulses pounding in his temples—the tight hard fury of resentment which time had failed to soften—brooding on that agony of childhood, which was not, and could not be, the will of Allah—not the hurting of a child—

The captain's whistle roused him: shrill blasts which called the crew—to shorten sail, he thought, for he had read the sky. He got heavily to his feet, feeling with his wooden leg for the jars beneath the straw, to rest his weight on them; and he found the sack and swung it to his shoulder and went slowly up the ladder, hopping from rung to rung, lifting easily with his arms—to make entrance on the scene at his appointed time, responding to his cue in the impending drama.

If—if—if—

If the Little One had not been bored. If she had not remembered, at the moment when she did, the pictures of America; if she had not suggested drawing straws. If Gil or Juan or Pablo had been loser in the contest. If Rosa had accepted Juan's offer to go with her, which her heart urged her to do; or had accepted Gil's to take her place, as Teresa would have done without a second thought. If Kerch had been asleep—

And he would have been asleep but for a line of thought he was trying to resolve—lying on his bed in a faded dressing gown, half drugged with sedatives, struggling to keep awake, to follow out the thread of abstraction in his mind, not thinking very clearly, losing track of where he was and then finding it again—

Was corruption inescapable?—That's where it began.—Was it of sterner stuff than the social phenomena so widely credited with its creation? Was it cause and not effect?—independent of conditioning, of indoctrination, not deriving from, but creating and constructing the Adult Party Line?—Were greed and fear, whence all corruption stemmed, inherent in the human organism?—That was in fact the doctrine of the Church, but not to be discarded for that reason, for the source of superstition was likely to be rational, intuitively sound. —Was infection in the child when it was born?—not immediately discernible, but planted none the less in the embryonic cell, not to be extirpated or separated from it, but to develop with it in the process of its growth?—Was corruption biological?

If that were true then there was no escape.—He moved and turned his pillow which was soaked with sweat. The air was heavy, stifling. Through the partly open skylight he could see the middle segment of the wheel and the captain's legs behind it. His eyes were closing but he forced himself to think—

There must be some escape. But in what direction was it to be found? —If the individual life was a down stroke on the graph, descending from the high point at its birth, then the life span of the species must decline in positive ratio, moving steadily toward destruction.—Was this true or was it not? Was there any way to measure it?—Human history was too short, and geologic time was unexplored.—Was a tree a higher type of life than man? For stature and complexity were not to be confused. Was human thought perhaps at the bottom of the scale?—an exchange of sensitivity for a superficial process which the so-called lower creatures would disdain?—Was chaos at the end of it?—or the silence of the fossil, when degeneration stopped like an arthritic joint turned into stone, frozen and dead forever?—Was this to be the end, and was there no escape?

He dozed and woke, and found the place again.—Repentance, said the Church. But repentance was a gesture, a confession, an admission, as to say, "I am sorry I'm a scoundrel." But the fact was not dissolved by the regret. Greed and fear were not disposed of by admitting you possessed them, that you were the victim of them.—Was there any solid ground beneath this clumsy notion of repentance?—any rational meaning to it—

Wait now!—He had touched the edge of something, and he dragged himself awake.—Was it possible the life span was a circle, a curved line on the graph?—departing from the child to return to it again, retracing all its steps in a moment or an eon?—Then repentance might claim sanction of biology—as a natural turning point, misnamed, misapprehended, distorted and confused by superstitious dogma; but an actual point in arc, at the nadir of the curve, when Life started back again toward its entrance in the world—back to childhood whence it came, to the gateway of salvation—

"Suffer the little children to come unto me, and forbid them not—forbid them not—" He fumbled for the words beneath his breath. "For of such is the kingdom of heaven."—Yes, that was it: the words of Christ which meant, if they meant anything, that Life returned, or might return. Only then could repentance be a fact—not a gesture of negation, but assertion of an actual state of being: "I am a child again. I have forgotten all I have learned from men, have outgrown all their toys—the painted trifles that they fight and die for, the phantom terrors that they fly from. I have wakened from a dream, an ugly nightmare. I am free from Greed and Fear; nor will those monsters trouble me again, for I have struggled with them, lived through them, and survived them. The germs of them are dead, the virus immunized; for the living of my life has provided a vaccine which is permanent in effect." —Yes, that would seem to fit, biologically at least—

He nodded drowsily.—But how and when?—in time and space, in the life span of a man? At what point in the circle? At the nadir. Where was that?—At no given time or place. Perhaps when Death drew near. You could sometimes see it in the eyes of dying men—eyes suddenly awakened. Or when Life became intolerable, could no longer be endured, and men let go of it, released their desperate grasp. Or never. Salvation was not guaranteed. Life had a lavish hand and was careless of its fruit; not every acorn grew into an oak.—But there was no other gateway, no crack you could slip through, no path except the one path that led back. "For of such is the kingdom of heaven."—Yes, of such, of such—and no other had been mentioned—

He started slightly, smiling to himself.—Then God must be a child. What an absurd idea! In another moment he would have been asleep, and he would not have heard the timid knock, which would not have been repeated.

"Look!" the children cried. "She's going in."

"Oh, good for Rosa!"

"Now he'll bring the pictures."

They waited by the galley, with their eyes upon the door. And the moments fled away—

"What can she be doing?"

"If she doesn't hurry Mamud will come back."

"And he'll be very angry."

"What will he do?"

"I know—" Pablo grinned. "He'll cut her up in pieces with his knife."

They laughed at the idea, but shivered too, beginning to be sorry and a little anxious.

"Maybe she's looking at the pictures by herself?"

"No," objected Juan. "Rosa wouldn't do that."

"Then why doesn't she come back?"

And now the captain's whistle blew in shrill command; and he was shouting orders to the crew. They came running to their tasks, and while some untied the ropes which were fastened to the rail, others swarmed like monkeys up the ladders to the mast. The children were absorbed; they forgot about Rosa and the pictures of America—

Up, up they climbed until they looked like flies, swinging to and fro as the mast tipped back and forth, hanging far over the sea, then swinging back again, like a pendulum inverted. It was thrilling, horrifying—

"They will fall into the sea," the children said.

"Not if they hold on tight."

The men on deck were pulling at the ropes, shouting to the ones upon the mast, who shouted faintly back; pulleys squeaked and rattled; the canvas of the skysail flapped and rose—

"What are they doing now?"

"Rolling up the sail."

"Why are they doing that?"

"Because a storm is coming."

They glanced at the sky which had grown very dark; and there was a flare of lightning far away, and the distant roll of thunder; but there was not any wind. The air was like a blanket rolled tight around your head—

"A storm?" The Little One considered and rejected the idea. "A storm couldn't hurt a Fairy ship."

"Then why are they rolling up the sail?"

"Why?" She tossed her head. "Because it's going to rain. They don't want them to get wet."

The sail was cleanly furled, the gaskets fast around it; the men came scrambling back, and down, and out again upon the spar beneath—the royal yard. The shouting recommenced, the pulleys squeaked, the canvas flapped and shrank—

Mohammed's shoulders rose out of the hatch. But they did not see him coming; their eyes were fixed aloft. He moved among them, his eyes as dark and sullen as the sky, the aura of his memories clinging round him—seeing them, not seeing them. But suddenly he started, aware that one was missing, checking with his eye, glancing quickly all about—

"Rosa?" he demanded in a voice they'd never heard.

And they remembered now, huddling close together, chilled with guilt, staring in dismay at a face they hardly knew, furious and threatening. They looked and looked away.

"Rosa?" he repeated, coming closer.

"Don't tell him," whispered Gil from the corner of his mouth.

"Rosa? Rosa?" He singled out the boy and gripped his arm and twisted it; and Gil cried out with pain and sank upon his knees. But suddenly he turned his head and caught his captor's hand between his teeth and bit into the flesh at the bottom of the thumb—bit with all his might.

"Akhs!" The black man jerked his hand away and struck him in the face—an openhanded blow, but it knocked the wits out of him for a moment. "Rosa?"

It was Teresa who gave the thing away, sobbing, terrified, pointing to the cabin at the back, expecting he would kill her. But instead he turned away, with a rasping, groaning sound, and ran back along the deck, his wooden leg tap-tapping.

"See what you've done!" stormed Gil.

"I—" She sat on the deck, dissolved in tears, face hidden in her hands. "I—I couldn't help it." It had been too much to bear—even for a child.

"Don't cry, Teresa." Juan came and put his hand upon her shoulder.

"But," she sobbed, "what will he do to Rosa?"

They peeked around the corner of the galley. He had not gone to the door, but up the ladder at its side—in a single bound, it seemed—

"He won't find her there," they gloated fearfully.

But then things came so fast—as swiftly as the lightning that was forking in the sky, piling one upon another so you couldn't really see them, or know, or understand, or ever put them back the way they were.

Kerch heard the timid knock in the shallow edge of sleep, thinking, if he thought, that it was the black come to ask or bring him something. "Come in," he said in Arabic.

The child heard the muffled voice, assuming its intent; and she turned the knob, opening the door enough to see into the room, but not venturing to step across the threshold which was higher than the deck—seeing in a glance an unfamiliar wealth of pretty things, luxurious and soft, like the things that one might see in the Palace of a King—or so it seemed to her. And there was a smell of perfume, like flowers in a garden. She was torn at this moment between dread and curiosity, shyness and desire—a longing to look closely, to touch the pretty things. If only the man had not been there!

He was lying on the bed with his face turned from the door, with a rich soft gown around him. Perhaps she had awakened him. She had a sudden impulse to turn and run away, but she waited in the door. And then he spoke again, sleepily and impatiently, words she didn't understand.

"The—pictures—" she said faintly.

"Pictures?" He jerked his head to see her, and sat up on the bed; his hair was mussed and funny, comical to look at; his little mouselike eyes staring at her strangely—in a way that made her shiver. "But come in," he said. "Come in."

She came a step into the room and the door swung to behind her. She heard the clicking latch above the thudding of her heart.

"Pictures?" he repeated.

"The—the pictures of America," she stammered.

"Oh, pictures of America!" He sat there looking at her, not making any move, not seeming pleased or angry, as if the words meant nothing. He was thinking so many things at once: pictures of America, the slender childish innocence, the face like a Madonna. Why? Oh why? Not even St. Francis had been more cruelly tempted. Was God determined to destroy him?—It was twilight in the room. The shrill call of the whistle came through the open skylight, the voice of the Greek shouting orders to the crew, feet scampering on the deck.—Why had this child come here? A kind of fury swept him, at the tortures God devised, inextricably mixed with relief, with gratitude. God both cursed and blessed him—

"I can come again," she gulped, backing toward the door, frantic to be out, outside this horrid room, away from its prettiness and soft-ness—out of reach of those eyes, like a snake's eyes crawling on her. Still, she tried to be polite—"Perhaps another day—" feeling for the knob behind her back.

"Yes, another day," he said, nodding her away, motioning toward the door with a gesture of impatience.

She was struggling with the latch; it was different on the inside and she couldn't turn the handle. She pulled and twisted but in vain. She heard him muttering crossly, heard the bed as he got up, the scuff-ling of his slippers on the floor—felt his arm reach past her shoulder, brush against her hair—saw his hand extended, fingers curving to the knob. But instead he shot the bolt which was beneath it—as if he had not meant to, as if his hand had acted independent of his will, counter-manding his intention—staring at the door, as if he were surprised.

But then he laughed, a disagreeable sound, drawing back his hand so that it brushed her cheek, his wrist against her neck. "Pictures of America—" He nodded, smiling at her. "Today will do as well. But come and we will look." His hand closed on her neck, gathering her dress so it pulled against her throat, the fingers twitching, pinching—

"Oh please—" She twisted loose, but a button had come off, and there were not many others. Her dress was slipping down; she caught it up and held it with her hand behind her neck. "My dress—" she gasped. "The button—"

"Button?" He stared. But then he saw it on the floor and stooped to pick it up.

"Thank you—" She snatched it from him, keeping out of reach.

"You—" He fought down a flush of anger, to keep it from his face. "You are not very friendly—" But then he laughed again. And suddenly he jerked away and ran across the room, mumbling to himself, "Pictures of America—pictures of America—we will find them in a moment." He knelt besides a locker and began to throw things out upon the floor—papers and books, scattering them about. "Yes, of course, they must be here—"

She stood beside the door, not knowing what to do, not daring to unbolt it, not knowing how to open it—not wanting to be rude; suddenly remembering that Mamud would be angry. She had not meant to stay, not even for a moment—

"I—I must go now," she said.

"Go?" He stood up, glaring at her. "Well then, why did you come?"

"To—to ask about the pictures—"

"Oh, the pictures!" he exclaimed, as if he had forgotten. "But I am searching for them." And he ran across the room, stumbling over things, to another locker, raking in the contents.

"Please let me go—" she faltered, tears welling in her eyes.

"Ah, here!" he cried triumphantly, and took it from the locker—a thick red-covered book, spread open on the floor. "Pictures of America!" He struck it with his hand. "Come and we will look.—Come, come!" he beckoned her.

"Oh no—" She shook her head. "I would rather look—with them."

"With them?" he questioned dully.

"With the other children."

"Other children?" he repeated.

"I promised them," she said.

"I see." He nodded slowly. And then there was a pause—so long that she wondered if perhaps he had forgotten. She had time to look around, seeing that the room was not filled with pretty things, but shabby and untidy; the carpet worn through; the canopy above the bed, of gold and purple silk, but with ragged holes in it; a lamp shade with a picture painted on it, but the chimney black with soot; a chair which leaned against the wall because a leg was broken; a table, dirty dishes, and stains upon the cloth; an ugly-looking gun fastened to the wall in a kind of wooden box; cobwebs everywhere—

But then at last he spoke, indifferently and wearily, "Well, come and get the book." And he pushed it with his foot, sitting on the floor.

"You mean that I may take it?" She was incredulous. "Take it out to them?"

"Yes, take it, take it," he insisted irritably.

"Oh, thank you—" And she came to get the book, lying open on the floor beneath the skylight, kneeling down to pick it up, needing both her hands to do it, for the book was big and heavy—seeing his hand reach to help her. But instead the fingers closed around her wrist. She looked up, startled, wondering—

"You are forgetting something," he said thickly.

"Forgetting?" she repeated.

"To thank me for the book."

"Oh yes," she said, "I do."

"But how?" he urged.

"How?" She shook her head, embarrassed and confused.

"Well, we will make a bargain—" He was smiling, a twitching kind of smile that was not nice to see. "You shall pay me with a kiss."

"A kiss—" She thought he must be joking.

"Is that too much to ask?"

"Oh no—" she answered hastily, wanting to be polite, not to hurt his feelings. It wasn't much to ask. And if she closed her eyes it would be over quickly, and she could take the book—take it to the others and be glad that she had done it, that she hadn't been afraid. She felt his face come closer, the hot breath on her cheek—

But it was not to be—the defilement of a child, the last poor prayer of an international scoundrel; for the matter had been otherwise arranged, all the factors set in motion and converging to their end.

Hark now!—He listened, jerking to his knees, dreadful memory flashing back to that day in Bucharest—and the black man looking at him from the doorway of the galley.—What folly, folly!

"Mamud—" She gasped. She had heard it at the moment, striking terror to her heart: the hollow, clumping sound on the deck above their heads.

"Go! Go!" he urged in panic, struggling to his feet, pulling at her wrist, the book clutched in her arms—pushing her away: that's what he willed to do, his hand loosed from her wrist, pushing at her shoulder —*pushing*, so he meant. But his fingers disobeyed, clinging to her dress which tore open down her back, slipping from her shoulders—

11

IT WAS THIS MOHAMMED SAW—CROUCHING ON THE deck, looking through the slit beneath the cabin skylight: the sobbing child, half naked, in the grasp of the Effendi—missaw, if you like; but only in relation to the element of Time. At all events it was enough to snap a thread already stretched to the limit of its tolerance.

The Greek had watched him bounding up the ladder, clumping to the skylight, crouching down to look beneath it—watched with vacant wonder, with only half an eye, his attention centered elsewhere, staring past the negro at a riffle on the sea, a churning green and white where a squall was racing in on the *Flying Virgin's* bow, which might take the ship aback with the royals still half furled. He was putting down the helm in frantic haste, spinning the heavy wheel, for the ship had little headway and responded sluggishly—shouting warning to the men in the rigging and on deck. But then he heard a sound and looked again—

"What now?" he mumbled stupidly, scarcely crediting his eyes. For the negro was smashing in the skylight, poking out the glass with his wooden leg, raking round the frame to clear the fragments.

The glass came crashing down into the cabin, showering on the floor. And they saw his face above them, contorted, wild with fury—saw him reaching for his knife, poise himself to spring upon them—

The child was free at last from the restraining hand which pushed and pulled her back. The book fell from her arms. She fled blindly to the door, pulling back the bolt, twisting at the latch, never doubting that the black man's rage was directed at her crime, her fatal disobedience.

But Kerch knew better, knew he had no option but to kill or to be killed. His brain was clear again, as he ran to snatch the gun from the rack upon the wall—his whole life flashing by, in the moment that it took, like a strip of flying film.—Yes, he deserved to die, but not for this.—His hand was on the weapon when he heard the negro thud upon the floor, and the crinkling of the glass. But before he could have turned the knife sped through the air, like an arrow to its mark—through his neck, the long sharp blade projecting from his throat. He crumpled, coughing, choking, blood gushing from his mouth, and the gun clattered down across his body.

But the child saw nothing of this, not daring to look back, clawing at the latch, expecting every moment Mamud's hands would clutch her.—If only she were not alone! If only Juan had come!—But it was not Juan's name she cried in her dispair—

"Gil!" she screamed. "Gil, help me!" The stubborn latch let loose and she sprawled across the threshold, scrambling up again, running like a streak to the shelter of the galley, meeting Gil halfway; for he had heard her cry and had not hesitated. "Oh, Gil—" she gasped.

"What happened, Rosa?" But then he saw her tears and the terror in her eyes and her dress half torn off. "What is it? What?"

"Mamud—" she sobbed, and could not tell him more. They ran back to the galley hand in hand. And then things went on happening so fast—so very fast—

They saw the hairy man standing by the skylight looking down into the room, holding the wheel with his hand behind his back; and they heard the explosion of a gun, not knowing what it was, for the sound of it was muffled, not much different from the thunder which was rumbling in the sky. But the hairy man fell down, or seemed to fall, out of sight behind the skylight, and did not get up again.

The men who were nearby against the rail, stopped pulling on the

ropes, and one of them ran back along the deck. And suddenly Mamud
was standing in the door with a gun held in his hands. The man stood
still, looking back across his shoulder, saying something to the others.
And while his head was turned Mamud raised the gun and shot him,
and he fell down on his face, not moving any more. The other men let
go the ropes, and there was a flapping sound from the canvas overhead,
and angry shouting from the men high on the mast who were wrapping
up the sail.

The children stared in fascinated horror. But Juan had turned away,
leaning with his face against the galley wall, his stomach getting sick.

"Why? Oh why?" they questioned.

"Maybe he is crazy?"

"Yes, crazy," they agreed, "like the man that killed the cow and
little pigs."

And they were right: Mohammed had gone mad, with grief and rage
and fear—a simple, gentle black man run amok, unable to endure the
ways of men. And now he had no option but to kill or to be killed.

But though mad he was also shrewdly sane, as he came on toward
the galley with the gun across his breast and smoke still oozing from
it, toward the five remaining men huddled close against the bulwark,
shrinking one behind the other. He was planning craftily how he
could dispose of them: the longboat was afloat, still towing at the
stern where the lazy Greek had left it. But he must not come too
close: if they rushed him he was lost. The others in the rigging he was
not concerned about—struggling with the canvas which had suddenly
gone slack and impossible to drag into the furl, not knowing what
had happened on the deck, shouting angry imprecations at their
fellows. Them he could dispose of at his leisure, pick them off like
flies if need be. He did not even trouble to look up.

Nor did he see the ally that was coming to his aid, to resolve that
problem for him: the green-white churning water racing toward the
bow, out of sight behind the mainsail, no longer on the quarter, for
the ship, without a helm, had wallowed round to meet it—into the
very trap the Greek had feared and struggled to avert. No doubt the
mermaid saw it from her niche beneath the bowsprit, and perhaps
her wooden heart was quaking at the menace. But the matter was
beyond the will of men or mermaids.

The negro paused with the gun across his arm, and the muzzle of it swaying back and forth along the men. The children held their breath—

"Will he kill them all?" they whispered.

"And the ones up on the mast?"

"And maybe us?"

But he was not killing them. He was shouting something at them, motioning them to jump into the sea, pointing back at something in the water—perhaps the little boat which was fastened with a rope. But they did not want to go, begging him to stay, hiding from the gun. And one man ran away, but he did not go far because the gun went off and he ran back to the others. Mamud's face was very angry now, and he shouted loudly at them, pointing the gun at one and then another. And after that they went, squirming across the rail, slipping down into the sea. And Mamud ran to watch them, and then came running back, directly toward the galley. They fled around the corner, peeking out. But he was not seeking them. He snatched the ax which was sticking in the block and went clumping down the deck, up the ladder, out of sight. They could not see what he did, but they heard the ax chop down and far-off cries—

He had severed the towline of the longboat: those five were finished with; and five and three were eight. There were eight more aloft, fighting the stubborn canvas on the topmast, spread out along the royal and topgallant yards—like flies caught on a flypaper, unable to let go, as he had known they could not. The timing had been faultless—

"Look out!" the children screamed, clutching at each other, clinging to the handrail on the galley wall. And in another moment they were blinded by the scud and pelting rain, choked and battered by the wind.

The squall had struck. But it was more than that: precursor of a gale, a hurricane perhaps—a vagrant fragment of it, which could strike from any quarter, box the compass, hit and run. It struck like an assassin out of breathless silence, with a dreadful howl of fury, with shattering brutal force.

The *Flying Virgin* reared like a frightened horse, quivering from the impact, squatting back upon her haunches, driven back and down until the high decked poop dipped water from the sea and the mermaid's trident pointed at the sky. The canvas tore out of the furler's hands, billowing back against the mast, ballooning into pockets, jerking at the ship as a dog would shake a rat, the tangled clew lines screaming through the blocks until they snagged or parted.

The royal stay gave way above the foremast crosstrees, snapping like a gunshot; and then in quick succession the flying jibstay went, the topgallant and topmast—crack—crack—crack—like popping corks. The topmast, unsustained, bent to the wind, oscillating like a coach whip, jerking at the backstays. A man came hurtling down with a strangled shriek of terror, bouncing through the canvas, thudding on the deck. Another lost his hold, dangling head down from the yard, his foot caught in the stirrup of the footrope. They were being shaken off—shaken off like crawling bugs. But then in a moment it was over—

The topmast broke off short above the trestletrees—no doubt a stout, sound spar, but not designed for punishment like this—broke off below the yards to which the men were clinging, and fell into the sea, ripping through shrouds and backstays, tearing loose the top- and mainsails, which were blown out to rags; falling aft to port, still fastened to the ship by a tangled mass of wreckage, dragging down her side till the rail was under water.

The children had crawled behind the galley where they were a little sheltered from the wind. They did not know what had happened; it had gone too fast for that. And there was not much to see through the blackness of the storm, illumined now and then by streaks of lightning. They heard the man cry out, and saw him fall—almost at their feet; and caught a fleeting glimpse of the other figure hanging upside down. But then the mast broke off and crashed into the sea, and the ship tipped so far over they had to scurry back from the water reaching for them, and the dead man on the deck washed away out of their sight. Then the lightning flared again and they saw the black man coming—coming back along the rail, waist deep in foaming water, chopping with the ax, cutting through the tangled ropes—

"He is coming back," they cried.

"Coming back to kill us."

"Where can we hide?"

"Where the animals are kept."

"Good!" they agreed. "He'll never look down there."

They fled around the corner of the galley, scrambling down the ladder to the storeroom, pausing in amazement. Everything was upside down and the floor was deep in things which had fallen from the shelves, even barrels had tipped over.

"Wait!" said Gil. "Let's take some things to eat."

They hastily filled their pockets: biscuit and dried fruit and strips of sun-cured meat and sugar that had spilled out of a barrel. The Little One scooped handfuls from the floor, and could scarce be parted from it, protesting that the storeroom was as good a place to hide as any other.

They ran on into the stable. The animals were moving restlessly, making frightened sounds, the chickens cackling mournfully. It was dark and hot and smelly; they went carefully, holding hands. But suddenly Gil yelled and his hand tore loose from Rosa's. He had stumbled on the coaming and fallen through the hatch into the hold— the same that Mamud had left open. But it was not far to fall and he landed comfortably in a soft spot in the straw—

"Take care!" he warned. "There's a big hole in the floor." He crawled and felt around. "But wait, there is a ladder."

"Well then, come back," they urged.

"No, you come down." He could not see anything, but he had a sense of space—that there was room to run.

"But why?" they questioned fearfully, peering down into the blackness.

"Because it's safer here," he cried impatiently. "And the floor is made of straw."

"Of straw? What good is that?"

"It's soft," he said. "If he tries to catch us his wooden leg will sink."

They hesitated, whispering. But then they heard the black man's voice shouting in the storeroom, calling them by name; and the sound of it struck terror to their hearts. "He is coming," they exclaimed, fumbling in panic for the ladder, getting in each other's way. "Oh, hurry! Hurry!"

Mohammed had cut loose the wreckage of the topmast, which was dragging the ship to certain death, wading through water which reached above his waist and sometimes buried him, clinging to the bulwark with one hand while he wielded the cleaver with the other, depending on the

lightning to show him what to do—chopping, chopping, chopping—
exhausted, nearly drowned. Half a dozen times Death had snatched
at him; once he had been dragged across the rail, clinging with one hand
while the sea washed over him, escaping by a miracle. But at last the
wreckage cleared and the ship reeled free from it, tossing like a cork,
rolling on its beams, but rolling free, unbound.

Not till then did he think about the children, and now his heart
stood still. Perhaps they had been washed away and drowned. "Little
children—" he cried into the storm, running to the galley where he
had seen them last, groping his way around it. "Little children, please
come back—"

There was no sign of them, no answering voice. But then it crossed
his mind they might have gone below, and he went down the ladder
to the storeroom, holding his breath to listen, thinking that he heard
them above the howling wind—voices on the halfdeck where the
animals were moaning, though he was not sure of it.

"Little children!—Rosa!—Gil!" There was anguish in his voice, but
not to be distinguished from revengeful fury. "Mohammed would not
hurt you. Mohammed is your friend." He found and lit the lantern;
he was certain that he heard them. And he ran from the storeroom,
stumbling through the debris.—Yes, there they were—scrambling
through the hatch into the hold.—"Wait, little children! Wait!" He
ran and reached in vain.

Juan had been last, and he had jumped. The black man's fingers
brushed his shoulder, tore his sleeve. But Gil was waiting for him,
dragging him away. They were all scampering, crawling, rattling
through the straw, pausing at safe distance to look back, seeing Mamud's
face framed in the open hatch, with the lantern flaring on it.

He held the lantern wide, searching the shadows for them.—Yes,
they were safe, all six. Allah had heard his prayer. He kneeled against
the coaming of the hatch, trembling with relief, as yet but half aware
of the crimes he had committed and their fearful implications. The
ship dove steeply, with a shuddering jolt, as a sea swept over her and
came pouring down the hatch, through the storeroom to the halfdeck,
washing on into the hold. The animals were trampling, wild with
fright. The lantern was extinguished.

He dragged the cover on the hatch, found the battens in the dark and made them fast. There was nothing else to do—nothing but to leave them in that place of dreadful memories, locked in against escape to perils that were worse. And there was no time to lose. Another sea like that might put an end to her. He must get to the helm before it was too late.

"He's gone," the children cried, crawling close together, feeling for each other. But then they heard the grating of the cover on the hatch.

"What's he doing now?"

"Covering up the hole."

"Then we can't get out."

"And he can't come and catch us."

"It's like being in a prison."

"Yes, a prison," they agreed. They were not disturbed about it; on the whole they felt relieved. They began to explore the contents of their pockets, the goodies they had garnered in the storeroom. It was a kind of game: discovering what you had when you couldn't see it.

"He didn't look very angry," said Teresa.

"And he didn't sound very angry," added Pablo.

"Maybe not," Gil shrugged. "That was just a trick to catch us."

"But why does he want to kill us?"

"It's my fault," Rosa said.

"No, it isn't," Juan assured her.

"Then tell us why," they urged.

"I know why," the Little One said cheerfully, licking sugar from her fingers. "Mamud is bewitched."

"Bewitched?" They laughed, not very scornfully.

"I don't believe in Witches," Gil said firmly, though they didn't seem unlikely at the moment.

"If—" objected Pablo, with his mouth stuffed full of figs, "—if he was bewitched he could run across the straw."

"No, he couldn't," the Little One replied. "Not unless the Witch had thought of it."

This was unanswerable.

"But who has bewitched him?" they inquired.

"Why a Witch of course," she said.

"Well, what Witch?" they insisted.

"What Witch?" She considered. "Maybe the mouse-man is a Witch."

"Oh, the mouse-man!" They laughed, but it didn't seem impossible.

"Witches are ladies," Teresa interposed.

"Yes, of course, I know," the Little One admitted, though in fact she had forgotten all about it. "And the mouse-man could be a lady in disguise."

This also was unanswerable.

"And how will Mamud get out of it?" they asked.

"He must be disenchanted."

"Well, how?"

But the Little One was tired of the subject.

12

THE *FLYING VIRGIN* FLED BEFORE THE STORM: a battered wreck; all of her canvas gone, save for a rag of jib which served to keep her headed with the gale; her waist a swimming web of ropes and broken spars, surging from side to side as the seas washed over her; the meat block torn loose, thundering across the deck like an engine of destruction, charging against the bulwarks, hurled back to ram the galley which threatened to collapse; the ship's bell tolling dolefully, a premonitory dirge—tolling, tolling in the night—

And the black man at the helm, lashed to it with a rope, beaten breathless by the wind, half smothered by the scud, racing the following seas which seemed certain to engulf her, which curled and broke upon him, dragging at him like wild horses. Or the ship would yaw and wallow in the trough, rolling on her beams. But he would pull her out by some miracle of instinct, leaning all his strength upon the wheel which resisted as if it were alive and determined to defeat him.

There was nothing to be seen save when the lightning flashed, momentarily disclosing the tumbling hills and valleys of the sea, as they towered or caverned against the schooner's side, their summits curling green and flecked with white, wide-jawed to crush and swallow at a gulp. But even when unseen he had the sense of them, and his hands would feel the ship out of the threat in time to meet another —and another, and another, for there was no end to them, no moment to relax—like a man on a tightrope, catching balance by a hair, not thinking what to do but instinctively responding, clinging to Life with incredible agility.

Once when the lightning flared he saw the dead man rolling across the cabin floor, washing in the litter, rolling on his back, face up and staring at him—accusingly, it seemed. But the picture was blacked out before his memory stirred, before he saw again—the child's face stained with tears, her dress half torn off, her little body naked—the Effendi clinging to her, running for the gun—And he had killed him—standing beneath the shattered skylight where he would have room to swing his arm, taking time to measure it—had hurled his knife and caught him through the neck, as if he were a rabbit; and blood had spurted out, gushing like a hose—He touched the knife which hung against his leg, as if for confirmation of the fact; it seemed unreal, impossible. —Yes, he had killed the man, and not in self-defense, for he would have killed him anyway: that's why he had come, being certain what he'd find, and with murder in his heart.—He had plucked his knife away and snatched the gun. And then, and then—

He saw the Greek's face staring through the skylight, jaw hanging loose and terror in his eyes. "What now? What have you done?" the man had stuttered stupidly. And he had raised the gun and shot him through the heart, without a word of warning. There was nothing else to do. And the sailor on the deck—He groaned as memory widened. Yes, he had shot him, too, standing alone and helpless. But there was no place to stop once killing had begun.

And the ones he had compelled to jump into the sea, watching them swim back and climb into the longboat, which he had cut adrift to perish in the storm. And the others in the rigging, whose deaths were

at his door. Yes, he had murdered them.—How many? Oh, how many?
—He could not even count them, add up the dreadful score.—And the
children whom he loved, for whom he would so gladly give his life,
locked in the hold of a nearly foundering ship which could scarce survive the night—locked there by his hand, as he had once been locked
in the bottom of a slave ship. He cried aloud in anguish.

Yes, the time for remorse had now arrived—to catalog his sins, to
relive each detail of them, to estimate their value and their cost. A
murderer, an assassin, an outcast, a pariah!—Strange paradox of justice,
both human and divine, that deeds one does for love should be described as crimes. *Crimes of passion* they are called in civil codes, to
distinguish them from less emotional matters, and some allowance made
for motivations, be they actual or imagined, though rarely very much.
But the word of God provides for no mitigating promptings: "Thou
shalt not kill," is all that Jehovah says about it. So it would seem that
men, with all their faults, are more merciful than God.

He wept with choking sobs. But remorse requires leisure, and a man
on a tightrope has little time to spare for reflecting how he got there.
A sea came thundering down upon the poop and put an end to it.

The children were not suffering the tortures of remorse, and they
had no expectation of disaster; for the moment they were safe and the
moment filled their thought. It was snug and cozy in the hold; the storm
was shut away, the howling of the wind and all the awful sounds; and
deep in the ship the motion was less violent. The straw was soft and
fragrant, reminiscent of the granary; and the darkness did not matter
if they were close together.

They were busily occupied with the food that filled their pockets,
exclaiming with delight over something specially good—or even something bad, in the hope of promoting an offer of exchange. The Little
One was eager to sample everything, and she still had a pocket full of
sugar which was greatly in demand, which she doled out cautiously,
having started very badly with a fragment of dried fish which Teresa
had insisted was delicious. She was being canny now, as she asked with
fine indifference—

"What have you got, Pablo?"

"I don't know," said Pablo thickly, "but it's very good."

"Sweet or sour?"

"Sweet."

"Hard or soft?"

"It's sticky—" And it was—a chunk of damp, tough figs.

"So is sugar sticky," the Little One remarked with studied carelessness.

"Do you want to trade?" said Pablo.

"Not until I taste it."

"Well, here—" He held it out.

"Um—" She tasted warily. It wasn't bad. "All right," she said and put a pinch of sugar in his hand.

"No," protested Pablo. "It isn't half enough."

"Then give it back."

"No, I won't." But he shortened his grip upon the figs. "If you want it bite it off.—Ouch! That's my finger."

She set her teeth in it and tore a morsel loose. It was sweet but very sticky; she could hardly move her jaws. And then suddenly a dreadful thing occurred: there was something hard and gritty in the sticky lump, something that had not been there to start—

"Oh, oh, oh—" she shrieked.

"What is it? What's the matter?"

"My tooth came out."

"Oh!" They laughed, relieved. "Well, that is nothing."

"Yes, it is," she howled.

"Witches," Gil suggested. "Maybe you've been bewitched."

"No, no, no—" She clung to Rosa, sobbing.

"Gil is only teasing," Rosa reassured her.

"But my tooth is out. I've got it in my hand."

"A new one will grow in."

"I don't want a new one."

"The new one will be bigger."

"I don't want a bigger one."

"Ho!" jeered Gil. "Do you want to be a baby all your life?"

"Of course I do," she said. "I don't want to change a bit. And I want my old tooth back."

"Wait till you see the new one," they consoled her.

"I won't, and I won't like it." She raised her head from Rosa's lap, still sobbing but impressed. "Do they hurt when they come back?"

"Not a bit," they promised. "You wake up in the morning and there is a new one."

"Tomorrow morning?"

"Maybe not as soon as that."

"But when?"

"Oh, soon enough."

"Well—" She sighed, not completely reconciled, feeling with her tongue the gaping hole, and the sharp little tooth clutched in her hand. "Anyway," she said, "Pablo ought to give it back."

"What?" gulped Pablo, startled.

"The sugar that I gave you."

"But I traded something for it."

"What you traded wasn't good."

"You had a chance to taste it, and you said you wanted it."

"Well, I don't. I want my sugar."

"I've eaten it," said Pablo with an air of satisfaction, and licked his sticky fingers.

"That was cheating," the Little One declared and was silent for a moment, turning matters in her mind. "Perhaps," she suggested, "I'd forget about my tooth if Teresa told a story."

"Yes, a story," Pablo urged, glad to change the subject.

"But which?" Teresa said.

"A frightening story," the Little One demanded.

"Yes, good," they agreed. "A frightening one, Teresa."

"Well—" Teresa assumed her storytelling voice, which sent shivers up their spines—even Gil was not immune. "Once upon a time—"

The story of the Saragossa Sorcerer, which they had heard many times before, but never in more scary circumstances. It was about a Prince and his lovely Princess wife and a very evil Sorcerer. The Prince was everything a Prince should be, but he had one little weakness: he could not remember which was right and which was left. And this was the cause of all the trouble, for once when the Sorcerer came to dinner at the Palace, the Prince became confused and put the guest upon his left instead of on his right. The Sorcerer was furious at this indignity, and he went back to his house and made an incantation, and the Princess was changed into a statue. That was his revenge.

The Prince was brokenhearted, but he girded himself and went forth to slay the Sorcerer, pursuing him through perilous adventures. But in the end he caught him and killed him with his sword, and even cut his head off. And when the head was off the Princess came to life; but only from a point upon her neck where the Sorcerer's head was severed from his body. She could smile and she could speak, but the rest of her was dead—a cold and stony statue.

The Prince was in despair, for the Sorcerer was dead and the incantation undissolved. The Princess could not help him, but she said if he would go to the far end of the earth, he would find an aged Wizard who might know what to do. And so the Prince set out across the stormy sea, over deserts and mountains, beset by savage beasts. And he often lost his way, because he got mixed up—not remembering which was right and which was left. But his courage never faltered and at last he found the Wizard in a cave. And when he had explained the situation, the Wizard got a great book from a shelf and hunted through the pages until he found the answer, which was a truly horrifying one—

The Sorcerer was not dead, for his heart was still alive. Cutting off his head had failed to kill his heart which was very tough indeed. The head of the Princess had returned to life because the Sorcerer's head was separated from his body, and the power of enchantment much reduced. But so long as the heart continued to survive, the rest of the Princess would remain a frozen statue.—What was he to do, the poor Prince asked in grief. And the Wizard turned the pages until he found the answer: the Prince must dig the Sorcerer from his grave and drive a pointed stake into his heart. But he must be very careful that the heart should not get out, not making any hole through which it could escape before the stick went through it, for it would run away if it got a chance, and as long as it lived the enchantment would continue.

The Prince went journeying back across the sea, and found the Sorcerer's grave and dug him up, and brought him to the Palace where the Princess was waiting on her pedestal. When everything was ready the wooden stake was brought, sharpened like a needle. But just at the moment that he aimed it, to drive it straight and true into the Sorcerer's breast, a voice cried out a warning. "No, no," it said, "you are making a mistake. The heart is on the other side." It was the evil heart that spoke these words, cunningly assuming the voice of the Princess. The poor Prince was deceived, and before he could be stopped he drove the stake into the other side. In the twinkling of an eye out jumped the living heart and bounced away across the floor and through an open window.—"Alas—" the Princess moaned. Tears rolled down her cheeks and dripped upon her body where they were turned to stone.

It was all to do again, and there was another chapter of desperate undertakings. Indeed, the story might never have been finished but for the intervention of a friendly Fairy who came finally to their aid and tricked the wicked heart into a dead pig's body. This time, though the heart made an effort to confuse him, the Prince had learned his lesson and would not again forget which was right and which was left. So the Sorcerer's heart was pierced, and the blood ran out like ink. The Princess was restored to her own sweet lovely self. And they both lived happily ever after.

The children sighed, lying snugly in the straw, beginning to be sleepy despite the chilling horrors. The Little One was wriggling, with her head in Rosa's lap—

"I can hear it," she announced.

"Hear what?"

"My heart. It's ticking like a clock."

"Well, you better not forget which side it's on," Gil warned her, pretending to be solemn.

"No, I won't," she said. "I'll put my tooth in that hand so I will remember." She was silent for a while, debating in her mind a new idea. "Perhaps—" she suggested, "perhaps he is a Sorcerer."

"A Sorcerer? Who?"

"The mouse-man."

"Oh, the mouse-man!" They laughed, but shivered too.

"Well, he could be," she insisted.

They didn't answer that. He *could* be: that was true. Almost anything *could* be.

"I don't believe in Sorcerers," grumbled Gil.

"Oh, you don't believe in Sorcerers," the Little One said scornfully. "And you don't believe in Fairies, and you don't believe in Witches! Well then, what do you believe in?"

Gil muttered in the darkness.

"Oh well—" She sighed indulgently, cuddling her head in Rosa's lap, too sleepy to continue the discussion. "This is right—" she crooned, wiggling fingers on one hand. "And this is left—where my tooth is and my heart—"

Presently they were asleep.

The *Flying Virgin* reeled on through the night, like a drunken prostitute, befuddled and bedraggled, escaping by a hair as many perils as the luckless Prince. But the black man at her helm did not falter in his guidance, nor forget for a moment which was right and which was left.

The dawn came at his back: a dirty, pallid lifting of the night, revealing the implacable aspect of the sea—a brutal, callous monster, without pity or compassion. Its hilltops were like mountains whose summits were sheared off, sliced and lifted by the gale, and hurled upon the ship in sheets of yellow foam; its valleys gaping chasms, bottomless as funnels, the sides of them spun smooth, like sucking whirlpools. The ship was no more than a pygmy craft adrift in a battle of the giants, creaking and groaning in a weak and puny voice, scarcely to be heard through the bedlam of the Titans, pleading for relief from its frightful punishment.

Bruised and aching with exhaustion, he climbed upon his feet, whence he could see the deck—the surging wreckage battering at the bulwarks. The galley had collapsed and the roof had washed away; the meat block rolled and thundered, and the bell still tolled its melancholy dirge. He was looking for the bodies of the dead. But they were not in sight; the sea had swallowed them. For a moment he believed it had been all a dream. But then his glance fell through the empty skylight.—No, it was not a dream, for there was the Effendi, washing back and forth across the floor, rolling to and fro in the soggy litter—dishes, books and papers, valises, cushions, clothing— sometimes swimming like a man when the water leveled deeply to the high sill of the door, or again looking limply like a fragment of the debris, a crumpled, shapeless blanket, like nothing that had ever been alive. But then it would roll over and lie upon its back, its arms and legs all loose, its head grotesquely tipped where the knife had nearly severed it, and its eyes wide open, staring.

He groaned and looked away. And now a peril met his eye, to blot the sight and memory from his mind: a tumbling streak of white at the margin of the sky beyond the bow. The ship dove steeply and his view of it was lost; and his heart stood still until she climbed again.— Yes, there against the sky, dead ahead and inescapable: the writhing crest of surf, as far as he could see to left or right—a barrier of savage, foaming breakers. He listened and could hear the booming of them, deep and sullen.—A reef or coast?—He thought the sky was blacker at their back, as if there might be mountains hidden in the clouds. But this he could not tell in the half-light and the murk, nor did it matter much. She could not live through the surf, and the rocks on which it broke would tear her bottom out—tear it out like paper.—Yes, this would be the end.—And the children in the hold—

He watched the tattered fringe of lace draw near, curving like a noose till the ship was in a pocket with the lace spread far around her—his eyes half blind with salt, searching the tightening rim. But there was not any gap, the wall of surf was solid, the lace that trimmed the schooner's shroud was flawless in design. The booming of the breakers mounted into thunder.

"Please save the children, Allah, before you punish me." In the obvious circumstances no prayer could seem more futile, yet it came from his heart and his lips repeated it. There was nothing to be done but to hold the schooner's head upon her course, driving straight into the surf which no longer looked like lace but like a boiling cauldron.

And then, when in another moment he would have closed his eyes against the fatal impact; when he had abandoned hope, but not his prayer; when his heart had ceased to stumble and leap into his throat; when he had given up everything except his effort, had surrendered all decision in the matter, and already felt the quiet hand of Death and did not push nor try to hold it off—just then, when all was lost and Fear had fled, he saw, without elation or surprise, a passage through the wall, a hole in it, a gap—which perhaps had not been there until that moment, which perhaps the hand of God had spread apart.— But who can answer that?—Still, there it was: a channel through the reef, scarcely wider than the ship—the eye of a needle through which to guide a thread. There would only be one chance; you could not draw back your hand and try again. He leaned upon the helm, watching

the rag of jib which gave him steerageway, steering her head into it
—a fluttering scrap of thread, and the eye of a needle with destruction
all around it—

"Please save the children, Allah, before you punish me." And no
doubt God's hand was there, resting gently on the wheel, for the miracle
occurred. The *Flying Virgin* seemed to understand what was demanded
of her, shaking herself alert, rising on her heels to see the mark, taking
careful aim at it—then settling to her task, darting like an arrow, riding
high on a providential sea—scraping bottom even then, but as lightly
as a feather—missing by an oar's length jagged teeth of rock which
reached and snapped at her—

In a moment it was over. But there was no breathing space for
ship or man. He saw the land ahead, a fleeting glimpse through the
curtain of the storm—the looming, shadowy form of it. But there was no
time to act, nor anything to do. And perhaps she saw it too, with her
carved and painted eyes, or the mermaid screamed a warning; for she
seemed to lose her head, to try to veer away, rolling broadside, bulwark under. Again she straightened out, heedless of control—perhaps
God's hand was finished with the matter—hurled on by her momentum
and the sluice gate at her back, reeling from beam to beam, rasping
over rocks which were tearing out her bottom, plunging headlong
through the shore surf. And then at last she struck—a crunching,
splintering crash.

The wreckage on the deck leaped up from the shock. The masts
snapped off like matchsticks and fell this way and that, tearing
through the bulwarks, ripping up the deck till it buckled like a washboard. The wheel collapsed and bore the black man with it, mauling
the breath out of him; and a spar came hurtling down upon his head,
mercifully completing his oblivion. The dead man in the cabin
bounced up and was at rest, lying spread upon his back, staring widely
through the skylight, grinning emptily at nothing. The tolling bell
clanged crazily and was still.

The children were awakened when she struck, hurled about like nine-
pins. But they fell back in the straw, unhurt and unalarmed, not
really wide awake. And then it was quiet and they went to sleep again.

But the *Flying Virgin* would never fly again. Her bow was high
and dry, wedged in a cleft of rock which held her like a vise. Below the

mermaid's tail she was shattered like an egg—a gaping, mortal wound through which could be discerned the contents of her belly: undigested straw, and broken earthen jars from which the oil was trickling—trickling down like tears out of her painted eyes. No, she would not fly again on any evil errand. She no longer presented the appearance of a ship, formless and dismantled, squatting flatly in the surf with her nose high in the air, the top of her a tangle of unfamiliar rubbish festooned with greasy kelp. But the mermaid was intact, wedged safely in the crevice of the rock, gazing through it to the land with placid, watery eyes, her trident pointing boldly straight ahead.

13

THE STORM HAD SPENT ITSELF AND LAIN DOWN
to rest, like an exhausted dog content with its achievement,
growling in its sleep from force of habit, dreaming of the
rabbit it had run to earth.

The sun broke through the clouds which began to drift apart, disclosing silver linings and facets of the sky set deeply in their folds. The angry sea subsided, and the waves resumed their pretty white lace caps, nodding once again in cheerful, friendly fashion, though still against the reef they boomed like thunder and hurled their ragged fringe high in the air. The tide ran out, receding from the *Flying Virgin's* corpse, leaving her broken bones, draped with seaweed for the funeral, to settle in the sand. But the mermaid could not turn her head to look, nor perhaps was tempted, for the sight that met her eyes must have claimed her full attention.

At her feet was a strip of broad white beach, shelving gently to the sea, curving seaward from her vision at the sides; and scattered widely on it, in groups or pairs or singly, were monolithic pillars—heroic granite figures sculptured by the sea, grotesquely carved in strangely human form. There were others in the water behind the mermaid's back; indeed, between a pair of them the ship had wedged her bow, in a cleft beneath which they were joined like Siamese twins. But these were too close to resemble anything. It was the others, scattered all around—

"Giants!" exclaimed the Little One, when her eyes first rested on them.

"Stones," they told her. "They are nothing but big stones."

"Giants," she insisted. "Giants turned into stones."

"Oh well—" They laughed. But now it was suggested, they did resemble Giants—husbands and wives strolling arm in arm; and smaller Giants, who could have been their children, walking sedately or romping at their heels; and tired Giants reclining on the beach; and others in the water wading through the waves, or far, far out with just their heads in sight.—Yes, Giants, big families of them—fathers, mothers, children, relatives and friends—enchanted into stone, frozen in a moment at their happy occupations, not to be restored until—until—

It was Juan who wakened first, noting with surprise that it was no longer dark. And then he was aware of the unfamiliar stillness—sound and motion both suspended. He climbed toward the light, crawling over hummocks in the straw in which were broken, sharp-edged things; and there was a smell of oil and his hands were greasy with it. But now the light was brighter and he saw that the fragments were bits of earthen jars which had been buried in the straw and in some way cast up from it. He could not imagine what had happened in the night to occasion such destruction. And then he scaled a final mound, strewn thick with shattered jars and reeking of the oil, and stared in stupefaction.

He was looking through a great hole in the ship—looking at a picture framed in walls of rock. He thought he must be dreaming; but when he had crept closer he began to understand, for he saw the broken bowsprit and the mermaid overhead, and beneath him was the sand whence the tide had run away. The ship had come to land.

His eye flew back to it, across the sparkling beach with its company of Giants, beyond the rocky bluff which bordered it, to a green and lovely forest—trunks of mighty trees twined with clinging vines and garlanded with flowers, and tall and slender ones with trunks like leaning poles, with fronded leaves that overhung the sand. And the forest was alive with many sounds—the twitter of small birds, and the raucous cries of big ones which fluttered here and there in streaks of brilliant color. And there was the smell of it—richly warm and soft, and the perfume of the flowers. He saw it all in one long breathless glance, and then turned back to shout—

"Wake up! Wake up! We're there."

They came swarming up the haystack, wading through the greasy straw, scratching arms and legs on fragments of the jars. And soon they were beside him, speechless with amazement, with wonder and delight, murmuring "Ohs" and "Ahs", not finding any words except the brief exchange about the Giants, even the Little One reduced to silent rapture. The clouds were rolling back and melting in the sun, disclosing rounded hills rising one above another.

"Mountains!" they exclaimed.—Yes, mountains hemmed the forest, rearing steeply from the green-clad slopes, towering gaunt and barren in the sky, their peaks still high above the lifting curtain.

"And snow!" they cried. For now the cone-shaped peaks were drifting into view, not easy to distinguish in the tangle of the clouds.

"Like Spain," Teresa whispered.

"No—" They shook their heads.—No, it was not like Spain, nor anything they'd known.

"It's America," said Juan.

"Yes, America," they cried. "America of course."

"But I thought there would be cinemas," sighed Pablo.

"Cinemas?" They laughed. But they had thought so too; it was not at all as they had thought America would be.

"Maybe behind the mountains," the Little One suggested.

"Oh—" Pablo sighed again. The mountains presented a formidable aspect.

"Look! A waterfall—" Gil pointed.

"Oh yes!" They saw it now: a silver ribbon tumbling down the bluff into a rocky pool, whence it overflowed and trickled in the sand.

"Let's go and look," he cried, and crawled ahead across the bridge that bound the Giants together. "Come on," he shouted, disappearing from their view. There was in fact a shoulder of the rock sloping gently to the beach, and anyway it was not far to jump.

"Go on," they called, pushing one another. But the Little One delayed them, her attention attracted by something in the straw—a little chamois bag lying in the fragments of a broken jar. "Go on! Go on!" they urged.

"No, please, I want it."

"It's nothing. Go ahead!"

"I want it for my tooth." She reached for it and got it. It was greasy, soaked with oil; and there was something in it, but she didn't stop to look, for just then she caught a glimpse of something else—something bright and shiny slipping through the straw, and she grabbed it just in time. "Oh, see what I've found now!" And she held it out for them to look—a golden sovereign.

"It's money," they explained, impatient of the matter.

"What is it for?"

"To buy things."

"But what is there to buy?"

"Nothing," they told her. "And it isn't any good. Go on," they pleaded. "Hurry!"

"Money—" she repeated and popped it in the bag. "Anyway, it's pretty and I'll keep it with my tooth."

Away they went at last, scrambling down the rock, racing through the sand, exclaiming rapturously—

"How soft and white it is!"

"We can build castles in it."

"See, there is a crab!"

"Look at him running sideways." It made them think of Rafael, but only for a moment. Gil was far ahead, urging them to hurry.

They ran around a sprawling Giant and came upon the pool, plunging their faces in, for the sun was high and hot now. The tall trees leaned above them from the bank, like a protecting canopy; and in the tops of some were clusters of gigantic nuts, bigger than their heads. And there were others scattered in the sand. They broke one with a rock and tasted cautiously—

"It's good," they cried. "It's milk."

"If only we could live here—" Juan said half to himself.

"Live here?" They were startled.

"Up there in the forest."

"Maybe we can," said Gil. Already he was climbing up the bluff beside the waterfall.

"But will they let us stay?" Teresa questioned doubtfully.

"Let us? Who?"

"The men who live here."

"Yes—" They nodded, spirits dampened. "Yes, the men who live here—what will they say?"

"Ho!" Gil shrugged, but he was doubtful too. "I don't see any men."

"But there must be men in America," they said.

"Indians anyway," amended Pablo.

"Maybe they're far away," suggested Juan. "Far away behind the mountains."

"And suppose they come and find us?"

"Maybe—" The Little One peered thoughtfully at the forest. "Maybe it's a Fairyland and they can't get into it."

"Yes, maybe—" They laughed, not altogether scornfully. But Rosa started suddenly, shivering with remembrance—

"Mamud! What of Mamud?"

"Mamud!" they exclaimed. They had forgotten him. "Will Mamud let us live here?" They stared at one another in growing consternation. "And where is Mamud now?"

They turned to look, back across the playground of the Giants: the pretty pool, designed for sailing boats, the soft white sand where castles could be built—from which they might be snatched and again imprisoned somewhere, in an ugly cheerless granary or a dark and smelly ship—

Yes, there it was. But it no longer bore resemblance to a ship. They were silent for a moment, feeling a little sad to see it crushed and broken—like a toy ship that a careless foot had trod on.

"The Fairy ship," jeered Gil.

"Anyway, it brought us," the Little One said stoutly.

"And see," cried Rosa, "the mermaid is still there."

Yes, the mermaid was still there, pointing with her trident, gazing

moistly at them with friendly, cowlike eyes. But where was Mamud?—
They searched the deck. There was the little house, flattened out to
nothing—the proud masts spread like oars, with their ends dipped
in the water—twisted heaps of spars, kindling trimmed with rags; but
not any sign of Mamud or the mouse-man or the others—

"Maybe they're dead," Gil said. "Washed away and drowned."

They nodded, shivering at the thought. But then they brightened—

"Then we can stay," they murmured. "Live here in the forest, and
build a little house."

"And castles in the sand," the Little One exclaimed. "I'll go and
build one now."

"No, wait!" cried Juan whose eyes were on the mermaid. "Look!
Someone is coming."

They looked and caught their breath. Yes, someone was coming,
creeping through the hole beneath the mermaid's tail. "Mamud—" they
gasped.

"No—" Gil laughed, albeit nervously. "No, it isn't Mamud."

"Then who?"

"It's just the sheep."

And the sheep in fact it was, with her lambs beside her; and behind
her was the goat accompanied by her kids. The halfdeck had been
shattered, cracked open like a nut, and the animals had found their
way out of the ship. Some chickens fluttered cautiously behind them,
escaped out of their broken crate. They came slowly down the shoulder
of the rock, in tentative procession, with the mother sheep in front,
and stood upon the sand in a bedraggled group—like prisoners freed
from cells and suddenly turned loose in an unfamiliar world.

"They are coming home to us," the Little One remarked. "Here
we are," she called.

The sheep and goat looked up, but they made no move to come.

"Up here," she urged, and stood to wave to them.

"Be still!" they cautioned. And Pablo pulled her down in the long
grass that grew against the bluff.

"He must be dead," they whispered.

"Or hiding," Gil said grimly.

"Yes, hiding—" they agreed, shuddering at the idea: Mamud peeking at them from the shelter of the ship, watching everything they did,

waiting like a spider till they walked into his trap, or waiting for the night when he could creep and find them—not a very cheerful prospect. "But how can we find out?" they questioned anxiously.

"That's easy," Gil said boldly, coming down the bluff from where he had been sitting a little way above them. "I'll go and look for him, and the rest of you stay here until I wave my hand."

"But if he should catch you—" stammered Rosa.

"He won't. I'm not afraid."

And he was off, running across the beach, in and out among the Giants—up the rocky path, through the cleft between the Twins, disappearing for a moment to reappear again, climbing up the mermaid, swinging on her trident, reaching for the bowsprit, crawling to the deck—

The Little One sat in the grass, with Juana in her lap, and explored the chamois bag, pouring out the contents: the tooth, the golden coin, and—diamonds, emeralds, pearls, a teacupful at least—the ransom of an international scoundrel. "Why, Juana," she exclaimed in pleased surprise, "just see what I have found—these pretty bits of glass." She cupped the precious stones in both her hands, allowing them to sift between her fingers, repeating to herself, "Pretty, pretty, pretty—"

But the others gave no heed, absorbed in watching Gil, fearful lest some dreadful thing should happen—losing sight of him, holding their breath until he reappeared. And then, at last, they saw him on the deck.

"Good for Gil!" they murmured. "Gil is not afraid."

But in fact he was a little. It had been fun at first, darting off alone upon a dangerous errand, knowing they were watching and admiring. But the fun was over when he stood upon the bow looking down upon the wreckage, dismal and deserted, coated green with slime, with strands of twining kelp which resembled crawling snakes. He almost wished he hadn't been so brave.

Still, he never thought of turning back, but went on warily, down the ladder from the forecastle, scrambling over debris, his bare feet slipping on the greasy planks.—There was Mamud's house, or what was left of it—the vagrant meat block in the middle of the wreck, hung with pots and pans. He half expected Mamud to rise out of the ruins with the long knife in his hand. But nothing happened.—There was the scuttle with the ladder to the storeroom where there were things to eat

—boxes, barrels, tins, which could later be collected and carried to the forest, if there was need of them. But the forest itself might be full of things to eat—like the milk nuts, only better.—The stillness was oppressive, like a burden on his back; his knees were trembling from it, from the listening, waiting tension.—Yes, the scuttle through which Mamud had so often made appearance, and might now appear again. He edged cautiously around it, watching back over his shoulder—

A big white bird came swooping, squawking at him, and his heart nearly jumped out of his breast.—A bird, yes, that was all. He tried to laugh about it, but it didn't sound like laughing.—There was the cleaver lying on the deck—the ax that Mamud used to chop the sheep, that sheep they had mistaken for a child. Well, it was not a child, but a child would look like that.—He hastily changed the current of his thought: the ax would be good to have, to chop wood for the fire when Rosa cooked their food. Yes, Rosa would be the one to do it; she knew about such things, had often helped the woman when they were at the farm. And she could teach Teresa, but Teresa wouldn't care about it much—would prefer to sing and dance and lie around, putting flowers in her hair and things like that.

He himself would hunt and fish. He would take Pablo with him and teach him to be a hunter. An objection that arose he quickly brushed aside: he had never hunted anything; but he would teach himself. He didn't think that Juan would be a hunter; for to be a hunter you mustn't care about things being dead, nor mind the sight of blood. And Juan had but one arm, and a hunter needed two. Still, Juan could do almost anything that he could. Well, Juan could build a house and make the chairs and table—carve them out of wood.— From the corner of his eye he could see them watching him. He was glad that they were there—

Something cold and slimy wriggled from his toes, and stood his hair on end. It was a crab, scuttling to the shelter of the seaweed.— There was the door into the mouse-man's house. He kept his eyes upon it, edging on tiptoe to the ladder at its side. The mouse-man might be there, peeking through a crack, waiting for a chance to take him unaware.—Witches, Giants, and Sorcerers!—No, it wasn't likely. Just stories made for children. But in fact he was a child, a frightened little boy—not sure about Sorcerers, nor Giants nor Witches either.

The wind had died away; the fleecy clouds had scattered to the far rim of the sky, resuming old disguises of dragons, castles, monsters; the waves had doffed their caps, and the distant fringe of lace had subsided to a feather. The sun blazed hot and dazzling, and the shadows of the Giants drew closer on the sand, wrapping tightly round their feet. White vapor, like the stuff that Sorcerers burn when they are casting spells, rose from the reeking seaweed, drifting on the deck. And the air was thick with the smell of rotting kelp. If there were such things as Sorcerers, this would be a place where they would feel at home—

He started up the ladder to the poop, where he had never been, where the hairy man had stayed to steer the ship, where he had last been seen—where he might be waiting now.—There was the skylight coming into view, the glass all broken out of it. A clammy length of kelp slithered from the ladder and wrapped around his ankle. He was sure he was caught—caught in a trap. But then it let him loose and slid away.

He took a cautious step—another and another. No, there was nothing there. But yes, there was! He crouched behind the coaming, peeking gingerly: something crumpled on the deck, half buried in a tangled heap of ropes and broken spars.—Yes, it was Mamud! There was the long sharp knife; and the wooden leg stuck out, like a fragment of the wreckage. The eyes were closed; and the blackness of his face was blacker for a stain of blood upon it—blood that had dripped in a pool upon the deck.—Yes, Mamud still and dead!

He turned to run away out of the dreadful place. But suddenly he paused, arrested by a thought: the knife—he should have that. As a hunter he would need it. Did he dare to go and get it?—to slip it from the cord around the dead man's waist?—He mustered all his courage, with a side glance at the shore. Yes, they were there and watching, though they couldn't see what he saw, with the skylight in between.—Imagine their amazement when he displayed the knife. The pleasure of that gesture was not to be resisted, must be had at any cost.—He crept out of his shelter, into the shallow cockpit, watching like a hawk, ready to fly back—reached for it and got it; it slipped easily from the noose. And with it in his hand his courage mounted. Mamud was dead, and weaponless as well—not dangerous any more.—

But suppose he wasn't dead? Suppose he was enchanted, and might wriggle out of it—might somehow come alive?—Well, now was the time to settle that, and there might not be another.—And what would they say then? He could see their faces, incredulous, admiring; and Rosa smiling at him, her eyes so soft and warm.—Yes, now was the time!—His heart was in his throat and beating like a hammer, but he crept a little closer—

"Where is he?" they were asking, for they could not see him now.

"Behind the mouse-man's roof."

"Why doesn't he come back?"

They waited anxiously. But the Little One was playing with the bits of broken glass, arranging them in piles of different colors; and Juan was not attending. He was sitting by himself, gazing at the mermaid with an air of rapt attention. And suddenly he said, half to himself—

"I know who she looks like."

"Who?—looks like what?" they questioned.

"The mermaid."

"Looks like who?"

"Like God's mother," he explained.

"God's mother?" They were startled.

"The time I saw her with the baby in her arms, and the people kneeling down; and she had a crown with jewels. You can see the way her arms are—as if she held God in them."

"But there isn't any baby," they objected.

"Well, maybe I could carve one that would fit into her arms."

"And she hasn't got a crown."

"I could make a crown if I had a piece of tin."

"What about the jewels?"

"I know," cried the Little One. "I'll give Juan some of mine."

"Just broken glass!" They laughed.

"They look like jewels," she said. "Maybe God's mother wouldn't know the difference."

"Did she have a spear?" they asked, concerned about the trident.

"No, not a spear," Juan said. "But she had a scepter. And if it stood up straight—" He paused, with narrowed eyes, reconstructing in his mind.

"Did she have a fishtail?" inquired Pablo doubtfully.

"We could fix that," Juan explained, "so the vines would grow around it."

"And her face is full of cracks."

"In a church you wouldn't see them."

"A church?" They stared. "But where is there a church?"

"Not a real one," he admitted. "But some place in the forest—"

"Oh—" They laughed again, a little disappointed.

"We could find a place," Juan said, "where there was a stump, or something like a throne. And it would be like church—"

But the others had lost interest, watching again for Gil to reappear—

"What can he be doing?"

"Why doesn't he come back?"

And Gil was coming back, crawling from the cockpit, when his glance fell through the skylight. And now his heart did stop, for there was the mouse-man staring straight into his eyes, grinning at him horribly. It was the end, he thought: he would be turned to stone, frozen like the Giants, never to explore the lovely forest, to hunt and fish and play—a cold and lonely statue. It was already happening, for he couldn't move or breathe, couldn't even shift his eyes from those awful grinning ones. But then—his toes were wriggling; they hadn't turned to stone.—His legs, his arms?—Yes, he could move them. He felt his heart again, scrambling wildly to get out.

And suddenly he realized the mouse-man was dead—not really looking at him, or anyway not seeing him—lying in the water, with his arms and legs all crooked, in a mess of soggy papers and things turned upside down, with a big red book close beside his head, and wisps of seaweed clinging to his hair. And his head!—Icy fingers clutched his spine.—His head was half cut off, hanging on one side.— Yes, he was dead, like Mamud.—The spell was broken—

"There he is," they cried.

"Look! He's waving to us."

"Come on, let's go!"

They raced across the beach. The tide had ebbed still farther and the sand was bare to the middle of the ship; and Gil was waiting there, leaning on the bulwark. They came running, shouting questions—"May we stay here?—Where is Mamud?"

He laughed and flung down something shiny to the sand.

"What's that?" They stared, not venturing to come close.

"Pick it up," he urged.

Pablo went and got it, shaking off the sand.

"Mamud's knife!" they gasped.

"Wait now!" He ducked behind the bulwark and reappeared with something in his arms. "Look out!" He pushed it over, and it fell with a plump, squashing in the sand.

"What's that?" They backed away.

"Go and look," he grinned.

They came closer to the object, poking with their toes—

"Mamud's leg!" cried Juan. And it flashed into his mind that the shape and size of it was not unlike a baby.

"Mamud's leg—" they echoed, shrinking back in horror.

"Pick it up," jeered Gil. "It will not bite."

But they didn't pick it up. It was Juan who came and got it, and went back a little way, till he could see the mermaid, measuring with his eye, intent on an idea.

"I cut it off," said Gill, "the strap that held it on."

"Oh—" They nodded, terribly impressed. "Is Mamud dead?" they asked.

"Yes, dead."

"Enchanted," the Little One said firmly.

"Enchanted?" Gil leaned across the rail. "Well, he won't run and catch us, not while we have his leg."

"No—" they chorused faintly. They were safe from Mamud's fury. "But the mouse-man?" they exclaimed.

"Dead," Gil said contemptuously.

"How do you know?"

"Because I saw him lying in his house, with his head almost cut off."

"Oh—" It was too awful.

"Maybe—" The Little One considered, nodding to herself. "Maybe his wicked heart is still alive."

But they were not listening to her. "The hairy man?" they asked. "And all the others?"

"Gone," he told them.

"You mean—" incredulously, "—there are no men at all?"

"Not one."

"Just children left?"

"Just us." He sat on the rail and swung his legs, and Rosa clambered up and sat beside him. It wasn't very high, nor hard to climb because there was a scupper for a foothold, and Gil reached down to help her.

"Then we can live here always," she said softly, gazing at the forest —the soft green roof of it sloping gently toward the mountains, looking almost solid, like something you could walk on, like a magic carpet.

"And build a house," said Pablo.

"And castles in the sand," the Little One amended. And she sat down in the shadow of a Giant, close by the water's edge where the sand was damp and firm, and began at once to build one.

"But the men behind the mountains—" Teresa ventured doubtfully. "If they come and drive us out—"

"Look!" Gil pointed. The clouds had spread apart, revealing snowy peaks spread all around the forest, like a mighty wall. "They can't get in," he said.

"And we can't get out," said Pablo.

"Who wants to?" laughed Teresa, reassured.

"No one—" he agreed. But he had a reservation: he would like to see a cinema—anyway, just once. "Here, catch!" he called, and tossed a milk nut to her.

"Perhaps it is a Fairyland," mused Rosa. "Perhaps the Giants were men who wanted to get in. And they were turned to stone."

"Ho!" Gil grinned. "Then we'll be turned to stone when we grow up."

"Perhaps we won't grow up."

"Oh yes, we will," he said.

"I suppose we will—" she sighed. "But not for a long time."

They were silent for a while, their shoulders touching, drinking in the beauty of the scene—the mountains and the forest, busy with their dreams which had not much in common. For the dream of the girl could not have been expressed, translated into words; it was much too nebulous—just a thread of warm wellbeing, a sense of belonging to the beauty of the world, of being part of it. And the dream of the boy—

"I'd like to know," Gil said, "what's behind those mountains."

"Would you, Gil?" She glanced at him and shivered. "But it would be cold up there."

"I wouldn't care." He laughed. "And some day I'll climb up and find out what's behind them."

She nodded absently; then suddenly remembering, "If we had the pictures maybe we could tell?"

"Pictures?"

"The pictures of America. They were in a big red book—" She shuddered at the memory. "But I didn't see inside it."

"Big red book!" He started, recollecting. "Wait! I'll go and get it."

"Oh no—" She caught his arm. "It's in the mouse-man's house."

"No matter," he said boldly. "I'm not afraid of him." And he jumped down from the rail and ran back along the deck.

But already he was sorry, wishing he hadn't been so hasty, not caring very much about the pictures, not enough to venture back into that awful place. But he had no option now. And it wasn't so bad as it had been before, when he had been alone, not knowing what he'd find. —He looked across the rail and was relieved to see the others close at hand.

Pablo and Teresa were sitting in the sand, playing with a milk nut, tossing it between them like a ball. And Juan sat between them with Mamud's wooden leg clenched between his knees. He was turning it around, poking at it with his knife.

"It ought to fit into her arms—" he said half to himself.

"Maybe—" Pablo shrugged with the milk nut in his lap. "But it's not shaped like a baby and the neck is much too long."

"Like a stork's," Teresa giggled.

"I could cut it off—right here." Juan nicked it with his knife.

"Then it won't have any head," objected Pablo.

"Maybe I can make one and stick it on the neck."

"Make it out of what?"

Juan turned the matter in his mind and was suddenly inspired. "I know what," he cried. "The very thing—that milk nut!"

"Milk nut?" Pablo stared. It did look like a head, though a rather shriveled one.

"It won't look like a baby." Teresa laughed disdainfully. "It's got hair all over it, and the skin is almost black."

"Well, so is mine," said Pablo, "and maybe so is God's."

Juan took the milk nut from him, considering aloud, "I could make a hole in it and stick it on the neck."

"And it hasn't any feet," Teresa added scornfully.

"Of course it has," he said, rapping with his knife on the thick end of the thing. "The feet are in there underneath the dress."

"Oh well—" She lay back in the sand, growing tired of the subject. "It's just a wooden leg turned upside down."

"You wait, you'll see," he promised.

"It won't look like a baby, no matter what you do." She stretched out languidly. "When I have a baby, it won't look like that."

"When you have one!" said Pablo, hugely startled.

"When I grow up," she said.

"Oh—" His jaw hung open. Teresa with a baby! It was a new idea, both intriguing and unpleasant. "And who will be the father?" he asked suspiciously.

"Who?" She shook the sand out of her hair. "Maybe Gil," she said.

Pablo thought about it. "No, not Gil." He frowned.—Gil might be the father if Rosa had a baby. He glanced up at her, sitting on the rail. —"No." He said again.

"Well, maybe Juan?"

But Juan did not look up. He was nicking at the wood where he meant to cut the neck; but the wood was hard and tough and the knife was very dull.

"No." Pablo shook his head. He felt certain that Juan would not be a party to it. "Then who?" he said.

"Maybe you," Teresa chuckled, teasing him of course.

"Me?" Pablo scrambled to his feet, feeling furious and pleased and terribly embarrassed.

"But there's no one else," she said.

"Oh, isn't there!" he stormed. "Well, I won't. Don't fool yourself." And suddenly he turned and went running toward the bluff, kicking at the sand.

"Pablo!" she sat up, watching him. "Where are you going, Pablo?— I was only fooling." He slowed his step but didn't look around. "Pablo! Wait for me!" She ran to overtake him, and presently they were climbing up the bluff beside the waterfall—climbing hand in hand.

Gil stood before the mouse-man's door and reached to turn the knob.

But then it crossed his mind that it might be as well to look in through the skylight before he ventured closer, to make certain there had not been any change. So he climbed the ladder, glancing back over his shoulder, seeing Rosa on the railing watching him, waving an assurance that he was not afraid; but he really was—a little. And then he took a step and cautiously peeked down.—There was the mouse-man, still lying on his back, with his head almost cut off—just as dead as ever. And there the big red book, half buried in the water! It was likely enough the pictures would be spoiled and not worth looking at—

His heart caught in his throat, for he had heard a sound—a rasping hollow groan. He stared in frozen terror. The mouse-man had not moved; his lips remained half open, the sneering grin unchanged. But there it was again—that dreadful moaning sound. And it was not the mouse-man; it came from somewhere else. He jerked his head to look, and then he turned and fled with panic in his legs, tumbling down the ladder, tripping in the kelp—

"Run!" he shouted. "Run!"

"What is it?" Rosa cried.

"Mamud isn't dead."

In another moment he had squirmed across the bulwark and dropped into the sand—into the water really, for the tide was coming back, but it wasn't very deep. Rosa and Juan were waiting when he waded out; and the wooden leg was safe beneath Juan's arm.—No, Mamud would not catch them, not while they had his leg! But still they were not tempted to linger on the scene.

They didn't see the others, and they didn't pause to look. The Little One was safe, they thought, with Pablo and Teresa. Afterwards they thought they must have thought this. But perhaps they had thought nothing; there was little time for thinking. For who could say what the black man might contrive? Indeed, at the moment, they would not have been surprised if he had come flying at them on a broomstick.

In any case the forest was a safer place to be—

14

A T THE TOP OF THE BLUFF THEY STOPPED FOR breath, crouching in the bushes that grew along its edge, fearfully looking back across the beach. Between a pair of Giants they could see the mouse-man's house, but not any sign of Mamud. The ship lay flatly in the sand, silent and deserted.

"Perhaps you were mistaken—" ventured Rosa.

"No, I wasn't," mumbled Gil.

"Anyway," said Juan, "I've got his wooden leg." And he stuck it in the ground, postponing further operation on it.

Yes, they had his wooden leg, and he wouldn't run and catch them. Their confidence revived, but they waited for a while, with their eyes upon the ship. There was no sign of life.

"Maybe now he's really dead," Gil grudgingly admitted, beginning to be doubtful of that awful moaning sound, wondering if his eyes could have deceived him—if he had really seen the black man move, beneath the tangled web of ropes and spars.

"Yes, maybe—" they agreed. They could hear Pablo shouting, remotely in the forest—exploring, having fun. There was nothing to be gained by staring at the ship. "Let's go," they cried. "Come on!"

And they ran into the forest, leaving Mamud's wooden leg stuck in the ground. In the twinkling of an eye the sky was shut away by a canopy of green, a tent of lofty foliage. And in another moment both Mamud and his leg had been forgotten.

Great trees were everywhere: mahogany and mango, waving manaca palms and feathery bamboo, papaya and banana, nutmeg and ceiba, and the slender trunks of coconuts whose tops were lost to sight. And flung among them was a net of vines and creepers, festooned from limb to limb and tree to tree; and sacks of moss in crotches of the branches, with orchids dripping from them. The air was sweet with perfume, and filled with pleasant sounds—of rustling leaves and singing birds, and the murmur of the brook chattering softly over pebbles and cascading to the beach.

It was like nothing they had ever seen; but like things they had imagined when Teresa told them stories—fabled lands of Princes, where they wandered with their sweethearts, or hunted with their courtiers; like places they remembered in their dreams—

"Like a church—" Juan murmured.—And it was like a church: a vast cathedral, with long straight aisles that led toward hidden shrines, with shafts of golden sunlight sifting through stained glass—a church at Easter, decked with green and flowers, dim and cool and peaceful. And the smell of it, like incense. And the music of the forest, like the music of an organ and the chanting of a choir.—It would be good, he thought, looking out a likely spot: God's mother on her throne, with her fishtail wrapped in vines, and the baby in her arms—

But Gil and Rosa were already far ahead and calling him to come. And he ran to overtake them.

But the black man was not dead. He was waking from a stupor, as a patient wakes from ether when the surgeon's job is done, to bruised and aching misery. Indeed a sorry figure! His hair and beard were matted with his blood, from a deep gash in his head where the falling spar had struck him; his lips puffed thick and blistered from the sun; his bloodshot eyes half open and the lashes white with salt.

He wakened from a dream, a nightmare of his childhood, in which he was a child again, a happy little boy, tending his father's cattle in the hills of Galla Land—seeing the white-clad figures coming stealthily through the bush, curious at first and unalarmed. And then suddenly he knew, for he had been often warned; and he sprang up from the grass with wildly beating heart, prepared to run away, home to his mother's arms. But alas it was too late! The Arabs were upon him, his hands bound tight behind him, a cord about his leg, a gag shoved in his mouth to still his frantic cries—

From such a dream he woke, to sobbing pain and terror, not asleep and not awake—in that narrow edge of madness which is never far away from suffering men, where the unreal and the real are inextricably mixed, where time and space are canceled. At first he could not move, pinned down by broken pieces of the wheel and webbed in tangled ropes. But he fumbled patiently until he freed himself, still deep within the aura of the dream—struggling with the cords which in the dream had bound him, his parched throat thick and strangling with the gag. At last he was free, sitting up amidst the wreckage, rising to his knees. But he crumpled helplessly. Again he tried and failed, not understanding why, not seeing what was wrong. And then he sat and stared—as, in grief and wonder, he had sat and stared fifty years ago, wakening from this dream, on a pallet in a slave pen.—His leg was gone. His leg had been cut off.—Hot tears ran down his cheeks, and all the years dissolved, as if they'd never been.—Again he heard the voices of the children in the slave pen, the lamenting of a child—

And this indeed he heard. The Little One was wailing in anger and despair. The ripples of the tide had undermined the castle's outer walls; and now a big one came and swept them quite away, and the castle was collapsing. She was packing sand against it, but in vain.

"Go back! Go back!" she ordered, stamping at the waves. But another one came rushing, splashing on her legs, and the castle was in ruins. There was nothing to be done. She paused to retrieve some bits of colored glass with which she had adorned the melting tower's roof—some diamonds, pearls, and emeralds disappearing in the sand. But she did not spend much time to look for them because she was too grieved to care about it, and there were plenty more in the little chamois bag.

"Rosa," she demanded, "come and see what's happened!"

But Rosa didn't answer. And when she ran around the Giant to look she found they had all gone—gone away and left her. "I don't care," she said, but in fact she did. She sat crossly in the sand, brooding on her injuries. They had gone away and left her, ignored and brushed aside—the common lot of children and of thinkers. But this dubious consolation did not occur to her. She had been badly treated and she went no further with it; abstract consideration would not mitigate the sting. "I hate them all," she said and dried her eyes. And then she scraped her pockets which were wet and sticky, but there was no sugar left in an edible condition.

An ungainly yellow bird with big black spectacles, hopped around the corner of a rock and stared at her with an air of disapproval. "Go away," she scolded and shooed it with her hand. But the bird only laughed in a nasty, spiteful way. "Go away, I tell you!" She threw a pebble at it, and it spread its wings and staggered off, screeching with derision. "And don't come back," she added. The bird might be a Witch. Its chin was hooked like one, and its face was full of wrinkles. Her irritation shifted to this fresh indignity, and presently took flight as a butterfly came by and attracted her attention—a big and gorgeous one with golden wings, and a black stripe—like a Wand. Yes, like a Fairy's Wand, tucked underneath its wing—

Suppose it was a Fairy!—She was tingling with excitement. It came and circled round her head in the most friendly fashion.—Suppose it should begin to talk and ask her what she wished!—It fluttered past her eyes and settled on a blade of grass in the crevice of a Giant, very still and looking at her.—Oh dear, what should she wish?—A pocket filled with sugar, that you could never empty—But she caught herself in time, remembering the disasters in a story—the story of a Prince who had wished for silly things, and was lucky in the end to get back where he had started. He had had three wishes, which was usually the case, but every wish he made got him deeper into trouble.—No, it should be something wonderful, like a golden Palace. But did she want a Palace? She must make her mind up quickly.—"Good Fairy—" she began, but then she hesitated. And the butterfly took wing and sailed away—

"Oh dear!" Now it had gone, out of patience with her maybe. She hastily stuffed the chamois bag in the pocket of her dress and set out in pursuit. Intent upon the Fairy she did not look around, and so she

did not see the black face staring at her from the railing of the ship
—the black man on his knee, with his arms spread on the bulwark,
looking down upon the beach, watching with wondering eyes every
move she made. The butterfly went on around the Giant and came to
rest again on another blade of grass. She approached it cautiously, tip-
toeing through the sand, saying over to herself, "I must wish for something wonderful—" And the Fairy waited for her. Now it was very
close, level with her face, looking straight into her eyes—

"I wish—" she breathed, "I wish—" But what was she to wish? She
had not made up her mind. The Fairy shook itself, as if annoyed; and
then it flew away.

"Oh dear! Oh dear!" she sighed, almost crying with vexation, and
ran to overtake it. Now and then she would lose sight of it, in and out
among the Giants, and think that it was gone. But then it would come
gliding down, its golden wings spread wide, and lazily flutter on in a
tantalizing way, pausing to hover over this and that, but never settling
down so she could come up with it. Sometimes it would fly quite close,
back and forth and round and round—teasing her until her eyes were
wet with tears. A reproof to indecision; she was certain that was it. The
Fairy was displeased and out of patience. And as she scampered after
it she was busy with her wish, so that she might be ready with the
words upon her lips, if she had another chance—

Not a Palace, she decided, not even made of gold. For if she had
a Palace she would have to live in it. And that couldn't be as nice as
living in a forest.—A pretty dress perhaps: silk and lace and ribbons,
like the ones Princesses wore. But when she went to play it would get
mussed and torn. And that would not be fun.—A dog, like Trictrac!
Yes, that would be good, but not terribly important: for a second wish
perhaps, if she had a second one. But the first wish ought to be more
wonderful than that.—What?—What?—She racked her mind. And
then suddenly she knew—

"Why yes, of course," she cried. And at this very moment the Fairy
glided down and came to rest upon the sand, with folded wings, the
magic Wand displayed and ready to be waved—as if it knew her
thought and was no longer vexed.—No, she would not fail this time.
And she tiptoed very carefully, with her hands clasped at her breast,
scarcely daring to breathe lest she frighten it away.—Closer—closer.—

She sank upon her knees and bowed her head. She could see the Fairy's eyes, watching her intently—friendly little eyes.

"Good Fairy," she said softly, "prithee grant my boon—" That was the way to ask, she remembered from the stories. "I would like to live here always in the lovely forest—for ever and ever."

The Fairy made no answer, but one wing fluttered slightly—as if it waved its Wand. There wasn't any doubt the wish was being granted.

"Thank you very much," said the Little One politely, quite over-whelmed with joy. And then she added doubtfully, not sure just how far one ought to go, and not wanting to appear unreasonable or greedy —some dreadful things had happened to people of that sort—"May I have another wish?"

The Fairy seemed to nod, as if to say, "Why certainly, my child."

"Oh, thank you—" She yearned to hug the Fairy in her arms, and half put out her hands. But of course that wouldn't do, and the Fairy might not like such informality. "Well, prithee then—" she stammered. "I mean—for my second wish I'd like to have a dog—a dog like Trictrac." She wasn't sure if the Fairy understood, and she hastened to explain, "A little woolly black one—about as big as that." And she held her hands to indicate the size.

Again the Fairy seemed to nod, with careless reassurance, as if to say, "Don't worry. Of course I understand." And then there was a pause. But the Fairy made no move to go away.

"You mean—" The Little One was eager but restrained. "You mean I may have another wish?" The Fairy didn't move, gazing at her steadily, obviously assenting. "Oh, thank you very much—" But alas she didn't have another wish ready on her tongue, a dreadful situation. She should have known there would be three and should have been prepared.— Another wish, but what?—There was no time to lose: the Fairy's wings were quivering, as if to take to flight, and its little eyes looked sad and disappointed.—Oh dear, what could she wish?—And then inspiration came flashing to her aid. "Yes, I know," she cried. "Good Fairy, prithee please make Mamud disenchanted."

She was not certain what response the Fairy made, because at this moment something made her turn her head, some sound behind her. She turned to look and saw to her surprise she had come back to the ship, to the very spot from which the chase had started. There was the ruined castle, just a tiny bit of it sticking from the water. And there—

"O-h-h—" she shrieked. And well she might, for, intent upon her quest, not looking where she went, oblivious of the danger, she had walked into a trap—like a silly little fly into a spider's web. For there was Mamud sitting in the sand—a horrifying sight, his face all caked with blood, and his beard and matted hair white with the salt, looking like a Sorcerer taken unaware—sitting in the sand between her and the safety of the forest, so close that he could easily reach and grab her. No good remembering now, no chance to run or hide. "O-h-h—" she squealed again and turned back to the Fairy—"Good Fairy, save me, save me—" But the Fairy was not there. A golden butterfly was lazily winging off, disappearing in the distance.

In the meanwhile, in the forest, Pablo and Teresa had found a teeter-totter—a nicely balanced log across a fallen tree. They were sitting on the ends of it, riding briskly up and down, exclaiming with delight. Juan and Rosa came upon them in the midst of the affair—

"It's wonderful," they cried. "Just wait until you try it."

It was then that Rosa missed the Little One, not seeing her or hearing her, looking anxiously around—

"Where is she?"

"Where is who?"

"The Little One."

"She hasn't been with us. We thought she was with you."

"No." Rosa shook her head, beginning to be frightened.

"Maybe with Gil."

"No, not with Gil." They could hear Gil calling to them, but he was far ahead and his voice was growing fainter.

"Maybe building castles in the sand," suggested Pablo.

Castles in the sand! Rosa caught her breath. Juan was explaining to them: Mamud wasn't dead; anyway, it wasn't sure. Gil had seen him waking up and they had run away. The teeter-totter stopped, with Teresa on the ground and Pablo in the air.—Suppose he wasn't dead, and that he'd someway caught her!—Teresa scrambled off the log without a word of warning, and Pablo came crashing down with a rather painful bump.

"That wasn't fair," he whimpered, sitting glumly in the grass. "You always cheat, Teresa." But he got no sympathy. The matter was alarming.

"Gil! Come back!" they shouted. But he didn't answer, and they could no longer hear his voice.

By common impulse they ran back to the bluff, crouching in the bushes, peering through the leaves. The afternoon was waning, the shadows of the Giants stretching blackly toward the sea, but the Little One was not in sight; the beach and ship were silent and deserted.

"Little One!" they called.

"No, don't," Juan cautioned them. "If Mamud isn't dead we mustn't let him know." He was staring at the sand, at curlicues of footprints weaving in and out among the Giants, coming almost to the bluff, then circling back again. "See there," he said and pointed out her path. "She's been running all around."

They nodded earnestly. "But why?" they wondered.

"Maybe he was chasing her," said Pablo.

"No." Juan shook his head. "He couldn't on one leg." He looked and saw the leg, sticking safely in the ground where he had left it. "And anyway," he added, "her footprints are alone."

"What could she have been doing?"

"I don't know," he said. "But we'd better go and look."

They scrambled down the bluff in single file, with Juan in front, then Rosa, then Pablo and Teresa, frightened but excited, like conspirators or hunters, and crept across the beach, following the little footprints which were easy to distinguish from their own because they were so small—from one Giant to another, and all the way around it, and maybe back again, a completely aimless progress, or so it seemed to them. Here she had paused to scuffle or sit down, and there she had described a perfect figure eight. But for all their divagations the little footprints were leading to the sea, returning to the ship. Juan pursued them silently, stopping now and then when he was in doubt, when they were obscured or tangled in a maze that they had made. But then he would make certain and cautiously go on, while they followed at his heels. It was terribly exciting—

At last he stopped, a stone's throw from the sea, pointing to a humpbacked Giant between them and the ship. "See—" he whispered, "the footprints go behind it. But they don't come out again."

"Yes—" they nodded. This was plainly true: the footprints disappeared, and there were none returning on the other side. The sand was smooth and bare. "Then she must be there," they said.

"Wait," Juan bade them, "and I will go and look." And he crept away alone, crawling on his knees. They watched with bated breath. He went on till he could see what was behind the Giant, peeking around its knee, and then rose to his feet and came running back to them—

"Well?" they questioned tensely. But they saw in his eyes that it was something bad.

"Mamud is there," he said.

"And the Little One?" moaned Rosa.

"Yes—" He nodded bleakly. "Mamud must have caught her."

"Oh, Juan!"

"Is she dead?" asked Pablo.

No, she wasn't dead, Juan said. He couldn't see her plainly because Mamud was between them, sitting in the sand. But he had seen her move, so he knew she wasn't dead.

"Maybe tied with ropes?" Teresa ventured.

"Anyway," said Pablo, "he can't cut her up, because I've got his knife"; and he drew it, like a sword, from the cord around his waist and waved it in the air.

"But Juan—" Rosa seized his hand. "Oh Juan, what shall we do?" She wished with all her heart that Gil were there.

"I don't know," Juan said, looking very sad and helpless.

"But we've got to save her, Juan."

"Yes, of course, we've got to." His hand was trembling and drops of sweat were rolling down his face. "Don't worry, Rosa." Suddenly he snatched his hand away, and took the knife from Pablo—Mamud's long sharp knife—

"Oh Juan—" they gasped, admiring and incredulous. "Juan, what will you do?"

"I must kill him," gulped the boy, his face like chalk.

"But if he bleeds?" said Pablo. "And it makes you sick?"

"Yes, I know," he muttered. "But I'll try to kill him first." And he turned away and went running toward the Giant, the knife clutched in his hand, running straight, not faltering, not pausing to look back.

"Oh, good for Juan," they whispered, quaking on their knees.

And good for Juan it was. Good for Gil it would have been, had Gil been there to undertake the task, which he would have undertaken without any hesitation, with assurance and bravado, not thinking or imagining all the dreadful implications, not foreseeing his reactions which action would have clouded, not frightened until fright would be too late. But Juan was different—

His heart was like a bumping lump of lead. He was terribly afraid —not of Death, lurking there behind the Giant, nor of injury which might be inflicted or sustained, but of *violence* in itself, the bare idea of it, of hurting anyone or being hurt. But he wasn't analyzing what he felt. He could see the mermaid from the corner of his eye. He wished that God were there, tucked in his mother's arms—God about whom there could not be any doubt, whom he himself had seen, and who must be more important than Sorcerers or Witches—

He came to the Giant and peeked around its leg.—Yes, there they were, exactly as they had been, a few short steps away. The black man's back was toward him. He couldn't see the Little One, but he knew that she was there because he heard her voice.—He felt so sick and faint, his knees were wobbling; but with gritted teeth he tiptoed closer. He had decided what to do—to plunge the knife into the black man's back. But he must be close enough so he could not miss his aim, for when he struck the blow he meant to close his eyes. Another step would do it. He mustered all his strength and raised the knife to strike—

But suddenly the Little One came into his view, and he paused in stupefaction. She wasn't tied with ropes, but sitting at her ease—not sobbing in distress but giggling with amusement. The treasure bag was open and things spilled out of it, in her lap and in the sand: her tooth, the golden coin, and bits of broken glass. She was making little piles of different colors. And the big black hands were helping—

The knife dropped from his hand. The scene began to blur—the figures on the sand, the Giants, the ship, the sky, all whirling dizzily round him.

15

GIL RAN ON ALONE INTO THE FOREST, following the brook, splashing back and forth across it. He kept calling Juan and Rosa, urging them to hurry; he wanted them to be with him, to share this fine adventure. But he didn't wait for them, and then at last he could no longer hear their answering voices and gave up shouting to them. He felt a little hurt, neglected and abandoned—as men are like to do when they have run away and left their friends behind.

But he was not a man; he was still a little boy, and so his sense of injury quickly ebbed away, and was presently forgotten in the wonders of the forest: gold and silver fishes darting to the shelter of pebbles in the brook; a flight of bright green parrots diving through the air, like jewels with wings; four-footed creatures rustling through the grass. Rabbits perhaps, he thought. But they were not rabbits.

And there were trees with ripe and luscious fruit and bushes filled with berries—all unfamiliar to him, but most of them were good and he ate his fill of them, and crammed his shallow pockets with trophies of the chase to take back to the others—to show where he had been. He felt himself a hunter, an explorer. It was good to be alone, to find things by yourself. He might even find the mountains, the place where they began. The brook would lead him there; it was sliding down a gentle slope, gurgling as it ran, coming from the mountains. He could follow the brook all the way across the forest, to the very end of it, to where the mountains started, where he could look closely at them and really see how hard they'd be to climb. Yes, that would be exciting, and something to relate—

On and on he went, careless of the waning day, of the deepening shadows. But once he stopped abruptly, with panic in his heart, staring at a monster on a boulder in the brook, basking in a vagrant ray of sunlight. He had almost stepped upon it, thinking it a log, but it had moved and wriggled. It was horrible to look at, with an awful, scaly back and a horn upon its head.—A Dragon, he was sure, and almost turned and fled. But then he was relieved to see that no smoke came from its nostrils or fire from its mouth; and at length he mustered courage to poke it with a stick. It opened sleepy eyes, regarding him without any visible resentment, and slowly crawled away.—"Just a lizard," he assured himself. And so in fact it was, but a lizard like no lizard he had ever seen.

He went on, not running now, looking carefully where he stepped. But indeed it was no longer possible to run, for the jungle was tightening like a net, and the surface of the ground was thick with tangled roots, spread out in all directions, designed to trip your feet. The fresh air of the shore was left behind and it was stifling hot, even in the shade beneath the rustling canopy of leaves where it was always twilight. The forest fairly steamed, the greenery of its curtains wrapped in pallid vapor—like incense wafting up from Witches' cauldrons. And the smell was suffocating: the thick rank smell of lushness, of crowded living things battling for their lives, of Death and damp decay. Rotten logs caved in when he set foot on them and dissolved in reeking dust. Thorns and brambles tore and scratched him. The vines and creepers hung like webs of monstrous spiders, their waxy flowers peeking through the leaves like evil eyes. Sometimes he could hardly wriggle through, and would have to break the stems and tear his way.

Once, in a tangle of them, he was startled to observe a green stalk swaying strangely, out of pressure of his hand, not acting like a vine. He stopped to watch and hastily backed away. It was a snake, thicker than his arm, with wicked beady eyes, curling up into a tree.

He looked, with dampened spirits, for another way around, but a splashing waterfall barred his passage in the brook and the curtain of the forest seemed to be impenetrable. At length he gave it up and sat to rest himself. The quest of the mountains must await another time. Some day he would come back, with Juan and Rosa, and they would find a way—

The day had fled. The sun slid down behind the snow-clad peaks, and flames of gold and crimson leaped out from crest to crest and reached into the sky to paint the clouds. Blue shadows spread like stains and came creeping down the slopes, shimmering hazily in the valleys above the frozen rivers. The darkening forest massed itself against the mountains' knees; its nodding plumes and fronded leaves stood still. A breath of chill swept through it—

He shivered and jumped up, suddenly reminded that he was alone. He could hardly remember when he had been alone—out of sight and sound of them. It wasn't any fun, not when the sun had gone. Suppose he couldn't find his way and the night should come upon him—night in the forest, by himself!—In frantic haste he dove into the labyrinth, this way and that, his sense of direction lost in panic.—But at last, there was the brook! He heard the waterfall before he saw it, a friendly voice to guide him.

But it wasn't any fun—not going back. In the deepening dusk the forest was a dark and gloomy place, threatening and deceptive: stumps and logs assumed strange forms, boulders in the brook suggested crouching beasts, and every swaying vine might be a coiling snake. And the evening came alive with new and frightening sounds: creatures that slept by day and were wakening to the night—hooting, whistling, screeching; and rustling in the grass of things you couldn't see.—No, it wasn't any fun.—He ran, splashing back and forth across the brook, slipping on the stones which were thick with slimy moss, bruising his tired feet, careless of the lizards which brushed against his toes. The spirit of adventure had been quenched; he no longer felt himself a hunter or explorer.

Once, crawling through a maze of twisted roots, something leaped out of the tree above his head. He heard the branch snap back and a terrifying growl, and looked up just in time to see a shadowy object sailing through the air. It landed with a crash and went rustling away, with awful snarling sounds. He did not know what it was—a wolf or lion or tiger? But it was not a rabbit; he was sure about that. He lay flat upon the ground and held his breath till he could no longer hear it. And there was one dreadful moment when something whacked his neck and screeched into his ear, flapping in his face. This time he was certain that it was a Witch. But then, with vast relief, he saw it was an owl. It fluttered to a branch and looked down at him severely, hooting with annoyance.

He struggled on, clawing through the vines which curled about his arms and legs and clung to him like fingers, often falling down from sheer exhaustion, half crying from his aching weariness. It was almost dark when he heard their voices and knew that he was safe. He had never been so glad of anything. He was about to shout the news of his return, but then he thought it would be fun to creep upon them stealthily and suddenly jump out, growling like the creature that had scared him half to death—or snarling, if he could. So he crawled upon his knees from tree to tree, forgetful of fatigue and the terrors of his journey, practicing a snarl beneath his breath—wondering if they had been anxious about him.

But they were not thinking of him, and they hadn't missed him. Only Rosa had, and kept watching through the dusk and listening for his voice. But they had been very busy. They had swarmed aboard the ship and carried off the contents of the storeroom—all sorts of things, including delicacies for the mouse-man's table. And now they were at supper, sitting in a circle on the grass beneath a mighty tree whose lofty branches spread above them like a tent—a ceiba tree it was, with a trunk so huge that all their arms together would not reach around it. They were sitting at their supper, pleasantly relaxed, tasting strange things out of tins, some of which were good and others bad; but with the bad ones they did not waste any time and threw the tins aside—

"They would be good," Juan said. "The empty ones, I mean."

"Good for what?" they asked.

"To make a crown for her."

"A crown?—for who?"

"For God's mother," he explained. "When we bring her to the forest."

"Yes, maybe—" they agreed, without enthusiasm.

Once while they were eating there was a diversion, a rustling in the

grass and glimpse of something moving. They cried out in alarm, clutching one another. But then they saw it was the mother goat, with her
kids beside her, hidden by the bushes, awaiting invitation. They coaxed
her nearer, throwing bits of food. And a little later the sheep came with
her lambs, and afterwards the chickens. They crumbled biscuits and
scattered them about, and the chickens ate them greedily and then
flew up to roost in the branches of the tree. They were getting sleepy
when—

"G-r-r-r-r—" snarled Gil, in the best imitation he could muster, and
sprang out from the cover of a bush. The effect was disappointing. The
goat and sheep looked up in mild concern and the chickens cackled
drowsily from their roost, but the children only laughed—

"It's Gil," they said.

"I scared you," he insisted.

"No, you didn't, not a bit."

"What did I sound like?"

"Like you," they said.

"Ho!" he scoffed without conviction. "Well anyway, you should have
gone with me. You should have seen what I've seen." He came a step
or two and then he saw what had been hidden from him. He could not
believe his eyes, crouching back in horror, his blood like trickling ice.
For there was the black man in the very circle of them, his wooden
leg recovered—so close to Rosa he could reach his hand and grab her.
No doubt he'd crept upon them, sneaked up behind their backs. But
still there might be time—"Mamud!" he shouted. "Run!" And he himself
was running, or anyway his legs were. But he caught his foot and
tripped, sprawling on the ground.

It was really very funny, the expression on his face and the caper
that he cut when his toe caught in the root. They laughed until they
choked. Yes, even Rosa laughed.

And perhaps that's where it started—the real beginning of it, of all
that was to come, though it must have started soon or late, in one way
or another, for the seeds of it were there when he was born. But perhaps
this was the point in Time from which it could be measured and the
progress of it charted—when the hidden could be seen. Not *what* it
was, for they had always laughed at one another, at falls and fears and
blunders; and there wasn't in her laughter any taunt or ridicule, any

new or subtle meaning. No, not *what* it was, but *when*—the inevitable moment, the location on the graph—that graph which Kerch had pondered, through a haze of drugs and torment, in the twilight of his life—a point in arc, in the circle of experience, when events still far removed project their shadows. However this may be he was never to forget it, as he always had forgotten until now. The sound and source of it would linger in his memory, sometimes dim and sometimes clear, but never quite forgotten.

They were explaining to him, still shaken by their laughter. They had missed the Little One and couldn't find her, and then at last they traced her, by her footprints in the sand. But it was Juan who found her, with the black man on the beach, concealed behind a Giant—captured, they supposed. And it was Juan who went to rescue her—went with Mamud's knife. He had gone alone to do it—

"Juan was brave," they chorused.

And perhaps this added something which had not been there before, or served to underline something as yet unnoticed. But he had no sense of that, nothing more than a resentment, of a sort with many others—as if Juan should outwrestle him or beat him in a race, as he very often did—resentments which would flare up and as quickly fade away. But there was a difference, for he would remember this one.—He was listening to the babble of their voices, in a whirlwind of confusion, still on guard and poised for flight.

Yes, Juan had gone to kill him, they were saying, to creep behind his back and stab him with the knife. And he had found him playing in the sand, playing with the Little One, with the bits of broken glass—playing like a child. At first they had been doubtful, not willing to believe it, afraid to venture close. But Mamud had been more afraid than they were. He had tried to run away, but without his leg he couldn't. Pablo had fetched the wooden one, and Juan had put it on. But at first he couldn't walk on it and they had to help him. He had been so shy and timid, watching every move they made, not trusting any of them except the Little One with whom he felt acquainted.

"Just look at him," they said. And he certainly looked frightened; there was no denying that—anything but dangerous, huddled up and whimpering, winking back his tears, while the Little One consoled him with soothing sounds and gestures, patting his big black hand where the tooth marks were still visible, where Gil's teeth had bitten deep into the flesh beneath his thumb. "He's friends with us," they added. "But he's still afraid of you."

"It—it's just a trick," Gil stammered. But it obviously wasn't, and he knew it sounded silly when he said it. He sat in the grass, staring at the black man, across the circle from him and safely out of reach, eating some food Rosa put into his hand, chagrined and unconvinced, his own adventures dwarfed and become of no account—even the tiger —he had settled on a tiger—which had leaped out of the tree above his head. And the trophies of the chase—the fruit and berries crushed to pulp and oozing through his pockets. He felt victimized and cheated. If this thing had to happen he should have been consulted.

"No, it's not a trick," they said. "He's just a child—like us."

And so in fact he was—let who will explain it, and with whatever symbols they are qualified to use. Mamud was a child, despite his great black body, his beard and whitened hair—a child about the age, they thought, of Pablo, or as Rafael would have been, older in some ways and not so old in others; and like Pablo in some ways but in others more like Rafael—very sensitive and gentle.

Perhaps the falling spar had cracked his skull and done injury to his brain, erasing from his memory a segment of his life, returning him to childhood—to that moment in the slave pen when, waking from a stupor, he found his leg was gone.—Yes, that could be the way of it.

Or perhaps he had arrived at the bottom of the graph, the nadir of that circle Kerch had pondered—the point in arc when Life turns back again toward the source from which it came, when the bottom has been plumbed, when there is no depth of agony unsounded, when experience is complete and its purpose has been served, when the road is at an end and there is no way to go save back the way you came, when the human soul cannot sustain another straw of burden—then all may be cast off, and the homeward journey start.

Perhaps—perhaps—perhaps—

The tropic night fell swiftly, like a descending curtain. They were very sleepy now, and one by one they stretched out in the grass, lying in a circle, like the spokes of a wheel, with all their heads together at the hub. Gil had been long silent, deep in thought. At length he said in a very gloomy voice—

"Suppose it doesn't last?"

"Not last?" They stirred uneasily.

"Suppose he changes back?—the way he was?"

"Oh—" They hadn't thought of that, and they sat up in their beds, peering at the black man who seemed to be asleep. Still, there was no way of telling—

But the Little One could contain herself no longer. She hadn't told them anything, not being sure if the Fairy would approve a disclosure of the matter, and which might jeopardize her other wishes, though nothing had been said about keeping it a secret. But she couldn't keep the secret any longer; she was almost bursting with it. "He won't go back," she cried. And the way she said it commanded their attention.

"What makes you think he won't?"

"Because he's disenchanted from the mouse-man's spell."

"Oh, disenchanted—" They laughed half-heartedly. "What makes you think he is?"

"Because I wished he would be, and—" She hesitated.

"And what?" they prompted her.

"And the Fairy granted it."

"Fairy?" They sat straighter. "What do you mean? What Fairy?"

"The one that came to see me when you went away and left me."

"But—you're just pretending."

"No, I'm not," she said. And they knew she wasn't.

"You didn't tell about it."

"No.—Well, I forgot." This was not true.

"Well, tell us now," they urged.

"It just came by and stopped."

"Oh!—What did it look like?"

"Like a Fairy."

"Yes, but how?"

"You know what Fairies look like."

"Tell us anyway."

"Well—" The Little One considered. "It was small and beautiful."

"How small?"

"Like this."

"Like what?"

"Both my hands together, with the fingers open." But it was too dark to see.

"All right, go on," they said, a little disappointed.

"It came and sat down on the sand, right in front of me."

"Did it have a Wand?" asked Pablo.

"Yes, a little black one, underneath its wing."

"Oh, then it had wings?"

"Of course—big golden ones."

"Fairy!" hooted Gil. "I know what it was." He had been listening closely, propped upon his elbow, both hopeful and incredulous. "It was just a butterfly. And there are millions of them in the forest."

"Yes, a butterfly—" they sighed in disillusioned chorus, sinking back upon their beds.

"It wasn't, it wasn't," the Little One protested.

"How do you know it wasn't?"

"If it was a butterfly—" She cocked her head in triumph. "—how could it grant my wish?"

This was unanswerable.

"I asked the Fairy to make Mamud disenchanted, and when I turned around it was already done."

"Why did you ask for that?" inquired Gil suspiciously.

"Because I couldn't think of anything to wish." And this was true.

"Pooh!" jeered Pablo. "You could have thought of a better wish than that."

"No, I couldn't," said the Little One, and went on to explain, "I already had two wishes and this one was the last, and I had no time to think."

"Oh!" Again they stirred and sat up in their beds. "What about the others?"

"I don't know if I should tell—"

"Why not?"

"The Fairy might not like it."

"You told us one."

"Yes, but not until I got it."

"Oh, go on," they urged. "The Fairy will not mind."

"Well—" She was dying to tell them. "I wished to have a dog."

"Good," they murmured, nodding with approval.

"A dog like Trictrac."

"I don't see any dog," Gil laughed contemptuously.

"Of course you don't, not yet," the Little One retorted. "You don't always get your wishes the moment that you wish them."

"Never mind," they said. "What was the other wish?"

"If I tell you will you promise not to laugh?"

"We promise," they agreed.

"All right, but don't forget."—She was silent for a moment. It was somehow hard to say, to tell that secret wish.—"I asked the Fairy to let me live here always in the forest, for ever and ever."

"Oh—" They didn't laugh.

Pablo had been pondering. "It doesn't matter much," he grumbled drowsily, "because she only wished it for herself."

"Yes, you should have put us in," Teresa said reproachfully.

"But—" The Little One was startled and contrite. "But how was I to know if you'd want a wish like that?" Though in truth she hadn't thought of them. "If the Fairy comes again," she added hastily, "I'll wish for all of you."

"Just a butterfly," Gil muttered, stretching out upon the grass. But he wasn't sure of it.

And it really makes no difference what or which. The point is that the Little One believed it was a Fairy. And in matters of this sort it is not *what* one believes, but *believing* that's important. So perhaps it was to her—the believing of a child—that Mamud owed his life, this strange renewal of it.—Perhaps—perhaps?—Who can say about these things?

The black man whimpered in his dreams—the deep voice of a man, but the whimper of a child. It seemed very strange and startling, a little disconcerting. And it was strange indeed! Though stranger things have happened and are happening every day, if one stops to think about them.

The stars popped from the sky and twinkled through the trees; and monstrous fireflies sailed among the branches, like swarms of dancing sparks—or Fairies carrying lanterns. Owls hooted, crickets sang, whip-poor-wills called out across the forest, and far-off hunting creatures gave voice to mournful cries.

The children snuggled closer. "What are those sounds?" they whispered.

"Wild beasts."

"Tigers," Gil said carelessly. But they were not tigers.

"Oh—" They nodded, yawning. It didn't really matter; they were not afraid of beasts, not while they were together.

"What shall we do tomorrow?"

"Tomorrow," said Teresa, "I'll make a wreath of flowers to wear around my neck."

"Tomorrow," said Rosa, "I'll gather oranges." She had seen them hanging from the branches of a tree. But they were not oranges.

"I'll build the house," said Pablo.

"Yes, good," they murmured. "But what shall we build it of?"

"We could build it out of sand," the Little One suggested. "And the roof could be of shells."

They laughed at the idea.

"We'll build it out of trees," said Gil, "so it will be strong."

They sighed contentedly. But it would be long before they built a house, and it would not be like any house they'd ever known or dreamed.

"And Juan? What will you do?"

"Me?" Juan thought about it. "Perhaps I'll find a piece of wood to make the baby's body."

"If you do," said Rosa, "we'll help you take the mermaid down and bring her to the forest."

"Yes, we'll help you," they agreed, hoping in their hearts that it wouldn't be tomorrow. And it wouldn't be tomorrow, nor for many of them.

The Little One was chuckling to herself. "I know what we'll do," she said, "tomorrow and tomorrow—all of the tomorrows."

"What?" they questioned sleepily.

"What they do in all the stories."

"Well, what?"

"You ought to know," she said, amazed at their simplicity. "Of course we'll just live happily ever after."

"Oh—" They nodded in the dark, repeating softly, "Yes, happily ever after." It seemed too good to be true. And so in fact it was.

One by one they fell asleep. But Gil remained awake, thinking of the mountains which some day he must climb, to find out for himself what was on the other side. They could not be far away, maybe not much farther than he'd gone this afternoon.—But they were farther than he dreamed.

Feeling Mamud's knife tucked against his side, fingering the edge of it—seeing in his mind Juan running through the sand with the knife grasped in his hand. But he hadn't killed the black man or done anything at all. He'd been sick and fallen down, though not until he knew that the Little One was safe.—Watching the stars twinkling through the leaves—wondering if it could have been a Fairy. If it hadn't been just Mamud! If it had been a dog—a dog like Trictrac! Well, he wasn't sure just how he would have felt, nor very sure now.

Thinking what he'd wish if a Fairy came to him; and it made his heart beat faster, even thinking of it.—His eyes were winking shut and he turned upon his side, cheek pillowed on his arm, snuggling close to Rosa.

And then he was asleep.

16

HAPPILY EVER AFTER—
Time fled, or it stood still. But what was time to them?
—that bridge contrived by men to bear their hopes and
sorrows. They had no hopes or sorrows, none they could
remember long enough to need a bridge. The moment was too full:
an overbrimming cup, like the magic pitcher which never could be
emptied. Yesterday was gone, merged with all the others; and tomorrow
was unborn, not borrowed to beguile the passing moment.

There were no milestones on the road. Time was not divided by dis-
tinguishable seasons, for it was always summer. The sun came bursting
from the sea and sped across the sky until it dipped from sight behind
the mountains. The great white clouds lay sleepily on the far rim of
the world; the little waves broke gently on the beach. It was light and
it was dark; that was the only measuring rod they had. There were no
anniversaries, fête days, birthdays, days with names and numbers.

They kept no record of them, cut no notches in a stick, in the way of shipwrecked men; inscribed no diaries. They couldn't read or write —only Gil and Rosa could a little bit, and they had almost forgotten.

Sometimes on the beach they would write things in the sand, where the tide had ebbed away and left it damp and firm: "Gil and Rosa" and the names of all the others, fearfully spelled and with letters upside down. Or one might leave a message for the other: "Am swimming." —"Gone to cave."—Things like that. Big letters you could read, even standing on the bluff, if you knew where to look; and if you were acquainted with the crazy hieroglyphs and incredible phonetics. But in time they learned to read the things they wrote, which the sea would smooth away when the tide came back again, never leaving any trace or any memory.

The days ran by like the water in the brook, singing through the pebbles, hurrying to the sea. There were so many things to do; they could never finish one before they were embarked upon another. And everything was new: the waterfall cascading down the bluff, and you could slide down with it, half smothered in the foam, till you splashed into the pool which was perfectly designed for sailing boats; and the long white beach with its company of Giants, and files of scurrying crabs; and caves in the bluff which the sea had hollowed out, whose narrow depths were dark and monsters might lurk in them. And the rocks with glistening seaweed when the tide ran out, and you could walk on the bottom of the sea among the wading Giants whose legs were crusted thick with shells and starfish; and pools with fishes in them, and shells that walked about. There was no end to wonders.

They did not go near the ship. Once the storeroom had been emptied there was nothing to attract them. But there was a better reason for avoiding it. The mouse-man was still there, inside his house. And, as the Little One reminded them, though his head was half cut off his heart might be alive and its power of enchantment undiminished. They had laughed at the idea, not unimpressed.

"You'd better not," she warned, "for if his heart's alive, it still can cast an evil spell—just like it did to Mamud."

Whatever they thought, they did not go near the ship; it was no use taking chances. And they presently forgot the mouse-man and his heart, even the ship itself, which more and more resembled the rocks on which it rested and came to be in time just a fragment of the scene,

like the Giants upon the beach. But the mermaid was still there, on
her perch between the Twins, and Juan did not forget her.

When the sun was high and hot the forest beckoned them into its
pleasant shade: trees that pleaded to be climbed, and the tall and
slender ones in which the milk nuts clustered—impossible to reach,
though Gil kept trying. But you could throw stones at them and sometimes bring one down, watching out it didn't fall upon your head. And
endless teeter-totters, and swings of hanging vines, and the friendly
little brook where the big brown lizards basked—dreadful looking
creatures when you first encountered them, but on close acquaintance
they proved to be quite harmless, as most things proved to be. To be
sure there were quantities of bugs, and savage little ants that nipped
as hard as crabs. But they could be avoided if you looked out where you
trod and were careful where you sat. The forest was a perfect place
to play at hide-and-seek, but you must not go too far away, not out of
sound of voice, for it would be very easy to be lost.

But they were not tempted to stray far into the forest. There was
too much at hand. Even Gil was content with the close familiar scene,
forgetful of the mountains, too happy to remember.

They forgot about the house they meant to build, remembering when
it rained—not the pleasant little showers which happened every day,
when vagrant clouds came tumbling down the mountains, quickly drifting by, melting in the sun; when everything was dry again as soon as
it was wet, when you could see the rainbows through the rain. No,
that they loved—the pattering on the leaves, the sweet damp smell and
the refreshing coolness. But there were storms, when drenching rain
poured down and lightning split the clouds and thunder crashed and
rumbled, when the wind came howling from the sea and the milk trees
bent like whips, and waves swept high upon the beach, breaking on
the Giants and burying them in spray.—Exciting times, not dreary
unless they lasted long, and they rarely did.

They would run to the shelter of the Tent tree, beneath whose
spreading branches they would be quite snug and cozy, though the roof
might leak a little. But that was no great matter: they had nothing that
would suffer from the weather. They had *nothing*: that was it. They
were free of all encumbrances, possessions to protect—nothing save the
rags upon their backs, grown very ragged now.

Teresa would tell stories to pass the time away. Juan would be carving something, as indeed he always was, in every idle moment.

"What is Juan making now?" somebody might ask. And one would look and answer—

"Another head for God."

"Oh that!" And they would laugh. It had come to be a joke.

He had made so many of them. God's body had been finished long ago, and lay beneath a bush, neglected and forgotten. And the crown, cut out of tins, had been fashioned, set with jewels; and was somewhere, thick with rust. But God's head was still unfinished, or rather there was none to satisfy the sculptor, not a milk nut in the lot. He would sort them over thoughtfully and reject them one by one.

"But this one," they'd suggest, selecting a lugubrious, wizened face, reminiscent of the melancholy Juana. "This one will do."

"No." Juan would shake his head.

"Well, this one then."—A baby Caliban, or another like a mummy, or one as blank as putty.

"It's not like God," he'd say.

"What difference does it make?"

"I want it to be like him, the way that I remember."

"But God won't care."

"No." He was not to be persuaded; and he would make another, and another, and another. There was quite a pile of them.

"Look!" they'd cry. "The sun is coming out." And God's head would be forgotten, and the house they meant to build.

They forgot—forgot—forgot—

They forgot that Mamud had ever been a man, forgot to be surprised that a child should have a beard and a rumbling voice like thunder, They had accepted him—as a little boy about the ago of Pablo, or as Rafael would have been, in some ways older, and not so old in others.— For example—

He could catch fish, with a hook made from a sea bird's bone he found upon the beach. And this was good for the tins were soon exhausted. He knew many things to eat, growing in the forest and underneath the ground, which they might not have found or thought to sample; and he had names for all the forest things—strange sounding names that were difficult to say. He knew about the chickens, where they laid their eggs; and how to milk the goat and where the sheep would graze. If they did not come home he could always go and find them, though he didn't always want to. And he could hunt, stalking careless little creatures with a spear—a slender shaft of wood with a sharp stone at the end, bound fast with strong tough grass—a harmless looking weapon, but deadly when he cast it with a wide sweep of his arm. He could even make a fire without matches—a miraculous affair till you learned how it was done. And they would learn from him, acquiring his skills in great or less degree; and he would learn from them, their way of life. Strange blending of experience. Even their language came to be in time a mixture of the two, of Galla and of Spanish, and words that they made up to serve for things unknown in either language.

There was one thing very strange: it seemed as though he knew things that he didn't know he knew—

Once, fishing on the rocks, he stepped off a ledge into deep water. And there were fearful splashings and frightened, strangled cries; and then he sank from sight. But before he disappeared they saw his face—the terror in his eyes.

"Mamud will be drowned," they cried. They did not know what to do; he was too far out to reach. But then he reappeared, not crying out or splashing, and began to swim around—as if he hadn't known he could, or ever tried before—swimming like a fish, whisking through the water and laughing with delight.

"But he's swimming," they exclaimed, staring in relief, and a little envious too, for none of them could swim.

"Oh, it's easy," Gil remarked with affected nonchalance.

"Easy?" They were doubtful. "What makes you think it is?"

"Well, look at Mamud."

"But maybe he knew how and then forgot."

"Anyone can do it," Gil assured them.

"Let's see you," said Pablo.

"Me?" He had no idea of trying, but then he noticed Rosa looking at him—

"Don't, Gil!" She shook her head.

"It's easy," he repeated. And he gritted his teeth and valiantly jumped in. But it was not so easy as he hoped, and his secret doubts about it were immediately confirmed, for despite his frantic efforts he could not stay afloat. Through a blur of spray he saw the others watching from the rocks, and caught a fleeting glimpse of Rosa's face. He tried to cry for help, but he was choking, strangling. And then the water closed above his head and he knew that he was drowning—

And no doubt he would have drowned if Mamud had not come in answer to their shouts, and quickly fished him out—waterlogged and scared and gagging from the salt, but otherwise unharmed.

"Oh yes, easy!" gloated Pablo when the danger was resolved.

"You wait—" he gulped, "—till next time."

And if not the next time, still, in time he learned to swim. All of them did, and could dart about like fishes, quite as well as Mamud, even Juan with his one arm—swimming under water, which was so crystal clear they could plainly see the bottom: the rippled sand and shiny leaves and waving stalks of kelp, and shells for which they dived in eager competition—playing hide-and-seek among the wading Giants, whose shoulders they would use for diving platforms, and whose laps were basking places, like bath chairs in the sea—swimming far out to the reef where the big waves roared and pounded, and the white lace hung above them.

Things like these they learned from Mamud, challenged or encouraged by example; and might not have learned without him. But in other ways he seemed much younger—

He loved to play—childish games which even Pablo would not condescend to. The Little One was his adored companion. They were a funny pair, comical to look at, for in the beginning her head reached not much higher than his wooden leg—the great black figure and the tiny girl, trotting off together.—Yes, it was a funny sight, but they soon forgot it was.—He would sit with her for hours, building castles in the sand. And they collected things: shells and pebbles and the empty claws of crabs, and flowers from the forest, wandering here and there till she was tired; and then she would command—

"Carry me, Mamud!" And he would pick her up as if she were a feather and whisk her to his shoulder, with her feet locked round his neck, clinging tightly to his head. And away he would go, running like the wind, while she shouted in his ear, "Faster, Mamud! Faster!"

Perhaps, next to the Little One, he liked Teresa best, for she was easy going and rarely interfered with what he chose to do. And he loved to listen to her stories and would clap his hands with joy when she began, though he didn't at the start understand a single word. But sitting in the evening in the circle round the fire, he would follow the proceedings with riveted attention, laughing when they laughed and sharing their excitement, seeming to absorb from her performance what was taking place upon the stage which was peopled with Teresas impersonating Witches, Fairies, Sorcerers, Princesses and Princes escaping desperate hazards by the slim breadth of a hair.

Sometimes she would dance; and then he was in raptures, and would jump to his feet and imitate her steps, or improvise strange dancing of his own, hopping up and down, and making funny sounds in a shrill and altered voice. And he even made a drum: a hollow end of log with the skin of some dead creature stretched across it. And when Teresa danced he would rap it with his knuckles, while Juan blew on the whistle—its three melancholy notes.

He was a happy child—about the age of Pablo, though he sometimes seemed much younger. But then something would occur to upset the calculation. For the skills of his hands were not forgotten—even those he had acquired in the dead span of his manhood, of which not any memory had survived, no moment since that one when he wakened in the slave pen and found his leg was gone. But the skills were still alive, buried deeply in the flesh, from which they could be summoned when there was need to use them. Like the way he flung the spear. It was really not a spear; it was too short. And he held it in his hand more as one would hold a knife, flatly on the palm with the thumb across the haft, flinging widely to the side, not as one would cast a spear.

Gil had watched him like a hawk, to find out how it was done. And he had been practicing—practicing in private, stealing off alone, not wanting to be laughed at, but determined all the same. He would aim at a mark, a stump or tree, and pelt away at it until his arm was tired; and now and then he'd hit it, but more often not. It was very hard to do and he almost gave it up. But then at last one day he seemed to get the hang of it. Time after time the spear sped straight and true, and the sharp flint in its head was buried in the target—not always just the spot at which he aimed, but always close to it. He was very much elated, proud and happy, eager for the moment when he could really try it—

And the moment was at hand. For hurrying homeward through the forest twilight he saw a small green bird perched on a branch—a pretty little bird, sitting all alone, cheeping to itself. Cuddlebirds they'd named them, because nearly always there would be two of them, billing and cooing, cuddling close to one another. And the name had been well chosen, for in the world of men they are known as lovebirds—diminutive parrots that show, or seem to show, great affection for their mates. But there was only one sitting on the branch. Perhaps it was waiting for the other to come home.

He didn't think he'd hit it, if he thought at all. He had no expectation of success as he poised the spear, held flatly on his hand with his thumb across the shaft, testing the balance of it. It was done without reflection, without intent or malice—just aiming at a mark he was certain he would miss.

And at first he thought he had. The spear appeared to strike the branch and drop into the grass; the bird had vanished—fluttered off, he thought. But when he went to get the spear he could scarce believe his eyes, for the little thing was lying there, on the ground beside it. He stooped to pick it up, with a sharp pang of remorse, cupping it in his hands, looking for a wound. But there was no sign of one, no drops of blood; the feathers were unruffled. He turned it in his hands and pressed it to his cheek, as if to give it life out of himself. And then he felt it move, softly quiver in his hand; and remorse took instant flight. No, it wasn't dead. The spear had only grazed it and knocked it from its perch. Elation flooded back. He had hit it, a target no broader than a leaf, and from a decent distance—a feat of arms which Mamud couldn't equal or surpass.

He tucked the bird inside his shirt and went running home to find them, to show them what he'd done, the fruit of perseverance, of all the hours he had spent alone, pelting at the stumps with aching arm. And as he ran there flashed into his mind a thrilling idea: He would give the bird to Rosa, give it to her for a pet; he would make a cage for her to keep it in. A real live cuddlebird! Not something made of wood, like the things that Juan kept carving—little figures, heads, and boxes, which he made and gave to Rosa, or sometimes to Teresa, which were no good for anything. But they were always thanking him and saying it was wonderful. But a real live bird was a substantial gift, not easy to be got and deserving to be cherished. It would make her think of him every time she saw it. Maybe she could teach it to sit upon her shoulder and go with her everywhere. For a moment he was tempted to keep the bird himself. But no, it was for Rosa; the gesture was compelling. And he had captured it, had struck it with the spear, not hard enough to hurt it, but just to knock it down. He felt himself a hunter.

They were all of them together, as he had hoped they would be, when he ran into their midst, breathless and excited, calling out before he got there—

"Just wait until you see—" And when they had jumped up and gathered round him, properly impressed, curious and eager to know what he had found, while he reached into his shirt, feeling the soft warm body—but it did seem very still. "It's for Rosa," he explained as he drew it from his shirt. And he put it in her hands.

"Oh Gil—" she said. And warmth went surging through him. He was repaid and glad.

"A cuddlebird!" they cried, amazed and wondering. "However did you catch it?"

"With the spear," he told them. "It was sitting on a branch, as far away as that—" He pointed to a bush which perhaps was somewhat farther. "I threw the spear and knocked it off its perch."

"Oh—" They looked distressed.

"But I didn't hit it hard," he added quickly.

"Oh Gil—" she said again. But it didn't sound as she had said it first, and he felt a sudden chill of apprehension.

"Don't you want it, Rosa?"

"It—it's dead."

"Dead?" He stared at her. "No, it isn't dead. It was alive; it moved." He snatched it back and held it to his cheek. But it wasn't moving now. Its little head hung limply on its breast.

"Oh Gil," she said, "how could you?" And there was such reproach in her voice and eyes! It shriveled him inside.

None of the others spoke, their eyes upon the bird. But there was condemnation in their silence.

"I didn't mean to kill it," he said defensively; and then he added, mumbling, "Mamud kills things."

Still nobody spoke. But he knew what was passing in their minds: Mamud didn't kill little cuddlebirds.

"All right, it's dead." He threw it on the ground. "And I don't care," he said, scowling and defiant. And he turned his back on them and stalked off to the beach.

Mamud and the Little One took the cuddlebird away and made a grave for it. They bordered it with pretty shells, and in the very center placed a bit of broken glass—the last one that remained in the chamois treasure bag.

17

IT MIGHT HAVE BEEN THE NEXT DAY, OR THE NEXT, that he announced abruptly, when they were eating breakfast, "I am going off exploring."

It was said provocatively, but it failed of its intent—not for any special reason: they had no reservation in their minds, no shadow of resentment. They had forgotten all about the cuddlebird, though he had not. He addressed the Little One, who had not made any comment. "You can't go," he said, "because you are too small." And this evoked response.

"Exploring?—where?" they asked.

"In the forest." He waved his hand expansively.

"Oh, the forest—" They nodded, but it didn't sound exciting.

"Maybe clear across it."

"No—" They shook their heads. "You never could."

"Oh yes, I can," he said. "And once I did—almost to the end of it, where the mountains start."

"When?" They were startled and suspicious. "You never told about it."

"Didn't I?" He shrugged. "Maybe I forgot." And so in fact he had—till yesterday.

"Did you climb them to the top?" inquired Pablo.

"Climb them to the top?" He laughed indulgently. "Why, that would take all day. But I almost got to the place where they begin."

"Oh, just the bottom of them—" They nodded, unimpressed.

"It's a long, long way," he said.

"What is it like back there?"

"Wonderful," he told them. "Much more beautiful than this."

"But how?"

"Oh, the trees are thicker, and—and you should see the milk nuts. They're twice as big as these."

"Twice as big—" Juan murmured, his eyes agleam with interest.

"Are there flowers?" asked Teresa.

"Better ones than here."

"But if you get lost?" said Pablo.

"You can't get lost if you stay beside the brook."

"Does the brook come from the mountains?"

"Of course it does. Where else?"

"I'd like to go," said Rosa, dreamily to herself. "I'd like to see the mountains, to really see them close."

"Would you?" It was this that he was waiting for and hoping. "All right, I'll take you with me," he said gruffly. But that was what he wanted more than anything on earth: to show her how he'd find his way across the forest, and guide her safely through it, protect her every step. He turned to the Little One again, repeating his original admonition. "But you can't go," he said, "because you are too small."

"I don't want to go," she answered. "And Mamud doesn't either."

Juan was listening thoughtfully, not saying anything.

"Let's all go," cried Pablo.

"If you want to," Gil said glumly. He had been afraid of this. "But it's hot back there," he added.

"Hotter than the beach?" asked Teresa anxiously.

"Twice as hot," he warned. "And the vines are so thick sometimes you have to crawl on your hands and knees."

"No—" She sighed regretfully. "I think I'll stay at home."

"I don't care," said Pablo. "I'm going anyway."

"All right—if you want to." Gil was silent for a moment, communing with himself. "When I went the other time I saw a snake," he said, "as big around as I am."—"As my arm," he meant to say, but the other words came out. "It was hanging from a branch. It looked just like a vine."

Pablo shivered slightly. "What did it do?" he questioned.

"Nothing—" Gil admitted. "But once—" He scooped the final morsels of his breakfast from the bowl. "Once I was almost killed."

"Killed?—How?"

"A savage beast jumped at me from a tree."

"What kind of beast?"

"A tiger—or it might have been a lion."

"Oh—" Pablo caught his breath.

"It landed on my back." He was hastily combining the adventure with the owl. "Its claws were on my shoulder."

"What did you do?"

"I fell down flat and pretended I was dead, and then it went away."

"Weren't you scared?"

"Of course I was—a little."

He got up from the log on which he sat and went to find the spear; and when he returned he observed with satisfaction that Pablo wasn't there. The others called to him but there was no response. Pablo had disappeared.

"No matter," Gil said cheerfully. "We've got no time to wait." And he motioned Rosa to come on. But then he saw with blank dismay that Juan was doing something—taking down a rucksack from the branch on which it hung. "What's that for?" he muttered.

"For the milk nuts," Juan explained. "To bring them back."

"Oh good!" cried Rosa, seeming very pleased about it. "Juan is going with us."

"Milk nuts—" mumbled Gil. "But the trees are full of milk nuts."

"Big ones," Juan replied. "Like the ones you said we'd find."

"Oh those!" He could have bit his tongue off for the useless fabrication. "They aren't so very big," he stammered weakly.

"Anyway," said Juan, buckling on the rucksack, "anyway, I'd like to see them."

"I could take the sack—" Gil was thinking fast. "And bring some back to you—if you don't want to go."

"No." Juan shook his head. "I want to see the flowers, and what it's like back there."

"Well, there are snakes and beasts—"

But Juan was not to be discouraged or diverted—not ever when he had a notion in his head. And he had one now: a bigger, better milk nut for God's head. And so they started off, the three of them, on very different quests.

It wasn't a success, not from the start.

They followed the brook, splashing back and forth across it—a familiar easy path, at least in the beginning, though even at the start there were annoying aspects, for Juan could not be hurried and was always lagging back to look at this or that—the color of a pebble or the shape of some old stump, endless worthless trifles which only wasted time. And Rosa wouldn't go ahead without him, and was always running back to see what he had found. So every little while Gil would find himself alone, shouting back to them to hurry, shouting and waiting, his patience wearing thin—

"We'll never, never get there," he kept warning them, "if you don't hurry up." And they'd promise to do better, and for a while they would, but then it would be the same again.—It wasn't fun, not at all as he had pictured it—tearing through the forest with Rosa at his side, always at his side or close upon his heels, holding back the vines for her to pass, taking her hand to guide her. If only they had come alone, just the two of them!—He stopped again to shout, "Hurry! Hurry up or I won't wait for you." But of course he waited. What else was there to do?

And they did make progress, for at last the forest tightened in the way that he remembered. They came a little faster now, or perhaps his pace was slowed. And if he was far ahead, or even out of sight, it was Rosa who was calling—

"Gil! Where are you?"

"Here!"

"Please wait for me."

"I'm waiting. Hurry up!" And he'd wait until she came, and then they'd wait for Juan, sitting on a log, sitting close together.

"It's so hot—" she said. And it was stifling.

"Yes, but I don't mind." He was simply drenched in sweat.

"What makes it smell so funny?"—The sweetish, rotten smell of dampness and decay.

"I don't know." He was prodding with the spearhead in the rotten log. "But I kind of like it."—This wasn't true. It was a sickening smell.

"Do you?—Oh!" She puckered up her nose. "And it's so dark and gloomy."—And it was dark and gloomy, doomed to perpetual twilight, for the sun could never penetrate its depths.

"If it wasn't," he said, "it would be hotter."

"Yes, perhaps—" She nodded. "The forest is so thick, not like ours at home—" She glanced around and shivered. "It's almost like a net." —And it was like a net: the mata-palos vines dripping from the trees— tree-killers, they are called, because they wrap around them, even mighty ones, and strangle them to death.

"Oh, this is nothing yet," he told her carelessly.

"Is it much farther, Gil?"

"Farther?" He laughed. "Why, we haven't even started."

"Oh—" She could not repress a sigh.

Then Juan caught up with them. He had found a lovely flower, a purple orchid bigger than his hand. He displayed it with delight and put it in the sack with other souvenirs he had gathered by the way. But he hadn't found the milk nuts, not any that were bigger than the ones at home, and he was growing anxious.

"Farther," Gil said briefly.

On and on they trudged, scrambling over, crawling under things, tripped by hidden roots and scratched by unseen brambles; and though Juan would lag behind, Rosa stayed close by him. Still, it wasn't fun, like it had been the first time, as he remembered it. But then it had been new, and the newness was exciting.

The jungle tightened and the twilight deepened. The friendly little brook flowed blackly through a tunnel, so narrow that at times they couldn't wriggle through and must leave its course and find a way around. At length there was a waterfall which was too steep to climb, and when they had crawled out to seek another path, they faced a wall of tightly woven creepers hanging from a tree, in a maze of twisted roots that grew above the ground—a forbidding and impenetrable labyrinth.

There was something reminiscent in the look of it, and the slippery waterfall. Yes, it was here, he thought, or in a similar place, that, peering through the leaves on that other trip, he had seen the green stalk swaying, out of pressure of his hand—and had seen it was a snake, the color of the leaves and thicker than his arm, with wicked beady eyes, curling up into the tree. He approached with cautious steps, the spear poised in his hand, but he saw nothing disturbing in the somber, tangled depths.

"Gil—"

"What?"

"Are we nearly there?"

"About halfway," he said. But this was pure conjecture.

"Only halfway?" She sank down in the grass.

"Well, maybe a little more—" He was debating whether to crawl into the tangle or try to find a better way around.

"Gil—"

"Yes?"

"Let's not go any farther."

"What?" He turned and came back to her. "But we're going to the mountains."

"No, this is far enough."

"But you haven't seen them yet."

"I've seen them far away."

"You haven't seen them close."

"I don't care," she pleaded. "I don't want to see them close."

"Why not?" he grumbled, startled and disgusted.

"Because I don't, I don't. You said it would be beautiful—more beautiful than home."

"Well—" But he couldn't think of an appropriate answer.

"Well, it isn't," she said, half crying with fatigue and aching misery. "The forest isn't good, the way it is at home. It's ugly and it's horrid."

"You wait, you'll see," he muttered, and turned and strode away.

"No, Gil!" She jumped up in alarm. "Where are you going?"

"Over here to look if there's an easy way."

"No, please—" But he was gone.

She stood where he had left her, afraid to move, in a strange un-
reasoning panic—more afraid than she had been that awful day in the
mouse-man's house; and afraid in that same way, of something that
could not be rationalized, something deeply hidden, but the air was
filled with it, a suffocating terror. Interminable moments ticked away.
She heard a sound behind her and dared to turn her head. It was
one of those ugly yellow birds with big black spectacles. Witchbirds,
the Little One had named them, insisting that they were, or might be
anyway. Not Witches probably, she told herself, but ill-tempered
and unpleasant. It sat there staring at her in a disapproving manner,
making scornful, croaking sounds; and she moved a step away, closer to
the vines, beneath a thick brown limb, around which another branch
was twined.

Gil went back toward the brook, poking with the spear, searching
for a way around the tree. It was only a few steps. He was angry, out
of patience, with her and with himself. Nothing had turned out as he
had hoped it would, which is the usual way of too much hoping. And he
was tired too and beginning to be doubtful that the mountains would
be reached, though he wasn't yet prepared to admit that to himself. He
wished he'd come alone, or hadn't come at all. It was no place for a
girl, even one like Rosa, and Juan was not much better, stopping
every minute to look at silly things or pick a flower. Well, that was
not the way to find the mountains. He heard Juan coming now,
splashing through the brook, and shouted irritably for him to hurry up.

He had found a place where it seemed to be more open. And he
hadn't wasted time; it hadn't taken long, only a few moments. He called
to her to come, but she didn't answer him, nor when he called again.
And then, a little anxious but mostly irritated, he went running back to
get her—

"Rosa! Rosa!"

Yes, there she was, standing where he'd left her—standing with
her back to him, looking up into the tree, gazing at the branches
which were twined above her head. But one of them was not, for it
was hanging down, swaying gently back and forth—

"Rosa—" But the sound caught in his throat, entangled with his
heart. That swaying thing was not a branch. It was a snake, thicker than
his arm, swaying back and forth, swinging lower, lower—till its head

was almost level with her face. He could see the beady eyes, like great black buttons—the partly open jaws and dripping fangs. And there was a hissing sound, like the steaming of a kettle.—His feet had turned to lead, but at last he found his voice—

"Rosa! Run!" he yelled.

But still she didn't move. And then—oh horrible to see!—the snake whipped out like lightning and coiled around her body, wrapping round and round, pinning her arms against her sides, its great flat head above her, waving slowly back and forth.

She screamed—the breath crushed out of her. He saw her feet lifting from the ground. And there he stood, as if turned into stone, the spear dangling loosely at his side, useless and forgotten. Suddenly he felt it slip out of his hand, and thought that he had dropped it—if he thought at all.

Then Juan brushed past him, pushing him aside. And he saw, as one sees things in a dream, in a helpless, fleeting moment, Juan running at the snake with the spear clutched in his hand, not holding it to fling not knowing how to do it—but running straight upon it, close up within its reach, and stabbing with the spear, as one would stab a knife. Stabbing, stabbing, stabbing at the soft wide yellow throat, from which the blood came gushing—dodging in and out to avoid the darting head which dove at him in fury and tried to strike him down, rearing through the vines, ripping them to shreds, hissing in its anguish like a thousand boiling kettles.

All in a fleeting moment, the figment of a dream. The coils relaxed, unwrapped, and Rosa tumbled from them, scrambling on her knees, sobbing, sick with terror, but uninjured. And still Juan went on stabbing till the throat was filled with holes, spattering blood like rain. A moment more the snake clung to the branch, and then came crashing down among the roots—threshing, twisting, writhing, then rustling in the leaves, and the hissing dying out.

And Juan lay stretched upon the ground, the spear still in his hand, his white face streaked with blood. And Rosa crawling to him, sitting in the grass with his head upon her lap, leaning to press her cheek against his face—

And he just standing there, not doing anything. What had there been to do?—the spear snatched from his hand, his weapon stolen from him before he had a chance. In another moment he would have thought of it.—But would he? And what would have happened in that moment of delay?—He tried to kill the doubt, as he should have killed the snake, stifling his shame and nourishing his injury. Yes, he would have killed it, not poking it to death, but taking careful aim, flinging straight and true, piercing through the yellow throat. If Juan hadn't interfered, if he'd had another moment—

She raised her head and looked at him, with eyes that were ablaze behind her tears. The gentle, kindly Rosa, not kind or gentle now, but hysterical with fright and grief, and bitterly reproachful—

"See what you've done," she sobbed. "He's dead and it's your fault."

"He isn't dead," he mumbled, sullen and defiant, not knowing if he was, not caring very much—not at the moment. He came a step or two, staring down at Juan, and saw he wasn't dead, for he was breathing, moving. "He isn't hurt a bit," he said contemptuously. "He's sick, that's all, the way he always is when there's any blood around."

But she wasn't listening to him. She wet her dress against her tongue and wiped the blood streaks from Juan's face, tears running down her cheeks and dripping onto his.

"I would have killed it if—"

Again she raised her head. "No," she cried, "you wouldn't." Still sobbing and hysterical, not knowing what she said, not really meaning it, "You just kill cuddlebirds."

It was as if the spear had pierced his heart. He waited for a moment, kicking at the grass, and then he stooped and took it from Juan's hand, and walked away into the thicket.—Well, it was plain enough: Juan was the one she liked.—"I don't care," he said.

The snake was dead, still wriggling. He poked it with the spear but it offered no resistance. Yes, it was dead all right; its throat was cut to shreds, the head almost cut off. He dragged it from its coils and stretched it out. It was thicker than his arm and very long—a formidable reptile. He wondered, with a shudder, if there might be another, and looked carefully in the branches and down among the roots which grew above the ground in an amazing tangle. There was no sign of one, of anything that moved.

But then he thought he heard a sound and poised himself for flight. —Yes, there it was again—like a baby crying, or a little creature whining. He searched the shadows with his eyes but he couldn't see a thing. It wasn't in the tree but somewhere on the ground, underneath the roots. He scrambled over them, peering underneath, poking with the spear, getting colder, getting warmer. And then at last he found it, hidden in a burrow deep under a root. Lying flat among the roots he could look in and see it—a little creature scarcely bigger than a kitten, with fur as black as coal and tawny, playful eyes. It was all alone and crying, sort of whining to itself. He reached in cautiously and got it by the neck and dragged it out.

A little baby creature all alone. Why had it been left? Where were its mother and its father? Perhaps the snake had eaten them, and its brothers and its sisters, all the family but this one, which perhaps it couldn't reach. He hugged it in his arms, fondling the silky head against his cheek. It was just like a puppy, though its big soft paws had claws as sharp as needles—so wobbly on its feet, hardly able to stand up.

He ran back to them with it in his arms. Juan was sitting up, all right again; and Rosa wasn't crying. For the moment he forgot.

"Look," he cried, "what I've found."

"A kitten!" Juan exclaimed.

"No, a puppy," Rosa said. "Oh, let me hold it, Gil."

"It's a baby animal," he told them gruffly, and put it in her lap.

"What kind of animal?"

He shrugged indifferently, avoiding looking at them—the two of them together sitting in the grass—his brief elation melting, feeling ill at ease, self-conscious and unwanted—feeling these emotions for the first time in his life in relation to his friends, his own, his family, not knowing what they were, not yet acquainted with them. "Anyway," he said, "I'll take it home."

"But its mother?" ventured Rosa.

"It hasn't any mother. It was all alone in there, hiding from the snake. It's an orphan, I suppose."

"Oh—" She nodded, sighing. "But how can you carry it?"

"I'll put it in the sack." And he picked up the rucksack which Juan had flung aside when he charged upon the snake.

"But the milk nuts," Juan objected.

"Milk nuts?" He'd forgotten.

"The big ones that I came to get, the ones you said we'd find."

"Oh those!" He shrugged again. "Maybe they weren't so big as I thought they were."

"But—" Juan was disappointed. "Aren't we going to look? You mean we're going home now?"

"Yes, home," said Rosa quickly, scrambling to her feet.

And he did not protest. He was ready to go home. And so they started back—a tedious, silent journey, the little creature whining and clawing in the sack, but still at last and probably asleep. Juan was far behind, but they didn't stop to wait for him, nor call to him to hurry.

Once on the way she said, toiling painfully at his heels—

"I'm sorry, Gil."

"Sorry?" He didn't look around.

"For what I said."

"Oh, that's all right," he mumbled.

But it was not all right. And now there were two of them with something to remember.

18

"TRICTRAC!" CRIED THE LITTLE ONE.

"Trictrac—" They were startled.

"I knew it," she exclaimed with rapturous delight. "I knew it all the time." She took the little creature and hugged it in her arms.

"Knew what?" they asked.

"That I would get my wish."

"What wish?"

"The wish the Fairy granted."

"Oh that—" They laughed, but staring, incredulous and wondering.

"But it's not a dog," Gil said.

"Oh, isn't it?" She smiled with airy condescension. "Then tell me what it is."

"What?" He scratched his head, as many an authority has done in similar circumstance. It was not a lion or tiger; he was sure about that.—It was in fact a panther, but of panthers he knew nothing.—"Just an animal," he told her.

"Well what's a dog?" she said.

"A wild one," he amended.

"Oh, a wild one!" And she laughed with amiable indulgence.—It did seem silly to dispose of it like that—the playful little creature with its head against her cheek.

"You'll see," he muttered grimly.

"I see now," she said. "It's a baby Trictrac—just exactly what I asked for."

"Humph!" He grunted scornfully, but without much confidence. It did resemble Trictrac—what Trictrac might have looked like when he was a puppy.

"I've got all my wishes," she announced ecstatically. "All three of them are finished."

"All three—" they said suspiciously. "What about the first one?"

"Oh that!" She tossed her head. "I've had that all the time."

And it seemed as though she had.

Time fled, or it stood still.—They grew—outgrew their rags, which were gradually replaced with garments that they made, which Rosa and Teresa plaited out of grass, and skins of animals that Mamud brought them—enough for decent covering, though they were not prompted by a sense of modesty. They had no shame of their bodies and swam together naked as the fishes, but the habit of their clothing was not easily put aside.

They grew tall and strong and brown—as brown as Pablo now. Only Mamud stayed the same, a permanent guide to growth. Gil's head reached to his shoulder, and the Little One's had risen to his waist. They grew beautiful in fact: lithe slender bodies, with rippling muscles under satin skin.

But Trictrac grew the fastest. Lying stretched upon her side, from the whiskers on her nose to the tip of her long tail, she was as tall as Mamud.—Yes, *her* side, for, as it turned out, Trictrac was a girl: a matter, when discovered, which cast a shade of doubt on the transaction—

"But—" the Little One indignantly protested when the matter was called to her attention. "But I didn't ask the Fairy for a boy dog."

"You asked for a Trictrac, and Trictrac was a boy."

"What difference does it make?"

"It makes a lot of difference."

"Well, what?"

"A boy dog can't have children."

"Oh, is that all?" She dismissed it. "Well, I think it would be nice for Trictrac to have children, and I'm glad the Fairy thought of it."

"But it isn't Trictrac," they insisted.

"Of course it is," she said. "It is for me." And that ended the discussion.

But that was long ago and long forgotten, when the panther was a baby and no one could foresee what she would become. She had grown up among the lambs and kids, which themselves had grown up and indeed had multiplied; and she was still friendly with them, though not the way she had been. She would lie and watch them with her head between her paws and a curious expression in her sleepy, yellow eyes— thoughtful and perplexed, as if she might be pondering their old relationship, weighing and considering in her mind. The chickens which had used to scratch around her, even perching on her back, scurried off when she came near and kept respectful distance.

She did not resemble Trictrac, not remotely. But they had forgotten that, or what Trictrac had looked like. They had accepted her: Trictrac was Trictrac—black and sleek and graceful, soft-footed as a cat, with long cruel claws discreetly hidden in their velvet pads—except when she was fishing. She would stretch out in the sun on a rock beside a tide pool, indolent and beautiful, apparently asleep, but with one wakeful eye. Her tail would wave a little; then suddenly a paw would reach into the pool and scoop a careless fish onto the rock. She would play with it a while and finally eat it, leisurely and daintily, picking out the bones and pushing them aside.

Gil was her favorite. She went with him everywhere, following like a dog, carrying the spear between her teeth. And she was jealous too, of attentions he bestowed or that were bestowed on him. Sometimes when they were playing, being rough or wrestling, she would snarl with disapproval—watching Gil, springing lightly here and there to keep him in her view; her back would arch, hair bristling on her neck. At night she slept against his feet. She did not care for Rosa or Teresa, and never followed them.

They grew older. Only Mamud didn't, and the Little One not much, for they still spent endless hours building castles in the sand and playing with the treasures in the little chamois bag—the tooth and golden coin, and pebbles they'd collected to replace the bits of glass which were finally exhausted—all the things they had done. But you could no longer say that Mamud was a child about the age of Pablo. He was definitely younger; and so it must be Pablo who was getting older. Still, aside from such devious computation, there wasn't any yardstick to measure what was changing, any visible progression such as children have in school. They grew older all together, unaware of what was happening, not seeing any change. Certain games stopped being fun, but they stopped for everyone; and then they were forgotten.

Somewhere along the way the house was built.

It turned out to be an endless undertaking, having its beginning when Trictrac was a puppy; and it was still unfinished when she was grown up.

It had been Gil's idea. A day when he was bored, not for a fleeting moment between this thing and that, but restless and unhappy, seeking desperately for engrossing occupation to absorb his mind and muscles, to leave no room for memories which kept circling through his head: the cuddlebird, the snake, the things she'd said; and the sight of them together—they were much together now, Juan always carving something out of wood and Rosa watching him, or helping him to hold it. Though in fact the fault was his, for it was he who shunned them, who would shake his head ungraciously in response to invitation, who would go to swim alone, not telling them or asking them, never leaving any message written in the sand—playing childish games with Pablo and Teresa, pretending it was fun—even condescending to Mamud and the Little One, building castles in the sand. But he only tried this once, and monopolized the matter, finding fault with their construction, until at length they sat and would have no part in it. And then he lost his patience and kicked it all to pieces. They were glad when he went and left them to themselves.

Something had gone wrong, very wrong indeed. But only Gil and Rosa were much aware of it, and by no means constantly, for there were many interludes when things seemed to be the same as they had always been. But they weren't the same, not quite, and could never be again.

However this may be, one day he said abruptly, "I'm going to build the house."

"Yes, good!" they cried, delighted with the idea.

"Where shall we build it, Gil?"

"Come on," he said, "I'll show you." And he led them to a spot, deeper in the forest, but not very far away—a damp and dismal hollow where the ground was thick with ferns, and the branches overhead so tightly laced that the sun could never pierce them.

"Why here?" they questioned doubtfully, enthusiasm waning.

"Because I like it here."

"Oh—" They gazed uncomfortably, thinking of the Tent tree which was in a pretty glade, always bright and cheerful. "Why not at home?" they asked.

"Because it's safer here."

"Safer?—from what?"

"Storms and beasts," he told them. "Everything," he added.

"But it's so dark," said Pablo.

"Gloomy," said Teresa, wrinkling up her nose.

Mamud and the Little One had already run away, without interest in the matter. And Juan had made no comment, his eyes fixed on the burl of a dead, contorted tree, admiring its design.

"It's lonely," Rosa said.—And lonely was the word.—Likely enough that was why he chose it, feeling in the place something kindred to his mood, for he was lonely too.

Anyway, that's where they built it.

It was Mamud in the end, after several futile starts, who had known how to do it, though he was of little use when it was once begun, for he would sneak away at every opportunity, and even hide from them, abetted by the Little One. And Pablo was not faithful; he would go to cut a pole and simply not come back. Teresa made no pretense of assistance.

So it was the three of them—Gil and Juan and Rosa—who really built the house. But in a way Gil built it all alone, for Juan spent half his time carving pictures on the poles, paying scant attention to the things that were important; and Rosa came and went, exclaiming with delight at some new piece of sculpture, scarcely noticing the house. She would help them for a while, or sit and watch, and then she'd go away.

Only Trictrac was devoted, loyal and unfaltering: at first a tiny puppy playing in the grass—then almost grown up, lying by the hour in a bed of soft green ferns, with her muzzle on her paws and one keen eye watching him, waiting patiently until he should be done—till he flung the ax aside. She would raise her head alertly, wrinkling her nose, smiling with delight, waiting for the moment he would call to her to come. And then she would leap up, with the spear between her teeth, whining with excitement, bounding after him—to go swimming in the sea or hunting in the forest, treading close upon his heels, obedient and content.

But this wasn't every day, for the house did not progress in a consistent fashion, but by fits and starts. There were long periods when it would be forgotten, when nobody went near it. But then the restless boredom would come on him again, and he would remember and plunge back at the task. And they would come and help him when it suited their convenience. But he often worked alone, with only Trictrac there —cutting poles and digging holes in which to fix them, lacing them together with strands of twisted grass, which Mamud knew to do but never would—then, near the end, making bundles out of leaves to thatch the roof, broad flat leaves that would shed the rain like shingles. It was a tedious business, tying them together, then climbing up to bind them into place. He sometimes wondered why he bothered with it, for no one seemed to care except himself.

It was a funny house, ridiculous in size: the seven of them couldn't have got into it at once, unless they all stood up, and then their heads would have bumped against the roof, and Mamud's gone right through it. But even if they could have crowded in, it is doubtful if the house would have sustained their weight, for it leaned this way and that, and everything was crooked. There was no way that Trictrac could get into it at all, because it stood on stilts—like a beehive in the air. The door of it was higher than the top of Mamud's head, and you had to climb a ladder to get in. It did not have any windows, but excellent ventilation through the cracks between the poles, in the walls and through the floor.

Yes, it was a funny house, built out of Mamud's memory. And it was safe from beasts, even lions and tigers, none of whom could reach it—safe from storms no doubt, in the shelter of the trees and the hollow of the ground—safe from everything, once you were inside with the ladder pulled up after you—safe from prying eyes—

He was thinking this one day, when the house was almost finished, working on the roof, fastening on the thatch. Juan had been helping him, climbing up the ladder with bundles of the leaves and standing in the house to reach them through the roof—a pretty easy job. But there had been long delays, when he waited empty-handed. And he was waiting now, his patience wearing thin—

"Juan!"

"What?"

"I need another bundle."

"All right—"

He waited, crouched uncomfortably upon the slippery thatch, chopping with the ax at a knothole in a pole. "Juan!"

"Yes?"

"What are you doing?"

"I'm coming right away."

"Well, hurry up! I'm waiting."

"All right. I'm coming now."

But he didn't come. Gil couldn't see him, though he craned his neck to look. He was under the edge of the overhanging roof, doing something. Yes, but what? There were bundles of thatch ready waiting on the ground; and Trictrac was in view, lying in her fern bed, her head cocked watching him, hopeful and expectant. His patience was exhausted and he swung down to the floor, with the ax gripped in his hand. Kneeling on the floor he could see between the cracks. Juan was standing by the ladder, doing something to a pole. He listened and could hear the nicking of the knife—just as he'd expected.

"So that's why you don't come!" he shouted angrily, and went scrambling down the ladder.

"I—I'm coming now," Juan stammered, guilty and contrite. "I was just starting, Gil." And he turned to get a bundle of the leaves. But Gil already had one in his arms.

"Well, you needn't," he said, almost crying with vexation. "I don't want any help, from you or anyone. You just waste time, that's all. You'd never build a house."

And then his eye took in the sculpture on the pole—a smooth, round pole beneath the door, where everyone would see it, where it couldn't be avoided. He had carved a snake around it, round and round the pole, its flat head reaching up—reaching toward a bird whose wings were spread for flight.—A little cuddlebird!—Though probably it wasn't; nor was there probably, in the artist's thought, any meaning or intent —just a pole that lent itself to that sort of composition. But to a guilty conscience all things have significance.

"God damn you," he said. And if not the first time he had ever said those words, the first time anyway he had ever said and meant them.

Juan gulped and stared at him, incredulous and hurt, not seeing in the matter any cause for such abuse. Often enough he had delayed when Gil was waiting for him. The panther stood up in the ferns, arching her back and watching, her long tail swaying gently.

"You let my house alone." And that was new—"*my* house." He dropped the thatch and gripped the ax in both his hands, chopping at the pole, ripping off the carving—the head, the cuddlebird. "I'll show you," he kept shouting.

"But why?" Juan mumbled.

"Because I don't want it there."

"It's just a picture, Gil."

"No matter, I don't want it."

"But—"

"It's my house. Mine."

"Yes—all right," Juan said. And he turned and walked away, stumbling through the ferns.

Gil watched him go, his passion flickering out. "Juan!" he called. "Juan, wait!" Perhaps he didn't call as loudly as he thought; or perhaps it was too late. Anyway, Juan kept on going, not even looking back.

"Juan, come back!" he cried. But Juan was gone, vanished in the forest.

He sat down on the ground, and Trictrac crouched beside him, making little whining sounds, looking up into his face.—His friend was gone—his gentle, faithful friend. Oh, they had quarreled sometimes —but not like this.—He was alone at last; he had come as far as that.—

He wept hot, burning tears—tears for himself, for all the yesterdays, nostalgic tears of grief and of remorse—staring through them at the house: the crazy, crooked hut stuck up on stilts, and the dismal spot he had selected for it. Yes, it was safe all right, but safe from what?

Suddenly it all seemed folly to him, childish and absurd: the house, his life, the forest and the sea, everything he knew. He choked his tears away and scrambled to his feet—

"Come on," he said, "let's go!" And he strode off toward the beach, the panther at his heels, with the spear between her teeth.

Rosa saw him sitting in the sand—saw him from the bluff where she was idly strolling, not knowing what to do, feeling restless and unhappy, but not knowing why she did. Pablo and Teresa had gone swimming. They had called to her to come but she hadn't wanted to. She could see them splashing through the waves and hear their laughing voices. Mamud and the Little One were playing in the forest. She could hear their voices too, chattering with delight over something they had found. She wished that she were young again—as young as they, or even as young as Pablo and Teresa who couldn't be much younger than herself. She wished that yesterday could be brought back again. She wished, she wished—She did not know what she wished.

It was then that she saw Gil, sitting in the sand in the shadow of a Giant, with Trictrac stretched beside him, writing something in the sand with the handle of the spear.

She hurried down the bluff and ran across the beach under cover of the Giants, coming up behind him softly, meaning to surprise him, catching sight across his shoulder of her name writ in the sand, and an unfamiliar word she didn't know. But Trictrac growled and spoiled it; and she had no time to look; for he quickly brushed his arm across the sand and rubbed it out. His face was flushed and angry, but she had no notion why. She sat down at his side and Trictrac edged away, hair bristling on her neck.

"What were you writing, Gil?"

"Nothing—" he mumbled, poking at the sand.

"But I saw my name."

No answer.

"What was the other word?"

"Nothing."

"But I saw it."

"Well, then you know," he muttered, digging with the spear.

"No, I don't. You rubbed it out before I had a chance."

"Humph!" He scowled suspiciously.

"What was it, Gil?"

"No matter."

"Write it again and see if I can read it."

"No." He jerked away. "And you had no business sneaking up to look."

"Oh, Gil—" Quick tears welled in her eyes. "I wasn't doing that, not sneaking up to look."

"Yes, you were," he grumbled. "Anyway, you wouldn't care."

"Care?—for what?"

"For anything I wrote."

"All right—" She stood up, hurt and angry.—Why must he be so mean?—always saying hateful things and spoiling everything. And the word?—what did it matter?—"If that's the way you feel—" She lingered for a moment but he didn't look around. And then she turned and trudged back toward the bluff, pausing once or twice, pretending to pick something from the sand, hoping he would call her. But he didn't call or look.

Juan was standing on the bluff within her view. She saw him with relief, with a stir of expectation.—Good, kind Juan—sometimes irritating when he was carving pictures and didn't even hear you when you spoke—but never cross or hateful.—She waved to him and ran, climbing nimbly up the path beside the waterfall—

"Juan—" she cried, a note of desperation in her voice, and came running through the bushes to his side. "Let's do something, Juan."

"Something, Rosa?—What?"

"Anything," she said.

"Well—" He thought about it. "We might take the mermaid down."

"The mermaid?—Oh!" Her heart sank miserably.

"And bring her to the forest, the way we said we would. And put her in a church, with the baby in her arms."

"Yes—" She nodded wearily and sank down in the grass, gazing at the mermaid in the cleft between the Twins—the weather-beaten face and rusty trident.

"I was looking at her now," he went on with mounting interest. "It would be nice, I think, to have her in the forest."

"Yes, nice—" Again she nodded.

"We could do it, too, if the other ones would help. Mamud could carry her."

"Yes, some day, Juan." And then there was a pause until suddenly she said, almost breathless with her eagerness to know, "Are you always happy, Juan?"

"Happy?" He looked startled.

"I mean, here in the forest?—living here?—just us?"

"Why yes, of course," he smiled, sitting down beside her in the grass.

"You don't need anything?"

"Anything?" He pondered. "I'd like a better knife, and—"

"No," she interrupted. "I don't mean things like that."

"Oh!" He reflected and then he shook his head.

"Yes—" She nodded to herself, as if she had expected him to answer in that way.

"Aren't you?" he asked.

"What, Juan?"

"Aren't you happy, too?"

"Oh yes—" she said, confused and stammering. "Well, I don't know. I used to be." And then she faced it honestly. "No, not very, Juan."

"But why?"

"I don't know why. Sometimes I think—"

"Think what?"

"Nothing," she said and laughed, for she was at the end of what there was to say.

"But the forest hasn't changed." He studied her with anxious eyes. "Everything is just the same."

"Yes, just the same—" She plucked a blade of grass and drew it through her teeth, not looking at him.—Yes, everything was just the same: the trees and hanging vines, the flowers and the birds, the playground of the Giants, the forest and the sea—everything unchanged but like castles in the sand, like the games of yesterday.—"Yes, everything—" she whispered. "Everything but me."

Gil sat moodily in the sand, writing with the handle of the spear.

And this is what he wrote, in twisted crazy letters: "*I love Trictrac.*"
But it wasn't spelled like that. He smoothed the sand beneath it and
composed another line: "*Trictrac loves me.*" And then he looked around
and saw them on the bluff, sitting close together in the grass.

So that's where she had gone!—Well, let her!—But in his heart he
had hoped she would come back. Suddenly he jumped up from the
sand, tramping out what he had written, running toward the sea, calling
Trictrac to come with him, diving through the surf, swimming like an
otter. And the panther swam beside him, with the spear between her
teeth.

Far out they swam, to the farthest of the Giants, buried deeply to
his elbows, facing the open sea with folded arms—a narrow ledge of
rock on which they clambered out. The forest and the mountains were
no longer in his view; there was nothing to be seen but the flutter of the
lace above the reef, and the wide blue sea beyond it. He was safe from
prying eyes, from reminders of defeat. Pablo and Teresa were much
closer to the shore; they had called to him to come and dive for shells,
but he hadn't answered them. The panther shook the water from her
coat and stretched out lazily on the ledge, with graceful, languorous
ease. There was just room for both of them. He lay against her, with
his head upon her shoulder.

It was cool in the shadow of the Giant, against the smooth wet
rock, with the ripples of the sea spreading thinly on it. The water and
the air were soft as down, fragrant and caressing; and the sound of the
sea was like a song—a tender, whispering voice. Trictrac's fur kept
brushing, tickling on his neck as she moved to lick her paws, wrinkling
her dainty nose at the flavor of the salt—

"Don't," he said. "Be still." He closed his eyes, hands clasped above
his head, feeling the fur beneath them, and the muscles in her shoulders
moving up and down—soft and warm and living, and the beating
of her heart. He snuggled closer to her, in the hollow of her flank,
beneath her leg which drooped across his shoulder. When she reached
to lick her paw, her breath was on his cheek; she was purring in his
ear, languidly content. Lying there against her living warmth, his eyes
half closed, feeling her, not seeing her, she did not seem like an
animal; and he forgot she was—

"I love—" he said, and caught his breath, for he had never said the word aloud before. "I love—Trictrac." And he added softly, "Trictrac loves me."

He felt her licking tongue upon his cheek. And suddenly he turned and flung his arms around her—tight around her neck, hugging her close to him, burrowing his head against her—"I love you—love you—"

Perhaps the panther only meant to play, postponing her submission with feline modesty. Or perhaps it was too new, she herself but just emerging from her childhood to a strange, uncharted segment of the graph—that biologic circle Kerch had pondered.—Perhaps, perhaps?— At all events she snarled, drew back, her yellow eyes half closed and startled danger in them. The long sharp claws shot from their velvet pad and struck at him like lightning—ripping across his arm.

"Trictrac!" He jerked away, staring at his arm, at the blood oozing slowly from the deep and ugly scratches—amazed, incredulous. "Trictrac—" he gasped. But then his anger flamed. "You—you—" he gulped, half sobbing. And he struck her in the face, cuffing back and forth with all his might.

She cowered from him, whining, holding up her paw to shield her face—she who could have felled him with one blow, who could have sprung upon him and torn him to pieces with a fraction of her strength —cringing from his hand, whimpering like a child.

"I hate you—hate you." He struck and struck until his arm was weary, until his fury dulled; and then he turned and dove into the sea, swimming blindly toward the shore, not looking back. And the panther swam behind him, with the spear between her teeth.

I love you—I hate you.—Poor unmeaning words, inextricably tangled; or words so vast with meaning that no meaning can contain them.— Poor Trictrac and poor Gil.

She dropped the spear upon the sand and crouched beside it, waiting, her muzzle on her paws and her yellow eyes upon him, soft and pleading. He stooped to snatch the spear, looking at his arm—the red, raw scratches, tingling from the salt—

"Go on," he said. "Get out!" And he jabbed her with the spearpoint, in the soft flesh of her neck.

She cried and stood and backed away, backing step by step, her nose against the sand, begging with her eyes, saying she was sorry. But there was no forgiveness in the prodding spear. At last she turned from it and went slinking toward the bluff, pausing to look back, to listen for a word. But there was none. And she went on again—up the path into the forest.

He watched her out of sight, and when he turned his head—there was Teresa lying in the sand, almost at his feet, propped upon her elbows, staring at him—

"But why?" she said, wide eyed.

"Because—" He stood there, scuffing at the sand.

"What has she done?"

"Nothing—"

"Why did you hurt her then?"

"Because—"

"What's happened to your arm?"

"Nothing," he mumbled. "I scratched it on a rock."

"Oh—" She stretched out lazily, too indolent to probe the matter further. But she thought there must be more to it than that.

He stood there looking at her, scuffing at the sand. And suddenly he saw her, as he'd seen her every day since Time began and yet had never seen her until now—like a figure carved in driftwood, a slender graceful figure, warm and brown, basking naked in the sun, her long black hair like a cape around her shoulders, half concealing the near promise of her breasts—desirable and beautiful, and evil. He scowled, his face flushed red, sweat trickling on his neck—

"You—you—" he muttered.

She looked up, startled.

"You should be ashamed," he stormed.

"Ashamed?" She sat up in amazement. "Ashamed of what?"

"Lying there—with nothing on."

"But why?" She stared, bewildered.

"Because—because—" he stammered.

But she waited for no more. There was something in his face that frightened her, and she sprang up like a deer and ran away.

Trictrac did not come home for supper. But no one made any mention of her absence, for Teresa had reported what she had seen and heard—not the part about herself, which she thought would just sound silly, which for some other reason she didn't want to say, but the rest of it in full. They listened, grieved and puzzled.

"But what had she done?" they asked.

"Nothing," Teresa said. She had come out of the sea with the spear between her teeth, the way she always did, and dropped it in the sand. And he had picked it up and driven her away, sticking the pointed end into her neck until she cried with pain.

They shook their heads in horrified dismay.

"The Fairy will not like it," the Little One remarked, looking very solemn.

"Fairy?—What Fairy?"

"The one that Trictrac came from."

"Oh—" They nodded thoughtfully.

"Maybe he is crazy," suggested Pablo gloomily.

"Bewitched," the Little One said firmly.

"How would he get bewitched?"

But that she couldn't tell. There were many ways, she said, and no way to tell which one, unless he himself should know.

"Oh well—" They turned the matter in their minds, impressed but unconvinced. It was not a pleasant idea.

He had thought they would ask questions and was prepared for that with some answers he'd invented. But they asked no questions. Trictrac wasn't there, in her accustomed place, but they didn't look around or call to her, as they would have done any other time. Nor did they ask about his arm, pretending not to notice the way he tried to hide it. He thought that Rosa glanced at it with a sorrowful expression in her eyes, but when he caught her looking she quickly looked away. None of the others seemed to notice it at all, or really notice him. It was not a cheerful meal; even Mamud and the Little One were silent and depressed, missing Trictrac from the circle, wondering where she was and why she didn't come.

He sat by himself, sullen and detached, aware of something hostile in the air—something he had never felt before—just a breath of it perhaps when he killed the cuddlebird, long long ago. But this was something else, of another sort than that, or maybe a deepening of it— something hostile and suspicious, impossible to cope with. He felt himself alone in the very midst of them.

"I don't care," he kept saying to himself. "I don't care what they think." He was watching for Trictrac from the corner of his eye, listening for the sound of her approaching through the grass. He was sure she'd come home before it was quite dark. But when the darkness came she wasn't there.

That night he couldn't sleep, tormented by his aching arm, by grief, humiliation—by bewildered wretchedness. He kept straining his ears for the snapping of a twig, raising on his elbow to peer into the night, thinking he saw the glint of yellow eyes, but they would be fireflies flitting through the trees—feeling certain she would come, rustling softly through the leaves, to cuddle at his feet.

19

TRICTRAC DID NOT COME HOME.
They called and searched for a day or two or three, and then gave up the quest, convinced that she was gone. Only Gil did not give up nor cease to grieve. Day after day he went trudging through the forest—whistling, calling, looking, searching tangled thickets where she might be hiding—

"Trictrac!—Trictrac!"

Standing still with pounding heart, thinking he heard her whine, or the rustling of her paws among the leaves, or that he glimpsed her crouching in the shadows—

"Trictrac!—Trictrac!"

But it would turn out to be a root or log. Often at the start he had been so sure of it, certain he had found her; and sometimes he had cried with disappointment—tears that rolled unheeded down his cheeks, for there was no one to see and so it didn't matter—

"Trictrac!—Trictrac!"

Calling, tramping on, all the places they had used to go together, all the forest paths they'd known so well, returning in the twilight, weary and discouraged.

"Did you find her?" they would shout, in the beginning, when they saw him coming home—a gesture of politeness, for they knew he never would.

"Not yet," he'd answer gruffly. And after a while they didn't even ask.

He never went to swim with them, nor joined in any games. In the morning he'd be gone and would not come back till night; and then he'd sit apart, outside the circle of them, silent and detached. It was hard to laugh when he was there, and their chatter would subside. Teresa rarely told them stories any more, and Mamud begged in vain. They would watch him covertly, half wishing in their hearts he'd stayed away. Not that they accused him or were grieving about Trictrac. That was past and gone and infrequently remembered. It was something much more subtle, which they didn't understand or try to analyze. But he was like a stranger, no longer one of them, almost like a—But they never went so far as to put that into words, or ever really think it. They were just uncomfortable when he was there. Mamud and the Little One kept well out of his way. He was short and sharp with them. And though Rosa often watched him, with a pucker in her brow and sadness in her eyes, she could hardly ever think of anything to say. He seemed so far away—so very far.

"Trictrac!—Trictrac!"—They'd hear him all day long, calling in the forest. But as time went on they didn't notice, or stop to think about it.

And one day he gave it up. He had looked in every place they'd ever been together, not once but many times. It was no use to search; he was at the end of it. He had come back past the house—the crazy, crooked beehive stuck up upon its stilts, just as he had left it that day he'd quarreled with Juan, when he'd claimed it for his own—an empty claim which no one had debated. There it stood, unfinished, the ladder propped against it, part of the roof still missing, and some bundles of the thatch still scattered on the ground. There was the pole on which Juan had carved the picture, and the ax with which he'd sliced it off lying close beside it. The picture was effaced, every vestige of it vanished; but when he ran his hand along the wood he could feel, or thought he could, the contour of the snake.

There was the hollow in the ferns where Trictrac made her bed, which it seemed might still be warm from the pressure of her body— the flattened fronds and broken stems where she had waited for him so many patient hours, first a little puppy playing in the grass, then slowly growing older, growing up.

He lay down in the fern bed, hands clasped beneath his head, his eyes half closed, thinking back upon those bygone days with sad nostalgic yearning—as one thinks about one's childhood, when the world was good and beautiful and there was no end to it, when there were no problems in it, not any to remember, no bitterness or grief, nothing to regret—when each day was like another, like a never ending song, and you could scarcely wait for the sun to rise again. He was thinking of these things when he saw the butterfly, scarcely noticing at first. A golden butterfly, with stripes of black upon its wings—like little Wands they were. Just a butterfly, like millions that flitted through the forest. But still the crazy notion popped into his head—

Suppose it was a Fairy! Suppose it really was!—He watched it with a tightening of attention, winging lazily up and down, but not going far away and always coming back to circle round him. He sat up in the ferns with quickening pulse, observing what it did—curious behavior when you stopped to think about it, as if it were inviting him to take an interest in it. He rose upon his knees, being careful not to frighten it; when it disappeared behind a bush he quickly crawled to look, fearful for a moment that it had gone away. But it was coming back. It came very close indeed—so close that he could see its tiny eyes which seemed to be regarding him with critical precaution—but unafraid and friendly. And then it settled down upon a blade of grass, so near he could have reached it with his hand. And there it sat, as if it meant to stay, motionless and waiting.

"Good Fairy—" he began, and almost went no further, for the sound of his voice was funny in his ears, and the words he had spoken were funnier than that.—Kneeling on the ground, with his hands clasped like a priest, talking to a butterfly, asking it for things!—Just suppose someone had heard him!—He glanced anxiously around.

But suppose it was a Fairy!—It hadn't flown away. It appeared to be waiting, looking at him closely, inquiringly, he thought—perhaps a little mournfully, as if it were regretful of delay.

"Good Fairy—" he repeated, fumbling in his memory for the proper formula. It seemed to shake its wings, suggesting that its patience was drawing to a close. But he remembered now, before it was too late. "Good Fairy, prithee grant my boon—" It was waiting, listening to him, its little head cocked on one side so as not to miss a word. "Please bring Trictrac back. Please bring her right away." It appeared to nod its head, but still it sat there waiting. "That's all I want," he said. "My only wish." And then it spread its wings and slowly fluttered off.

"Just a butterfly," he muttered, feeling silly and ashamed. But still he looked around with faintly hopeful eyes, half expecting Trictrac to come bounding into view—but only half expecting. He even tried a long forgotten game, closing his eyes and repeating to himself, "When I open them again she will be here." And then you must count ten before you opened them. He tried it several times but nothing came of it. "Just a butterfly," he said with a disdainful shrug. Still, hurrying home along the trodden path, he kept peering through the dusk, watching like a hawk, seeing for an instant in a log or stump resemblance to the dear, familiar figure—thinking once or twice the bushes swayed or that he heard the crackling of a twig, listening for a sound above the noisy beating of his heart—saying all the time beneath his breath to excuse what he was doing, "It was just a butterfly—"

Yet, when he approached the Tent tree, he was treading on his toes, straining his ears to listen. He could hear their voices chattering and exclaiming, with unusual gaiety—or so his quickened fancy made it seem. It was here, quite naturally, that the Fairy might elect, if such a thing could be, to produce the missing Trictrac, in the spot that was her home. Even now she might be there and waiting for him, lying in the circle with her nose upon her paws, in her old place next to his. He was half convinced she was—but only half. Else why would they be chattering in such excited fashion—though they were always chattering, about a thousand things.

He came quickly on the path, taking cover of the bushes, creeping close till he could see them, so he might be certain of it before they should have sight of his joy or disappointment.—Yes, there they were, already at their supper—chattering to be sure, but apparently at nothing.

The place beside his own was as empty as it had been. He searched the circle of them, and the long grass at their backs.—No, Trictrac wasn't there.—"Just a butterfly," he said with hard contempt.

He came and took his place, and the chatter died away.

While he was eating supper a butterfly came winging through the twilight—a golden one with Wands, exactly like the other. But the Wands were only stripes upon its wings. It fluttered over them, as butterflies were fluttering all day long, hardly ever noticed, for there were so many of them—round and round the circle, close above their heads, not offering to alight.

He watched it with resentment, with bitter, spreading anger, groping on the ground for a pebble or a stick. He was angry at himself for being such a fool, for betrayal he had suffered, for his own childish folly. And this fresh indignity was more than he could bear, an open mockery of him. Now it was coming back, directly toward him. He tore a clod of earth out of the ground. "Go on, get out!" he said and hurled it at the butterfly, not hitting it of course, but coming close enough to send it hurrying off.

No one made any comment, not a single word, nor even seemed to notice what he'd done. But he knew what they were thinking.

"Just a butterfly," he stormed at them, as if he'd been attacked. Still, nobody spoke, and the dreadful silent moments ticked away. "Well, I don't care," he muttered. He got up from the grass and went to take a rucksack from the branch where they were hanging; and then he kneeled beside it and put some things into it—things that were his own. They watched in silence from the corners of their eyes, pretending not to see. Only Rosa dared at last to speak, with a tremor in her voice—

"What are you doing, Gil?"

"Nothing—" he mumbled, going on about it.

"But—where are you going?"

"To the house."

"The house?" She caught her breath. "Alone at night?—What for?"

"To live there," he said shortly.

"But why?"

"Because—" He hesitated, fumbling with the straps. "Because Trictrac might come back there looking for me." It was pretty lame, he knew, not much of an excuse. "Anyway," he added, "that's what I

built it for, to have a house to live in. I'm sick of living this way—
just underneath a tree, sleeping on the ground."

"Oh—" She nodded, sighing. None of the others spoke. Impossible
to say what they were thinking.

He stood up, with the rucksack on his shoulder and the spear gripped
in his hand, not even glancing at them. He hadn't told the truth, not
any of it. He had no hope that Trictrac would come back, to the house
or any place; and he loved his home beneath the Tent tree, and sleeping in the fragrant, crinkly grass. His decision had been the impulse
of a moment—to go and live alone in the house that he had built, that
house which was his own. He simply couldn't stand it to be with them
any longer, to be constantly reminded of the vanished past, of everything he'd had and someway lost—aware of disapproval and eternal
accusation, as if he were shut out, regarded with suspicion, as an enemy
in fact. It was horrible and lonely, more lonely than the lonesomeness
of being by yourself.

He went slowly back along the path, in the gathering darkness—
more slowly than he needed, for he knew each step of it, every root and
rock. He could have run along it, blindfolded perhaps.—If she should
have called to him, "Shall I come with you, Gil?"—If she should have
said, "We can live there together."—It was in his mind she might; that's
why he went so slowly. But he knew she wouldn't, though in fact she
almost did.—If he had said to her, "Come with me, Rosa." Which he
would have given anything to say, and couldn't have.—If he had
waited just a moment longer, if he had looked at her! If he could have
told the truth with his words or with his eyes!—But he had passed the
point on the circle of the graph when saying what is in your heart is
an easy thing to do, reasonable and natural. Truth was no longer possible. And so he went alone, save for the fireflies that danced around
him.

There was the house, a crooked shadow in the starlight. He quickly
climbed the ladder, whistling to himself to keep his spirits up, and
dragged it after him. There was scarcely room for both of them inside.
It should have been exciting, coming in the night to the home that
you had built, a house on stilts which no one could get into when you
pulled the ladder up—like the drawbridge of a castle; where you were
safe from beasts and prying eyes, though no beasts had ever threatened

the shelter of the Tent tree, and there were no eyes to see, save those he'd used to think of as almost like his own, from which he'd had no secrets; safe from Sorcerers and Witches, if such there really were; not safe from butterflies, nor from snakes which coiled about and wriggled up a pole. Safe from storms, but not from memories.—Yes, it should have been exciting, and perhaps it was a little, for there are compensations in the emptiest of things.

He stretched out on the floor, with the rucksack for a pillow, a very flat one, for there was little in it; the packing of his things had been a gesture; he hadn't any things. It was not a comfortable bed, not as level as the ground and not as soft; the poles, of different thickness, had unpleasant hollows in them, and ragged knots which dug into his spine—like lying on a washboard. When he turned upon his side he bumped against the drawbridge. He was thankful the roof had not been finished. It was good to see the stars drifting through the tree tops, to know that they were there—the same ones he had watched from his bed beneath the Tent tree, with Rosa close beside him. It somehow made him feel near to her again. He wished he hadn't come, and he was glad he had.

But sleep evaded him.—What should he do tomorrow?—What indeed?—He tossed and turned upon the crooked poles, selecting and rejecting occupations, aching with homesickness. And then he thought of something, a rush of things in fact, a tangle of them. But it was with Trictrac that it started, thinking back to all the places they had gone together and where he'd searched for her, trying to remember if he could have missed one, thinking with a start: Why yes, of course, he had—that place where he had found her. Strange thing he'd never thought of it before. But the mountains had not tempted him since that far distant day when he and Juan and Rosa had made their fatal journey, which had ended with the snake, with Trictrac too—an orphaned puppy crying in a burrow of the roots. Still, that had been her home, the first one she had known—to which she might return when she had been mistreated, when she was sad and lonely.

Yes, perhaps she had gone back there, far across the forest—or maybe even farther, to the mountains. Perhaps she'd climbed them to the top and found her way across them to the other side. If he went to look for her he ought to be prepared to go on until he found her, to climb and cross the mountains, as he had dreamed of doing when his eyes first rested on them, as he had known he must and some day would—not stopped by snakes or beasts, or anything at all.—And what would it be like, beyond the mountains?—on the other side of them?—If he only knew, if there were some way to tell!—If he had that big red book with the pictures of America—

That was where it started.

He hardly slept a wink, aquiver with excitement, waiting for the dawn. At the first pale hint of it he flung the drawbridge down and went running to the beach, the empty rucksack flapping on his shoulder, skirting wide around the Tent tree, down the bluff where it was steep, but there was a way he knew. He ran across the sand, dodging craftily in and out among the Giants, not taking any chance of being seen, though he was pretty sure they wouldn't be awake yet. The sun was coming now, the golden rim of it swimming up out of the sea. He ran along the edge, splashing through the water, where his footsteps were effaced, where his path could not be traced.

There was the ship.—He saw it with a thrill of satisfaction. He hadn't been quite certain that anything was left of it, hadn't noticed for so long.—But there it was, spread flatly in the sea, the hull of it thick plastered with clinging shells and seaweed, looking like the rocks on which it rested—looking so much like them it could hardly be distinguished, and in fact had ceased to be. As a ship it had been long ago forgotten. No one had gone near it since Mamud was a man, since the day the thing had happened and he had become a child. They had taken from the storeroom what they could find to eat, and that had been the end of interest in it. There had been good reason then to stay away from it; and the habit had persisted though the reason had grown faint. But it came back to him now, as he stood there in the sand, staring at the wreck: the mouse-man in his house, with his head almost cut off—lying in the water, with his arms and legs all twisted, with a big red book beside him. Dead of course.—But his heart might be alive —his wicked Sorcerer's heart; and that had been the reason.—Just a silly childish story!—He laughed contemptuously, but the joy of his adventure was a little shadowed.

The tide was in, lapping high upon the sunken stern, almost to the rail, within arm's reach of it. He looked behind him at the bluff, peeking stealthily from the cover of a Giant. There was no one to be seen, and no suspicious waving of the bushes which were as still and silent as the sea, hushed in the breathless dawn. And then he waded in till the water reached his shoulders, then swam with easy strokes around the stern, looking for a likely spot to reach up to the rail and scramble to the deck. It wasn't much to climb, though harder than it looked, for the greasy seaweed slithered through his hands or broke off when he put his weight upon it; and the shells and barnacles with which the hull was covered, scratched his flesh like rusty nails. But at last he got a grip upon the solid rail and dragged himself across it into the shallow cockpit where the wheel had been. He was on board the ship and safely out of sight in the shelter of the skylight, his secret undertaking undetected. He stood and looked around.

The wreck was unfamiliar; there was nothing reminiscent of a ship. The masts had long since washed away, the tangled spars and ropes succumbed to time and storms; the cockpit where he stood was filled with sand. Of Mamud's house no vestige now remained. In the place where it had stood there was a yawning crater, for the belly of the ship had split apart—from the very bow of it, on which the mermaid hung, wedged fast between the Twins, back to the mouse-man's door. The ancient teak had cracked and spread apart, like the broken skin of an over ripe banana. The bowels of the ship lay open to his view, looking scarcely different than the bottom of the sea—a stagnant, limpid pool, with seaweed growing in it, clinging to the rocks—

But no, those were not rocks that lined the bottom of it. He stared in puzzled wonder: a monstrous bird nest filled with monstrous eggs. For the straw which once had covered them had rotted and dissolved, exposing to view the earthen jars of oil, nestling in the sea, coated green with slime—with broken ones among them, as if the eggs had hatched and their feathered inmates flown.—A bird nest in the sea, with eggs as big as pumpkins!—But he suddenly remembered what they were, remembering how the Little One had found, in the fragments of a jar, the oil-soaked treasure bag with its bits of broken glass, and the golden coin as well. It flashed into his mind that there might be more of them within those earthen eggs, and when the tide was low they could be easily reached. But he gave no thought to it, for golden coins were not the object of his quest.

He crept near to the skylight, an empty frame from which the glass had vanished, and cautiously peeked in, not certain what he'd find and prepared for instant flight. But to his amazement the mouse-man wasn't there, not the slightest sign of him. There was the awful litter of things turned upside down—furniture and dishes, open chests and satchels with things spilled out of them, broken glass and scraps of clothing, books and papers—a stained and wrinkled mess, burned yellow by the sun, half buried in the sand and crinkly seaweed. And yes, there was the book with the pictures of America, lying just where he remembered, safe and sound, though of course it had been soaked and the pictures might be spoiled.—But the mouse-man? Where was he to whom the book belonged, who had lain dead beside it, with his head almost cut off? He searched the room, the floor, the empty bed on which the ragged covers lay like rumpled dust.—If he had been really dead he couldn't disappear.—And suppose he wasn't dead, but had managed to survive—as perhaps a Sorcerer might. Suppose he should be hiding in some corner of the ship!—The hair rose on his head at the bare idea of it.

But then he caught a chilling, yet reassuring glimpse of something in the sand: in a litter of the papers, close beside the big red book—a naked, whitened bone. And yes, there was another, and another, and another, half hidden by the seaweed—bones of different sizes, not of sea birds nor of fishes—a scattered heap of them.—He began to breathe again.—They were the mouse-man's bones, and could be nothing else, all that was left of him—harmless, crumbling bones.—He could laugh at his alarm.

He swung down from the skylight, hanging by his hands, dropping lightly to the floor, and ran straight to get the book, lifting it carefully, brushing off the sand—a thick and bulky book, damaged but not ruined, the pages stained with water, some of them stuck together, some of the pictures blurred so you could hardly see them, but lots of them you could. He didn't wait to determine more than that, anxious to be gone out of the gruesome place. He meant to take the book back to the house, where in perfect safety, with the drawbridge drawn up, he'd have leisure to examine it with care, to separate the pages that were stuck together—to begin at the beginning and look at everything, expecting he must come to a picture of the forest—the playground of the Giants he would surely recognize—and the mountains at the back. He would know them if he saw them. And no doubt there would be pictures of what was concealed behind them, a guide to exploration, to the future that awaited if some day he should climb them—or so he hoped and thought.

He wrapped a rag around the book and put it in the rucksack, strapped high upon his neck where he could keep it dry, and was hurrying toward the door, which had fallen from its hinges, when he paused to stare at something—a weather-beaten shoe, half buried in the sand. The mouse-man's shoe it must be.—He had almost forgotten there were such things as shoes, and himself had never owned one. He stooped to pick it up and empty out the sand—the stiff, cracked leather as unyielding as cement; then sat to try it on, cramming his foot into it, though it pinched and bruised his toes like an instrument of medieval torture. But at last he got it on and stood and walked about, regarding it with pride, though every step was painful. But in time, with practice, he'd get used to it, he thought. And shoes might be the very thing with which to climb the mountains, to tramp through snow and ice. But one shoe wouldn't do. There must be another somewhere. He looked around for it, poking in the sand, lifting up the seaweed with his toes.

He couldn't find the shoe, but he came on something else that diverted his attention—a faded old felt hat, as hard as iron. He put it on his head with a thrill of satisfaction. With a hat and shoes, he felt, he would be equipped for anything. But then he was reminded there were many other things in the mouse-man's house which might serve his purpose —odds and ends of garments whose use he didn't know, or had long since forgotten, but still they might come handy; and who could tell what else might be hidden in the sand. He poked around, considering what to do: he could come again, as often as he chose, once the book had been explored, when he should be ready to take a final step. He could come and go through everything, and pick out what he wanted—

But his planning ended there, for he suddenly looked up to confront an utter stranger—miraculously come, for he hadn't heard a sound—a strange face staring at him, not an arm's length from his own—a face with long black hair, almost to the shoulders, with grim, defiant eyes, though they looked a little scared—staring straight into his own. It was too abrupt for terror; there wasn't time to think. He raised one arm defensively and the other one to strike, and saw the stranger mimic what he did. But even then he didn't understand. It was the hat perhaps that gave the thing away—the funny looking hat perched high upon his head, for it was much too small—the hat the stranger wore, which he finally recognized, though he didn't know himself. He was looking in a mirror that was hanging on the wall.

And even when he knew he couldn't quite believe that this could be himself, not until he'd put his fingers on the glass. For a long time he stood there staring at it, smiling, frowning, coming closer, moving back, turning one way, then another.—Did he really look like that?—What had he thought he looked like?—But he hadn't thought about it; he hadn't any memory, any image of himself. He had thought, if he thought anything, that he must look like a child. But the face in the mirror, whatever else it was, was not a child's.

He was thrilled and he was frightened.

20

SECRETS ARE DANGEROUS THINGS—DANGEROUS to a child, incompatible with childhood, denoting nothing less than a thickening of the shell which surrounds the human soul and cuts it off from Life.

Rosa had one too. Something strange and new had happened to her—disturbing and unpleasant but not really frightening, because she had the feeling that it ought to happen, as if she had in some way known it would, and been waiting and expecting it. It went away but then it came again, and she was not surprised. She did not know what it meant, the threat and promise of it; but she felt it had mysteriously changed her, that she would never be again as she had been before, that something had been lost which could never be recovered, and something else had come to take its place.

It was a secret thing which she could not confide, not even to Teresa, as she had always done with everything that happened, as she might have done, and longed to do to someone. But not to them. When it came she went away, long walks into the forest by herself. She wouldn't answer when she heard them calling; sometimes she hid from them. It was the first real secret of her life, her first possession, and the weight of it was heavy. It made a gulf between them; she felt herself apart, removed by an experience which they couldn't share, unique and lonely.

She was desperately unhappy. Often she would sit and watch them at their play—Pablo and Teresa swimming in the sea, diving after shells; Mamud and the Little One building castles in the sand, as they had always done, as they might do forever—wishing with all her heart she could take part with them as she had used to do, that Time could be turned back. Distressing thoughts would flit across her mind and she would drive them off, saying to herself, "I have everything I want—my companions whom I love, the forest and the sea." But a hidden voice would whisper, "All that is not enough."

Or she would sit near Juan when he was carving something, watching his hand chipping gently at the wood—so sure of himself, so patient and exact, so happy and content if he was making something, no matter what it was or who would care about it.—Watching Juan, and thinking about Gil—wondering where he was and what he could be doing for she no longer heard him calling Trictrac in the forest. Sometimes he would come when they were eating supper, sitting by himself, silent and detached, and then he would be off without a word. She hadn't dared to ask.

But one day she went to look, unable to endure her anxiety about him—along the forest path to the ugly little house.

He heard her coming, and saw her through the cracks between the poles—coming slowly through the ferns, with her eyes upon the house. He was safe inside it, with the drawbridge drawn up, with his secret to himself. It was not a day on which to suffer an intrusion, for he had found at last what he was seeking, near the long end of the book—a tedious, patient search which he had begun to dread might never be rewarded. But there it was, spread out before his eyes: a picture of the forest, with the curving beach before it and the mountains at the back, exactly as it was—or so it seemed to be, though he hadn't yet had time to examine it with care when he was interrupted.

Day after day he had pored over the pages, studying blurred and faded pictures of every sort of thing—beaches and mountains too, some with caps of snow, not unlike the ones he knew and yet not like enough—villages, and cities with streets of towering buildings—motor-cars and trams, trains and boats and bridges—deserts, plains, and forests—engines and machines—many kinds of things he'd never seen, for which he had no names. And there were people too—men with hats and shoes and other things he'd noticed in the mouse-man's house; and women in rich dresses of velvet or of silk, with jewels upon their arms and even in their ears, and their hair not hanging down but piled upon their heads—very beautiful they looked.

Day after day, with the book upon his knees, or lying on the crooked floor, propped on aching elbows, going through the pages, making certain not to miss a single one, spending endless time when they were stuck together. Good thing the roof was open to the sky, that he had never finished it, for then it would have been too dark to see. A long and trying job, but it was exciting too, like a trip around the world. America was big and wonderful indeed!—The springboard of his effort, which had been the missing Trictrac, was gradually submerged in a wave of mounting interest. Of course it would be Trictrac that he was looking for, but there were so many things—

"Gil—" She called him softly, standing in the ferns which reached almost to her shoulders.

He lay flat upon the floor against the wall, watching through a crack between the poles. He knew she couldn't see him, couldn't guess that he was there. But he could see her plainly in a vagrant shaft of sunlight, like a golden halo round her—the straight and slender figure in a garment made of grass, standing very still with her eyes upon the house.

"Gil—"

He held his breath, the thick red book spread open underneath his body.—Why had she come? What did she want with him?—Her long dark hair, parted in the middle, hung low around her shoulders.—How would it look, he wondered, piled upon her head, like the pictures in the book?

"Please, Gil—"

He wriggled with annoyance. It was silly to keep calling when she knew he wasn't there.—Her hands were clasped, bare arms against her breast.—How would they look with bands of jewels around them?—if she wore a silken gown, or one of velvet?

"What are you doing, Gil?"

So that's why she had come—a scheme to learn his secret! No doubt
they'd talked it over and sent her on the errand, to find out what she
could. Well, he knew how to guard it; they'd never, never know.—It
seemed as though her eyes were looking into his—gazing at him sadly.
But why should she be sad? She had everything she wanted—Juan and
all of them.

"Why won't you answer me?"

And then there was a pause—an endless one it seemed, for he didn't
dare to move, and the book and crooked floor were digging in his
flesh.—What was she waiting for? Why must she stand there staring
at the empty house?—But she knew it wasn't empty, knew that he was
there although she couldn't see him, for the end of the ladder was
projecting through the door. He hadn't thought of that.

She didn't speak again, and at last she went away, slowly through
the ferns, not looking back. He raised upon his elbow, watching till she
vanished from his sight among the trees. And then he quickly spread
the book beneath the open roof, bending close to see the picture, for
it was growing dusk.

She walked along the path with dragging steps and aching heart.
She had never been more wretched.—Why was he hiding in the ugly
little house? What was he doing there? Why would he not answer?
What had happened to him?—to them?—to everything?—She turned
the questions in her mind but could find no explanation, except a
sudden dreadful one she didn't want to think, but it wouldn't be
denied.—Could it be he was bewitched, as the Little One had said?

"Bewitched—" she mused aloud and caught her breath with horror
at a new and awful thought.—Perhaps she too had been the victim of
it—an evil spell which had come she knew not whence, to steal away
her joy, to rob her of her happiness, of everything she'd cherished—
which had even changed her body, as it had changed her heart. "No,
no," she cried, standing still upon the path, in the grasp of a fear she
had never known before.—Oh yes, she had been frightened many times
—in the mouse-man's house, when the Little One was lost, when the
snake had wrapped around her! But this was something new, of another
kind and quality, quite different from the fearing of a child.

"Oh God—" she said, looking up into the sky. "Please help me,

God."—And never in her life had she called on God before, nor felt the need to do so—perhaps because she had never until now been separated from Him.—"God, please—" Standing still upon the path, with her hands clasped at her breast and her eyes upon the sky.—Her first long distance prayer.

But God seemed very far away in heaven, too far away to hear or be concerned. Nor was she sure what to say to him, how he should be addressed or his interest be invoked. She stood dejectedly, staring at the sky—a tiny patch of blue in the tall tops of the trees, so very far away, so impossibly remote. It was then the idea popped into her head, and hope came flooding back. "Yes, yes, of course—" she said. And suddenly she ran, fleet-footed on the path—running toward the Tent tree.

Gil lay propped upon his elbows, with the picture spread before him. Part of it was blurry but most of it was plain—the forest and the mountains, exactly as they were—the ragged snow-capped peaks which were so familiar to him. The forest was no more than a solid mass of trees, but he saw the milk nut ones sticking up above the others, and the bluff that ringed the beach, with the bushes at its edge. Still, there might be other forests with similar bluffs and bushes.—But wait! For bending close he detected something else: the tumbling waterfall—just a thread against the bluff; it might even be a wrinkle. He rubbed it with his thumb but it remained. Yes, it was the waterfall, with the rocky pool beneath it!

And now the beach!—But the bottom of the picture was badly blurred and faded. The figures of the Giants could not be seen. He sat and took the book upon his knees to get a better light. There were spots upon the page, little blots of ink where no doubt the Giants had been, but the water had effaced them. Still, they'd been there, he was sure from the remnants that survived. He thought he saw a blot right where the Twins should be, and there were other specks he seemed to recognize.—Yes, of course the Giants had been there, till the sea had soaked them out.

Anyway, it didn't matter; there was evidence enough. The picture was a faithful reproduction of the forest, not to be denied because some stones were missing from the beach. He could put his finger on places that he knew: there would be the Tent tree—and here the house where he was sitting now. He could even trace the brook, meandering through the forest, winding back to find the mountains, as he'd always known it must. Here might be the place where they'd come upon the snake, where Trictrac had been found, where she might be waiting for him.

And the mountains!—He studied them with care: a formidable foe, with steep and barren sides, with peaks of snow and ice, like lofty jagged teeth. Yet no doubt they could be climbed; he was not frightened by them or discouraged.—The mouse-man's shoes would be needed for the trip—if he could find the other. Well, tomorrow he would go and search for it.—There were words upon the page beneath the picture, but he couldn't read them. And even if he could they would have told him nothing.

And now!—He turned the page with eager, trembling fingers. He was terribly excited, feeling sure he would find upon the other side what was behind the mountains.—A reasonable idea: if you could read a book, the reading must go on from one thing to the next, or it would make no sense. And pictures, he supposed, would be the same—would have a continuity, one place behind another.

He turned the page and stared with racing heart.—A city met his eye—bigger and more wonderful than any he'd encountered. The biggest in the book, in America perhaps. A city like Madrid!—Enormous buildings reared against the sky, like the Palaces of Kings—streets that swarmed with people, with motorcars and trams.—Cinemas no doubt. He thought that he could see one on a busy street, with people hurrying in, crowding at the door.—Yes, a city close behind him, with nothing in between but the forest and the mountains—seeming scarcely farther off than the page that he had turned.—And he would climb those mountains, however hard and steep—climb them to the top and down the other side, till the city should be reached.—He could hardly bear to think of the time that he had wasted.

Tomorrow he would go and search the mouse-man's house, to find the missing shoe, and other things as well. In a city he'd need clothing —not ugly, ragged garments made of grass and skins, but the kind the pictures showed. He must look like other people, so he wouldn't be embarrassed or ashamed of his appearance—must cover up his body and cut his hair off short, like other people did, so there would be no difference between himself and them—and they wouldn't turn and

stare when he walked along the street, and make remarks about him.—
Perhaps he wouldn't understand anything they said, but he would
learn in time. If he looked and acted like them, if he was very careful,
they might be friendly to him—might ask him in their houses, to have
his supper with them.

And some day, when he'd learned to walk about the streets as carelessly as they did, when he could drive a motorcar himself, when he
had one of his own and a pretty house to live in—not a crazy, crooked
beehive; some day when he knew as much as they did, and looked
exactly like them—some day he would find her, a lovely lady in a silk
or velvet dress, with jewels upon her arms and her hair piled on her
head—like the pictures in the book. She would be his friend and would
come to live with him. They would go in the motorcar, tearing through
the streets to visit cinemas; they would always be together. At night
she would be near him, sleeping at his side. If he woke he could reach
and touch her with his hand; and he would not be lonely, not ever
any more.—He would know her when he saw her—maybe on the street
or inside a cinema; it might happen anywhere. But he'd know her in-
stantly—the straight and slender figure, the dark soft hair, the warm
brown eyes that always spoke the truth.—He would know her—yes,
of course, because she'd look like Rosa.—But he hastily changed the
current of his thought to safer ground.

Tomorrow he would go and collect the things he needed. And then
he would be ready to set out upon his journey, properly equipped.
He'd keep his secret to the end. He'd never say a word, not to any of
them—though perhaps he'd leave for her a message in the sand, just
a word to say good-by. In the morning, when they woke, he would be
gone. And they would never know what had happened to him, nor
likely care about it.

A sharp nostalgic twinge pinched at his heart; and he changed his
thought again, bending close to see the picture. But by now it was too
dark.

They were gathered at the Tent tree when Rosa burst upon them,
breathless from her haste—

"Let's do it, Juan," she cried before she even got there. They looked
up in surprise. And Pablo dropped abruptly from a limb where he was
hanging, chinning himself and counting. "Let's do it," she repeated.

"Do what?" they asked.

"Let's take the mermaid down and bring her to the forest."

"Is that all?" grumbled Pablo. "And now you made me spoil it. Anyway, I broke Gil's record; I chinned myself twelve times."

"Eleven," said the Little One who had been watching closely.

"Twelve," insisted Pablo. "You don't know how to count."

"No matter," pleaded Rosa, aglow with her idea. "Let's bring her to the forest, with the baby in her arms, and find a church for her."

"A church?" they echoed vaguely, beginning to remember.

"I know the very place," Juan said, eager and excited. "I found it long ago. There's a stump for her to stand on, with vines that grow around it. And it's almost like a church."

"Yes, good—" They nodded, interest mounting. It would be fun, they thought, an exciting undertaking.

"But she is so big and heavy," Teresa ventured doubtfully. "How could we ever bring her?"

"Perhaps if Gil would help—" But they knew he wouldn't, and they wouldn't ask him.

"We don't need Gil," said Pablo, sounding very bold and confident —quite like Gil in fact. "We can do it by ourselves. We can make a rope of vines to let her down. And then—" He frowned, considering.

"Mamud could carry her," the Little One suggested.

"Yes, Mamud," they agreed. And Mamud looked dejected but offered no objection.

Now what?—"The baby!" they exclaimed, and ran to find God's body. It was there beneath the Tent tree, half buried in the grass, a seasoned lump of wood not much resembling anything.—The crown!— And that was found, though a bush had grown through it. It was thick with rust, and the jewels looked dull and moldy.

"Like glass—" said Pablo mournfully.

"Like jewels," Juan cried. "You'll see."

"Well, maybe—" they conceded. But they did look like glass.

And now?—God's head! They scampered to the pile of graven milk nuts, black with age and shriveled, and spread them in a row—like proofs from a photographer, kneeling in the grass to make selection—

"This one."

"No, this."

"But that one looks too cross."

"This one is smiling—see?"

"No, its mouth is open, like a fish."

"Well, here is one that's shut."

"But that's the ugliest."

"Here! This one; it looks—sweet."

"Sweet?" They clustered round it with their heads together, while the sculptor stood in silence, in his own peculiar agony.—It did not look sweet exactly, but it was not revolting. Its withered reddish hair was banged across its forehead; its face was round and flat, and empty of expression—

"Like its mother," Pablo said.

They nodded earnestly. It did look like its mother. "Yes, this one," they decided.

"Well—" Juan sighed regretfully. "It doesn't look much like him— the way that I remember."

"No matter, it will do." They dismissed debate of it.—Anyway, by now it was too dark to see.

21

H^E THOUGHT HE WAS DISCOVERED, AND HIS heart sank to his shoe.—Yes, shoe, for the missing one had not yet been found. He hadn't taken time to really look for it, intent on other matters. He had found a lot of things which he thought might come in handy—scattered on the floor, in bags and chests and lockers—

Quantities of clothing, shirts and coats and trousers—some of them so rotten you could stick your fingers through them, but some were good as new when the sand was shaken out. A brush and comb; a rusty scissors with which to cut his hair. He'd sheared it off close to his neck, and snipped it on the top till his head was nearly bald.—"Yes, better—" he confided to himself, staring at the glass a little doubtfully. —And if not better, it was certainly more like the pictures in the book.

A plate and cup, a knife and fork and spoon: things he'd need when he went out to supper. A bottle full of black stuff—ink, he guessed, for near it was a pen. And they would come in handy when he had learned to write. He might even write a letter back to them, an account of his adventures and description of the city. But none of them could read it, not even Rosa could—that easy word he'd written in the sand, and had hurried to rub it out, not wanting her to see it, but hoping that she had.—Anyway, no letters ever came into the forest.

Bullets for a gun, but the gun itself was missing—probably the one with which Mamud shot the men. A pocketknife with seven blades—something Juan would want if he ever knew about it, but he never would. A bunch of keys, a pin with colored glass—Teresa would like that, but she wouldn't get it. A pair of spectacles. He tried them on to see how he would look, but he couldn't see through them. No matter, he would keep them; they might be useful sometime.

And now!—There were a lot of shirts, all white with stiff high collars. He selected one at random, but it was much too tight and impossible to button. However, when he stretched his arms it ripped apart behind, and then it buttoned easily. It looked all right in front and no one could see the back, underneath a coat. He drew the trousers on; they were snug around the waist, not likely to slip down. He walked about, regarding them with pride. They were a little short, only reaching to his ankles, but his nakedness was covered. The coat came next, a clumsy, scratchy garment of thick and heavy cloth. The shoe—the hat, nicely balanced on his ears. He felt himself equipped at last, prepared to face the issue; and he hobbled to the mirror.

"Yes, good!" he cried. The image in the glass was smiling, nodding at him. And indeed the transformation was incredibly effective; he would not have known himself; there was nothing left of him except his startled eyes. He did look like the pictures in the book, or near enough so he wouldn't be ashamed. They might not even guess he was a stranger.—Sweat trickled down his face; his shirt was soaked and sticking to his skin, uncomfortable and clammy. The trousers pinched between his legs and clung around his knees, like casings made of stovepipe; the shoe was torture. The coat confined his arms, as if they were in manacles; and the iron collar round his neck was threatening to behead him. He was choking, suffocating, but he was supremely happy.

It was then he heard them coming and was certain he was caught, that his secret was discovered. He climbed on a transom whence he could see the beach.—Yes, there they were, all six of them, with

Pablo in the lead, racing toward the ship, dragging something with them—like a rope made out of vines. He jumped down in a panic, tearing off his clothes which he rolled into a bundle with all his other treasures and hid beneath the bed. He expected every moment they would burst in upon him.

But they didn't come. He could hear them chattering somewhere—behind the Twins, he thought. At last he went to look, to see what they were up to, creeping along the deck under cover of the rail until he reached the bow. He could hear them plainly now; through a crack beside the bowsprit he could look down upon them—standing in a group at the bottom of the Twins—staring up at him, or so it seemed.

"Now listen," Pablo said, elated at the prospect of conducting the affair, "and I'll tell you how to do it."

Do what?—He caught his breath.

"Yes, how?" they questioned anxiously, gazing at the mermaid who looked very large and heavy, suspended high above them.

"I'll climb up with the rope—" Pablo paused, considering.

The rope?—for what?—He squirmed with apprehension.—Maybe nothing more than Pablo showing off!

"I'll fasten it around her neck—"

Her neck?—Whose neck?—And suddenly he knew: they had come to get the mermaid and take her to the forest—to set her on a stump and pretend it was a church. A silly, childish business! He shrugged contemptuously, albeit with relief.

Pablo was explaining in response to eager questions: he would tie the rope around the mermaid's neck—like a person being hung, with the bowsprit for a gibbet. And when they got her loose they could let her gently down—

Not a bad idea, Gil grudgingly admitted.

"But if she should fall—" protested Juan.

"Yes, on us?" they cried.

"She won't," he told them firmly, "if you don't let go the rope."

"But how shall we get her loose?"

"That's easy," he replied. "Mamud must climb up and—" He suddenly broke off to shout, "Mamud, you come back!"

And he was just in time, for Mamud was crawling off upon his hands and knees, about to disappear behind a Giant.

"Yes, you come back," they ordered.

Mamud hesitated, but then he came back slowly, the picture of dejection.

"You ought to be ashamed," Teresa scolded.

"He wasn't going anywhere," the Little One objected, with a twinkle in her eye. She had been watching him and had hoped he'd get away. Mamud grinned and nodded.

"No matter, you stay here," Pablo warned him sternly. "When I get the rope around her neck you climb up with the spear and pry her loose." And he took the rope and ran nimbly up the path to the cleft between the Twins, then climbing up the mermaid's tail—a hazardous adventure—

"Look out!" they called. "Take care!"

"Ho!" he jeered. "It's easy."

"You sound like Gil," Teresa said.—And he did sound like Gil, remarkably in fact.

Humph!—Gil muttered to himself, watching through the crack. It occurred to him unpleasantly that Pablo might succeed him.

He was on the mermaid's shoulders, reaching for the bowsprit, now swung astraddle of it, sitting at his ease. He leaned to drop the noose around the mermaid's neck, and flung the end to them. "Now Mamud," he instructed, "climb up and pry her loose. And the rest of you hold fast."

"Yes, good," they said. And Mamud climbed up to the cleft, prying with the spear behind the mermaid's back, as Pablo gave direction.

"Be careful not to break her," pleaded Juan.

But Pablo made no answer, intent upon the job, looking down and shouting orders—"Now this side! Now the other!"—The mermaid creaked alarmingly.

"She's breaking," Juan protested.

"No, she isn't. Go ahead!"

Gil craned his neck to see. It was an exciting business and he wished that he was in it.

The handle of the spear was having its effect: the rusted bolts were breaking, ripping through the rotten planks. The mermaid twitched and sagged—

"Now, Mamud! Now!"

A final splitting creak. The woven vines pulled tight and she was swinging free, hanging from the bowsprit with the noose around her neck.

"Hold fast!" exhorted Pablo. But the rope was slipping, the mermaid's weight too great for the ones upon the ground. They were being dragged along, though they pulled with all their might, shouting desperately for help.

Gil hugged himself, expectant of disaster, which was imminent indeed. He was tempted to rush forth and take charge of the affair.

But disaster was averted, for Pablo saw the danger and did a daring thing. He swung down from the bowsprit, twined his legs around the rope, and came down hand over hand. And the added weight of him was enough to turn the scales.

"Oh, good for Pablo!"—In another moment he was safely on the ground and Mamud came to help—all six of them to hold the rope; and the mermaid safe and sound, swinging gently in the air.

Gil groaned aloud. He could not, himself, have done it any better.

Down, down she came until she was at rest upon the sand, lying lumpily on her back, staring at the sky with her faded, placid eyes.

"She isn't very pretty," the Little One said sadly. "Not when you see her close."

"No, not very," they admitted. But this was understatement: she was really very plain. Her face was full of cracks, but it wouldn't have been pretty anyway. It was round and flat and wooden.

"Still," Rosa murmured hopefully, "she looks kind."

"Like a bowl with nothing in it," Mamud said.

But Juan came to her defense. "You wait, you'll see—" he promised. "When she's sitting on her throne with the baby in her arms and her fish tail covered up, and the crown upon her head! You'll hardly know her then."

"Yes, maybe—" Rosa nodded. But it was hard to think that the mermaid and the baby could be of any help.

Gil was bored, but he lingered with his eye against the crack; he didn't want to take a chance on missing anything.

"How can we get her to the forest?" they were asking.

"Let Mamud carry her," Teresa said.

"Yes, Mamud," they agreed. And they caught him just in time; he was sneaking off again.

He could lift her in his arms, but then he couldn't walk because his wooden leg sank so deep into the sand, almost out of sight.

"We must drag her," Pablo said, "with the rope around her neck."

"No, no," protested Juan. "She'll get broken; she'll get scratched."

"No matter," they insisted. "That's the only way to do it."

Chatter, chatter, chatter!—Gil was quivering with impatience.

But off they went at last, all harnessed to the rope, dragging the bulky mermaid squeaking through the sand—like a wanton or a saint, for both have shared excursions of this sort. But if she was concerned she gave no sign; her faded eyes gazed widely at the sky, placid and resigned—in the fine tradition of the Faithful. Or perhaps she sensed her present degradation as a step toward elevation, as indeed, with her disreputable past, any step was bound to be.

Gil sighed with vast relief and hurried back to find the missing shoe. He looked and looked, in vain. He could hear them chattering, shouting, climbing up the bluff, going on into the forest. But he couldn't find the shoe; he had searched in every corner, under everything. There was only one place left that hadn't been explored—the little mound of sand with the white bones sticking out. He had avoided that, not even going near it. But that's where it must be—

He kneeled beside it, raking off the seaweed—like dead and wilted flowers on a grave; poking with his fingers, very gingerly at first. If a thing felt like a bone he would jerk his hand away and try another place. But at last he was rewarded, feeling something like a shoe, like the toe of it perhaps. He scraped the sand away and there it was—as stiff and hard as iron, exactly like the other. There was nothing more he wanted, nothing to detain him. He dragged the bundle from beneath the bed and stuffed the shoe into it. The tide was low; he could toss it to the sand and then climb down and get it. There was no one to observe him, for they were in the forest, busy with the mermaid. Anyway, it didn't matter; in the morning he'd be gone.

He was about to turn away when something caught his eye, in the hole left by the shoe—a bit of shiny chain. He kneeled again and carefully drew it out. There was something on the end of it, unrecognized at first, but then he remembered and saw it was a watch—a big one, thick with rust; but when he scraped it clean, beneath was gleaming gold.—The mouse-man's watch! What luck!—His finger pressed the knob and the lid of it flew open, revealing the face and hands that told the time.—He had almost forgotten there was such a thing as Time, in measurable amounts. But in the city he would need to know about it.—He held it to his ear but there was no sound of ticking. Perhaps it had been broken or the water had got in. Anyway, it was a watch!

But then the thought occurred to him: there might be other treasures hidden in the sand.—He prodded with his fingers, careless of the bones, and unearthed—a pocketbook. But when he tore it open it was empty, save for some scraps of faded paper.—Bank of England notes they were, in considerable amount.—He discarded them as worthless. But the pocketbook he'd keep.—Too bad he didn't have something to put in it.

And this gave rise to a disturbing idea. You couldn't get a motorcar just by asking for it; you would have to buy it in a shop and pay for it with money. Even at the cinema they wouldn't let you in unless you bought a ticket. Yes, money he would need—more than anything perhaps. And the mouse-man must have had some.—He dug deep into the sand, raking through it carefully. No sign of any money; but there was something else. He had it in his hands before he really saw—

It was the mouse-man's skull, leering at him horribly with empty grinning eyes.—He dropped it with a strangled gasp and scrambled to his feet; and something moved beneath his toes, wriggling in the sand as he jerked his foot away. He was sure that he saw it—just a fleeting glimpse, for his eyes were on the skull—something small and round, bouncing from his foot—like those seaweed balls that pop when you chance to tread upon them. But this one hadn't popped, and he didn't see it now.

It flashed across his mind: about the size and shape, the way a heart might look when it was old and dry. It was not a pleasant thought: the mouse-man's evil heart awakened from its slumber, probably enraged, plotting vengeance to the person who had disturbed its grave.— Of course it wasn't that—just a piece of dried up seaweed—

Funny thing he couldn't see it. There was seaweed everywhere, but not any of those shriveled balls that pop when they are pinched, nothing that resembled the thing he thought he'd seen. He got down on his knees and searched the floor, even underneath the bed, uncomfortably aware of the mouse-man's sightless eyes which seemed to follow him no matter where he was—grinning, mocking him. At last he snatched a pillow from the bed and covered up the skull. But the thing that had squirmed beneath his foot—like a rubber ball, like a thing that was alive—well, it simply wasn't there.

The mouse-man's house was like an oven. He was giddy with the heat and sick with apprehension, with bitter disappointment. He fled out to the deck and sat upon the edge beside the mouse-man's door, where the planks had split apart, staring down into the belly of the ship—the greasy, stagnant water thick with stinking seaweed, and the slimy earthen jars clustered at the bottom, like monstrous rotten eggs. But he scarcely saw them, for his thoughts were somewhere else—

"Money, money, money—" he kept saying to himself. And there was none inside the mouse-man's house. Anyway, he'd had enough of the mouse-man and his skull, and that other thing that wriggled, whatever it might be. He wasn't going back again to look.—"But money, money—" What a silly fool he'd been not to have thought of that! Nothing that he'd found would be any use without it—the watch and chain, and an empty pocketbook! The hat and coat and shoes wouldn't help the situation. There was nothing in the world of men unless you had some money. It would be no use to go, no use to climb the mountains. Likely enough they would send you back again. But even if they didn't it would not be any fun. No motorcar, no cinema, no food when you were hungry, no house in which to sleep, probably no friend.—He groaned and shook his head, as well he might. For his bridges had been burned: there was nothing for him here; and, without money, there was nothing anywhere.—"Money, money—" He shrunk against the mouse-man's house, in the scanty shadow of it, racking his aching head.—He could hear them in the forest, shouting, having fun. He wished that he were with them, but it was too late for that.

And they were having fun. The procession was advancing, near its place of destination, the mermaid plowing bumpily through the grass, with Mamud, Juan, and Pablo hauling on the rope, and the three girls close behind with God's body and his head and his mother's rusty crown.

"Here we are," Juan cried.

"Yes, good!" They looked about, exclaiming with delight, stirred by unremembered memories. It did seem like a church, they thought—the way a church should be. And so indeed it was.

Two rows of milk nut trees, with slender, tapering stems of Byzantine design, and lofty, fronded tops arched together like a dome, served to form a narrow nave which ended in a shrine where a tree had broken off and left a stump, overgrown thick with vines in which were waxy flowers, white and yellow ones, like candles on an altar: a throne on which God's mother might be regally installed. Beyond the stump was a tight-laced screen of vines, extending far around it: a church with walls and roof, dim and cool and quiet. The grassy floor was level, and there were scattered logs, disposed like pews.

"Do you like it?" Juan was beaming.

"It's beautiful," they said. But they were too excited to spend much time in looking, busy with the mermaid and the scepter and the crown, getting everything arranged, while Juan went rushing here and there, advising and directing. Only Rosa took no part, sitting in the grass with God's little shriveled head upon her lap, gazing at it sadly, not feeling very hopeful.

"Now ready! Up she goes!" They went at it with a will. Even Mamud was intrigued, lifting with all his might. "Now carefully, let her down!" The stump was hollow and the mermaid's tail went in it, almost out of sight, a perfect fit. There she sat upon her throne, with the crown upon her head, and her trident sticking up exactly like a scepter.

"Now the baby!" They ran and got the head and stuck it on the body. In the twinkling of an eye it was in its mother's arms, cuddled safe and sound against her wooden breast.

"Hooray!" A cheer burst from them. It was a thrilling sight, something to be proud of. "And now what must we do?"

"Flowers," Juan suggested. "There should be lots of them—the way it was when I saw him in the cart."

"All right!" They ran to gather flowers and hurried back with armfuls which they strewed upon the altar, all around the mermaid's throne. "And now what?"

"Maybe," said Teresa, "we ought to give him presents."

"Yes, good!" they cried, for in Teresa's stories they were always giving presents to the Princes. "But what?—what kind of presents?"

"Anything," said Pablo, and climbed a tree to pluck some fruit which he thought would serve the purpose. Teresa gave a necklace made of shells; and Rosa, who had nothing, wove a chaplet out of flowers to hang around the baby's withered neck. Juan ran to get a precious wooden bowl that he had carved, in which he said the presents could be kept. He arranged it on the stump underneath the baby's head, while the others gathered round to make their offerings.

Even Mamud was impressed. On the Little One's persuasion he parted with a fishhook, a very special one. But he did it with reluctance, and he hoped to get it back when nobody was looking.

The Little One herself was confronted with a problem, the contents of the treasure bag poured out into her hand—bits of this and that, and her two most loved possessions: the tooth and golden coin. It was hard to make a choice between these cherished objects, impossible in fact. She settled it at last with Mamud's help, closing both her hands and making Mamud choose.

The golden coin it was!—She marched up bravely and dropped it in the bowl where it glittered beautifully—much the nicest present that the baby got. The idea was consoling. And it would still be hers, she thought; she could come and look at it as often as she liked, and even take it out and hold it in her hand—just borrow it of course. The baby wouldn't mind. It might be safer in the bowl than in the treasure bag which had several times been lost. She stood upon her toes again to see it: the lovely, shiny coin in the bottom of the bowl—like the golden sun when it popped out of the sea to begin another day. "Good-by," she whispered softly and kissed her fingers to it.

Gil was half asleep, sitting on the deck outside the mouse-man's door, his elbows on his knees and his chin cupped in his hands, the gutted belly of the ship wide open at his feet—a wooden bowl in which the tide was rising, like the water in a well, slowly creeping higher, stirring the greasy seaweed.

Perhaps he dreamed it; afterwards he wasn't sure. But he saw, or thought he saw, through the tangled mat of kelp, something round and shiny at the bottom of the bowl among the slimy jars—not a pebble or a shell.—A golden coin!—He was wide awake and quivering with excitement, searching with his eyes. But the mat of leaves had shifted and he couldn't see it now.—No matter, he had glimpsed it. He caught his breath, remembering in a flash that other which the Little One had found in the fragments of a jar. And where there had been one there must be more—

Not worthless earthen jars, but precious golden eggs, neglected and forgotten, waiting for someone to loose the treasure from them!—Money! There it was, underneath his nose, enough to fill his hands. He cupped them eagerly, debating what they'd hold—twenty, maybe fifty. But how much would be enough?—No, he might need more than that, more than his hands would hold. He'd fill the rucksack with them, all that he could carry loaded on his back, and the pockets of his coat.—He sprang to his feet, impatient to be at it. But the day was nearly done, the shadows of the Giants reaching blackly toward the sea; and he would need the ax to smash the earthen jars; and the water in the bowl was now too deep. There was nothing to be done until tomorrow. He groaned disgustedly, thinking with chagrin of the day that he had wasted.

"But tomorrow—" he promised, nodding grimly to himself. Yes, tomorrow he would come and bring the ax, and when the tide was low he'd smash those golden eggs—till every one was broken and all the treasure gathered. Not a single golden coin would get away. And they'd never know about it, never dream what he was doing; they couldn't hear the ax blows underneath the water—

He paused, reminded of them, listening for their voices. But he didn't hear them now—no shouting in the forest. What could they be doing in their silly church? Not that he cared about it or had the slightest interest, but still he wished he knew.—He was in fact consumed with curiosity.—It would serve to pass the time, he told himself, to go and have a look—sneak up, unseen, and peek. He had nothing else to do—nothing until morning.—Yes, it might be fun, and it might be the last time that he would ever see them.—He glanced into the mouse-man's house to make sure all was well. The skull was covered up and nothing moved or wriggled. His bundle and his watch —they would be safer there than in the house where someone might come prying. Yes, he'd leave them where they were—

He slid across the rail and waded to the beach, and in another minute was scrambling up the bluff.—The church?—He did not know where it was but he had no trouble finding it, for the mermaid's path was plain. He walked as quickly as he could, pretending not to hurry, but secretly afraid he might be missing something. It wasn't very far, beyond the Tent tree, near the bluff. He came upon it suddenly, and stopped with quickened breath behind a screen of bushes, peeking through the leaves—

Yes, there she was, perched snugly on her throne, with her fishtail out of sight and flowers piled around her. He could scarce believe his eyes, for she looked almost pretty. You couldn't see the cracks. Still, he wasn't very close, and it wasn't very light inside the church. The rusty old tin crown was on her head. It didn't fit exactly, but it was quite becoming. When the sunlight flickered through the leaves the rust turned into gold, and the glass jewels really sparkled, the way that real ones might. And her spear was sticking up, like a Queen would hold a scepter.—No, she didn't look as silly as he had thought she would.

And there was God!—You couldn't see much of him, tucked behind her arms—just his head was sticking out. Of course his face was black, but that could be a shadow if you didn't know about it. There was a string of flowers tied around his neck. He looked quite nice—no use denying it.—Just a chunk of wood with a milk nut for a head!—But—but—

He was startled by a voice, almost at his feet.—Yes, there they were, four of them at least: Pablo and Teresa, and the Little One and Mamud—just lying in the grass, not doing anything. It was Mamud who had spoken, asking for a story—

"Teresa, please—" he begged.

"No—" She shook her head.

"Yes, please, Teresa—" the Little One joined in.

"Well, what kind of story?"

"About a Fairy," Mamud said. "A Fairy and a Prince."

"No," protested Pablo. "I don't want to hear it. I'm sick of all those stories."

"I'm not," cried the Little One. "And Mamud isn't either. And there are two of us and only one of you.—Please! Oh please!" she pleaded.

"Well—" Teresa yawned, languidly indulgent. She was in truth a little sick of Fairy tales herself. But she sat up in the grass and presently began, "Once upon a time—"

"Ugh!" Pablo groaned disgustedly and covered up his head.

So that's what they were up to! Gil felt a little cheated.—And the others, where were they? He searched the shadowed ground and then he saw them, half hidden by a log, kneeling side by side before the throne.—Of course they'd be together! He might have known they would, but he wished he hadn't seen them, wished he hadn't come— not on this last day.—He watched with a contemptuous grin, but only half a grin, for only half of him was in a grinning mood.—They were praying, he supposed—asking God for something. He would have liked to know for what, and he would have been surprised—

Juan's head wasn't bowed. He was gazing at the work of his creation, thinking reverently how beautiful it was—praising and adoring it. But there were some minor things that wanted fixing. The scepter wasn't just the way it should be, because it hid her face—the crown was not quite straight—God's head might be improved if he made some ears for it—and the vines were thin in one place; he could see the fish scales through them—

And Rosa?—"Please, God," she was saying, whispering to herself, hoping God would hear her, though he hadn't any ears. "Please make us unbewitched—both Gil and me. And bring him home again. And let things be the way they were before, when we were little children." But she only half believed that God was there; and even if he was, that he would hear or care, or would or could do anything about it.

"Humph!" Gil shrugged disdainfully, but only half a shrug, for he wasn't unimpressed.—Well, they could have their silly church, and the mermaid and the baby. He had something better, or would have by tomorrow when those earthen jars were smashed.

He slipped back through the bushes, and then he turned and ran.

22

I T WAS PABLO WHO DISCOVERED HIM.
He was running on the beach when he came upon the footprints in the sand, leading to the sea—but not coming out again. He searched for quite a distance but there were no more of them. And then he called Teresa who was lying in the shade behind a Giant.

"Look there," he said.

"Look where?"

"Those footprints."

"Well, what of it?"

"They went into the sea but they don't come out again."

"Oh—" She was impressed. "But whose could they be?"

"Gil's," he said.

"How do you know?"

He explained impatiently: they were not his, and Juan was in the church making ears for God, and the footprints were too big for any of the others, excepting Mamud who of course had only one. And so they must be Gil's.

"Maybe he went swimming?"

"Maybe—" Pablo pondered. The tide had ebbed away and left a

253

wide bare space between the final footprints and the water. If he had gone swimming it must have been this morning, and now the afternoon was drawing to a close.

They scanned the sea but there was no sign of him. Still, he could be hidden behind a wading Giant.

"Maybe he's been drowned?" Teresa ventured.

"Well, maybe—" Pablo nodded, not thinking it was likely and not caring very much. "Let's go and see," he said, "where the footprints come from."

They followed them across the beach, in and out among the Giants. Where the sand was loose and dry there were quite a lot of them, old and new, in both directions—as if whoever made them had come and gone repeatedly. They ended at the bluff, where it was high and steep, where no one had ever climbed it. But that was where they ended, and where he must have come from.

"Come on," said Pablo. "Let's climb up and see."

It wasn't very difficult, not as hard as it had looked, for someone else had done it—many times, it seemed—and so there was the vestige of a trail, broken rocks and crumpled shrubs to mark the easy way. And when they stood upon the top they saw there was a path, too plain to be mistaken, leading through the bushes, straight back into the forest.

They ran along it quickly, curious and eager, until Pablo stopped abruptly, pointing through the trees. It had led them to the house.— There it was, stuck on its crooked stilts in the hollow of the ferns— apparently deserted. They stood and stared at it from a respectful distance. The drawbridge wasn't down nor anywhere in sight.

"Perhaps he has come back," Teresa whispered.

"He couldn't," Pablo said. "Not without his footprints."

"Maybe some other way?"

"No." Pablo shook his head.

"But how can you be sure?"

"I'll show you how," he said. And he picked up a pebble and tossed it through the door. They heard it rattle on the poles but not any other sound. It was clear he wasn't there and they ventured to come closer.

Below the door, where the ferns were trampled down, were a

kettle and a bowl, ashes of the fire over which he cooked his solitary suppers, and the debris of them, rinds of fruit and the empty claws of crabs—messy and depressing. And the house itself looked ready to fall down, leaning all askew, with the big hole in its roof—uglier and gloomier than they had remembered.

"When I build my house," Pablo said, "it won't be like that."

"What will it be like?"

"Bigger," he assured her. "And not stuck up in the air, and with lots of windows."

"Yes—" She nodded with a hint of speculation in her eyes. "And will you go and live in it alone?"

"Alone?" He frowned. He had never thought of living anywhere alone—anywhere without her. "Well, you can come and live in it," he said ungraciously.

"Maybe I won't want to."

"Why not?"

"Oh, just because—" She tossed her head coquettishly.

"I don't care," he mumbled, his feelings slightly ruffled.

But she knew he did, and that had been her purpose.

They poked around in silence for a while, busy with their thoughts which were new and rather startling, till they came upon the ladder buried deeply in the ferns—where he'd carefully hidden it.—The same idea was in both their minds at once—

"Let's look inside," said Pablo.

"Gil wouldn't like it."

"He'll never know."

"But if he should?"

"How could he?"

"Well—" She yielded, consumed with curiosity.

They dragged the ladder out and set it up against the door, and Pablo had his foot upon the bottom rung—

"But just suppose—" she said.

"Suppose?" He hesitated.

"He might be coming back."

"Hum—" Pablo paused, considering. Gil might be coming back, climbing up the bluff, approaching on the path, about to make appearance, bursting suddenly upon them, furiously angry that his things

should be disturbed and his house should be explored. "Yes, maybe—"
he agreed, and hurriedly got down. It would only take a minute to
find out. "All right, I'll see," he said. "You wait till I come back."
And he ran off toward the bluff.

"Hurry up!" Teresa urged, impatient of delay, wishing she hadn't
suggested the idea. She sat down in the ferns to wait, but curiosity
was stronger than discretion. She might as well climb up, she thought,
and take a hasty peek—just to pass the time. And so she climbed the
ladder and looked into the house, which at first appeared quite empty.
But then—"Oh!" she exclaimed with pleased surprise, and squirmed
across the threshold to disappear within.

Pablo ran at full speed to the bluff. The coast was clear: there
was no one on the beach or swimming in the sea, and the footprints in
the sand appeared unchanged. He came running back again—

"It's all right," he called. But she wasn't where he'd left her nor
anywhere in sight. "Teresa! Where are you?"

"Up here."

"Up where?"

"Inside the house."

"Oh!" He paused to get his breath. "What are you doing?"

"Come and see."

"All right—" He scampered up the ladder and looked in. For a
moment he was frightened; he didn't recognize her; and for another
moment he couldn't tell the reason—what had happened to her to make
her look so different, like someone whom he knew and had never
seen before. She was sitting on the floor and laughing at him. "But
what—" he gasped, clinging to the ladder, wide-eyed and open-mouthed.
And then he saw—

It was her hair—not hanging down her back, almost to her waist, but
braided into ropes, and the ropes all wound around and piled upon
her head in a very startling fashion. She looked like a lady—like a
lady grown up. And beautiful, he thought. His heart was thumping
strangely but of course he had been running. Still, it wasn't only that.

"Well?" She cocked her head. "How do you like me now?"

"You—you look so funny—" But that was not exactly what he
meant, and she knew it wasn't. "What made you think of doing it?"

"That," she said and pointed to something on the floor.

The big red book spread open beneath the gaping roof.—But he didn't immediately identify the object, not until he'd scrambled in and was kneeling at her side. And then it took a moment to remember what it was and find a name for it—time to turn the pages and see that there were pictures—

"Why, it's a book—" he muttered.

"It was lying here," she said.

And then the memory stirred. "The mouse-man's book!" he cried.

"Oh—" She nodded vaguely. She hadn't thought about it, thought anything at all, too absorbed in what she'd found between the covers. "But how did it get here?"

He shook his head.

"Gil must have brought it."

"Yes, Gil!"—They stared at one another across the open book. The mystery was resolved, the secret of the days when no one ever saw him, when it seemed that he had vanished from the forest: the empty house, the beaten path, the footprints in the sand—

"That's where he goes," said Pablo.

"That's where he spends all day."

"That's where he is right now."

And that is where he was, where it seemed to him he'd always been —waist deep in greasy water, chopping with the ax—

It hadn't been as easy as it looked: uncertain of his footing, tangled in the seaweed which would wrap around the ax, and, no matter how you cleared it, would come floating back again. And the water dulled the blows, so he must strike with all his strength to even nick the jars.—Still, at first it had been fun. The mere act of destruction was thrilling in itself; then gazing down to see, not knowing what you'd find.

But the oil spread a film on the surface of the pool, blurring and distorting what lay upon the bottom. He had to duck beneath it to see anything at all; and when he raised his head it dripped out of his hair and ran into his eyes and spread a film on them. And then he'd rub them, rubbing in the salt until they itched and burned. It nearly drove him wild. And the smell and taste of oil would make him sick, gagging and retching till he was weak and breathless.—But he wouldn't be defeated; he'd go back at it again: smashing, ducking, looking, groping blindly with his hands—tripping in the kelp, slipping on the slimy jars, cutting his hands and feet on the broken fragments of them.

No, it hadn't been much fun; a fatiguing, dirty job. And the ones he broke were empty of everything but oil; not a single golden coin had been revealed. Once he thought he saw one and went diving after it, but it turned out to be a scuttling crab. Again he saw a glitter and ducked and fetched it up—something big and heavy.—A bell!—And so it was, crusted deep with rust: the *Flying Virgin's* bell, the same that tolled her death knell in the storm. He flung it to the deck.—Glints of shells and pebbles, but not any golden coins—

Still, where there had been one there must be more!—Anyway, he couldn't quit, for the thing had reached the point of an obsession. And so, day after day, he would come back, to smash and duck and search, until the rising tide would drive him to the deck. And there he'd lie exhausted, bruised and cut and spent, repeating to himself, "Tomorrow. Yes, tomorrow—"

And the tide was rising now, the greasy seaweed swimming at his armpits. He could no longer reach the jars, strike hard enough to break them. Nor were there many left that he could ever reach, for those upon the bottom would always be too deep, when the tide was at its lowest. He climbed out to the deck and sat upon the edge against the mouse-man's house with the blunted ax beside him.—"Tomorrow—" he insisted as bravely as he could, reflecting dismally: It had better be tomorrow, for in another day he'd be at the end of it, of all his painful effort could accomplish.

He was thinking of the stories in Teresa's repertoire which had to do with treasures: of Fairies who produced them by the waving of a wand—a Palace or a Princess, or both of them at once—to whom it would be nothing to deliver golden coins; of Genii who appeared when you chanced to rub a lamp, and accepted any order, for anything you wanted. If the treasure was remote they would have a magic carpet on which to whisk you off—across the highest mountains in the twinkling of an eye.—He turned his head to see them—the ragged peaks with the setting sun behind them, and shivered at the notion. It would be cold up there, and a little frightening, riding through the sky with nothing to hang onto but a scrap of flimsy carpet. Still, the Genie would be there, sitting close behind you, directing the affair.

But the question had no point, for the treasure was at hand, right beneath his eyes at the bottom of the well. And all that was needed was to take away the water—simply dry it up, a negligible task for any Genie. Yet even that would be a waste of time. Just order golden coins, with no effort of your own. Yes, that would be the easy way to do it.—His hand encountered the *Flying Virgin's* bell—not a lamp but not unlike one, and old enough and rusty. He closed his eyes and rubbed it, smiling wanly to himself, addressing an imaginary Genie. "Bring some money," he commanded. "Enough to fill my hands." But he hastily reconsidered and added with a frown, "I mean, to fill the sack." And then he peeked to see—just pretending, just for fun, thinking what it would be like if such things really happened. But the rucksack at his knees was flat and empty.

Alas, there were no Genii, no Fairies, and no Magic—no easy way to scale the mountain peaks, and no way to fill a sack with golden coins unless you were lucky and could fill it by yourself.—He groaned and shook his head. And then suddenly he thought, or the words came to his lips: "But there is God!"—He sat up straighter, intrigued by the idea. Yes, God, he mused, a Genie of a sort, whose existence was generally admitted, whom even men believed in, for there were priests and churches. He'd never really given any thought to it before, never called on God for help or asked for anything. "Wasting time on Fairies!" he said contemptuously.—But how could God be reached?— Not rubbing on a lamp—

And then he saw again the figures on their knees before the stump, inside the silly church. But perhaps it wasn't silly, or as silly as it seemed. They were asking God for something—and maybe they had got it. His spirits had been rising but now they sank abruptly, for he suddenly remembered the puny little baby with a milk nut for a head; and though of course it wasn't God, still, it must be somehow like him, as he'd looked when Juan had seen him. Anyway, God was a child—not likely to be able to help this present matter, or even understand why he'd want a sack of money.—"No—" He shook his head. God might be all right for children, but he'd be no use to him. He sighed as he stood up and strapped the empty rucksack on his shoulders. —Still, he thought, it could do no harm to try—

They saw his bobbing head, swimming in the sea. They had left the book spread open on the floor, and scrambled down the ladder and hidden it away, in the ferns where they had found it, not leaving any trace; and had run straight to the bluff—lying on their stomachs, watching through the bushes—

"There!" cried Pablo.

"Where?"

"Close behind the ship."

"Oh yes!" She saw it now, the bobbing head circling widely toward the beach. He was coming from the ship, for there was no place else from which he could have come.

They watched him wade ashore and run along the edge, the empty rucksack flapping on his shoulders, to the very spot where they had found the footprints. And then he turned and headed for the bluff.

"Come on, let's go," they said, for they had seen enough.

And away they went, racing through the forest to the Tent tree, where the other four were gathered, for it was supper time and growing dark—bursting on the circle to relate in breathless gasps an account of their adventure: the footprints disappearing in the sea—the beaten path that led straight to the house—the ladder hidden in the ferns—the mouse-man's big red book with the pictures of America—the bobbing head returning from the ship—

There was silence when they finished, incredulous amazement. Supper was forgotten; even Mamud had put down his bowl to stare.

"The ship? But are you sure?" Rosa asked, shivering with the dread of some hidden implication.

"Yes, sure," they insisted. And of course he must have gone there to get the big red book which was in the mouse-man's house.

"But why would he go again?"

"Every day," Teresa said.

"And stay there," added Pablo, "all day long."

They turned the matter in their minds but could make nothing of it.

"He must be crazy," Juan admitted sadly.

"Yes, crazy," they agreed, disposing of the matter, though of course it didn't really dispose of it at all, and they knew that when they said it.

"Enchanted," the Little One corrected amiably, and reached to fill her bowl from the kettle on the fire.

They stirred uneasily, busy with their thoughts. The idea wasn't new. Rosa had been thinking from the start—half thinking, trying not to: enchanted and bewitched would be similar in effect, only differing in their source. But no one made any comment. Only Mamud, who believed in everything, was inquiring anxiously and demanding the particulars.

"It's as plain as it can be," the Little One explained. "The mouse-man was a Sorcerer—"

"Just a silly story!" Pablo interrupted. "And even if it wasn't, the mouse-man's dead and gone."

"But not his heart," she said.

"Humph!" He grunted scornfully. "Anyway," he added, "I don't want to hear about it."

"I'm telling it to Mamud," the Little One said sweetly. "And you don't need to listen."

But all of them were listening.

"It could be like this," she said, using very simple words for Mamud's benefit. He had gone to get the book, nobody could say why and it didn't matter. But he had gone to get it, inside the mouse-man's house, where the Sorcerer's evil heart was still alive—

"But what makes you think it is?" Teresa questioned doubtfully.

"Why, that's easy," she replied. "If the heart was not alive how could he be enchanted?"

Pablo groaned and covered up his ears. But he didn't miss a word.

So the heart had worked its will, the Little One continued, and cast a spell upon him—just the way it did on Mamud. She gave his hand a reassuring pat, adding with a smile, "Before the Fairy came and we got you out of it."

"Um—" Mamud hugged himself, divided between horror and delight.

"But why would he go back?" asked Juan. "Back to the ship again?"

"Yes, why?" they echoed eagerly, suspecting they had found a loop-hole in the matter.

"Maybe because he has to go," the Little One replied without the slightest hint of hesitation.

"But why would he have to go?"

"Because the mouse-man wants him."

"Wants him, for what?" they said.

"I don't know." She shook her head. "But maybe that's the spell: that he must go back and back, every day until he dies, or until the spell is broken."

"Oh—" They nodded bleakly. A pretty dismal outlook for the unlucky Gil! And it didn't sound unreasonable, not to any of them; not to Rosa though she felt that there must be more to it, some aspect of the thing deeply hidden from her eyes, that she didn't want to see; not to Pablo though he scoffed—

"It's just a Fairy story," he said contemptuously and began to eat his supper.

The Little One was deep in thought but she suddenly looked up—

"Did you touch it?" she demanded.

"Did who touch what?" they asked.

"The mouse-man's book."

"Of course," Teresa chuckled. "I fixed my hair like a picture in the book and Pablo didn't know me."

"Oh yes, I did," he said. "I knew you right away. But you certainly looked funny." He laughed extravagantly to cover his confusion, but in the midst of it he caught her anxious eye and his laughter died abruptly. "Well, if we did, what of it?" And he scowled at the Little One who was gazing at him sadly.

"You shouldn't have," she said.

"Why not?" he growled. But he already knew, and the pleasant glow of warmth which the memory had evoked, was turning into creepy little chills.

"Because—" She hesitated. "Because the mouse-man's book must be enchanted too, like everything he had. And so—" She shook her head.

"Oh dear—" Teresa groaned. "You mean, just touching it?"

"Well, it could happen," the Little One said cautiously. And Teresa should have known it, for there were many cases of similar indiscretions in the stories that she told.

"No, it couldn't," shouted Pablo. And then he laughed again with a very hollow sound. "It's just a picture book and I'm not afraid of it, or the mouse-man, or his heart." He picked up his bowl but he was no longer hungry.

And in fact there were three of them who had no appetite. For Rosa had remembered, with a sinking heart: she too had touched the book, had held it in her hands, that awful day inside the mouse-man's house —that day so long ago. But perhaps it had been then that everything began. Perhaps some spells were like that, not immediately effective, or seeming to be so—like a seed when it was planted, unseen beneath the ground, but growing all the time. And at first you didn't know that anything was happening—and then it was too late.

Teresa was reflecting: wondering if she felt any different than she had before she touched the book. She didn't think she did, and found it hard to keep her mind upon the question, for the book kept popping back into her thought—the picture of the lady with her hair piled on her head, and the lovely dress she wore, probably of velvet but certainly not grass. She had noticed that the lady had rings upon her fingers and bracelets on her arms, even earrings in her ears, set with precious jewels. Of course she had no jewels, but perhaps she could make some earrings out of shells—maybe Juan could fix them so she could tie them on. She could never hope to look like the lady in the picture, no matter what she did. Still, if she had the book and time to study it! Anyway, she'd like to try.—And then, she wondered, what would Pablo say? She would like to see his face.—But if the book was dangerous! She was forgetting that.—"Oh dear—" She sighed regretfully.

Pablo was less sanguine: the book was just a book, he kept saying to himself, and could not hurt anybody. He was not enchanted; he felt just the same as he had before he touched it. But he had a suspicion that this was not the truth—that something had occurred inside the crooked house, when he stood upon the ladder looking in—when he first saw Teresa and didn't recognize her. It seemed to be just then. But that was before he'd even touched the book. Well, it was hard to put your finger on the moment, to remember it exactly. It might have been while he was kneeling by her on the floor, looking at the picture. He'd barely touched the page—still, one touch might be enough.

Anyway, since then he hadn't felt the same. and there was no use denying it. He kept glancing at her now from the corner of his eye, wondering what had happened to make everything seem different.—It couldn't be the book, he insisted to himself. But he wished the mouse-man's heart had been accounted for. He saw it in his thought, a black and shriveled object, like a piece of dried up seaweed, hiding in a corner of the mouse-man's house. If the heart was really dead all its, spells would be dissolved.—Of course it was a lie, a silly Fairy story. Anyway, he'd like to have it, stuck upon the spear. And then, just to make sure, he'd roast it in the fire till there was nothing left of it but ashes. Yes, that would end the matter.—But you couldn't cook a fish until you caught it—

Juan hadn't touched the book and wasn't thinking of it. He was thinking of the church, how much nicer God looked now with the ears that he had made, though one of them was bigger than the other; but tomorrow he would fix it. And the Little One and Mamud were not thinking anything that could be reduced to language. They were eating their supper and enjoying every mouthful.

The darkness fell. A sheep bleated mournfully in the pen—not far off from the Tent tree, where long ago they had fenced a place for them. Mamud had known how but he hadn't helped much. The fence had long since fallen down, but the animals still stayed inside as if they didn't know it. The chickens had arrived and were roosting in the branches, clucking drowsily. Some of them had died but others had been hatched, and their habits were unchanged.

The fireflies came out from wherever they were hidden, and sailed among the leaves like dancing sparks. Owls hooted, crickets sang, night birds gave their calls—all the medley of the forest; and the odor of the night, the sweet damp smell, so homelike and familiar. The moon swam up out of the sea like an immense balloon, and climbed into the sky. The embers of the fire glowed red beneath the kettle. Pablo's eyes were on it, and suddenly he said—

"If it wasn't there he couldn't."

"Who?—couldn't what?" they questioned absently.

"Gil." But it was not of Gil that he was thinking.

"Couldn't what?"

"Go back there every day."

"Back where?"

"Back to the ship."

"Oh—" They thought about it. "But the ship *is* there," they said.

"Yes, but if it wasn't?"

"No, he couldn't," they admitted.

"Then let's get rid of it."

"Rid of it? But how?"

"Burn it up," he said.

"What—" They sat up, wide awake, in a flutter of excitement.—A heroic remedy, with startling implications! The spell, if spell there was, would certainly be broken; and the mouse-man's heart, if such there was, was bound to be consumed—

Rosa didn't know; she was terribly confused. But if the ship were gone he could go to it no more, whatever was the reason of his going. And then he might come home. If it was more than that, if there was some evil thing affecting both of them, it too might be disposed of. God hadn't helped. And the ship was at best a place of bitter memory. It could do no harm to try—

Juan was impressed but a little vague about it. He was very thankful that the mermaid had escaped. Teresa was elated: when the ship had been destroyed she could look, with perfect safety, at the pictures in the book. The Little One was jubilant and hopeful of the issue, but cautious of prediction, for the heart was tough and sly. And Mamud was asleep.

Decision was the matter of a moment. "Yes, good!" they cried. "Let's burn it up."

"But when?"

"Tonight," said Pablo firmly. He was quivering with impatience to get the matter done.

They barely hesitated. "All right, tonight—" they nodded. The affair began to shine with a radiance of its own, independent of its issues.

"But how?"

Pablo had already considered the details and hurriedly explained: no one would need to go inside the mouse-man's house; they would set the fire at the door and quickly run away.

"But will it burn?" they wondered.

"Of course. It's made of wood."

"And filled with papers," Rosa said.

"Well, good!—And who will light it?"

"Mamud," Pablo answered. He had figured that out too.

"But will he?"

"If we make him."

"Why must Mamud do it?" the Little One protested.

"Because—" Pablo was ready with his brief: Juan couldn't with one hand.—And that was true, or true enough; he could with time and effort, but time might be the essence of the matter.

"Well, why not you?" she said.

"Because I'm not as good at it as Mamud"—And this was true, though he had often boasted he was better.

"You're always saying that you are," the Little One replied.

But the course seemed indicated. "Yes, Mamud," they agreed.

They woke him up and told him. And now they struck a snag, for Mamud was obdurate, sleepy and determined.

"Why not?" They gathered round and shook him. He was hard to understand, mumbling and complaining.

"He says Gil might not like it," the Little One translated.

"Gil won't know," they said. "He'll be sleeping in his house; he won't know a thing about it. In the morning he'll think it just burned up itself." But Mamud was pretending to be asleep again. "Come on, we know you're fooling!" They propped him up and held him, while he stammered plaintively.

"He says—" the Little One interpreting—"he doesn't want to go near the mouse-man's wicked heart."

"There's no such thing," stormed Pablo.

"Then why should he burn it up?—that's what he wants to know."

"Oh, just for fun," they said.

"No." Mamud shook his head. It would not be any fun—not at any rate for him.

They tried another tack; they coaxed and threatened. It went on interminably. Even the Little One was getting out of patience, knowing as she did that Mamud ran no risk, for he had been enchanted and it wouldn't work again. But there was no use attempting to explain these facts to him. At last she thought of something else—

"Would you like to have your fishhook back?—the one you gave to God?"

Yes, he would like to have it.

"Well, if you go—" she promised.

"No—" But he was weakening.

Juan thought of something else: there had been a bell upon the ship, hanging by the mast—a big brass bell with a sweet and mellow sound. He had used to listen for it and count the times it rang, as in the long ago he had listened to the church bells. It would be wonderful to have, to hang up in the church. And maybe he could find it. Suddenly he volunteered—

"I'll go with you, Mamud."

"Good for Juan!" they cried. And to Mamud, "There, you see!"

"No—" But the fishhook was at work, having its effect; and he wouldn't be alone. He felt around, objecting that he couldn't find his sparking stones and did not know where he'd left them.

"Here! Take mine," said Pablo.

But Mamud spurned the offer: he couldn't light a fire unless he had his own.

"Why, here they are!" Teresa found them in the grass where he had tried to hide them.

He took them with a groan.

"All right, let's go!" they cried.

And off they went, the six of them, with Mamud in the middle where he couldn't sneak away. The moon had risen high; it was as bright as day. They came upon the bluff and stopped to look.—There was the ship, the naked bow of it stuck fast between the Twins, like the head of some dead monster sprawling in the sea. And it would soon be nothing—

They started down the path, keeping careful watch of Mamud. They had forgotten Gil. Only Rosa hadn't. She saw him in her thought, asleep in his lonely little house. But perhaps tomorrow he would come home again—

23

GIL WAS NOT ASLEEP IN THE CROOKED LITTLE house where no one but a turtle could have slept with any comfort. He had tried it only once and thereafter made his bed among the ferns, in the very spot which Trictrac had hallowed with her memory.

But tonight he wasn't there, nor anywhere that anyone could have reasonably expected. For he was in the church.—Oh, not as a communicant—nothing of that sort. He wasn't such a fool. Just strolling in the moonlight and chancing to look in—

He couldn't sleep, tormented by his desperate situation—the net of greed and fear in which he had been snared: the golden coins he wanted and the fear he wouldn't find them. He could think of nothing else, for he had lost the power to forget. His eyes would not stay shut. He turned and tossed; and then, when the moon had risen high, he gave it up at last and went to take a walk. An aimless stroll, he pretended to himself. But he knew where he was going.

He had passed close by the Tent tree, near enough to hear their voices, wondering absently why they were not asleep, but not curious enough to pause and listen to the chatter.—Pity that he didn't, or good thing he hadn't, though perhaps it could have made no difference in the end. Anyway, he had gone on—

"Why, there's the church—" he said in mock surprise, as if he'd come upon it quite by chance. He pushed aside the tapestry of vines and tiptoed down the aisle between the milk nut trees—like stately marble columns in the night, through speckled moonlight dancing on the grass—like a tessellated pavement. The scattered logs, like empty pews; the mermaid on her throne; the crown with glinting jewels.— "Just broken glass," he muttered. But they did look like jewels. His heart was beating fast; his breath was tight. It didn't seem as silly as he had thought it would. He came closer to the mermaid, gazing doubtfully at the little wooden figure in her arms, the black and shriveled head with the funny looking ears. He was face to face with God—the last resort of troubled treasure seekers.

But he wasn't sure how to proceed about the matter, nor convinced it wasn't silly; and the longer he postponed it the more difficult it got. He was edging away, feeling foolish and embarrassed, about to give it up, when he saw Juan's wooden bowl among the wilted flowers on the stump; and he came back to look in.—Teresa's necklace, Mamud's precious fishhook: presents they had brought. And perhaps he should have brought one.—There was something else in the bottom of the bowl. He felt and drew it out, and stared in startled wonder.—A shiny golden coin! The Little One's of course. But it seemed an answer to his prayer before he'd even made it, a sign of hopeful portent—as if God were inviting him to go ahead and ask—

"Like—like this," he stammered, holding the coin before God's face, where he couldn't fail to see it. But then he was reminded of his manners and dropped upon his knees, still holding up the coin, so there could be no mistake. "Please, God—" His lips were dry and he wet them with his tongue. "I need some more like this. A lot of them," he added. "Enough to fill the sack. And—and—" But there seemed no more to say.

He got back upon his feet, staring at the baby, whose wooden face had a melancholy air, as if it were displeased or disappointed. "Oh yes—" he said contritely, aware of the coin he was clutching in his hand. And he put it back into the bowl, a shade reluctantly, beginning again to feel foolish and embarrassed, for the moment of illusion had already taken flight. The mermaid had a fishtail and her crown was made of tin, the pews were scattered logs, the tessellated floor was just moonlight on the grass, the lofty marble columns were only milk nut trees. And God?—He didn't know. Still, he hoped that it might work—

He turned to go. It was then he saw, through the patchwork of the leaves, the crimson glow of fire in the sky.—"Why, what—" he gasped and ran, plunging through the forest to the bluff, a dreadful premonition of disaster in his heart, for there was nothing else to paint the empty sky—nothing but the ship.

Juan and Mamud had gone alone to do it, leaving the others waiting on the beach.—"On guard," as Pablo put it, though from what he didn't say. Juan had led the way and had fallen in the well where the ship was split apart. He was hanging by one hand when Mamud pulled him out. After that he was careful where he stepped. But he felt himself rewarded because he found the bell, without even looking for it—outside the mouse-man's door; and the ax was there beside it.

Mamud set the fire, but he was so frightened that it took him quite a while, and Juan must kneel to help him, blowing on the sparks until the seaweed kindled. But then at last it caught. They flung some blazing fragments into the mouse-man's house, and the littered papers flamed like an exploding lamp. They waited for no more, but grabbed the ax and the bell and scrambled for the rail—

"There she goes!" cried Pablo, as the flames shot through the skylight.

"But look—" they gulped, huddling closer in the sand, seeing Juan and Mamud squirm across the rail and come running back to them.

"I found it," Juan was shouting.

"The mouse-man's heart?"

"The bell." He held it up. "It's for the church," he said. But they barely glanced at it.

"Did anything jump out?" the Little One demanded.

Mamud shook his head. He had not seen anything, but in fact he hadn't looked, for most of the time he had kept his eyes tight shut.

"Then it must be in there," she exclaimed with satisfaction.

"Yes, good—" They nodded, but they scarcely thought about it. The spectacle itself was too absorbing.

The ship was like a tinderbox. In the twinkling of an eye the mouse-man's house was converted to a furnace, the skylight belching flames and sparks which rose into the languid air and gently drifted down, to kindle where they fell. And hidden tongues of fire ran along the deck, spreading like a fan, igniting heaps of seaweed which blazed and gnawed the planks. Melting tar oozed from the broken seams; smoke poured from her belly, for the oil was burning now, and the greasy straw that clung to the lining of her gullet. The crackling of the flames became a roar—

It was too hot for comfort where they sat, and they scuttled back to the shelter of a Giant. The ship was now ablaze from stem to stern, wrapped in thick black smoke through which the flames were stabbing. Behind its gaping seams the hull glowed like an oven; the painted eyes upon the bow were ringed around with fire.

This was what he saw when he stumbled through the bushes and stood upon the bluff. The end of all his hopes! A cry burst from his throat—a dreadful cry of anguish and despair.

"It's Gil—" they gasped in panic, and jerked their heads to look, scanning the empty bluff until at last they saw him—far from the house where he should have been asleep.

"He's coming—" And he was. He had disappeared from sight but they heard him crashing down in an avalanche of stones.

"Coming after us—"

They ran for their lives—ran by common impulse, without another word. Only Mamud didn't run; he couldn't in the sand. He was crawling after them as fast as he could go, begging them to wait. But they didn't wait, or pause to catch their breath, till they'd fled across the beach and scrambled up the path and were crouching safely hidden in the bushes at the top.

"There he is," they whispered. He was running toward the ship, as if he hadn't seen them.

And in fact he hadn't, hadn't even thought of them. He was running with no purpose in his mind, for he knew that it was useless, that everything was lost—the watch and chain, the hat and shoes and clothes, and those precious golden coins which he would have found tomorrow—all gone forever now. He was running in a daze when he came upon the ax—the tell-tale ax which Mamud had discarded in his flight.

The ax which he had left beside the mouse-man's door! And how had it come here?—He stooped to pick it up, a faint suspicion stirring in his muddled head.

"The ax," they groaned. "He's found the ax."

"And Mamud?" Where was Mamud?

So quickly had it happened that Mamud was still crawling through the sand, almost at the bluff, which, once his wooden leg had touched the solid rock, he could spring up as nimbly as a goat.

Would he make it? Would Gil see him?

The Little One could not contain her fear. She stood up in the bushes, crying out a warning before they dragged her down, "Oh, Mamud, hurry! Hurry!"

But, alas, the warning served a double purpose, for now Gil turned and saw him and ran to head him off.

"Mamud! Look out!" they screamed.

Too late.—They watched in horror as Gil caught and flung him back. Poor Mamud, crouching on his knees, with his head against the sand, like an ostrich seeking cover.

"My ax—" Gil gripped his arm and shook him. "Where did you get my ax?"

But Mamud didn't answer, blubbering with fright, mumbling words that made no sense.

"Where?" Gil dragged his face out of the sand. "Tell me or I'll kill you!" He shook the ax before his eyes, as if he meant to do it, and quite possibly he did, for he was beside himself with grief and fury and the poison of suspicion that was seeping in his heart.

"Oh, please—" Mamud cringed and whimpered, begging for his life.

"Then tell me!"

A gibberish of words: they'd made him go—they'd promised him his fishhook—they'd waked him up and made him—he hadn't wanted to—he'd tried to get away—but they had made him go—all of them had made him—Juan and Rosa too—

"Go where?" Gil grabbed his arm and twisted it until he howled with pain. "Then tell me! Tell me quick!"

"The ship—" he sobbed. But he hadn't gone alone. Juan had been there too; Juan had led the way and told him what to do. He had brought the ax and Juan had brought the bell.

"And my other things?" Gil shouted, for a desperate hope had come into his mind: they had gone to steal his things and carry them away. "Where have you hidden them?"

Mamud shook his head, groveling in the sand.

"My watch and chain and all my other things?—inside the mouse-man's house?—What have you done with them?"

Mamud stared dumbly through his tears, protesting piteously: he knew about no things; they hadn't gone inside or even looked; and they hadn't taken anything except the ax and bell.

"You lie." He poised the ax but could get no other answer. "Then why? Why did you go?"

Because they'd made him, Mamud shrieked.

"But why? For what?"

More gibberish—of evil hearts and spells—

"You mean—" he interrupted, with an inkling of the truth. "You mean you set the fire?"

Mamud bowed his head.

So that was it at last!—They knew; they'd spied upon him. And they'd gone to burn the ship, to rob him of his dreams. All of them were in it, Juan and Rosa too. They'd done it in the night when they thought he was asleep.—He leaped at Mamud who was edging out of reach, and struck him viciously, struck him in the face—the great black man whose hair and beard were white, but in fact a little boy, cowering in the sand.

"For shame!" they shouted from the bluff. "Oh stop! For shame!"

He jerked back, staring up, while Mamud crawled away in desperate haste.—So that's where they were hiding, spying on him now!—Fury overwhelmed him, and perhaps the bite of shame. He stood to shake his fist at the bushes where they hid. "You wait—" he shouted wildly and started up the path.

But they didn't wait. They ran for their lives, leaving Mamud to his fate, which wasn't like them; if it had been a beast or snake they would not have run away.—Of what were they afraid? They were five to one against him.—No, it wasn't that, not of what he'd do with his fists or with the ax. But still they were afraid, frightened and bewildered. They were shocked by his appearance, for none of them had seen him since he had cut his hair. He didn't look like Gil, nor anyone they knew. And he didn't sound like Gil. When he stood upon the bluff and saw the burning ship, the cry he uttered had struck terror to their hearts. The sound of despair was unfamiliar to them, outside of their experience; for despair is an emotion which requires concentration.—And he didn't act like Gil, for Gil, with all his faults, would not have struck poor Mamud in the face—a careless slap perhaps, but not a blow.—They were looking at a stranger, and an enemy as well. And so they ran away.

When he reached the top there was no one to be seen. He tramped among the bushes, flailing with the ax, shouting crazy threats. There was murder in his heart, a thirst for vengeance: to do to them what they had done to him. Yes, even Rosa, for she too had betrayed him. But mostly it was Juan on whom his fury focused, whom he could have seized and strangled with his hands or slain with the ax. "Come out!" he shouted, for he thought they might be near, still spying on him.—And they were not far away, huddled close together, watching through the leaves. Once he came so close they could have reached and touched him—could have sprung upon him and torn him to pieces. But they were not killers.

"Come out! Come out!" And then he'd stop to listen, but there was no sound save the roaring of the flames which blazed against the sky; it was as bright as noon upon the bluff. "Come out, I say!"—Perhaps they were not there. Then where? The Tent tree!—Yes, of course that's where they'd go, running home like frightened children. And he was off again, riding hard and fast in the saddle of his passion, tripping over roots, sprawling on the ground.

But the Tent tree was deserted. Their grassy beds were empty, drenched in moonlight. "Come out! Come out!" he shouted, suspecting they were hiding.—And again they were not far away, peeking through the leaves.—The forest was awakening to his voice: birds were calling fearfully, and the sleepy chickens, roosting in the branches, were cackling in alarm. He ran around the tree, round and round the trunk, as if it were a game, as he had used to run when they were playing tag. —It would have been amusing if it hadn't been so dreadful, if you couldn't see his face.—Round and round he went, and now and then he'd stop and run the other way, as if he thought to catch somebody unaware. But there was no one playing but himself.

At last he gave it up and turned to something else, searching in the grass, feeling with his hands. He found some wooden bowls and smashed them with the ax. But there was nothing else, nothing to destroy.—Vengeance! Yes, but how? How take from them that have not? The destitute are safe from theft, beyond the reach of vandals. He saw the supper kettle standing in the ashes which still glowed red beneath it, and overturned it with his foot—a silly, wanton gesture. But the embers caught his eye—

Fire! That was it, the very thing they'd done to him. He'd burn the roof that sheltered them, reduce their home to ashes—and the hateful forest too. He'd scorch the very earth till there was nothing left, no birds or beasts, no tree or bush or blade of grass—a barren waste of smoking stumps. Yes, that would pay them back!—He raked the embers with the ax and scattered them about, crouching on his knees to blow upon the sparks. But the green grass would not burn and the embers flickered out. The forest was impervious to his puny will. The Tent tree reared above him like a tower made of stone.

All right. He'd cut it down, bring their house down on their heads. If they were hiding, spying, they might be caught and crushed to death. He scrambled to his feet and struck it with the ax, but the blunted edge would no more than nick the bark, and not all their arms together could reach around the trunk. It would take forever, if it could be done at all.

He groaned and leaned with his back against the tree, the tantrum wearing off but his fury unabated, thinking now more calmly, with more deliberation.—Vengeance! Yes, but how? They had nothing he could take from them and nothing he could break.—And then he thought of something, with a thrill of exultation that made him laugh aloud. Yes, that would pay them back, or anyway pay Juan. "All right! Just wait!" he cried, and was gone out of their sight, lost among the trees.

"What does he mean?" they whispered.

"Now what will he do?"

But no one knew or ventured an opinion.

They crept out of their hiding, awed and silent, looking ruefully at the broken wooden bowls. But their loss was no great matter, for Juan could make some new ones. Mamud came limping home and crawled into his bed. His lip was cut and bleeding and he wouldn't speak to them. When the Little One came near he turned his back.

Thud-thud-thud—the sound of the ax, not very far away.

"What's that?" they muttered fearfully.

"What can he be doing?"

"Chopping down a tree."

"In the middle of the night?"

Thud-thud-thud—

"It sounds," suggested Pablo, "like it was in the church."

"The church—" Juan gasped. And suddenly he ran, jerking loose from Rosa who clutched his arm to stop him.

"Juan, don't! Come back!" she cried, and ran to follow him.

"Let's go and see," said Pablo without enthusiasm.

"Yes, let's—" Teresa yawned. But they made no move to go.

"If it's bad," advised the Little One, "it's better not to know." And she snuggled in her bed.

"Juan, wait!—Please wait—" But Rosa could not stop him, seeing his figure slicing through the moonbeams far ahead, for he was swift of foot, swiftest of them all.

Thud-thud-thud—

He came into the church, running like a deer. But then he stopped and stared, scarce believing what he saw, what he had known he'd find. —Incredible destruction!—The mermaid was unthroned, the crown gone from her head, the scepter from her hands. She lay starkly on her back, almost cut in two where her body changed to fishscales, while the executioner stood with his foot upon her breast, hacking with the ax.—And God?—Alas! God lay scattered in the grass, his body and his head from which the ears had vanished.

A sacrilege?—No doubt. But it was more than that.

"Oh Gil!" he cried in horror and dismay.

Gil stayed the ax and turned his head, his eyes as hard as stone.

"Why did you do it, Gil?"

"To pay you back for what you've done to me."

"I—I've never meant to hurt you."

"You burned my things."

"I didn't know about them."

"No matter what you knew." He was whipping up his fury for fear

that it would slip. "Anyway, I hate you, and your silly little God." He kicked the milk nut head.

"Please, Gil. Don't break them any worse. Maybe I can fix them."

"Not when I get through you can't." He laughed and raised the ax.

"No, don't!" Juan's voice rang out with a note he'd never heard, desperate and determined. "Don't, I say! You can't!" And he ran and caught the ax, locking his arm around the arm that held it.

"Let loose," Gil snarled and tried to fling him off. But Juan's one arm was strong and the ax was tightly pinned. They struggled back and forth, stumbling on the mermaid, trampling on her crown. "Let loose, I tell you!" His other hand was free and he clenched his fist and struck—short vicious jabs, till he saw the trickling blood on Juan's white face, ghost-like in the moonlight. But he couldn't see his eyes, for they were closed, and he was glad of that.

"I hate you, hate you, hate you—" The ax was still pinned tight. He caught Juan's leg crooked in his own and threw him to the ground, dragged down and falling with him, rolling in the grass. But now he was on top, feeling for Juan's throat. He got his hand upon it and squeezed with all his might. The blood smeared face was close to his, the gasping breath upon his cheek. Juan was choking, strangling, making dreadful sounds. But the ax was loosening now. At last he tore it free and flung it back to strike—

And perhaps he would have done so, but before the blow could fall his arm was caught and held, the ax wrenched from his hand. He hadn't heard her coming, not any conscious sound, but he knew that it was Rosa. He scrambled back and got upon his feet, wiping the sweat out of his eyes, the fury draining from him like water from a leaking jug, leaving nothing in its place but a sickening emptiness.

Yes, there she was, standing in the moonlight, staring at him strangely—as if she hardly knew him and was looking close to see; the ax still in her hand. She glanced at it and shivered and dropped it in the grass. She hadn't run to Juan, to take his head upon her lap and press her cheek to his, as she had done that other time when he had killed the snake. Well, she'd paid him back for that. Anyway, Juan wasn't hurt much; he was stirring, sitting up.—What was she staring at? Maybe at the mermaid and the baby. They weren't so

badly smashed; he'd only started on them. Juan could patch them up, as good as new or better.—But he knew it wasn't that.

"Oh Gil—" she cried, not accusing nor reproachful, but as if she'd said, "Poor Gil—" And she looked so very sad.—Maybe a trick of moonlight, and he moved a step to change the shadows on her face. But the look in her eyes remained the same.

"Well, what?" he said, as roughly as he could, for he was near to sobbing.

She didn't answer.

"Because I paid him back?"

She shook her head.

"Because I broke those silly things?"

"No, Gil."

"Then why?"

"Because—" She hesitated. "Because it's happened, Gil."

"Happened?—What?" he blustered.

But she only shook her head and looked away from him. He thought that she was crying. But he knew what she meant; he'd known it all the time.

"Well, I don't care," he said. And suddenly he turned and strode away, out of the silent church and speckled moonlight—strode deep into the forest, with tired aimless steps, this way and that. For there was not any way for him to go—nowhere in the forest.

24

NO DOUBT IN SIMILAR FASHION REBELLIOUS angels were dismissed from heaven, stripped of their harps and wings, expelled and banished into outer darkness.

And probably they went with mixed emotions: glad and sorry, resentful and dismayed, contrite and scornful, wistful and elated, hopeful and regretful, courageous and afraid; relieved that it was over, their crimes discovered and themselves found out; rejoiced to be released from the confinement of celestial space, from nectar and ambrosia—a pallid sort of pap, from harps and wings—encumbrances of virtue, biologically unsound except for little children. Yes, quite likely they were glad to be rid of it at last, to be off upon their way, no matter where—glad and very sorry. For they were leaving home, and that is hard to do, for men or angels.

"Well, I don't care," perhaps they told themselves, shrugging their shoulders from which the wings had vanished. But they couldn't shrug their hearts.

Anyway, it was like that when in the graying dawn he set out upon his journey—that journey of his dreams, a sad and bitter mockery of

the journey he'd imagined, when light of heart and foot, and the
rucksack filled with treasure, he should have marched away with a
song upon his lips and all his colors flying. But his feet were shod
with lead and his heart was not less heavy. An empty rucksack flapped
upon his shoulders—though not entirely empty, for there was something hidden deep in a corner of it. He hoped that it was there—and
hoped it wasn't. Sometimes he wasn't sure, for his memory of the
night, of what he'd done or had only thought to do, was tangled and
confused.—"Well, I don't care—"

And it was still like that when near the long day's end he climbed
the slope beside the waterfall and came upon the thicket where the
snake had been concealed: the wall of creepers hanging from the tree,
in the maze of roots that grew above the ground—exactly as it had
been. He paused with quickened heart, for Trictrac might be there,
in her home where he had found her when she was a baby.

"Trictrac! Trictrac!" He spread the curtain of the vines and
cautiously explored. No stirring stem, no coiling snake; even its bones
were gone, mysteriously vanished. He crawled among the roots, finding
again the burrow where the little thing had hid, lying on his stomach
to peer into its depths. But he knew she wasn't there, that she was
much too big to have hidden in it now; one of her paws would fill it.
—"Trictrac! Trictrac!"

He was aching with fatigue and disappointment. The rucksack had
become a heavy burden, for he had stopped along the way to fill it,
with fruit and even milk nuts, thinking perhaps he might not have
another chance. And many times he'd stopped, seeing a fleeting shadow,
hearing a crackling twig, hoping it might be Trictrac, waiting to call
and whistle, holding his breath to listen.—He had not come very fast,
not as he had fancied in the journey of his dreams. In them he'd
found the mountains and scaled them in a day. And now it was near
evening and perhaps he'd come halfway. Impossible to tell, for he
was at the spot where twice he had turned back, and beyond which
there would not be any landmarks.

"Trictrac! Trictrac!"—Perhaps this was her home and she'd only
gone away—maybe to hunt her supper? And then she would return?
But he didn't think she would. Perhaps she had gone on across the
mountains, and he would never find her. Yes, that was far more likely.
—"Well, I don't care—"

He swung the heavy rucksack to his shoulders, stumbled on a few short steps among the roots, tearing his way through a tangled net of vines, and suddenly emerged out of the somber thicket, into blazing sunshine—blinding for a moment—

"What—" he gasped, and stopped in stupefaction, unable to believe it: the forest was behind him; the end of it was here—only a step from where he'd been when he had come before. The mountains reared before his eyes, towering in the sky, their dazzling snow-capped peaks lost in the drifting clouds. He scrambled up a gentle slope, through grass as soft as velvet, and stood upon a little hill, looking down upon the forest—

It did not look very big, as if it could have taken such a time to get across it. It did not seem formidable—like a patch of ragged carpet, not hinting at the perils underneath. But he had met no perils on his way, no savage beasts or snakes. Perhaps they knew he wasn't coming back, and so had let him pass.

He turned to face the mountains, gazing with sinking heart at the wall that barred his path: the gaunt escarpments, pitted with crevasses; fields of snow and rivers made of ice; the ragged peaks that stretched away as far as he could see. A formidable foe, as he had known it would be. But the aspect of it was worse on close acquaintance. In contrast with it the forest seemed a trifle—as things are like to do once they are passed.—He searched with his eyes for some possible attack, a gap through which the fortress might be breached. But he saw no sign of any, no easy way to go, no way at all save up the awful sides till he should gain the top.—The sun went down behind a peak, and flames of gold and crimson leaped out from crest to crest and reached into the sky to paint the clouds. The light was dazzling, blinding, and he could no longer see.

He groaned and turned away. It was not a cheerful prospect—bare footed, clothed in grass, naked to the cold. If only he had his precious shoes and coat! If he were not alone!—Perhaps he'd never make it. Perhaps he would be frozen in his tracks and left to stand forever in the snow, like the Giants upon the beach, turned to ice instead of stone.—Still, tomorrow he must try; there was nothing else to do, for there was no way back.

He loosed the rucksack from his shoulders and emptied out the fruit and nuts he'd gathered, feeling in the corners of the sack for that other hidden thing, of which he wasn't sure.—Yes, it was there; he found it with his fingers, glad and sorry, but he didn't take it out. And he sat to eat his supper, in the shelter of some boulders, a cozy spot whence he could see the forest. But he wasn't very hungry.

The twilight fell; the distant sea turned black and purple shadows spread upon the mountains, creeping down their slopes. A gentle breeze came sighing from the snow—not cold but cool and pleasantly refreshing. The forest stirred and answered, like an orchestra of countless harps softly brushed by countless fingers; the birds began to call as they always did at evening. He leaned against the rock, beginning to be sleepy, watching the stars come out, keeping careful count of them so he couldn't think of anything. The breeze had died away and it was very still—

Wait now! What was that?—Ding-dong—the deep and mellow sound, all the way across the forest.—The bell! It must be that, the bell he'd left upon the ship, that Juan had found and taken.—Ding-dong —ding-dong.—Good-by, it seemed to say, but not sorrowly at all—as if it wished him well upon his journey. Maybe they were ringing it to send a message to him?—Ding-dong—ding-dong.—He saw them in the dark, sitting round the fire—and Teresa might be dancing, kicking up her heels, showing off her slim brown legs, not caring if you saw.—He frowned and shook his head, to shake the memory from it.—Yes, maybe they were having fun, not missing him at all, or glad he wasn't there.—Ding-dong—Ding-dong—

"Well, I don't care—" But nostalgia overwhelmed him, and he turned his face away and hid it in his arm, and sobbed and sobbed until he fell asleep.

"Gil!—Gil!"

The voice was in his dreams. But then he was awake, not knowing where he was, thinking he was home. But memory flooded back in a sickening, crushing wave. He sat up in his bed. The moon was creeping from the sea. He had been asleep and dreaming—

"Gil!—Gil!"

But he wasn't dreaming now. He scrambled to his feet, gazing fearfully all around—the silent mountains wrapped in winding sheets; the forest like the sea, with a silver bridge across it.—No, it couldn't be; he was imagining things.—But then he recollected he had heard